Praise for H. G. Parry

The Unlikely Escape of Uriah Heep

"If you've ever checked the back of your wardrobe for snow and lamplight—if you've ever longed to visit Pemberley House or 221B Baker Street, to battle the Jabberwock or wander through a fictional London fog—this book belongs to you. It's a star-studded literary tour and a tangled mystery and a reflection on reading itself; it's a pure delight."

—Alix E. Harrow, *New York Times* bestselling author

"Many have tried and some have succeeded in writing mash-ups with famed literary characters, but Parry knocks it out of the park.... Just plain wonderful." —*Kirkus* (starred review)

"Part mystery, all magical, *The Unlikely Escape of Uriah Heep* is both amusing and perceptive; the novel entertains as it reminds us of the power of words and how fiction can influence real life."

—*Locus*

"H. G. Parry has crafted an imaginative and unique exploration of how words shift our lives in ways big and small. *The Unlikely Escape of Uriah Heep* is a rollicking adventure that thrills like Neil Gaiman's *Neverwhere* mashed up with *Penny Dreadful* in the best postmodern way. Equal parts sibling rivalry, crackling mystery, and Dickensian battle royale, it'll be one of your most fun reads this year." —Mike Chen, author of *Here and Now and Then*

The Shadow Histories

"A first-rate blend of political drama and magic battle–action.... Absolutely superb." —*Kirkus* (starred review)

"A witty, riveting historical fantasy.... Parry has a historian's eye for period detail and weaves real figures from history—including Robespierre and Toussaint Louverture—throughout her poetic tale of justice, liberation, and dark magic. This is a knockout." —*Publishers Weekly* (starred review)

"An absolute delight to read; splendid and fluid, with beautiful and complex use of language." —Genevieve Cogman, author of *The Invisible Library*

"Magnificent.... [Turns] the part of history class you might have slept through into something new, exciting and deeply magical." —*BookPage*

THE MAGICIAN'S DAUGHTER

By H. G. Parry

The Magician's Daughter

THE SHADOW HISTORIES

A Declaration of the Rights of Magicians
A Radical Act of Free Magic

The Unlikely Escape of Uriah Heep

THE MAGICIAN'S DAUGHTER

H. G. PARRY

REDHOOK

Copyright © 2023 by H. G. Parry
Excerpt from *The Book of Gothel* copyright © 2022 by Mary McMyne

Cover design by Lisa Marie Pompilio
Cover illustrations by Shutterstock
Cover copyright © 2023 by Hachette Book Group, Inc.
Author photo by Fairlie Atkinson

Redhook Books/Orbit
Hachette Book Group
1290 Avenue of the Americas
New York, NY 10104
hachettebookgroup.com

First Edition: February 2023
Simultaneously published in Great Britain by Orbit

Redhook is an imprint of Orbit, a division of Hachette Book Group.
The Redhook name and logo are trademarks of Hachette Book Group, Inc.

The publisher is not responsible for websites (or their content) that are not owned by the publisher.

The Hachette Speakers Bureau provides a wide range of authors for speaking events. To find out more, go to hachettespeakersbureau.com or email HachetteSpeakers@hbgusa.com.

Redhook books may be purchased in bulk for business, educational, or promotional use. For information, please contact your local bookseller or the Hachette Book Group Special Markets Department at special.markets@hbgusa.com.

A signed limited edition has been privately printed by Charnel House Ltd
www.charnelhouse.com.

Library of Congress Cataloging-in-Publication Data
Names: Parry, H. G., author.
Title: The magician's daughter / H.G. Parry.
Description: First edition. | New York, NY : Redhook, 2023.
Identifiers: LCCN 2022026623 | ISBN 9780316383707 (trade paperback) |
ISBN 9780316383806 (ebook)
Subjects: LCGFT: Fantasy fiction. | Novels.
Classification: LCC PR9639.4.P376 M34 2023 | DDC 823/.92—dc23/eng/20220609
LC record available at https://lccn.loc.gov/2022026623

ISBNs: 9780316383707 (trade paperback), 9780316383806 (ebook)

Printed in the United States of America

LSC-C

Printing 1, 2022

To our Lockdown 2020 house. Nothing is ever forgotten.
And to Robin and Much, our lockdown mice.
Now and forever, my loves.

THE MAGICIAN'S DAUGHTER

Chapter One

*R*owan had left the island again last night.

He had done so quietly, as usual. Had Biddy not been lying awake, listening for his light tread on the stairs outside her bedroom, she would have never known he was gone. But he had slipped out of the castle once or twice too often lately while she slept, and this time she was ready. She got out of bed and went to the window, shivering at the touch of the early-autumn chill, in time to see him cross the moonlit fields where the black rabbits nibbled the grass. Her fingers clenched into fists, knowing what was coming, frustrated and annoyed and more worried than she wanted to admit. At the cliff edge he paused, and then his tall, thin form rippled and changed as wings burst from his back, his body shriveled, and a large black bird flew away into the night. Rowan was always a raven when he wasn't himself.

When she was very young, Biddy hadn't minded too much when Rowan flew away at night. As unpredictable as Rowan could be, he was also her guardian, and however far he went she trusted him to always be there if she needed him. In the meantime, she was used to fending for herself. She did so all day sometimes, when Rowan was shut up in his study or off in the forest and had no time for things like meals or conversation or common sense. Besides, Rowan always left Hutchincroft behind to watch over things. Hutch couldn't speak to her when he was a rabbit, it was true, but he would leap onto the bed beside her, lay his head flat, and let her curl around his soft golden fur. It made the castle less empty, and the darkness less hungry. She would lie there, dozing fitfully, until either she heard the flutter of feathers and the scrabble of claws at the window above hers or exhaustion won out and pulled her into deeper sleep.

And in the morning, Rowan would always be there, as if he'd never left.

———————————◆◆◆———————————

That morning was no exception. When she woke to slanting sunlight and came downstairs to the kitchen, Rowan was leaning against the bench with his fingers curled around a mug of tea. His brown hair was rumpled and his eyes were a little heavy, but still dancing.

"Morning," he said to her brightly. "Sleep all right?"

She would have let him get away with that once. Not now. She wasn't a very young girl anymore. She was sixteen, almost seventeen, and she minded very much.

"What time did you get in?" she asked severely, so he'd know she hadn't been fooled. He laughed ruefully.

"An hour or two before dawn?" He glanced at Hutchincroft, who was busily munching cabbage leaves and carrots by the stove. "Half past four, Hutch says. Why? Did I miss anything?"

"I was asleep," she said, which wasn't entirely true. "You'd have to tell me."

She pulled the last of yesterday's bread out of the cupboard, sneaking a look at Rowan as she did so. There was a new cut at the corner of one eyebrow, and when he straightened, it was with a wince that he turned into a smile when he saw her watching.

Biddy didn't think there had ever been a time when she had thought Rowan was her father, even before he had told her the story of how she first came to Hy-Brasil. The two of them looked nothing alike, for one thing. Rowan was slender and long-limbed like a young tree, eternally unkempt and wild and sparkling with mis-chief. She was smaller, darker, with serious eyes and a tendency to frown. And yet he wasn't an older brother either, or an uncle, or anything else she had read about in the castle's vast library. He was just Rowan, the magician of Hy-Brasil, and as long as she could remember there had been only him and Hutchincroft and herself. She knew them as well as she knew the castle, or the cliffs that bor-dered the island, or the forests that covered it. And she knew when he was hiding something from her.

He knew her too, at least well enough to know he was being scrutinized. He lasted until she had cut the bread and toasted one side above the kitchen fire, and then he set his mug down, amused and resigned.

"All right. I give up. What have I done now?"

"Where did you go last night?" she asked—bluntly, but without any hope of a real answer.

She wasn't disappointed. "Oh, you know. Here and there. I was in Dublin for a bit, then I got over to Edinburgh. And London," he added, with a nod to Hutchincroft, conceding a point Biddy couldn't hear. In her bleakest moments, she wished they wouldn't do that. It reminded her once again of all the magic from which she was locked out.

"And when did you get hurt?"

"I didn't—well, hardly. A few bruises. I got careless." He looked at her, more serious. "If you're worried, you don't have to be. I'm not doing anything I haven't been doing longer than you've been alive. I haven't died yet."

"Death isn't a habit you develop, you know, like tobacco or whis-key. It only takes once."

"In that case, I promise I'll let you know before I consider taking it up. Is that toast done?"

"Almost." She turned the bread belatedly. "But we need more milk."

"Well, talk to the goats about it." He checked the milk jug, none-theless, and made a face. "We do, don't we? And more jam. I need to take the boat out to the mainland for that."

This gave her the opening she'd been hoping for. She picked the slightly burnt bread off the fork and buttered it, trying for careful nonchalance. "I could come with you."

"No," he said, equally lightly. "You couldn't."

"Why not? You just pointed out that you've been leaving the island at night since long before I was born, and you're still alive. Why can't I at least come to get the supplies in broad daylight?"

"Because you don't go to the mainland, Biddy. I told you."

"You told me. You also told me it wouldn't be forever. You said I could go when I was older."

He frowned. "Did I? When did I say that?"

"Rowan! You said it when I was little. Seven or eight, I think. I asked if I could come with you when I was grown up, and you said, 'Yeah, of course.'"

She had held on to that across all the years in between, imagining what it would be like. Rowan clearly had no memory of it at all, but Hutchincroft nudged him pointedly and he shrugged. "All right. You're not grown up yet, though, are you?"

She couldn't argue with that. She had tried when she turned sixteen to think of herself as a woman, like Jane Eyre or Elizabeth Bennet or the multitudes of heroines who lived in her books, but in her head she wasn't there. They were all older than her, and had all, even Jane, seen more of life. And yet she was too old to be Sara Crewe or Alice or Wendy Darling either. She was a liminal person, trapped between a world she'd grown out of and another that wouldn't let her in. It was one reason why she wanted to leave the island so badly—the hope that leaving the place she'd grown up would help her leave her childhood behind. Not forever, not yet. But for a visit, to see what it was like.

"I'm not a child," she said instead. Of that, at least, she was sure. "I'm seventeen in December. I might be seventeen already—you don't know. I can't stay on this island my entire life."

"I know," he said. "I'll work something out, I promise. For now, it's not safe for you."

"You leave all the time."

"It's not exactly safe for me either, but that's different."

"Why?" She couldn't keep frustration out of her voice. "It should be safer for me than for you, surely. You're a mage. I'm nothing."

"You're not nothing," he corrected her, and he was truly serious now. "Don't say that."

She knew better than to push that further. Rowan, like her, had no patience for self-pity, and she didn't want to blur the lines of her argument by indulging in it.

"Well," she amended. "I can't channel magic. I'm not like you. I'm no different to any of the other millions of people living out there in the world right now, the ones I read about in books, and they're safe and well. If there's no threat to them, surely there's no threat to me." She hesitated, seized by doubt. "They *are* out there, aren't they? It really is like in the books?"

He laughed. "What, you mean are we the only people left in the world?"

"How should I know?" she pointed out, defensive. "I've never seen anyone else."

"There are millions of people out there. Of all shapes and sizes, colors and creeds, many of them very much like the people in books. Trust me. Where do you think the jam comes from?"

"I don't know where the jam comes from!" This wasn't strictly true—she knew both exactly how jam was made, thanks to the library, and how Rowan obtained it, thanks to Hutchincroft. But qualifying that would weaken her position, so she rushed on. "I've never seen that either. I've never seen anywhere except the island."

"Well, none of the rest of the world have ever seen the island. So you're not too badly off, considering."

"That isn't the point! I know why the rest of the world can't see us. I don't understand why I can't see the rest of the world."

"Biddy," he said, and the familiar note was in his voice, quiet but firm, that had stopped her in her tracks since she was old enough to recognize her name. "That's enough, all right?"

Against her own will, she fell silent, burning with resentment. It was directed at herself as much as anyone. Rowan rarely tried to guide any aspect of her behavior, and yet when he did she never dared to push back. No, *dared* was the wrong word—that sounded as though she was afraid of him, and Rowan had never done anything to make her so. The barrier came from inside her own head, from her own reluctance to lose Rowan's approval when he and Hutch were the only people in her world. She hated it. The heroines in her book would never care what anybody thought. And she hated most of all the reminder that her world was so small.

Rowan must have seen it, because the lines of his face softened. "Look, Bid—"

"Never mind." She laid down her butter knife and pushed her toast aside, trying for a dignified exit. It felt stiff and childish, only signifying that she had lost both the argument and, for some reason, her breakfast. "It was just a question, that's all. I need to see to the goats."

"All right." Rowan didn't sound happy, but he clearly had no intention of prolonging a discussion he himself had stopped. "I'll be in the study if you need me. We'll probably see you this afternoon?"

Biddy glanced at Hutch, who was watching her anxiously from the fireplace, and managed a wan smile for him. Then she went out the kitchen door, into the windswept courtyard where the chickens pecked. She wished, not for the first time lately, the hinges in the castle doors worked well enough to allow a remotely satisfying slam.

———✦————————✦———

There were three rules to living on the Isle of Hy-Brasil, or so Rowan always said.

The first was to never set foot under the trees after dark. That one wasn't much of a rule—Rowan broke it all the time. It was difficult not to in the short daylight hours of winter. The forest covered most of the island, tangled and grey green and wild, and they often needed to forage well into it to collect plants for food and spells. But certainly there was an edge of danger under the branches once the sun went down. The shadows had been known to misbehave; high lilting sounds like laughter or half-heard music drifted through the leaves when the wind was still. There were things in the depths of Hy-Brasil that none of them would ever know, not even Hutchincroft.

The second rule was to watch out for the Púca, and never accept a ride from it. Unlike the rule about the trees, which seemed something she had always known, Biddy could dimly remember being given this one when she was four years old. She had been picking dandelions in the fields beyond the castle, the summer's grass swishing past her knees, when she had seen a black horse beyond the crest of the hill. There were no horses on Hy-Brasil: She had recognized it at once from pictures in her books, and her heart had thrilled. Its golden eyes had held her, beckoned her, and she had been venturing forward open-mouthed to touch its wiry mane when Rowan and Hutch had come from nowhere. She could recollect very little after that, but afterward Rowan had sat her down in the library for a rare serious talk and told her all about the Púca—that it was a shapeshifter, a trickster spirit who loved nothing better than to tempt unwary travelers onto its back, take them for a wild and terrifying ride, and dump them in a patch of thorns miles from home. She had found the thought more funny than scary at the time, but she had steered clear of any golden-eyed creature ever since.

The third was to never harm the black rabbits that speckled the long grass behind the castle, along the cliff paths up to the ruins. This one was the easiest of all. Biddy couldn't imagine why anyone would want to harm a rabbit.

It wasn't until she was a good deal older that Biddy had realized the fourth rule of living on Hy-Brasil, the unspoken one, the only truly inviolable ultimatum and one that applied only to herself. She was never to leave it.

It took her a long time to notice this, and even longer to mind. Hy-Brasil was hidden from the rest of the world by centuries-old magic, only able to be seen once every seven years and only reached by a chosen few. Nobody had ever come to its shores in her lifetime.

As a child, she was curious about the world beyond the sea, but in a vague, half-sketched way, as she was curious about a lot of things she read in books. London and Treasure Island and horses and dragons were all equally imagined to her. She thought she would probably see them one day, when she was old. In the meantime, the island was hers to explore, and it took up more time than she could ever imagine having. There were books to read, thousands of them in the castle library, and Rowan brought back more all the time. There were trees to climb, caves along the beach to get lost in, traces of the fair folk who had once lived on the island to find and bring home. There was work to be done: Food needed to be grown and harvested; the livable parts of the castle, the parts that weren't a crumbling ruin, needed to be constantly fortified against the harsh salt winds; the rocks needed to be combed for useful things when the tide went out. She was a half-wild thing of ink and grass and sea breezes, raised by books and rabbits and fairy lore, and that was all she cared to be.

She didn't know now when that had changed—it had done so gradually, one question at a time wearing away at her like the relentless drops of rain on the ruins by the cliffs. She must have asked Rowan at some point how she had come to the island, but she couldn't remember it. It seemed she had always known the story: a violent storm that churned up the ocean and strewn the shoreline with driftwood; Rowan and Hutchincroft walking along the clifftops the morning afterward; the battered lifeboat on the rocks, half-flooded, with the little girl that had been her curled up in the very bottom. Rowan had since shown her the spot many times at her request. She had been no more than a year old when they found her, with a mop of chestnut curls and enormous eyes, wet through and crying but unscathed. There was no trace of her parents, or the shipwreck that had likely killed them. It was as though the island itself had reached out into the deadly seas and snatched her to safety. She liked to think of that—that Hy-Brasil, which rarely let anyone come to its shores, had for its own reasons welcomed her. It had to mean something. Perhaps she was the daughter of somebody important, a queen or a brilliant sorcerer; perhaps, like the orphan girls in her books, she had some great destiny to fulfill. It made up in some small way for not being a mage.

She could, though, distinctly remember reading *A Little Princess* when she was ten or eleven and stopping short at the realization that Sara Crewe, at seven, was being sent from her home to school. She wasn't sure why this struck her particularly—she had read other stories about children being sent to school, after all, without wondering why it didn't seem to apply to her. Perhaps it was that Sara's father, young and full of fun, reminded her a little of Rowan just as Sara reminded her a little of herself. Perhaps it was just that she was ready to question, and books, as they so often did, crystallized her question into words.

She'd tracked him down to the library that evening. "Rowan?"

"Yes, my love?" he'd said absently. It probably wasn't the right time—he was up on the bookshelves near the ceiling, balanced precariously as he tracked down a volume about poltergeists. Hutch lay on the rug by the fire, flopped on his side in a peaceful C shape.

"Why haven't I gone to school?"

She thought he focused his attention a little more carefully on the books in front of him, but he might have just been trying not to fall to his death. "Do you want to go to school?"

It wasn't what she had been asking, and the possibility had distracted her while she considered. "I think so," she said at last. "Someday."

"Well, then you will, someday," he said. "It might be a while, though. I'll see what I can do."

It was no different to the kind of thing he'd said before, but for the first time, far too late, she realized what he wasn't saying. He was telling her that she couldn't leave yet, and she trusted that he had a good reason. He was telling her that she would leave one day, and she trusted that too. But he wasn't telling her *why*. He never did.

Once she had noticed that, she began to notice other things he wasn't saying, lurking like predators in long grass amid the things he was saying instead.

She knew, for instance, that Rowan had grown up on the distant shoreline she could see from the cliffs on a clear day, the one she used to think of as the beginning of the world. Actually, it was Inishmore, one of the Aran Islands. Beyond it was the coast of western Ireland, and beyond that was Great Britain and then the great mass of Europe, over which Rowan and Hutch had wandered before coming to the island. Rowan would give her all the books and maps she could ever want, and in the right mood he would talk to her for hours about the countries inside their pages. Yet when she pressed him on any stories from his own childhood or travels, he would turn elusive.

"It was a long time ago," he said once, with a shrug.

"So was the Norman Conquest," she reminded him. "And we were just talking about that."

He laughed. "Well, it wasn't *that* long ago!"

"How long was it, then?" she countered. "I know you're a lot older than you look, because Hutch told me that magicians age slowly once they get their familiars. But he didn't know how old that made you, because rabbits aren't very good with time."

"Neither am I. A hundred years or so? I lost count around the Boer War."

She didn't believe that for a minute. Rowan could misplace a lot of things, but surely not entire years. But she had learned to accept it. It was useless to try to make Rowan talk when he didn't want to. And Hutchincroft, who when he could talk would do so happily at any time at all, knew Rowan too well to give Biddy information that she wasn't supposed to have.

Lately, though, things had been different. It wasn't only that she was getting older, more restless, her eyes pulled constantly to the bump of land on the horizon and her thoughts pulled even further. Rowan had been disappearing more and more often; he was bringing back a lot more injuries than he was artifacts, and some of them she suspected hurt more than he was letting on. Hutchincroft was restless when he wasn't there, on edge, possibly in constant silent communication and certainly in silent worry. It was possible, she supposed, that these things had been festering under the surface of her life for a long time, and she was only lately becoming aware of them. Either way, she could feel a bite of danger in the air like the first frost of autumn, and she didn't like it.

━▶■◀━════════════▶■◀━

It should have been a perfect morning. The day had unfurled crisp and bright, the kind to be taken advantage of on Hy-Brasil, where wind was common but sun was rare, and she had gone up the cliffs with a rug, three undersized apples, and a battered copy of *Jane Eyre*. The wind ruffled her hair and the grass behind the castle; the black rabbits grazing there, infected with the chaotic joy of it, flicked their ears and jumped in the air. It made her smile, despite everything. And yet she hadn't been able to focus as she usually did. The argument had tainted the morning like smoke, leaving an acrid taste in her throat and a grey pall over the sky. The world of her book seemed impossibly far away, full of strangers and schools and romances when she had never seen anything of the kind. Her self-righteous fury at Rowan's treatment of her gave way, predictably, to doubts about her own behavior, and then to guilt. It was a relief when shortly after midday a shadow fell across the pages.

"Hello," Rowan said. At his side, Hutchincroft nudged her book experimentally with his nose. "What are you up to, then?"

She shrugged, determined not to give him the satisfaction of a smile quite yet. "Not a lot."

"You're not still sulking, are you?"

"I don't *sulk*. You two sulk. I was reading."

"Any good?"

She glanced down at her book. " 'It is in vain to say human beings ought to be satisfied with tranquility: they must have action; and they will make it if they cannot find it. Millions are condemned to a stiller doom than mine, and millions are in silent revolt against their lot. Nobody knows how many rebellions besides political rebellions ferment in the masses of life which people earth.' "

His eyebrows went up. "And that's you not sulking, is it?"

"It's Charlotte Brontë, not me!" In fact, that part had been a few chapters earlier, but she had remembered it to make a point. "I'm just reading what she says."

"Well, tell her to lay off." He must have seen that pretending they hadn't argued wasn't working. She heard a faint sigh, and then he settled down beside her on the grass. "Look, I know it's not fair. I know it's lonely here for you. For what it's worth, I'm sure I did say you could come with me when you were older, and I'm sure I meant it. I thought things would be different by now. They might be soon—I'll do what I can, I promise—but I need more time. All right?"

It wasn't, really. But she knew Rowan was apologizing in his own way, and she wanted to apologize too. She didn't want there to be undercurrents of tension and struggle between the two of them, as there seemed to be more and more often these days. There never had been before. Oh, when she was thirteen and a prickly ball of existential angst, she would shout at him that he didn't *understand* her, and he would retort, a little frustrated and a lot more amused, that she was bloody right about that, and she would storm off fuming. But that had been about her own emotions flaring, easily solved once they settled down again. This was about Rowan, and she had enough common sense to see that if he wasn't going to budge, she could do nothing except keep pushing or back down.

And so she nodded, and tried to mean it.

"Thank you." His voice was so unexpectedly quiet and sincere that it caught her off guard. It was as though a curtain had flickered aside, and beyond it she could glimpse something shadowed and troubled. Then the moment passed, and he was stretching and getting back to his feet in one sure movement. "What time is it, by the way?"

Biddy resigned herself to the subject being closed and checked her coat pocket for her watch. "Ah . . . almost two."

"That late?" He glanced down at Hutch. "You were right. We do need to get a move on if we want to get back before tonight."

"Are you going somewhere tonight?" She made her voice deliberately innocent, and his look suggested he knew it.

"I might be. For now, I'm going out to the oak. Do you fancy a walk?"

She was half tempted to refuse, just to show she wasn't letting him off as easily as all that. But she *did* fancy a walk, and what was more, she fancied their company after her morning alone. So she got to her feet, brushing grass from her skirt.

"It isn't only about me leaving the island," she couldn't help adding. "I worry about you when I wake up at night and you're not there."

"I know you do. But you don't have to, I promise. I can take care of myself. I'm always back by morning."

"That doesn't mean you always will be."

"It doesn't mean I won't be either," he pointed out, which was technically accurate if infuriating.

They walked through the trees, the two of them on foot and Hutch scampering beside them before Rowan scooped him up to settle him against his shoulder. At this time of year, the path was like a dark green cathedral, dappled with sun, and Biddy told the other two about the words the Japanese had for different kinds of light: Light through leaves was called *komorebi*. Her mood lifted, and the trapped, resentful feeling sank back down in her chest where it belonged.

When they passed the familiar track where the elm trees grew, Rowan stopped.

"Think you can get up there now?" he asked, with a nod to the tallest branches.

She sighed. "Honestly, does it matter? When in my life am I ever going to need to get up a tree?"

"You never know," he said lightly. "Does that mean you can't?"

Reluctantly, she returned his grin. "What do you think?"

Children in the books Biddy read were always told not to climb trees, and getting in trouble for tearing their clothes when they did. Hutchincroft, it was true, did fuss over both her clothes and her safety, but Rowan had been teaching her to climb since she could walk, usually just a little higher and on branches a little more precarious than she would have preferred. Sometimes they made a game of seeing how far through the forest they could get without once setting foot on the ground; sometimes they raced to see who could get the highest branches first. Rowan always won, but she had grown to her full height over the summer, and she had been practicing.

"Good work," Rowan said approvingly, as she made a grab for a mossy branch and pulled herself up to him. "You'll be outclimbing me soon."

She rolled her eyes, pleased but disbelieving.

"No, I mean it! You're clever, and you're brave—that's all you need with trees. My reach is longer than yours, but you're lighter, and you're learning how to use that. You're mostly slower now because you're more cautious than me, and that's probably not a bad thing. Probably."

"Well, it means I'm not going to come back in the mornings covered with scratches and bruises," she couldn't resist saying, "so that's a good thing. *Probably.*"

He laughed. "Honestly, you and Hutch. If you had your way, I'd never do anything at all."

There was an edge to the laugh, and she knew there had been an edge to her words too. He couldn't quite hide that he was in an odd mood: restless, distant, too light and playful when he was talking to her and too prone to frowning silence when he wasn't. He took a great deal of magic from the oak as well, when they finally reached it. As though he intended to use it.

She said nothing more. It was his business, she reminded herself, and he had made it clear that he would answer no questions. If she trusted him—and she did, with all her heart—then that would have to be enough. Until she felt like starting another argument, at least.

That night, when she heard his footsteps soft and light on the stairs, she lay quiet. She kept her gaze trained on her window, until a darker speck of black flashed across the clouds and was gone. Then she closed her eyes, and tried to think of nothing at all.

＊ーー・ーーーーーー・ーーー＊

Biddy wasn't sure what woke her, only that she sat up so sharply in her bed that something certainly had. The sky was still dark, but faint traces of grey and gold glimmered on the horizon. Almost dawn.

She swung her legs out of bed and went to the window. The grass under the castle stretched out dark and tangled beneath them. On it, a square of light glowed from Rowan's study window in the turret. When she craned her neck up, she could see the shutters wide open and a candle burning on the ledge. That candle had been left there for a reason: to guide the raven back from its travels. When Rowan returned, he extinguished it. Right now, like the rest of the castle, it was still ready and waiting. A memory stirred uneasily. She frowned, trying through the last cobwebs of sleep to see what it was that troubled her. She had known he was going, after all.

It was then that she heard a sharp, sudden sound; the sound, she knew at once, was what had woken her in the first place. The warning thump of a rabbit's back feet against a hard wood floor. Hutchincroft.

The cobwebs cleared as if in a sudden gust, and her stomach turned cold.

The sky.

An hour or two before dawn, Rowan had said, when she had asked him what time he had gotten back. He had given her the same answer before, on many occasions. It was one sure thing she knew about his nighttime travels, the more valuable for being the only one: Wherever Rowan went, he was always back an hour or two before dawn.

Now dawn was almost here. And Rowan hadn't come home.

Chapter Two

*I*t didn't take long to find Hutchincroft. He was outside her bedroom when she opened the door, periscoped bolt upright, his sleek golden body rigid with tension.

"What's wrong?" Biddy dropped to her knees beside him. "Is something outside?"

Hy-Brasil, after all, had dangers of its own. Sometimes the Púca came too close to the castle to be entirely comfortable; sometimes shadows were shaken from the trees in a high wind. The fair folk were said to walk at this time of the year, and in the ocean the merrows grew restless. Sometimes Hutchincroft was unnerved by something as simple as an oncoming storm or a flock of black-backed gulls. She wasn't surprised, though, when Hutchincroft shook his head—one of the few human gestures he could mimic as a rabbit.

"It's Rowan, isn't it?" she said, as steadily as she could. "Something's happened to him. What is it?"

He dropped to all fours then, and the look he gave her clenched her chest. Hutch's fear always went to her heart, but this was more than fear. It was utter bewilderment, and terrible loss.

"You don't know, do you?" she whispered. "How can you not know?"

Rowan and Hutchincroft were mage and familiar—their communication went deeper than body or mind. They were part of each other. Hutch could reach Rowan through distance, through sleep, through the very worst pain. There were only two things that could separate them. One was magic, though she couldn't imagine what kind.

She wouldn't think about the other.

Whatever she had been dreading, whatever Rowan had been keeping from her, it was here.

"Hutch." Her voice trembled; she forced a deep breath. Rowan had said, only that afternoon, that she was brave. She had said, only that afternoon, that she wasn't a child anymore. "Hutch, if Rowan is in trouble, we need to find him. I need the scrying glass."

It was something she had considered often, when she lay awake wondering where he could be at nights. The only thing that had stopped her going to it then was the knowledge that Hutch would never let her. Sure enough, he growled faintly on reflex.

"Oh, for God's sake, I *know* I'm not allowed in Rowan's study without him. But this is an emergency, isn't it? And you can't use the glass, so it has to be me. Please."

Hutch must have known she was right—they *did* need the glass, and familiars couldn't use artifacts any more than they could be enchanted. They were too close to pure magic themselves. He hesitated only a further second, out of loyalty to Rowan's wishes. The next, he was bounding up the stairs, and Biddy was running behind him as fast as she could.

⋙══════════⋘

Biddy had been in Rowan's study many times, when she'd knocked at the door to see if he wanted to come on a walk, or he'd called her in to show her the latest artifact he'd found. She knew the small, curved room at the top of the turret well, with its haphazard piles of books and mingled clutter and charms. She knew the battered armchair by the tiny fireplace, one of the rare pieces of furniture that had been brought across from the mainland in the currach and not built on the island. But she had never been in it without Rowan. It

looked horribly empty and grey in the predawn light, as though he
had taken the colors with him. There was a cup of cold tea on the
mantelpiece, where Rowan had set it that evening, and a half-eaten
apple on the desk. He hadn't come down to supper.

She hadn't gone up to knock on the door for him. She'd sat
downstairs alone in the kitchen, resenting his absence when he'd
said that he'd see her again before she went to bed. It seemed a
thousand years ago, and now her resentment was a burning shard
of guilt in her chest. It didn't matter. The mainland didn't matter.
His disappearances didn't matter, nor his secrets, nor his moods. If
he could only be home and safe, she'd never want to leave the island
again. She'd never be angry at him again. *Just please*—she found
herself whispering it, as a mage would a spell—*please, please let him
be safe.*

Biddy found the scrying glass quickly, the size of a dinner plate
with a silver frame, and laid it flat on the desk. The weight of it
in her hands made her feel somewhat less useless. She might not
be a mage like Rowan; she couldn't take magic inside her, and she
couldn't cast spells. But enchanted objects had magic of their own,
and Rowan had taught her how to use most of them over the years.
This, at least, she could do. She paused only to lift Hutch onto the
table, so he could peer anxiously into the glass with her.

"Rowan of Hy-Brasil, please," she said—firmly, in the precise,
Hutchincroft-ish tone of voice Rowan had always told her sounded
like she was putting through a call on a telephone.

It took longer than usual. Perhaps, like Hutch, the magic had
difficulty finding him. But after several anxious seconds the glass
fogged, cleared, and resolved itself into an image of a room—
windowless and bare, utterly dark but for an eerie green-gold glow
that permeated the air like a mist. It was by that faint light alone
that she could make out Rowan's body on the floor. His eyes were
closed and his limbs crumpled beneath him, as though he had
fallen before he had a chance to catch himself. He might have
looked dead, had Biddy not noticed with a shiver of relief that his
chest rose and fell. Something silver glinted in his closed fist.

Hutchincroft's twitching nose pressed to the glass, desperate, as though he hoped to break through to the image behind it. Through her own fear, Biddy's heart ached for him. She couldn't imagine how it must feel for them to be separated.

"He's alive." She brushed her tangled hair from her eyes. *Stay firm, take a breath,* think. "And if you can't wake him, then he's under an enchantment. An enchanted sleep—I suppose they must be real, they're in so many stories. But I don't know what to do about it."

Hutchincroft thumped his back feet, miserably this time, and looked toward the window. Biddy looked too—the sky was pale grey now, almost white, the sun not far away. She wasn't sure why that mattered, but she was sure it did. Rowan was always back by sunrise. If he was still asleep when the sun rose, then she had no doubt he would be in danger. Perhaps he wouldn't be able to come back at all.

Rowan would know what to do. He always knew what to do. If she could just talk to him, even for a minute, he could tell her. But he was so far away in body and mind, and there was no way to get him back.

Or to get to him. The idea came like a candle catching light.

"Hutch! Does Rowan still have that ring he showed me last winter? The one that lets you walk into someone's dreams?"

She wouldn't have been at all surprised if Rowan had lost it. But Hutchincroft's ears pricked, and he hopped over the mirror to a shelf above the desk. Biddy saw the ring even before Hutchincroft picked it up in his delicate mouth. It was a small silver band—Rowan had brought it back one night and showed it to her at breakfast the following morning. She had been fascinated, though wary.

"Why would you want to go into someone's dreams?" she had asked.

"It's fun." He threw the ring in the air, caught it, inspected it. "Besides, you might need to talk to someone a long way away, and this is one way to do it. Bit of a weird way, though, and you can get very lost, so I wouldn't recommend it."

"Is it dangerous?"

He winked at her. "Well, it wouldn't be very fun if it weren't at least a *little* bit dangerous."

A weird way, and a dangerous way. But it was the only way, at least as far as she knew, to talk to someone who couldn't be woken.

"I'll go into his dreams and try to wake him up," she said to Hutch, with more assurance than she felt. "Or if I can't wake him, at least he can tell me where he is and what to do to help. I just need something of his. A scrap of hair would work, if there was some on a hairbrush, or..." Hutchincroft looked at her, and she smiled despite everything. "No, I know. I don't think Rowan's ever brushed his hair in his life."

She ran her eyes over the room quickly, catching on anything hopeful and bouncing off again in disappointment. It had to be a part of the person, Rowan said. Hair, fingernails—blood at a push, if you wanted to make things *really* weird. There was nothing like that in Rowan's study. Just books, paper, countless oddments, more cups and mugs than she thought they owned.

And—

Her eyes lit, at last, on Hutchincroft.

"Hutch," she said, slowly, over the quickening of her heart. "Would it work if I used you? You're his familiar. You're a part of each other."

It sounded like cheating to her—the two of them shared a soul, not a body. But magic loved cheating.

In answer, Hutchincroft pushed his head under her palm, burrowing until it reached his soft ears.

It was then, of all times, that the true seriousness of the situation sank in. Hutch cared about her safety more than almost anything in the world. He protested when she climbed too high, strayed too far, stayed out too long in rain and cold and sun. Yet now, when she had declared her intent to disappear into a dream—into an enchanted sleep that even Rowan couldn't escape—he was helping her without a murmur. There was only one reason he would let her take such a risk. Whatever danger Rowan was in, it was far worse.

Biddy drew a deep breath.

You're clever, and you're brave, Rowan had said to her that afternoon, and he had meant it. But he had been talking about climbing trees. It was easy to be brave when the greatest risk was in falling to the ground—that was real, tangible. Magic was perilous in ways that couldn't be predicted. You never knew what you might fall into. Rowan never cared what she climbed, but even he had never let her do magic alone. If he were here now, he would never let her do this.

But he wasn't here. And if she didn't, he might never be again.

She sat down at the desk first—you should always, Rowan said, be sitting down when you tried a new spell. Then she put the ring on her finger, buried the fingers of her other hand in Hutchincroft's fur, and entered Rowan's dream.

⬥━━━━━━━━⬥

Last summer, Biddy had slipped from the cliffs near the ruins and tumbled twenty feet into the sea. She had seen a glint of silver in a small hollow worn in the rocks: That close to the remnants of the old wall, she had wondered if it might be an artifact, even a magical one. It was a few feet down from the edge of the bank, the sea a dizzying grey-blue swirl below. Normally she would have mentioned it to Rowan and let him investigate later—he could fly, after all. But it was tantalizingly close, and the thought of how stupid she would look if it turned out to be nothing more than a trick of the light overcame her natural caution. Her boots had gripped the rock with reassuring firmness; she judged she could do it, and after she had swung herself over the edge, it was too late to change her mind. She was almost there when her foot shot from underneath her in a scree of pebbles, and she was falling.

Putting on the dream ring felt exactly like that plunge into icy water.

One moment she was on firm ground in the study with Hutch beside her; the next, her stomach lurched, and her grip was torn away. She was dropping, plummeting, a roar of wind in her ears and a surge of panic in her throat. Then, just as she had once hit the water and opened her eyes to a greenish haze shot through with sunlight, she opened her eyes and there was a new world about her.

A room. She was standing in a room. A room she had never seen before.

In all her life, the only rooms Biddy had ever known were those of the castle: the stone kitchen, cold in winter and hot in summer; her own room looking east out over the fields and the sea; Rowan's bedroom upstairs with its perpetually unmade bed; his study at the top of the turret; the massive oak-shelved library where she all but lived in the colder months; the frigid bathroom with its cracked washbasin; the crumbling gatehouse that had become dangerous with age and could be ventured into only with great care. This was smaller than any of them, and so much newer. The pale green walls formed a perfect square, with a flickering fireplace and darker green curtains half-drawn against the night. More surprising yet was what she could glimpse beyond those curtains. The glow of lamps, the rattle of wheels on cobbles, the sight—so terrifyingly close—of other windows across a narrow street.

This wasn't Hy-Brasil. For the first time in her memory, she was somewhere else.

She had only a moment to take all this in. She wasn't alone. Rowan stood facing the fireplace. It was him, exactly as he had left the island, even the same tiny cut above one eyebrow she'd noticed that morning. And yet something was different. His stance was open, less deliberately careless; his face, too, was unguarded, and softer than she had ever seen it. Opposite him, back to the fire, was a woman.

To Biddy's embarrassment, her first reaction was not curiosity or suspicion or fear but a thrill of wonder. A stranger. And not only a stranger, a woman. In all her life, she had only ever seen other women in books, in photographs, and once or twice—though she had never told Rowan or Hutch—in dreams as a small girl, when a lady about the age of a mother or older sister would come to her and smile and ask her about her day. This one looked the same age as Rowan, however old that was, but unlike him she was beautifully dressed. Her hair was darker than Biddy's, almost black; her face was paler, framed by precise curls. There was nothing unguarded about her. She faced Rowan firmly, proudly, a warrior primed for battle.

"I told you, I'm not going anywhere!" She had a cool, clear voice, yet by her side her hands were balled into fists. "You don't understand. It's too late."

"How is it too late?" Rowan demanded.

His voice jolted Biddy out of her fascination, and she flushed inwardly. For God's sake, this wasn't real. This was the inside of Rowan's head. She wasn't really away from the island, and the woman was no more solid than the one she herself had dreamed about as a child. A closer look at the woman's clothes confirmed that. Her dress was a soft grey green, the color of moss, and it drew to what seemed an uncomfortably tight waist before blossoming out into a voluminous bell-shaped skirt. Biddy had seen dresses like that in illustrations nestled in the text of *Jane Eyre* and *Oliver Twist*; it wasn't what people wore today. Not only was this a dream, it was a dream taking place at least fifty years ago, perhaps more.

Rowan was talking, low and urgent, not waiting for a response to his question. "Hutch and I have a rune door set up in Galway. We've had it years and never touched it, even Storm doesn't know. We can be out of this country in seconds—"

Biddy grabbed Rowan by the arm. "Rowan? It's me. I'm here."

It was like tugging at a statue. He didn't respond, not even to dislodge her. He didn't even know she was there.

This wasn't how it was meant to work. The ring was supposed to allow people to talk to each other in dreams. Surely she should be visible to the dreamer.

"There are places to hide for a while, just to get our bearings," Rowan was saying to the woman. "They won't find us."

"Suppose you're right, and you do manage to hide. Then what?"

"Then we fight back!"

"How?" She didn't wait for an answer either. "I can't leave London.

I can't leave the Council. We don't all have the luxury of running away, Rowan. Some of us have responsibilities."

"What *responsibilities*?" He shook his head, frustrated. "Jesus, Morgaine, you know what they've ordered us to do? What you would have to do to stay?"

"Of course I know!"

"Well, then. You can't tell me you're willing to pay that price."

"I already have." Her chin shot up, defiant, daring him to respond. "I did it this morning."

He laughed, a short, sharp bark of disbelief. "You didn't."

"I did. Look around, if you don't believe it. Look anywhere you like. Tilda's gone. She faded. She doesn't exist anymore."

"I don't believe it." But he did believe it, whatever it was. He took a step back, involuntarily. The color had leeched from his face like the blue from the sky as the sun went down. "You would never hurt her. You couldn't."

"She told me to!" Some of the brightness in the woman's eyes came from tears, Biddy thought. "They came for me this morning. Either I obeyed them, or I would be arrested. You know by arrested they meant killed."

Biddy tried again. "Rowan!"

It was useless. He couldn't see her; he couldn't hear her. His attention was fixed on the woman in front of him, and she had never seen him like that before—so horrified, so defenseless, so young and so hurt. It was frightening.

"She told me to do what they asked," the woman said, and there was an edge of defensiveness in her voice. "She told me to let her go."

"Of course she did!" Rowan snapped. "She wanted to keep you safe. How could you *listen*?"

"Because she was right! I'm no use to anyone in prison or dead. And I can't do anything hunted as a fugitive, scrabbling for the slightest hint of magic—neither can you. If we want to put this right, we need to keep our places on the Council and fight from the inside. It's our only chance."

Something hard glinted in his eyes. "You're worse than Vaughan. At least he doesn't pretend to be doing the right thing."

The woman's chin dropped then, at last. "Rowan—"

"Don't," he said flatly.

Biddy had no idea what they were talking about. She had no idea where they were. She was witnessing something horribly private, and she had no idea how to stop. But she knew that somewhere out there, the dawn was coming.

"Rowan." She said his name as loudly and as firmly as she could, because she could think of nothing else. "Rowan, this isn't real. You're in a dream somewhere. You have to wake up."

Something crossed his face—a frown, or a shadow of a frown. It was gone in a heartbeat, but she had seen it. Her heart leapt.

The woman was speaking again. Her voice trembled on the brink of calm. "You can hate me if you want. But if you're not going to join us, then you need to leave here, now. They're coming for you."

His attention went back to the woman, but it was weaker this time, divided. For a moment, Biddy could have sworn his eyes lit on her instead. "They're coming because of you, aren't they? You told them I would be here."

"For God's sake, Rowan, they knew! They've been watching you. They've been watching all of us for weeks. You have to go."

Biddy didn't wait for him to reply. She hit him on the shoulder, hard as she could, and then harder. "*Rowan!* Wake *up!*"

This time, at last, he heard her. With a strangled cry, he pulled back and dropped to his knees.

The room stilled. The woman froze, lips about to speak, eyes staring at nothing. Outside, the noise of the street quieted. Even the fire in the grate held steady, caught between flickers of flame.

The only things moving now were Biddy and Rowan. He rubbed at his eyes, firmly, as if to rid them of dust, and when he lowered his hands, his face was his own again—only puzzled, and wary. Biddy dropped to her own knees and threw her arms around him. He felt insubstantial to the touch, on the cusp of being a ghost, but he hugged her back.

"All right," he said, still dazed. "I'm here. What's wrong?"

"*You're* wrong." Biddy pulled back. She hadn't realized until then that her eyes had filled with tears. Just like the woman, who stood still now and silent, waiting to draw Rowan back. The room around them seemed to be holding its breath. The colors were subdued, with the cracked, faded quality of an old painting. "You're asleep somewhere, enchanted. This is a dream."

He blinked slowly. "A dream?"

"Hutch lost you. We didn't know what had happened, until we used the scrying glass."

"Hutch..." His eyes finally fixed on her. She could have sobbed with relief as he came back into them. "I should have known. He isn't here. I can't even hear him. And of course he *was* here, when this happened. I remember...Is he all right? Are you?"

"He's fine," she said. "I'm fine. We're both back at the castle. I used the ring to enter your dreams."

"You shouldn't have done that. I told you never to use any of the objects without me. I *definitely* told you never to use that ring, in particular."

"What else was I supposed to do?" she demanded. "You were lost. You're still lost—in body, at least. Where are you?"

The question distracted him from telling her off—she suspected his heart hadn't really been in it. "I..." He shook his head, frustrated. "I don't remember. I think...You said you saw me in the scrying glass?"

"You're underground, that's all I could make out. Like a cellar, or a dungeon. I think you were holding something silver."

His face cleared. "The amulet. I was in the vault, in the Undercastle. That was so bloody stupid—of course it was a trap. As soon as I picked it up it must have had me. Biddy, how long have I been asleep? What time is it?"

"Almost dawn."

He muttered something she wasn't meant to hear under his breath. "If I'm still there when the sun comes up, they'll check the trap and find me. It might be even earlier, if Storm has a bout of insomnia. I need to wake up."

"How? That's why I came. How do I wake you?"

"You don't have to. I can wake us both, with a bit of luck." He gave her shoulders one last comforting squeeze and rose to his feet. "There's always something not right in an enchanted dream, something that gives you a door out. The spells are woven that way, in case the mage doing the weaving is trapped inside by mistake. That's why they need to be something overwhelming—so the person you've enchanted doesn't have the sense to look for a way out. If you see me losing focus again, hit me as hard as you can. Don't hold back."

"Won't that hurt you?"

"Things don't hurt much in dreams. That's the point. I need you to remind me I'm dreaming."

She nodded conscientiously. "I won't hold back. But *who* will find you? Who did this to you?"

"Later. When I'm back home." He looked at her. "I meant what I said, Biddy. You shouldn't have come here. But I'm glad you did."

So was she, in that moment. Whatever she had entered, whatever dangers they were in, for the first time in her life she felt a part of them. And it would be worth all of it if they could, indeed, be back home.

<hr />

There was only one obvious door leading out of the room, and when Biddy tried it she found it locked.

"Check everything," Rowan told her. He was standing in the middle, eyes flickering over every inch of wall and furniture. "There has to be a way out, but it can be very small, and it won't be where you think."

Biddy checked everything. Door, window, fireplace; behind the bookshelf, behind the couch, under the rug. Her heart, which had quieted when Rowan had come back to her, was pounding again. She knew how close dawn was, and she had seen the underground room in which Rowan's body lay. She knew how little time they had. Perhaps time passed differently in a dream, but it couldn't stop forever.

She made sure to keep one eye on Rowan. Despite his best efforts, he still wasn't quite himself. He rubbed his eyes often, then shook his head. Once he stopped, and she saw the bewildered, half-fogged look creep across his face again. Luckily, she knew what to do. She hit him sharp and hard, right in the kidneys like he had shown her once, and he startled awake with a yelp and held up his hands in submission.

"All right, I'm back! Ow. I'm glad I *am* dreaming, or that would have had me on the floor."

"Well, I wouldn't have done it if you weren't," she reminded him.

"I'm glad to hear it. Get your hits in now rather than later, that's all I'm saying."

The dream had started moving again. Once more, sounds filtered through from the street outside, and shadows flickered on the wall.

"It's a good sign," Rowan said, catching her glance at the window. "The dream's getting stronger. It means we're getting close."

"Does it?"

"Well," he said cheerfully. "That, or I'm dying. I suppose we'll find out when I wake up."

Biddy shot him a very unamused look, right as the woman spoke from the center of the room.

"They're coming," she said, low and urgent. "You have to go."

Rowan ignored her.

"Who's coming?" Biddy asked. The room was definitely darkening. Outside, the wind roared. She hadn't heard it before, and now she wondered if it was the wind at all. "Does she mean the people who trapped you?"

"No," he said shortly. "It's nothing that can hurt us now. It's a warning from a long time ago. Never mind her."

Biddy took a step toward the woman. Morgaine, Rowan had called her, before she had said whatever had so shocked him and he had stopped calling her anything at all. Up close, there was something familiar about her face, though Biddy couldn't have said what—she couldn't, after all, have seen her before. It was a beautiful face, strong and determined, cold and luminous like moonlight. Biddy wondered if she really had been that lovely, or if it was simply how Rowan remembered her. Because it *was* a memory, and not a dream—she knew that now, had known it from the moment she had seen Rowan's expression. Dreams could hurt as much as anything, but not so deeply as this was hurting Rowan, or for so long.

"Who is she?" she asked quietly, not expecting an answer.

She didn't get one. Rowan had been feeling the edges of the locked door. He stood back, folded his arms, and let his breath out in a contemplative sigh.

"Perhaps I'm looking for the wrong thing," he said. "I'm trying to find a door. But perhaps the door is right in front of me. What I need is a key."

"Like the one around her neck?"

Rowan turned sharply. "What did you say?"

Biddy pointed at Morgaine. "Around her neck. On the chain. She has a key."

"She never had a key around her neck, on a chain or otherwise."

"Well, there is now."

And there was, gold against her grey-green bodice. Rowan was across the room in a moment. He took it between his fingers, and his smile this time was little more than a glint in the firelight.

"Of course." His laugh, low and unamused, sounded like a threat. "They knew. They knew I would never be brave enough to look closely at her."

Biddy watched him warily, uncertain of his mood. "So...we've found it?"

"We have." He saw her expression, and his own softened at once. "Or you did. Good work."

Morgaine was looking at him, motionless once more. He bowed to her, ironic, and slipped the chain over her head. "I'll take that, thank you, my love."

It made Biddy shiver. She had never heard that note in Rowan's voice before. It was bitter, almost cruel, and he was never cruel.

It was gone again by the time he had crossed the room. He put a reassuring hand on the small of her back, slipped the key into the lock, and twisted it sharply to one side. His face lit. "This is it."

Biddy watched it, skeptical. "The door hasn't opened."

"It will. Give it a minute. We're almost out."

"How do you know?"

"I'm getting cold. That's not the dream—that's me, outside, lying on some cold floor underground." He stretched his shoulders, and made a face. "Some cold, *hard* floor, by the feel of it."

She hoped he was right. Outside, the wind was getting even louder, and she was less and less sure it was the wind.

"Will you wake up alone in that cellar?" The thought struck her with a chill. She couldn't stay with him, after all, once there was no dream to share.

"I'll be in the cellar, but I won't be alone, will I? In fact, I wonder if—" He tilted his head upward, at the painted ceiling. "Hutch? Can you hear me yet?"

The voice was faint, but Biddy knew it at once. It was the voice she heard when Hutch was in human form, only clearer, higher, like the lilt of birdsong. *Rowan?*

"I'm here." Just for a moment, his eyes closed, as if trying to catch the fleeting warmth of a winter sunbeam. "I'm coming back, my friend. Just wait for me, all right?"

Always. Hutch's voice, which had been as soft as Rowan's, rose suddenly in far more familiar protest. *But where have you* been? *I thought you were* dead.

Rowan smiled ruefully. "Now I've done it. He'll never shut up." He turned back to Biddy. "I should wake up when we go through that door. When you find yourself back at home, you'll know I made it. Hutch will know anyway. Don't bother waiting up for me. I'll fly back, but I might be a bit slow."

"What if they're waiting for you when you wake up, whoever set the trap? It might be dawn by now."

He laughed. "Then I'll be *really* slow."

The door gave a very tiny click, and swung open. Beyond was

nothing but black, not darkness but the solid black of ink, of velvet, of the rabbits that grazed the fields on Hy-Brasil.

At their backs, the wind shrieked, a long earsplitting note like the scream of an animal in pain or about to kill. The windows smashed.

The gust whipped Biddy's hair in her face, pushed her forward a step, and wrenched a startled cry from her. Her hand flew up to cover her eyes from the shattered glass, but Rowan was already there, putting himself between her and the gust of air from the open window.

"Through the door," he said, over her shoulder. "Go."

She opened her mouth to ask why, what was coming through? Her eyes caught the first shimmer of movement, and the question died in her throat.

Nothing was coming through. Nothing had broken in. It was the glass. The shards of the window had fallen to the floor in a cascade and they were moving, swarming across the floorboards like glittering insects. They rippled together, transparent and sharp-edged, multiplying and coalescing into great wings and claws.

"Biddy!" Rowan urged, at the same time as Morgaine said, "Get out!"

She needed to move. Of course she needed to move.

But she couldn't. She couldn't even scream. She stared, wide-eyed, pinned by fascination and terror like a butterfly in a case, until Rowan grabbed her roughly by the shoulders and pushed her through the door and into nothing.

◆━━━━━◆

Biddy's eyes flew open with a gasp. The study was around her once more—once more she sat at Rowan's desk, ring on her finger. She barely took this in before twisting in panic toward the window.

Not dawn. Almost—the skies were pale, and the stars were gone. But not yet. They were in time.

Hutchincroft was perched on her lap, paws on her chest, bumping her chin with an anxious nose. She grabbed him tight, and buried her numb fingers in his fur as feeling and sense returned.

"Is he safe?" she asked, just to be sure, and Hutchincroft nudged her reassuringly. She could already tell he was. Hutch was still alert, still concerned, but the panic had faded. His lithe body was relaxed under her fingers, and she hugged him again just to feel it.

When you find yourself back at home, you'll know I made it, Rowan had said. She was home. She reminded herself of that, again and again. The shapes around her were those she'd known her whole life—the jumble of books on the desk, the dusty fireplace, the wind through the castle window with its smell of the sea.

And yet the world around her was different now. It was as though another door had opened, less tangible and yet more real than the one in Morgaine's house, and she had walked into something bigger and wilder than someone else's nightmare.

"He said he'd come back," she said out loud.

When he did, she had questions.

Chapter Three

*I*t was another three hours before the black bird that was Rowan returned home. Neither Biddy nor Hutchincroft had moved, or pretended to. They watched the horizon from the study, curled up in Rowan's worn chair by the cold fireplace, Hutchincroft nestled in Biddy's lap and the blanket from the back of the chair wrapped around them both. They watched the sun creep over the rim of the sea and the sky turn to red and then to blue. And then, at last, Hutchincroft stiffened in her arms and his ears swiveled. A short time later, Biddy saw the familiar black dot appear on the distance. It was aiming for the castle, but it didn't quite make it. The beat of the raven's wings was slow, laborious; as she watched, rising to her feet with Hutchincroft in her arms, it sank lower and lower and landed in the field outside.

They ran.

Hutchincroft was a swift blur as he leapt from her arms and disappeared down the hall. Biddy couldn't hope to keep up. By the time she made it downstairs, out the door, and across the fields, Rowan was lying on the dew-wet grass. She was just in time to catch the end of his transformation from raven to human. Usually, it was seamless and fluid; this time, his limbs twisted and distorted in painful spasms as the feathers vanished, and he rolled over white-faced and trembling. He managed a smile when he saw Biddy and Hutch, though, and even a soft laugh.

"I didn't expect a welcoming committee," he said. "I thought I told you not to wait?"

She didn't know whether she wanted to hug him or hit him. Both seemed childish, so she folded her arms tightly across her chest and tried to keep all the frustrations and worries of the long morning from entering her voice. "Where *were* you? What *happened*? I thought you were never coming back this time!"

So much for her resolve to never be angry at him again.

Beside her, Hutchincroft was poised with his legs stiff, his tail straight up, and his fur bristling angrily. She couldn't hear what he was saying to Rowan, but she could imagine it wasn't nice.

Rowan winced as he sat up. "Steady on. I can't take both of you going off at me at once. Hutch, I'm all right, I promise. Shut up a moment, yeah? You've been telling me off nonstop the whole way home, surely you must be getting bored by now…"

"I thought you were dead," Biddy said. She hadn't let herself put it into words, all the cold, frightening hours since she had woken to find him gone. "When dawn was coming, and there was no sign of you, I thought you'd been killed."

His face softened. "I didn't mean for you to worry. I go all the time, you know that. This wasn't supposed to be any more dangerous than all those other times."

"You said it was always dangerous to leave the island."

"Well, it's always a *little* bit dangerous," he admitted. "Not like that. But it came out all right, didn't it?" He reached out to stroke Hutchincroft's ears, and Hutchincroft scuttled backward firmly out of reach. He was in no mood to be reassured.

The sight of Rowan's outstretched hand distracted Biddy briefly. The palm was seared pink, with raised blisters in the center. "What happened?"

Rowan glanced down at his palm, and his fingers curled slightly as if to protect it. "That was where I picked up the amulet, the one bespelled to put me to sleep. You saw it in my hand, remember?"

"Does it hurt?"

He shrugged. "Stings a bit. It isn't going to kill me. I told you, I'm all right." He glanced at Hutch, who was still bristling, and sighed. "Oh, come on, both of you! Nothing happened!"

"Nothing—?" Biddy heard the familiar voice a moment before Hutchincroft bounded forward. In the blink of an eye, a human figure was standing beside her on the grass where the rabbit had been. He was small, with hair the color of honey and a round face that at that moment was incandescent with fury. Hutchincroft didn't shift into human form often—it took more magic than they usually had to spare. He might have done so now for her sake, so she could hear the conversation. Or maybe, as was sometimes the case, his feelings were just too big for a rabbit.

"Don't tell me nothing happened!" Hutchincroft snapped. His arms were folded, and his eyes, still bright blue and just a little too round to be fully human, blazed. "Biddy is absolutely right. You could easily have died. I would have faded without you. Biddy would have been left all on her own."

"Hutch," Rowan said firmly. "Stop."

Hutchincroft quieted, but he didn't back down. Neither, this time, did Biddy.

"I want to know everything," she said into the silence. "I want to know why you leave the island, I want to know where you go, and I want to know what happened tonight. I saved your life. I need to know."

"She does need to know," Hutchincroft agreed. "Things are getting worse. She needs to be told—about the cracks closing, and the magic leaving the world, and most of all about the Council. If anything happens to us, she won't be safe if she doesn't know."

If anything happens to us. That, out of nowhere, caught her breath in her throat. She'd been asking to know why Rowan left the island for a long time. But it had been like wanting to know the plot of a novel—she had never, despite what she had claimed, quite believed it was something she *needed* to know. Now she felt the vague, shadowy dangers of her childhood take on flesh and bone and blood.

Rowan sighed and rubbed his brow with his good hand, the way he did sometimes when he had been reading a long time and his eyes were getting tired. "Before I next leave the island, then. I promise. Not right now."

"Now," Hutchincroft said flatly.

"It's morning now. Biddy needs to go to bed. She's been up half the night."

"I'm not tired!" she protested. "Besides, you said once I could stay up all night if I wanted."

"Did I?" His eyebrow quirked. "That was a silly thing to say. Was I in the middle of something important when you asked, or just in a sulk?"

She smiled against her will. "Both, I think."

"I was in the middle of an important sulk?"

"Biddy needs breakfast before anything else, anyway," Hutchincroft interrupted. "We all do. You can tell her over breakfast."

"You're the one telling me how serious this is! Are you honestly thinking about breakfast?"

"I'm a rabbit," Hutchincroft pointed out. "I think about breakfast every morning."

Rowan laughed softly, and gave Biddy a long look that she couldn't quite read. She looked back, determined not to budge.

"All right," he said at last. He rose to his feet with a spark of his usual energy. "You go put some breakfast on. I'll go upstairs and get cleaned up. When I come back down, we'll have a talk."

Hutchincroft nodded. Some of the tension left him, though his eyes remained wary, as though expecting to be made angry again soon.

"Don't be too long," he warned.

"I won't be! I'm hungry too, you know."

Just before Biddy left, Rowan called her back and gave her a one-armed hug. "Thanks for coming after me," he said, very quietly, and she wondered if perhaps he did understand how scared she had been, just a little.

Hutchincroft didn't like human form. He could see better as a human, but only squarely in front of him; his hearing was muffled by rabbit standards; his sense of smell was almost nonexistent. He felt slow and clumsy on two legs. He couldn't run, he couldn't jump, he couldn't listen to the whispers of the world around him. There were only two things Hutchincroft liked about being a human, he had told Biddy once: eating human food, and talking to her. By "human food," he mostly meant bacon, and chocolate chip biscuits.

He was frying bacon now, and talking to her at top speed. Hutchincroft had a clear, precise voice that rose and fell with anger or joy, and often Biddy wouldn't even listen to the words, just enjoy the lilt of it in the way she might enjoy listening to a storm raging outside. It was strange to think that Rowan could hear it running through his mind all the time, even when to her Hutchincroft was a rabbit and all silence and softness and grace.

"He shouldn't leave the island without me," Hutchincroft was saying. His fury had burned to embers, but it hadn't yet burned out. "I tell him that, over and over, but he never listens."

"He never listens to anyone," Biddy agreed. She had heard all this before.

"He never listens to anyone! Exactly!" He turned the bacon in the pan, where it was beginning to crackle and spit in a satisfying way. "Do you want the crusts cut off your sandwich?"

She hadn't wanted the crusts cut off her sandwich since she was ten, but she didn't mind him always asking. Six years ago must seem like yesterday to a being of pure magic, especially when he was worried.

"I'll do the bread," she said, grateful for the distraction. There was half a loaf left on the counter—she cut six slices, for three sandwiches, and pulled the butter from the pantry. Two of the slices came out a little thick, and one was almost transparent at one end, so she gave herself the most uneven. It was exactly what she would have done on an ordinary morning, except that the sun was too high in the sky, and she was wearing her nightdress with her old grey jumper when she would normally have dressed before coming down, and Rowan was upstairs having nearly not come home at all. The world had a strange, too-bright precision, as though a veil had been pulled away.

"Hutch?" she said hesitantly. "Does Rowan leave you behind when he goes because of me? To watch over me?"

Hutchincroft caught his own tongue mid-rant. "No! Not only. That is... There are many reasons."

"Because he shouldn't. I can take care of myself."

"You need my protection as well," Hutchincroft said firmly. He turned to her, and his blue eyes were very clear. "And I want to give it to you. I tell him that too, often. It's his leaving I mind, not my being left with you. Don't ever think otherwise."

Biddy nodded, not trusting herself to reply. The cold grip around her stomach had loosened. "The bacon's burning," she said at last.

"Oh, bother!" Hutchincroft turned at once and flipped it with a deft hand.

"What's burning?" came a familiar voice, accompanied by a familiar tread. Biddy turned as Rowan came down the stairs, as usual jumping the last two.

He looked much better in some ways, and a little worse in others. He had washed and changed into a loose clean shirt, so that his face had a fresh-scrubbed look and his hair was, if not combed, at least damp. But he hadn't been able to wash away the worried lines around his eyes that seemed to have appeared overnight—or perhaps she was noticing them for the first time. Even his smile in her direction as he came up to the kitchen bench didn't quite do that.

"Why is something always burning around here?" he sighed, in mock resignation. "Is the tea on fire again? You know how I feel about that."

"Your tea is waiting in the teapot, and I think you'll find it's perfect," Hutchincroft said haughtily. "If you want to be useful, you could pour it."

"Well, I *always* want to be useful. Biddy, do you want tea?"

Rowan's idea of perfect tea was strong enough to melt half a spoon and keep the other half awake for weeks. "Can I have hot chocolate instead?"

"You could," he conceded, "if you wanted to upset me."

"I *always* want to upset you," she said seriously, and was rewarded with a smile.

His right hand was bandaged now, but it didn't stop him making hot chocolate the way he always had for her, wrapping his fingers around the mug and heating it with one perfect burst of magic. It was probably the most common spell performed on the island. Rowan had a habit of pouring drinks and forgetting about them for hours at a time, and his discipline about conserving magic broke down in the face of cold tea.

The three of them sat at the worn kitchen table together, and in the morning sun the terrors of the night seemed a very long way away. So far, in fact, that Biddy started to worry that this would be like any other breakfast, and she'd be left afterward with nothing.

She needn't have worried. As she took a grateful bite of her bacon sandwich, Rowan put down his tea and, after one quick glance at Hutchincroft, turned his attention to her.

"Right. You want to know where I go every night, don't you? It's a long story."

"I like stories."

That earned a quiet laugh. "I know you do." He paused. "I told you, didn't I, that there used to be magic in everything, every stone and every star and every grain of sand?"

She nodded without speaking. His voice had the softness she remembered from when she was very young and he would read her stories in front of the fire before bedtime. As then, it sent a shiver of anticipation down her back, as though any moment the world might open and something wonderful emerge.

"It used to come through cracks in the world, the way water leaks through a cracked bowl. It clung to trees and stones like pollen. Mages could collect it in great handfuls; familiars like Hutch could draw it through from the space beyond, whatever that was.

There were miracles everywhere then. We used it all the time, and never even gave it a second thought. And then, about seventy years ago, those cracks started to close, and magic started to die out."

"You told me that once," she said. "But you never told me why."

"Nobody ever knew why. For a long time—far too long—nobody even noticed. The world used to shimmer with it, and then it shimmered less, until one day we looked up and everything was grey. We had been looking somewhere else altogether."

Seventy years ago. It was 1912 now—they had celebrated the New Year together last winter. Biddy's history was patchy, skipping over whole centuries like a stone and landing hard on what she liked to read about. Still, she knew that seventy years ago was when Queen Victoria was on the throne, when the Treaty of Nanking was signed, when there was terrible famine in Ireland. When women wore dresses like the kind Morgaine had been wearing in Rowan's dream.

"This island is one of the last places where you can reliably find wild magic now," Rowan was saying. "And even here—there used to be a crack in the world over by the ruins, I'm fairly sure, but it closed like all the others. What we have left is just what's been drifting through the world for the last few decades, like dust lingering in an empty room."

She had to interrupt then. "And that's why you go every night. To find more."

Rowan nodded. "Yes."

He was looking at her as if waiting for another question, so she asked the first that came to her head. "Where do you go?"

"Everywhere. Wherever I can find a bit of magic clinging to a tree or an amulet or a stone. I take it, I keep what we absolutely need, and the rest I try to give away where it might be most helpful. Workhouses and poor neighborhoods, farms that are struggling, houses that are sick or grieving, places that need a small miracle to save them."

"That doesn't sound dangerous," she said cautiously.

"It isn't," Hutchincroft said, as severely as he could with his mouth full of crusts. He was on to his second sandwich. When Hutch was human, he liked to make the most of it. "If he kept to that, it would be fine."

Rowan gave Hutchincroft a warning glance, then returned his attention to Biddy. "Sometimes what magic I can find isn't enough," he said. "Not for everybody that needs it. Sometimes I have to steal it."

Her brow furrowed. "You mean...from other mages?"

She didn't even know if there were other mages left. Rowan was the only one she knew. But then, Rowan was the only person she knew of any kind. It had taken her until she was seven or eight to learn that most people couldn't do what he did with magic—that she herself would not be able to see and collect the magic that clung to the world as he did when she got older. She had cried for hours, as she never had before or since, and even Hutch had not been able to console her, because his tiny furry body against her chest had only reminded her that she would never have a familiar of her own. She loved Hutchincroft dearly, but he was a part of Rowan. She was just herself, alone, and she always would be.

"Yes," Rowan said. "From other mages." Something hard and fierce had crept into his words. His spine had straightened, his grip had tightened on his mug, and his eyes had a sharp glint like a reflection on the sea. "Have I ever talked about the Council?"

"No," she said. "Hutch did, just now."

Morgaine had mentioned them too, in Rowan's dream. *I can't leave London. I can't leave the Council.*

"Are they in charge of the other mages?" she prompted, when Rowan said nothing. "Like a government?"

"In a way." He paused, and she could see in his face different versions of his next words being turned over, examined, and rejected. This was the edge of what he was comfortable giving her. Up until now he had been telling a story he had meant to tell one day soon; from now on, he was off the page.

"There aren't a lot of mages, you know," he said at last. "A few thousand across Ireland and Great Britain; probably the same, proportionately, in other countries. Most of them get along fine on their own, living by the laws of wherever they happen to live. But the Councils make and enforce whatever decisions need to be made about magic. They seek out new mages, see that they're apprenticed to someone willing to teach them. They oversee experiments being done into new spells; they look after the archives in the Undercastle, where all the research takes place. All that kind of thing. There are thirteen on the British Council, and for most of its history it's been a council of old Englishmen, every one of them wealthy and titled and covered in dust." He must have caught the bitterness in his own voice, or just the startled look on her face, because he found a tight smile. "What you have to understand, Bid, is that mages are steeped in all the same prejudices as the rest of the world. They shouldn't be—it doesn't make any bloody *sense* to be, when magic doesn't discriminate between race or class or sex—but prejudices never do make sense. And mages live most of their lives among regular people; there aren't enough of us to do otherwise. We share the world's stupidities the way we share its food and fashions and books. Which means, among other things, that I would never normally have had a chance of getting anywhere near the Council."

Her heart was hammering; she longed to ask every question in her head, and yet worried any nudge would wake him up and remind him that he never told her anything like this, ever. "Why not?" she ventured.

"Why not?" He laughed a little. "Well, for starters, there had never been an Irish mage on the British Council. I don't know how much you know about relations between England and Ireland, but they're not good. An Anglo-Irish lord could have made it; I was a working-class nobody from the west who couldn't read or even speak proper English until I was thirteen." Biddy might have asked more, but he shifted in his seat, shaking off the subject. "Anyway. I did get there, let's leave it at that. Times were changing. I was appointed to the Council when I was thirty or so, along with a handful of other young mages who wouldn't have been there before."

I can't leave the Council. The words came back, and the defiance in them was now a puzzle piece locking into place.

"Like Morgaine," she said.

"I was dreaming about Morgaine," Rowan explained to Hutch, who had blinked in surprise. "Yeah, exactly like Morgaine. She was the first woman on the Council—probably still the only one, the way things went. The two of us were all set to change the world. And then, without warning, magic started to disappear. Nobody was prepared; nobody knew what to do." Another pause, another sorting through of words behind his eyes. She waited. "That was where Vaughan Carlisle came in."

The name sounded familiar—perhaps, like the Council, it had been mentioned in Rowan's dream. It was the tone of Rowan's voice, though, that made her sit up. He gave the first name a hard note of scorn and the second the distaste of touching something slimy.

"Who was he?"

Hutchincroft answered before Rowan could. "Vaughan Carlisle was a tiger in a business suit," he said. "Very tall and strong, and his teeth glittered when he smiled. He'd listen for a long time at Council meetings, so long and so still you'd forget he was there, and then his voice would come out of nowhere and startle you."

"I'm not sure tigers do half those things," Rowan said, with the ghost of good humor. It faded quickly. "He wasn't a tiger of any kind when we first met him. He was just an older member of the Council. Nothing special about him—he was the son of a factory owner up in Manchester, so practically in trade compared to some, but we were on the cusp of the Industrial Revolution and people like him were starting to count as gentlemen as long as they had enough money. He did have money, and what's more he had more ambition than the rest of them put together. Honestly, I liked him. He was clever, energetic, he had a sense of humor. None of those things made him good, but they didn't make him bad either—not then. Not until the magic started to disappear."

From what she had seen in Rowan's dream, that didn't bode well. "What happened?"

"He seized power, simple as that. It was just politics at first. The mage leading the Council was an old fool named Hubert Quirtle; Vaughan moved for a vote of no confidence in him a few weeks into the crisis, and to be honest I think he was grateful. We all were. The rest of the world was trying to find reasons, solutions, ways of coping—most of Europe outlawed all spells straight away, as a temporary measure. Quirtle had done nothing but dither. We all thought Vaughan would come up with a plan, at least. As it happened, he came up with about the worst one of all."

She waited.

"As soon as he took power, Vaughan declared that we needed to stop what he called squandering of magical resources. That didn't just mean holding off on using magic ourselves, as it did in other countries. We needed to stop letting magic drift free. We were no longer allowed to stand back as it worked its way into the lives of ordinary people, and on absolutely no account were we to help it on its way. Instead, we were to gather up all we could find and surrender it to the Council. They would then allocate it to the country's mages as they saw fit. Ordinary people wouldn't even know, according to him. Ordinary people had never known that magic was there, helping them when things were at their worst. They didn't know it was going in the first place; they would never know if the last of it never reached them."

The hard light behind his eyes was very bright now. His face was set, and there was no trace of a smile about it.

"Of course people knew. They didn't realize what they knew, but they knew something wasn't right. And even if they didn't, what difference did it make? Magic isn't there to be hoarded like dragon's treasure. Magic is kind. It comes into the world to help. Our job is to make sure it gets to where it needs to go."

"Is that what you told him?" Biddy asked quietly.

Rowan did laugh then, but the laugh was just as hard as his face had been before. "I did. So did a few others. I can't say it changed his mind very much."

He stood, suddenly restless, and snatched up his mug to take to the kitchen bench. His back was turned, but she could see his shoulders rise and fall as he drew a deep breath.

"Most English mages agreed with the Council's decision," Hutchincroft said into the silence. "When they gathered magic, it was delivered to the Undercastle and kept safe—the way we store magic in the great oak in the forest. Vaughan had mages traveling up and down the country to take it from them. He dictated who used it, and rewarded those who served him with more magic. We ignored him at first. We gave enough magic to the Council not to draw suspicion, but we also gave it away in secret. Vaughan must have suspected, with that eye of his—"

"Eye?" Biddy interrupted, without thinking.

Fortunately, Hutchincroft never minded talking, and now he had permission. "Vaughan had a glass eye," he said. "The sort you might have if your real eye was wounded in an accident and removed, only rumor was he'd dug out his own eye on purpose. He'd bespelled it to see into human hearts. Not in any detail— he couldn't read thoughts—but if he looked at you, your deepest desires and resentments would be laid bare to him."

The thought made her shudder.

"So he must have known what Rowan intended to do," Hutchincroft continued. "And he must have suspected we were doing it. We thought he was looking the other way deliberately—perhaps because we were on the Council, perhaps because he really didn't mind very much. We thought we were safe. Then, as magic kept getting scarce, things started to get...well, horrible."

"To say the least." Rowan turned, composed again. Only a certain tautness to his face betrayed him. "Overnight, without consulting the Council, Vaughan declared a state of emergency. The country needed to be scoured clean of every spare scrap of magic. Every bit of it needed to be handed over for public distribution. Anyone found keeping or using any would be branded a traitor and sentenced to death. It all came quickly in the end. The edict was issued first thing in the morning; exactly one minute later, the Council's collectors showed up at the houses of every mage who had defied them."

Biddy's grip tightened on her cocoa. The warmth of the mug didn't seem to reach her. "Was that you and Hutch?"

"It would have been," he agreed, "only we weren't at home. We had been out all night doing exactly what I was doing last night—looking for magic, and finding new places to put it. At that time we were living in London, on Primrose Hill. A young widow had come to me with a sick baby the day before, asking for my help or else the child would die. She was just scared and desperate enough to believe in magic, which is when magic does its best work. We managed to scrape enough from a tree up in Yorkshire after midnight, then took it back to her room in Whitechapel and blew it through the window. I hope it did something. I never found out. We got back at dawn, just in time to see the wisps converging on our house."

The terrible scream of the wind that wasn't wind. The glass cascading across the floor.

"They never saw us," Hutchincroft said, seeing the worry on Biddy's face. "We knew they'd started to watch us in the last few days, which is why we were working at night and only just returning home at dawn—very hungry, I might add, and very much looking forward to a nice soft bed."

"*You* were." Rowan was starting to sound more like himself. "I was trying to get you to come on a ride through Hyde Park with me. When we saw the wisps, we went straight into hiding. We tried to get to the house of a friend of ours, but by the time we got there the police had already been. His house was torn apart."

"And Morgaine?" Biddy asked. Things were beginning to fit.

"We went to Morgaine next," Rowan confirmed. "But by the time we got out to Kensington the sun had risen. As far as we could tell, her house was untouched and so was she. We didn't want to risk getting her into trouble, so we watched it all day, hiding from wisps and footsteps and any glimpse of stray magic. I knew if we could get out of London, we had a chance—I hadn't found Hy-Brasil then, but I had nooks and crannies up north where I thought we could hide. Only I didn't want to leave without Morgaine. I thought she was in danger. Before you ask, she had spoken against Vaughan too."

"I wasn't going to ask that," Biddy said. She was thinking of the frustration in his voice when he pleaded with Morgaine to come with them, the betrayal on his face when she refused. The anger, and worse than anger, when he'd taken the key from around her neck, as though she were painful to touch. "I was going to ask if you were in love with her."

It seemed a ridiculous question even as she asked. She'd known Rowan hadn't lived on Hy-Brasil his entire life; he'd explained courtship and sex to her quite matter-of-factly when she was ten, and if she'd thought about it at all she would have assumed it didn't all come from books. But love was something different. All her life he'd belonged to Hutchincroft and the island and to her; she couldn't imagine anyone else ever having had a claim on him. And yet he didn't seem surprised by it, or even fazed.

"We were engaged," he said, a little too carelessly. "I don't know if we would have gone through with it. We fought more often than we didn't. But I'd asked her, and she'd said yes. I thought she'd come with us." His jaw tightened. "Well. You saw how that went."

"She said she was going to work against them from the inside."

"That's what she said," he acknowledged. "I'm sure she meant it. But you can't work from inside the Council—not without having to do far more harm than good. I tried it myself for years. They're not stupid. They don't let people stay who make trouble. Vaughan certainly wouldn't."

"We were nearly *killed* because of her," Hutchincroft said. There was true fury in his voice, and what might almost have been disgust. "If you saw the wisps come in the dream, Biddy, then you know. She knew they were watching, and she didn't warn us away until it was almost too late. She betrayed us. And you *were* in love with her, Rowan. You know you were."

He shrugged, uncomfortable. "It was a long time ago. The point is, we barely got away. We'd spent nearly all our magic the night before. I had just enough to hold them off, and I had the ravenstone around my neck. I had to go up the chimney. Hutch too, of course."

Biddy had seen Hutch travel with Rowan in bird form before. He leapt into Rowan's arms, and then when Rowan transformed, Hutchincroft was somehow with him, in his head or in his heart.

"There's not much more to tell. We flew through the night. We made it as far as Liverpool, then I had to change or I would have been lost. I was already pretty far gone by then—Hutch had to talk me back. I wasn't so practiced at raven form in those days. But we'd lost them. We got on the next ferry to Dublin, out of England, and that was the last they saw of us for a long while."

"Was that when you came to Hy-Brasil?"

Somehow, it was the right thing to say. Some of the darkness lifted from his brow. "Not then. I spent over twenty years looking for Hy-Brasil before we found it. I'd glimpsed it once, when I was growing up on that coast you can see sometimes from the cliffs. An island cloaked in magic, visible only every seven years, that nobody could ever find on a map. There have been stories about it for centuries, but the mages didn't believe them. I'm not sure Hutch did either at first. We've been here ever since. Nobody's ever found us."

"Except me," Biddy pointed out, and was rewarded with a smile that was at least half as bright as usual.

"Well," he said, "you were only tiny. We could probably have fought you off, if it had come to it."

She couldn't stop a smile of her own.

"I knew we were all right, as soon as we were here," Rowan said. He was serious again, but at least this time he seemed more thoughtful than bitter. "The castle was waiting for us—in a worse state than it is now, but livable. We could start to fight back, instead of hiding. And we needed to fight back. There was barely any wild magic left by then. No lucky coincidences, no small miracles, nobody saved when things were at their very worst. At least we've been able to put a little of it right."

"But it's dangerous."

"Only when I'm out there," he assured her. "The Council did

catch me once, a few months before you came. They held me about a week before I escaped. But I told you, they've never come close to finding Hy-Brasil. You've always been safe, I promise."

"Do you really think I only care about me?" She felt more hurt than was probably fair. It had been a long night. "Is this why you won't let me leave the island?"

"I don't want you falling into the Council's hands," he said firmly. "Believe me, it is not a fun place to be."

She suspected there was more to it than that—he had spoken as though there was a danger to her, specifically—but she let it pass. Her head was teeming with too many new ideas as it was.

"Hutch said that things were getting worse."

"The Council do seem to be more powerful," he agreed. "Which is odd, considering there ought to be less magic as time goes on. I've been set upon by wisps three times in the last month, and now this trap tonight... Well. Either way, they're getting sick of me stealing from them. So am I, frankly. We can't go on like this forever."

Hutchincroft looked alarmed, as only a rabbit could. "What do you mean by that? As far as I'm concerned, we're already doing more than we can. I don't want you trapped again."

"That wasn't exactly my plan either. But something's not right about all this. I need to think."

"And I need you not to die!" Hutchincroft snapped. "Do you understand that? I can't live through another night like last night. It was horrible."

Rowan didn't seem to hear him, as Hutchincroft so often complained he didn't. His brow was furrowed, and his gaze was far away. It was only when the silence stretched out, expectant, that he came back to them.

"Well, it was definitely a waste of time," he said lightly. "I barely collected any magic at all, and I never got a chance to give away what I did take. Still. No real harm done."

"Are you sure there wasn't?" Biddy asked. "You don't look quite... right."

"Don't I?" He yawned, and made a face. "That's probably

because I'm dead on my feet. It's been a long night as well as a wasted one. Speaking of which, you should get up to bed."

"Oh, because *you're* tired? Shouldn't *you* go to bed?"

"Who taught you to answer back to your elders and betters?" His eyebrow raised, but his eyes were twinkling.

"Someone who also told me that just because someone is your elder it doesn't mean they're your better."

"It can't be me, then. I'm your elder, and I think I'm wonderful." He straightened, and the wince was a lot more pronounced than it had been yesterday morning. "For your information, I *will* go to bed, but I want to look at that amulet first. The spell's off it now—it should be safe, and I want to find out what it does. Seriously, are you all right? You've had a long night too, and a strange one."

Biddy nodded. She wasn't at all sure she was all right—her head was spinning—but she could tell that Rowan had gone beyond his limits of informative conversation for the time being. And this time, she wasn't sure she wanted to talk herself.

Rowan squeezed her shoulder comfortingly. "I'll be in my study if either of you needs me. Hutch, I'd appreciate your help when you're free. No hurry."

"Oh," Hutchincroft said knowingly. "And I suppose you're leaving the two of us to do the dishes, after we've already made the sandwiches and tea?"

"You know I'd do it," he said, regretfully, and held up his bandaged hand. "I'm just not sure I should get this dressing wet, you know? And it's a bit sore." He gave Biddy a wink, and she smiled reluctantly.

"You could put the dishes away," she reminded him. "That wouldn't get the bandage wet."

"Leave them for me, then. I'll come down and do it later."

"You're going to use magic, aren't you?" Hutchincroft sighed. "You're going to use magic to make them put themselves away, and you're going to break something, and you won't bother to sweep it up."

"Well, I might as well use this magic I'm holding for something. It'd be a waste otherwise."

Hutchincroft shook his head. "Unbelievable."

Biddy sat at the table quietly as Rowan's light footsteps receded up the stairs. He'd barely touched his sandwich, even though bacon was his favorite as well.

"Come on, then." Hutchincroft heaved himself to his feet, resigned. "I'll wash, if you like. Then you should get straight up to bed. You'll be tired when the effect of the ring and all that worry hits you."

Biddy rose slowly, deep in thought. "Hutch?" she asked. "Is Rowan all right?"

"Not when I'm finished with him, he won't be," Hutchincroft said grimly. "He's been far too careless lately, and he knows it. Something like this was bound to happen."

"But is he all *right*, though?" she persisted. She didn't know how to ask more clearly, or even what she meant. But she had never seen Rowan like he had been inside his own dreams, weak and frightened and hurt. She had known him all her life, and he was always the same: an accident of light and shadows, reckless and clever and crackling with magic. He was never sick, hardly ever tired, and when he came back from his travels with bumps and bruises, he would always laugh them off. For all her worries, it had never occurred to her that anyone would want to seriously hurt him, and it had certainly never occurred to her that anyone could.

"I mean," she added, when Hutchincroft didn't answer. "Is he *going* to be all right? Is he safe now?"

Hutchincroft turned to face her. His blue eyes were large and steady.

"When the magic started to go out of the world," he said, "it began to go out of us as well. The familiars. When those cracks closed, some link between us and what was beyond broke. Our mages would draw magic from us to cast spells, and no more would come to replace it. When there was no magic left in us, we would fade entirely and be nothing at all. Part of the edict decreed that every mage was to harvest what magic they could from their familiar, and let them fade."

Biddy felt hot and cold at the same time. In that moment, anger swallowed her fears. "Harvest it. You mean *steal* it? From you?"

He nodded, short and sharp. "Vaughan said that we would only fade anyway—it was better to take what magic they could first and use it themselves."

She faded. She doesn't exist anymore. The words came back to Biddy like a punch to the stomach, and she understood at last what the horror on Rowan's face had been. "Morgaine did that, didn't she? She took her familiar's magic and let her fade."

"She couldn't have stayed with the Council any other way," Hutchincroft said.

"She said her familiar told her to do it."

"I have no doubt at all that her familiar did," Hutchincroft said. "Because I said the same thing to Rowan. I would have given him my magic with all my heart. If I was to fade, I would rather have faded knowing that the very last of my magic had gone to keep him safe. But he wouldn't have it. He left me my magic, and what was more he shared what magic he kept for his own with me, so that I could remain in the world. He fled the Council in large part to save me. For that, and many other reasons, I love him. So he *will* be all right, always, because I will not allow anything to happen to him. And I will not allow anything to happen to you. Do you understand?"

Biddy nodded. Inside, her heart was a warm, fierce glow.

"Good. Now come wash up."

She grabbed the washcloth and came to stand beside him as he filled the basin with water.

"Hutch?" she said, struck by a sudden memory. "Have Morgaine and I ever met?"

Hutchincroft frowned. "We haven't seen Morgaine for years. I don't even know if she's still alive. I don't see how you could have. Why?"

"I don't know," she said. "Just a feeling."

Chapter Four

*B*iddy hadn't expected to actually sleep, despite what Hutchin-croft said, but apparently the familiar knew more about both magic and worry than she did. Once she lay down, relief and exhaustion enfolded her like a heavy blanket. She closed her eyes to morning sun, and opened them to gentle grey-blue skies and a whisper of wind from the sea. It was early afternoon, and the castle was as quiet as it should have been in the middle of the night.

The feeling of difference from that morning clung to her as she pulled back the covers. She felt older than she had only hours ago, more aware of her body in the familiar space. Yesterday she would have thought nothing of running downstairs in bare feet and faded skirt, or even in the pair of men's trousers Rowan had bought her for climbing trees. Now, studying herself in the age-freckled mirror, she couldn't help but remember Morgaine's immaculate hair and perfectly cut dress. It wasn't that she wanted to look like Morgaine, exactly—it was the knowledge that Morgaine could have walked down her street and looked *right*, as other women did, while she in the outside world would be odd and ill-fitting and strange. She found herself looking at her clothes critically, even though there was nobody to see her, just to feel as though she *could* be seen.

Unfortunately, there wasn't a lot that could be done, save making sure her shirtwaist had no grass stains and none of the darns in her stockings were visible under her good woolen skirt. She spent a few minutes trying to pin up her hair in a loose approximation of Morgaine's, but the wind the day before had whipped it into a froth of dark brown tangles and she finally had to give up in disgust. Morgaine's hairstyle would be seventy years out of date anyway. She wished she knew how grown women wore their hair, and most of all that she had someone to show her how to do it. Rowan knew more about dresses than might be supposed, but hairstyles were a mystery to him, and she felt self-conscious asking to use the scrying glass to watch women in the street and try to figure them out.

Rowan was sound asleep on the window seat in the main living room when she came downstairs, Hutchincroft back in rabbit form tucked against his chest. This wasn't too unusual—she didn't think she'd ever seen him go to bed. Sleep tended to be something that needed to catch Rowan off guard, to slip beneath his defenses once they had been lowered by sun or sea breezes or very dull spellbooks. He lay curled up in a patch of weak sunlight, head pillowed on one arm, his bandaged hand resting on Hutchincroft's soft fur. In the light his face looked soft and open, almost as it had in the dream, and the lines of tension she had seen earlier seemed deeper by contrast. Hutchincroft's ears pricked at Biddy's approach, and she smiled. She couldn't ask if all was well without waking Rowan, and Hutchincroft couldn't answer in words, but the rabbit laid his head flat to be stroked, and she knew it was, at least for now.

All was well outside too, when she pulled on an old jumper against the biting wind and went out to investigate. Either Rowan or Hutchincroft had evidently milked the two goats and let them out that morning—for once, she realized with a guilty squirm, she had forgotten. The eggs had been collected and were sitting in their basket on the window ledge (so probably Hutch—Rowan usually left them on the kitchen bench). The black rabbits were mostly asleep in their burrows, but one or two grazed on the meadow, periscoping every now and then to listen for danger. Everything looked as safe as it ever had.

Except she now knew that it never had been safe. The confusing shape of the things she had learned had solidified while she had slept, and she didn't like them. It wasn't the memories of Rowan's dream that bothered her, or the stories of what had happened in the last days of magic. Those were disturbing, but they were seventy years in the past, and she hadn't lived her whole life on a magic island without developing a strong streak of pragmatism. What worried her most was that, for the first time in her life, she knew they had enemies. They had tried to capture or kill Rowan the night before, and they would try again.

Her fears had been vague before. Now they had been given form by the Council and Morgaine and the memory of the terrible shriek before the glass shattered. She didn't want Rowan to go away again. When she looked in on him before she left the castle, he was still sleeping, and she willed him to stay that way, though she appreciated it wasn't a permanent solution.

━━━━━━━━━━━━━━━━

Hy-Brasil was not a large island. It was possible to walk around its edges in a few hours, provided you knew the way around the dangerous bits of the cliffs, you kept away from the rocks when the tide was coming in, and you kept a scrap of dry bread in your pocket to ward off the fair folk. Biddy knew both the cliffs and the tides by heart. They were her favorite parts of the island—not the forest, which she loved deeply but thought of as part of Rowan, or the fields, which belonged to the rabbits and in some way to Hutchincroft, but the in-between parts, the jagged ever-shifting line where the rocks met the sea and the horizon met the sky. She didn't plan to walk the whole path that afternoon, but she did want to walk it a short distance. Apart from wanting to leave Rowan in peace until after it was too late for him to fly away, she needed to think.

She walked farther than she meant to. By the time she reached the ruins on the northernmost cliffs, she was flushed and breathless, and the sun was much lower in the sky. She perched on the soundest of the old walls, careful not to further crumble the dark grey stone cobwebbed with green moss, and looked out to sea. In the distance something flashed beneath the waves—fish, perhaps, or seals, or merrows with their glittering tails and human faces.

Aside from their own castle, the ruins were the only sign that anyone else had ever lived on the island. According to legend, Hutchincroft had told her once, Hy-Brasil was the home of an ancient people, now lost forever. He couldn't tell her how true the legends were, or whether those people were mortal or fair folk or gods. He was a being of magic, but that didn't mean he knew everything about it.

Rowan said they were the Tuatha Dé Danann, the rulers of Ireland thousands of years ago. They had come from over the sea and burned their ships behind them when they landed, in a flare of fire and smoke that was seen across the world. The land was in the grip of a race of monsters then, and they fought many battles before the Tuatha Dé Danann were victorious. Hutchincroft said that Rowan knew even less about it than he did—he just liked the stories. Biddy didn't care, because she loved the stories too: Balor, the monstrous king of the Fomorians with a magic eye that could kill at a glance but needed ten soldiers to pull back its heavy eyelid; Lugh, Balor's half-god grandson, cast into the ocean at birth because he was prophesized to bring about his grandfather's downfall; Brigid, the goddess of wisdom and poetry and healing and blacksmiths, whose name she shared.

"What happened to them?" she remembered asking. She must have been very young at the time, because she was perched on Rowan's knee in his study to look at the pictures in one of his oldest books.

"What always happens," he said. "People came and took the land for themselves. They fought for a while, but in the end they were forced underground. They became the fair folk. You'll still find people who claim to have dealings with them, once in a while."

"Have you?"

"No." He said it lightly, but his hands around her waist had tightened. "No, I never have."

Whoever they were, they had left secrets behind them. The vast stone fortress must have once covered most of the northeast of the island, high stone walls and courtyards and towers raised high above the plunging cliffs. Over centuries the grass and trees and flowers had crept across them like a blanket over a sleeping child. Only odd bits remained, jutting out from the earth that buried them: the line of wall on which Biddy sat, the bones of a tower, a skeletal line of archways. An ancient yew tree grew nearby, its roots entwined with fragments of stone, and it seemed possible that the tree had once been at the center of a circular courtyard.

That courtyard had seemed empty when Biddy had climbed the hill. As she shifted her seat on the wall, a tickle of wind on the back of her neck made her turn. A black rabbit was at the base of the tree—no different to any of the others that peppered the fields at first glance, large, its thick winter coat coming through flecked with silver. And yet its eyes were not a rabbit's usual liquid brown, or even Hutchincroft's blue. They shone gold, startling in its fine-boned face.

The Púca. The trickster spirit that sent travelers on a wild ride through bog and thorn and whose breath turned autumn berries to poison. She had seen it before since the day she had nearly climbed on its back, but never so close. An odd thrill shot through her chest, at once fear and excitement and yearning when only the first made sense. She could remember none of the charms to ward off the fair folk, even had she wanted them. The ruins and the sea and the sky receded dizzyingly around her.

It only lasted a moment. Without warning, the Púca shook its ears, and turned tail across the fields as though it really were nothing more than a wild creature of the earth.

Biddy sat back, unsettled. It was a strange coincidence that the Púca should visit today, of all days. After the night's misadventures it seemed a bad omen, or perhaps a warning.

It was then that she saw the dots on the horizon.

A flock of birds, she thought at first. Against the sunlight they were black specks, seagulls perhaps, only their wingtips looked sharper and their silhouette impossibly thin. She shielded her eyes with her hand, frowning. It wasn't that she thought they were dangerous—in all her life, no danger from the outside had ever threatened Hy-Brasil. It was only that she had never seen anything quite like them.

Feeling slightly foolish, telling herself she was only on edge from the night before, she slipped off the wall. There was a branch about the length of her arm on the ground, presumably from the old yew; she picked it up. The feel of the bark beneath her fingers and the solid weight in her hand was comforting in some way beyond the practical, as though the tree itself was with her if she needed it. Not that she did. But still.

The birds, if that was what they were, were coming closer. The sun glinted on their wings. There was something strange about their flight—they might have been hunting, had they shown any interest in diving beneath the waves for fish.

Biddy was just starting to wonder if she should head back to the castle and wake Rowan after all when a short, sharp shriek came over the sea. It was no birdcall she knew: a dry rattle, a rasp of fingernails on rock. It froze her in place. She knew, without knowing how, that it was too late to go now. She had been seen.

As one, the swarm circled in the sky and headed straight for her. The sound of their wings came on the wind, a clicking and crunching like sticks and stones rattling together. Biddy just had time to scramble over the wall and hit the grassy bank behind it before they were on her.

They passed over her head like arrows, so close she felt the rush of air from their bodies. She pressed herself into the ground as hard as she could, heart thundering and thoughts racing. *What on* earth…?

Enemies weren't supposed to find Hy-Brasil. Birds weren't meant to be enemies. And yet these were here, and they had found her, and she was being hunted.

Biddy couldn't afford to stay down for long. As they wheeled around again, wings rattling, she clambered to her feet. This time, she swung the branch as hard as she could. It struck one of the birds; there was an audible crunch, and a shock of pain shot up her arm. Most of the flock veered off and scattered. The bird she had struck hit the ground with a shrill whistle, body crumpling and breaking apart.

It was made of bone. She saw the hooked skeleton wings and tiny vertebrae, stark white against the dirt and grass. They were not bird bones either, slender and featherlight. These were thick, yellow, brittle, from a much larger animal that had been dead a very long time. She had only a second to take it in, aghast, before the bone-creature reformed and launched itself at her eyes.

Biddy didn't stand and wait for it this time. She swung the branch again, not bothering to take aim, and ran for the row of arches across the field. Once she stumbled on the uneven ground, but she didn't pause. Her only thought was to get something solid and ancient between herself and the swarm of bones.

It worked better than she hoped. The bone-creatures broke off and circled, sharp heads turning as though searching once again. She remembered their uncertainty out at sea, the odd pattern of their flight. Of course. Hy-Brasil *had* protected itself, after all. She didn't know exactly what they could see—her, certainly—but the ruins were obviously making it as difficult for them as possible.

And yet not difficult enough. There was a rush of wings at her shoulder; on reflex, she turned and swung with the yew branch, and felt once again the shock as it hit bone seconds before it was on her. It was no use. There was nowhere to go—only the castle, at least half an hour away on foot, and the woods, closer but too far to run across open fields. She was trapped.

She swung again, tears of frustration and panic burning in her eyes. "Get away!"

The sound of her own voice, feeble as it felt, put a new idea in her head.

She had been gritting her teeth against any sound—partly on reflex, partly from stubborn pride, partly from trying not to show fear. Never show fear to a predator, Rowan said. But this was different. The bone-creatures didn't care about her fear.

Now, she fought past her own urge to be silent. Instead, she struggled for a deep breath, gathered all her strength, and screamed. It was all she could think: that Hutchincroft, who could hear everything on the island, might hear her; that he and Rowan might be close enough to come for her. The scream felt like a blade being withdrawn from a wound—sharp, thin, ending in a gasp that was nearly a sob.

Please. Please, somebody, help.

In answer, she heard a raven's harsh, guttural cry.

Her heart leapt. She glanced quickly toward the castle, and even as the bone-creatures came at her she saw the familiar black bird coming too, faster than the skeletons, faster than she had ever seen it fly before.

The raven swept in like the flight of an arrow. It pierced the center of the cloud of bone-creatures, scattering them in all directions.

The transformation was so fast this time she missed it: The raven was swooping in for a landing, and then it was gone and Rowan and Hutchincroft were on the ground.

Hutch's feet barely touched earth. His ears were flat against his back and his teeth were bared; he launched himself at the skeleton birds with one thrust of his back legs, a ball of muscle and claw and silent fury. He collided with the bird closest to Biddy and knocked it to the ground, kicking and biting as it jabbed with its beak.

Biddy had frozen in mixed relief and fear; the bone-creature's hoarse rattle as it stabbed at Hutch awakened her.

"Stop it!" she heard herself cry. She couldn't get close enough to disentangle Hutch from his opponent without hurting him too, but another was coming for him; she lashed at it with all the strength she could muster, and it crumpled to the ground. It was only then that she managed to glance back at Rowan.

Rowan had gotten to his feet too, but he hadn't moved forward to help them. Instead, he had pressed his hand to the base of the ancient yew tree in the center of the ruins. His eyes were narrowed in concentration, his eyebrows drawn together; Biddy, watching, saw his lips move and heard faint snatches of words under the skeletal screams.

The tree, already stirring in the wind, went wild. Its smooth limbs thrashed. The trunk creaked, so loud it was almost a shriek. The leaves crackled. And then, impossibly, they came to life.

Dark green specks filled the air like a swarm of insects, the rustle like the turning of a thousand pages. Biddy's first, confused impression was that the tree was shedding its leaves, as though autumn had ended and winter had come in the space of a heartbeat. But yew trees were evergreen, and there were far too many leaves for that. They were multiplying, flying from the tree, twisting into the forms of birds and spiraling into the air toward the bone-creatures.

The bone-creatures shrieked. As one, they rose to meet the birds made of leaves in the air. Hutchincroft fell back with a grunt, bristling; Biddy's knees gave way, and she hit the ground. Above their heads, the sky erupted into war. Leaf and bone clashed, the air filled with rattlings and rustlings and high, keening calls that seemed to come from neither side or both at once. At the trunk of the yew tree, Rowan held still, wind whipping around him as he worked the spell.

Something fell and struck Biddy on the shoulder: a fragment of bone. She flinched away with a gasp of disgust, but it wasn't reforming this time. It was already dissolving; as she watched, it shriveled into white dust, and then into nothing at all. Another fell, then another; a leaf struck the ground next, crumbling into green ash, but the shards of bone were falling thicker and faster, like ghastly hail. She put up her hands to shield herself, on instinct, and felt something hard and still-writhing strike the back of her head. The screeching overhead grew louder, higher, until it filled her ears and her lungs and her heart. She cried out, and couldn't hear her own voice.

Chapter Five

When it finally ended, it did so all at once. The sounds of unearthly combat died. Biddy dared to look up again. A few leaf-birds circled the air, green against the backdrop of the ocean. The creatures of bone were gone. She got to her feet, shakily, and saw Hutchincroft already periscoping beside her with ears pointed out to sea. Rowan, by the yew, had his eyes fixed in the same direction—toward the mainland, from where only moments ago the island had been under attack.

The three of them stood for a long silent moment, watching, waiting, Hutchincroft so rigid and alert it seemed he would shatter with a touch, Rowan still and straight as the tree beside him. The skies were clear again, pearlescent grey shot through with gold, the sun only just beginning to go down in the west. No new specks dotted the horizon. The last of the leaf-birds slowed, drifted apart, then fell as gently and softly as any leaves in autumn. One of them clung to Biddy's hair, tugged at a strand, and came to rest on the grass.

At last, Hutchincroft sank to four paws, satisfied. Rowan sighed heavily, and the tension left his shoulders. It was only then that he dropped his hand from the trunk.

Biddy had seen Rowan work spells before, many times, but it had always been small—domestic, even—candles lit, drinks warmed, vegetables helped to grow. Calling the birds to life out of the leaves had been magic of a different kind, wild and strange and powerful, and for a moment he had seemed a very different person. She almost felt shy of him, until he spoke, and his voice was the same as ever.

"Well. That was close. Are you all right?"

Biddy nodded, and clenched her fists to stop them from trembling. Part of her couldn't quite believe it was over. "What were they?"

"Wisps. Like the ones you saw in my dream—like the ones I just flung back at them. I haven't done that in a long time. Lucky I had a lot of magic left from last night, and the trees on Hy-Brasil are half-awake anyway."

"I thought—" She had to pause to steady her voice. "I thought wisps were made of glass."

"They're made of anything. Anything you can lay your hands on—anything you have an affinity with. They're elements animated by magic." He glanced sideways at Hutch. "Those came from Vaughan. He always did like using dead things."

Biddy couldn't hear Hutch's response, but it brought a faint twitch of a smile to Rowan's mouth.

"Were they after the island?"

"They were after me. But that's worse, considering."

He didn't need to explain. Enemies looking for Hy-Brasil could never find it. Enemies looking for Rowan might find him, and the island with him.

Wisps. The creatures of glass she had seen in Rowan's dream had been terrifying, of course, but insubstantial, as the name suggested. These had been vivid and vicious; their screams had curdled the flesh from her bones. Her jumper had a snag across the middle where the claws had caught and torn, and that faint touch was somehow more frightening than a real wound would be. It was a promise of something worse.

"What were you *doing* out here, anyway?" Rowan demanded, in a sudden, unexpected burst of exasperation. "I woke up to skeletons overhead and you were gone. I had no idea where to find you!"

"You never know where to find me!" She was more surprised than indignant. "I haven't told you where I was going since I could walk! How was I supposed to know today was any different? You said it was over."

"I know, I know." He pinched the bridge of his nose briefly, gathering himself. There was a thin line of blood across his neck from a razor-sharp beak. "My fault. I didn't mean to sleep the whole day out. And I never would have thought those things could see the island anyway."

"I don't think they could, quite," Biddy offered. "Not until they saw me. They knew something was here, but they weren't sure."

"The Council will be if they decide to come see why the Servant's favorite wisps vanished over the Atlantic." His voice was grim.

She must have shivered after all, despite her best efforts, because Rowan's voice softened and he ruffled her hair comfortingly. "I didn't mean that. They're gone. The Council will just think they dispersed without finding anything—wisps never last very long."

"But they're looking," Biddy reminded him. "That means they'll look again. They'll be back, sooner or later."

"I know." He glanced at Hutch one more time, in frustrating silent communication, then his eyes went back to Biddy. "I need to make sure there's nothing else on its way here, and it's probably best we get under cover tonight anyway. Will you come back to the turret with us?"

She nodded.

"Good. And then I have something to talk to you about."

Their castle's single surviving turret was in no state for any real battle. The battlements were cracked and worn, whittled down by wind and salt and rain, the stones overgrown with weeds and grass (which Hutchincroft happily helped to remedy). The outer stairs leading to the roof were unsafe unless climbed with absolute precision (Rowan kept promising to remedy that, but never had). The entire roof of the turret was unsafe, really—in any combat it would be more likely to be the death of its defenders than its attackers.

It was, however, the best vantage point to see over the entire island. To the east, the rocks sloped down to the bay and out past the stony beach to a vast ocean and the sky beyond; to the west, fields gave way to the thick tangle of woodland. Lately, on the wrong days, Biddy found it lonely, even oppressive—the emptiness of the world against the tiny circle of Hy-Brasil. Now, she breathed in the cold air gratefully, and her heart calmed for the first time since the attack.

"I don't see any wisps," she said unnecessarily. "And the seas look clear. Unless there's anything in the forest..."

"There's nothing in the forest that shouldn't be," Rowan said. He was turning over a slate-grey pebble in his fingers, as if examining it for cracks. "The trees are keeping watch. This'll do."

He cupped the pebble in his hands, raised it to his mouth, and whispered something too soft for her to catch. She recognized the lilt of a spell even though she couldn't see the magic pass from him to the stone, and wasn't surprised when he set it down on the wall beside her.

"What does that do?"

"It's a seeing stone. If it sees anything that shouldn't be there, I'll see it myself, wherever I am. Annoying, if you get a particularly jumpy bit of rock and have pictures of seagulls flashing in front of your eyes all day, but useful while it lasts. I should have put one up this morning, before I fell asleep, but..." He shrugged. "I didn't."

She suspected that hadn't been how he had been about to end that sentence. He was trying not to worry her. It didn't work—she could hear the unspoken endings too clearly. *But they had never needed such a thing before. But the magic around Hy-Brasil, ancient and strong, had always been enough. But their enemies were not supposed to be so powerful.*

"It's a nice afternoon," Rowan said. Perhaps he had seen her shiver again. "We should bring dinner up here." He glanced at

Hutch, and his eyebrows raised defensively. "What? You're allowed to be hungry after crises and I'm not? I think there's cake left in the pantry. Though I still have to pick up more jam from the mainland."

"We don't need it," Biddy said firmly. She would have happily lived on nothing but potatoes and boiled eggs forever, if it meant Rowan never left again. "We don't need anything."

"We do need *some* things, I'm sorry to say." Rowan had been leaning his elbows against the wall beside her; now he straightened. Something in him shifted at the same time. His eyes were serious, and his face was graver than she had ever seen it. "I have a proposition for you, Biddy, and I want you to know you can absolutely refuse. It's a lot to ask. I wouldn't, if it weren't important."

"What is it?"

He was silent for such a long time that she wondered if he was going to speak at all. When his question came, it dropped into the quiet evening like the skeleton birds had dropped from the sky.

"How would you feel about leaving the island for a few days?"

She didn't know what to say. She didn't know what she felt, except for an odd stirring in her stomach that might have been excitement or fear. Yesterday she would have known—she had been pleading to leave the island. The mainland had seemed so tantalizingly close, bustling with the kind of life and adventure she had read about. Now she had seen Rowan's nightmare. It had been a glimpse of what might be there for her, things that weren't there for the characters in books.

"Would it be safe?" she asked at last.

He made a face. "I hope so, but I also hope not. If things work out the way I plan, then they'll be both very dangerous and not at the same time. I'm not explaining this very well, am I?"

"No," she said evenly.

"Hutch is telling me to come out with it, so I will." Biddy glanced at Hutch, nibbling at the grass, but with an ear now pointed in their direction. "I want to use you as bait for the Council. I want to put you in the world, and when someone comes for you, I want to trap them myself and find out what they're up to. I need to know why they've been so desperate to catch me these last few months, and why they have the magic to do it. Something's wrong, I know it is. And until I find out what it is, I can't put it right."

"But why would they come for me? I'm nobody." She corrected herself before he could correct her. "I'm not a mage, you said."

"You're not a mage. I'm very sure of that. But there's something odd about you, something I've never told you. There's a fragment of magic in your heart."

At first she was too confused to be startled. "The way you hold magic inside you? When you collect it to put somewhere else?"

"No. No, not like that at all. Not the way the oak does, either. More like the way an amulet holds magic, or that ring you used last night, or that seeing stone I just made. It's a spell of some kind—it *does* something. It's buried right there." He tapped her chest with his finger lightly. "It's how I found you, all those years ago. It called to me. But I've never been able to get it out, or work out what it does—and I tried for months, when you first came."

"I'm like an amulet?"

"Maybe." He didn't sound very convinced. "There *are* times when a spell needs to be held inside a living soul—if the spell is too powerful to be contained by an amulet, and only to be used once. But I never heard of it being done to a non-mage, and definitely not to an infant who could neither benefit nor consent. And whoever hid it really locked it in."

Whoever did it. That, of all things, turned her stomach. She laid her hand on her chest, feeling the familiar flicker of her heart, and tried to imagine the shard of magic buried inside it. She pictured it like a fragment of shell in dark rock, the kind she saw on the cliffs when the tide went out.

"Is it dangerous?" she heard herself ask.

"*No,*" Rowan said emphatically. His eyes held hers. "I may not know very much about it yet, but I can tell you that whatever magic is inside you is not there to hurt you or anybody else. It's good magic—all magic is, until mages get their hands on it, and whatever mage got their hands on this didn't mean any harm. Trust me."

She did. "Who put it there? Was—was it my parents?"

"I don't know. I've tried a couple of spells to find who performed the magic, and they just reflect me back. It might have been your parents, yeah. I've looked for any word of who they might be for a long time, and I've never found any trace of them. They might have been mages. But one thing I do know: If you leave Hy-Brasil, sooner or later the Council will hear the magic in you as surely as I did. They'll send someone to find you, to investigate. And then Hutch and I will move in."

Biddy had almost forgotten what Rowan was asking her to do, in the shock of finding out what else he hadn't told her. It came back to her now. "Will they send wisps?"

"No. That's why we have to use you, and not me or Hutch. For us, they *would* send wisps—or they'd trap us some other way, like they tried last night. But you wouldn't be a fugitive to apprehend. All they'd sense is peculiar magic, and so they'd send a mage to investigate. Given the spell in question, they'll send a very good mage. And then that mage and I will have a talk."

"How do you know that mage won't capture you instead?"

He laughed. "Because I'm much too good for that?" Hutch growled, and he schooled his face into seriousness. "I *don't* know. I have Hutch, and they won't have any familiar at all. I'll be waiting for them, but they won't expect me. I think these things will be enough. I can't promise that they will. That's one reason why I will understand if you don't want to risk it."

"But you want me to risk it."

"Yes," he said, and his voice was quiet. "I do."

As long as magic wasn't involved, Rowan had always been relaxed about her taking risks. Since she could walk, he had let her wander where she liked, climb where she liked, swim and explore and play where she liked. When she had fallen or gotten stuck or been bitten by wood sprites, he had come to her aid with comfort or merciless teasing or both, depending on the situation. She had always assumed it was because he took so many risks himself he thought nothing of it. It had never occurred to her, though, that he might actually put her in danger. For the first time, doubt laid a cold finger on her heart with its secret magic.

"How long have you been planning this?" she asked. "Truthfully."

"Truthfully." He exhaled slowly, considering. "I suppose I thought of it a few months ago, when things first started to get dangerous out there. It struck me as a possible plan. I wasn't going to use it, though. This isn't your fight."

"Because I'm not a mage." Amid everything, she felt the familiar pang of exclusion.

"Because you're sixteen, with a life of your own to live, and you deserve better than to be caught up in the mess we all made decades ago," he said firmly. "But it's true, you're not a mage. Why should you care about magic?"

In fact, she cared desperately, but she didn't know how to say so. Magic was all she had ever known. It was a wonder and joy to her, just as it was to Rowan and Hutch, because they had raised her to see it that way. The thought of it leaving the world was terrible. But she could see, from Rowan's point of view, why that would make no sense.

"You said you weren't going to use me," she said instead. "What changed your mind?"

"I've run out of other ideas," he said. "That simple. I wanted to use something else as bait, some other spell, but nothing has the pull that the one in your heart does. And after last night, after this evening, we can't afford to go on as we have been. If I go out into the world again, sooner or later they'll catch me. But if I stay here, it's looking like that might draw them to Hy-Brasil, and I can't have that. I need to take the fight to them, which means I need to find out what I'm fighting and how I can win it, and this is the only way I know. Believe me, if I wasn't as sure as I could be that this will work, I would never ask you to do it."

"What does Hutch say?" she ventured. Of Hutch's love, at least, she had no doubt.

"He's not happy about it," Rowan said, so wryly she knew it was an understatement. "But he agrees as long as we stay by your side at all times. We will, you know. You might not see us, but we'll be there."

"Do you promise?"

"I promise," he said, and she knew it was true. Rowan never broke a promise.

Still she wasn't quite willing to agree. The world outside was one thing. But the Council were too new to her, and frightening.

Hutchincroft gave Rowan a warning glance, and he nodded. "Think it over," he said to Biddy. "You don't have to decide now. In the meantime, I have another important question."

"What is it?" she asked warily.

"Do you want to go downstairs and get cake?"

She knew it was a way out, but she accepted it, gratefully. She also accepted the cake.

It was what Rowan called a raid-the-kitchen dinner, and what Hutch more sniffily called eating scraps. Hutchincroft couldn't waste more magic turning human to cook, and Rowan couldn't be bothered. So they had bread and cheese and undersized tomatoes and cold sausages from last night, with the last of the sponge cake and tinned peaches for after, and took it up to the turret battlements as planned. It was late in the year to eat outdoors, and the wind was fierce from the shore, but the walls protected them as long as they sat on the still-warm flagstones. The sky above was shifting to purple, and when Biddy tilted her head back, she felt as though she could fall into it.

That evening, she loved the island more than anything that could be in the world.

⋯

The following morning, Biddy woke to find the house empty and a note from Rowan and Hutchincroft to say they had gone down to the great oak to gather more magic. There was no jam in the pantry, so Rowan probably hadn't left the island overnight, but if he thought he needed more magic there was little doubt he planned to go very soon. It strengthened Biddy's resolve.

She didn't wait for the other two to return—it might be all day, if Rowan got distracted. Instead, she set off down the path through the forest to the hollow where the great oak grew. It was the same path she had walked with Rowan and Hutch only two days ago, but it looked very different now in the cool, grey morning. Specks of rain were falling through the leaves, just enough to catch the light and dampen her face when she turned it to the sky. Things always did look different on the other side of a nightmare, particularly someone else's.

The grove where the old oak grew made its presence felt before she could see it—hushed, shadowed, expectant. Even on the warmest and most golden of days it smelled of damp grass after a thunderstorm. It sent a shiver across her skin, as though she had stepped out the door at night and into an unexpected breeze.

Hutchincroft had obviously heard her coming from miles away; he was waiting, alert, and when she came into view he gave her a happy flick of his ears. Rowan stood with his hand pressed to the oak and his eyes closed, and magic spilled from its trunk and thrummed under his skin. It didn't matter that Biddy couldn't see magic herself. She could see it the way she saw the wind—the ripples it created, the movement it stirred in the trees and the air. He breathed in, slowly, deeply, and the forest breathed and flexed with him. When his eyes flew open, they glittered in a flash of green and gold. Then they fell on her, and his face relaxed into a smile.

"Morning," he called.

"Good morning," she replied. He was crackling with magic—his movements were lighter, more restless, as though he could barely stay in his body. She felt a pang of familiar jealousy. She loved the great oak, and when she spent the afternoon curled up against its trunk reading, she thought she could feel something ancient and shimmering in the air of the grove. But that was as far as it went for her. Whatever magic she had nestled inside her, the magic of the world wouldn't let her glimpse past the veil.

But Hy-Brasil had chosen her. She clung to that, and it gave new steel to her night's resolve.

Rowan jumped off the twining roots to meet her as she scrambled down the bank. "Sleep well?"

"Not really," she said honestly. Hutchincroft nudged her ankle, and she crouched down beside him and stroked the hollow between his ears and cheek. His fur was slightly damp. "I was thinking."

Rowan nodded, unsurprised. "What about?"

She drew a deep breath. The leaves of the great oak rustled overhead. "If I don't go to the mainland, the way we talked about— is there a chance Hy-Brasil will be in danger? Could the Council find it?"

"As far as I know," he said, so precise that she knew he was being very careful, "nobody's looking for Hy-Brasil. When I was on the Council, nobody believed that it existed. They're looking for me. But if they keep looking—well, you saw how close they got yesterday. They could well find it at the same time. And if they do, they'll strip the island of its magic the same as they have the rest of the world. Don't worry," he added quickly, seeing her face. "I won't let that happen. If it comes to it, I'll leave you and Hutch safe here and go to the mainland. There are places there I can hide."

"But then _you'll_ be in danger. Again. Still."

"Well…yeah," he conceded. "Some. But don't worry about that either, Biddy. I can take care of us, and I can take care of Hy-Brasil. I want to find out what the Council's doing, that's all. It could be important, and your help could be important too. That's what matters."

But that wasn't what mattered to her, not really. She hadn't known the Council existed until yesterday, and she couldn't bring herself to care about what shadowy plans they may be making, out there in a wider world that was more shadowy to her yet. What mattered was Rowan's safety and the safety of her home. The terrible moments when she and Hutch had thought Rowan was lost to them forever were far too clear in her mind. She knew, with that same clarity, that she couldn't go through it again. She couldn't lose him. She couldn't lose the island. No matter what stirrings of rebellion she had felt against both over the last few months, they were rooted in the deepest part of her heart.

She nodded. "I'll do it. I'll go."

"You don't have to," he reminded her, though he had visibly relaxed. He smiled ruefully. "Hutch is telling me very emphatically right now that you don't have to. Especially, you don't have to do it to keep us safe."

It made her smile too. "I know." Hutchincroft had raised his head to look at her anxiously; she gave him a reassuring squeeze. "And it isn't just for that reason. I want to."

It wasn't a lie—it wasn't *just* for that reason. That reason, it was true, had pushed her most of the way to the edge during her sleepless night. But there were other feelings too, harder to define, that had pushed her over. For the first time in her entire life, Rowan was asking for her help, as though she were another mage, or at least another adult. She had wanted to be let into Rowan's secrets, to be allowed to leave the safety of the island, to share in all the dangers from which her childhood had protected her. Now she had been. However much she wanted to pull away from them again—and part of her did, very much—she found she couldn't, now she knew they were there.

And there was something else, an idea she hadn't thought about for a long time, an idea it made her blush to think about too directly now. Hy-Brasil had saved her as a child. When she was growing up, she had thought that perhaps it had saved her for a reason, as orphans so often were saved in stories, to fulfill some great and important destiny. Now here she was, with a spell in her heart, bound for the real world as the Council grew more powerful. She wasn't foolish enough to believe in such stories now, of course—or at least, not to admit it. But she couldn't help but feel she was trembling on the brink of something momentous.

Clever and brave, Rowan had called her. She wasn't sure if she was either. But she wanted to be both.

"All right, then," Rowan said. His smile had faded now, and she wasn't sure what had taken its place. She knew only three faces in the world: Rowan's, Hutchincroft's, and her own. It wasn't an expression she had seen before on any of them. "Let's have a go and see what happens."

Chapter Six

It was a week or so before they left. Rowan said that he was thinking, but Biddy wondered if he wasn't hesitating. He flew away from the island most nights, always returning well before dawn, and spent long hours every day in his study. Every time she spoke to him, he was filled with confidence and energy and plans. Yet often, when his attention lapsed and he thought she wasn't looking, his restless energy would still and a knot of worry crept between his eyes.

Hutchincroft was miserably worried, and made no attempts to hide it. He was at their side the entire time, but he refused to relax even for a moment. His ears remained upright, on alert, his movements as careful and deliberate as a windup toy.

"I can't help it," he said, when he and Biddy were alone in the kitchen making a pie for dinner. It was the first time she had seen his human face since her decision, and it was as tense and miserable as his rabbit body had been. He rolled the pastry as though furious with it. "I'm not saying it isn't the right thing to do, sending you in there. It might be. But it's reckless, and I'm a rabbit spirit. We don't like reckless."

Biddy wrapped her arms around his waist. Deep down, she didn't like reckless either. She was only calm because it didn't feel as if it was going to happen. The longer Rowan delayed, the more it came to seem like a story about somebody else.

In the meantime, every spare moment she had, she read. She scoured her books for everything she could find about England, about people, about life. When it came to it, she found she was far more worried about facing those things than she was about the Council. The Council she had learned of only days ago, and Rowan had promised to protect her from them; she had dreamed of meeting strangers for years, and however close Rowan and Hutch stayed in the shadows, she would face them on her own. She read Sherlock Holmes and Charles Dickens, *North and South* and *Howards End*, *Anne of Avonlea* and *Tom Brown's School Days*. She tried to become the people in their pages, so that when the time came to leave the island, she would already have done so a thousand times as Dr. Watson and Margaret Hale and Pip. It was necessary to read widely. She still didn't know where she would be going, or what she would be expected to do while she waited for the Council to come for her.

"Let me worry about that," Rowan said, when she pressed him. She had the impression he and Hutch had been fighting about it. It was difficult, when she could only hear half of every conversation between them, but Hutchincroft would turn his back very pointedly at that answer.

And yet in all other respects, Biddy had so many more answers that week than she had ever had before. Something had shifted in their relationship when he'd asked for her help, just as she'd hoped it would, and it hadn't shifted back now she'd agreed to give it. There was a new lightness in the air between them, almost an excitement. Rowan no longer attempted to hide his comings and goings, and she hadn't realized the strain it had been placing on them both. They often went for walks into the forest or along the cliff path, the wind off the sea crisp and the sky autumn bright. Even when Rowan was in his study, the door was left half-open; when she, greatly daring, brought her book to sit there and read, he gave her an abstracted smile and no indication he wanted her to leave. She would perch on the window ledge, sharing an apple with Hutchincroft and swinging her legs idly against the stone wall, and watch him over the pages.

"How are you going to capture the mage they send for me?" Biddy asked on one of those days.

Rowan was turning the silver amulet over in his fingers, lost in thought. He took a moment to hear her, but the frown cleared from his face when he did. "It's simple enough. Haven't I shown you a trap circle before?"

Biddy shook her head, and he threw down the amulet. "Here. I'm not getting anywhere with this anyway. It's some kind of invisibility charm, but I have no clue how it works. Bring me that bit of chalk, will you?"

She set her half-eaten apple and her volume of *Pickwick* down at once. The chalk was on the desk, leaving dust against the wood. Hutch growled faintly as she handed it over, and Rowan rolled his eyes.

"It doesn't take that much magic to do a trap circle!" he told him. "Stop fussing."

"Don't waste magic you don't have," Biddy said conscientiously, though she did want to see it.

"Not you too. I told you, we have it." Rowan crouched down on the floor, and Biddy followed suit. She noted, on reflex, that the rug could use a good beating and the floor desperately needed a sweep. "The chalk isn't important—it's not something you can enchant an object to do, or I'd just give you this and you could do it yourself. The trick is in asking the magic while you're drawing."

The rug underfoot was a muddy color that had once been dark green. The chalk showed stark white against it, and Biddy watched Rowan draw the circle clean and smooth, the spell coming in the lilting Gaelic tongue he always used for magic. It didn't matter what language a mage spoke their spells in, only that it was different to the one they spoke in their everyday conversation, and that it was one close to their own heart. Latin worked, or Old English, or the language an immigrant mage spoke at home. She often wondered which she would choose. She'd taught herself bits of French and German and Japanese, but they were for traveling, and none of them felt like home.

"The circle's bigger at one end than another," she pointed out, when Rowan joined the ends with a flourish. "It's more like a teardrop."

"Makes no difference." He got to his feet, a little breathless, more than a little pleased with himself. "It doesn't even have to be a circle, if you'd rather not—some mages do pentagrams, but that always seems a lot of fuss for effect to me. Go on, then. Try stepping in it."

Biddy glanced over at Hutch, who was watching with ears alert. "Don't you dare let him leave me in this thing," she warned, only half joking. "Or I won't bring you any dandelions for the next week."

Hutch flicked his ears.

She didn't really believe that the circle would work. Even though she had seen and felt the spell being done, the messy ring of chalk looked so innocuous, like something she would have drawn as a child. She felt nothing when she stepped in; the room looked no different from inside. And yet when she moved to step out, she found she couldn't. It wasn't that she encountered a barrier, seen or unseen. The barrier was in her mind. She could take tiny steps within the circle, no difficulty at all; as soon as she readied her foot to cross the line, her limbs and her will seized. It was fascinating and frightening in one heady rush.

"That's a good one," Rowan said. "Hopefully I can do as well as that when it counts."

"How do I get out?"

"Already? You just got in." She gave him a very unamused look, and he laughed. "It's easy enough to break. You just need someone outside to give you a hand."

He reached out his hand, and she took it before he changed his mind. It was his left hand, she noticed. The right was still bandaged from the night of the dream trap. He never mentioned it anymore, not even as an excuse to get out of whatever he didn't want to do, and from that she could tell it was bothering him.

Rowan only ever made a fuss about things he didn't mind. The ones that he did, he preferred not to think about.

He still hadn't told her where she would be going.

And then, very early one morning, Biddy was shaken gently awake by a hand on her shoulder.

"Time to go," Rowan whispered, though there was nobody but her to disturb. "The boat's ready."

She sat up, awake at once. It was still dark outside—she couldn't make out Rowan's face. "Now? You never said."

"There wasn't any point, was there? You would only have sat up all night worrying."

"Yes, but—" She didn't know how to put it into words. She could have said goodbye. The sun had gone down on the fields, and hadn't yet risen. She had looked at them for what might have been the last time, and she hadn't known. It felt as though something had been stolen from her.

The bed jumped as Rowan got to his feet. "We'll meet you down on the boat. Dress warm; it'll be cold on the sea."

The sea. It was enough to dash the confusion from her head. She had known the sea every day of her life: its shifting moods, its shifting colors, its playfulness and its dark heart. She had swum in it many times, even in the cold of winter. She had never been *on* it before.

It *was* cold, as Rowan had warned her. Even in her thickest jumper and duffle coat, she shivered as the currach pulled away from the cove where it was docked. But she barely noticed. Mist was coming off the sea; the sunrise colored it faint gold and orange, as though they were swimming through fiery haze. Behind them, their castle loomed high on the cliffs. The hill was dotted with black rabbits—some nibbling the grass, some poised and alert to the cry of seagulls overhead, some scampering for sheer joy of movement through the grass. The thought that she wouldn't see them again tomorrow, or the day after, or the day after that, tightened her throat. She tried to swallow it down.

"Where are we going?" she asked. Presumably he had planned it out by now.

"London," Rowan replied briefly. His attention was on guiding the ship past the sharp rocks that enclosed the bay. "Eventually. The mainland first, though."

London was the place she wanted third most to visit in the world, after Delhi and Tokyo. A thrill went through her alongside the cold off the sea.

Hutchincroft was perched at the prow of the ship, his ears straight up and his nose twitching in the sea air. Biddy followed his gaze out to the distance.

Her breath caught.

She had seen the horizon many times, from the cliff and from the beach and from the castle. She knew the way the water shimmered with light, in a clear path to where it touched the sky. But this time, they were moving *toward* it. Beneath her the boat skimmed the waves like a skipped stone. The wind from the sea blew her doubts away.

This was it. She was leaving her home at last. The world was ahead.

"You're not seasick, are you?" Rowan checked. "I *always* used to get seasick."

"No!" she protested. "It's wonderful." She turned to take a closer look at him, and grinned. "Wait, how long ago is 'used to'?"

He winked at her. "Wait until we reach the rough bits, and I'll let you know."

The horizon drew closer. Soon, the Isle of Hy-Brasil was a dot in the distance, and then it was nothing at all.

＊

It was a much longer journey than she had expected. When Rowan took the boat to pick up supplies, he could make the crossing to the mainland in a few hours and be back within the day. She knew the mainland was far from London, or even England, but though she'd had maps of other countries tacked to her bedroom walls for years she was vague on distances. Anything farther than a few miles had been theoretical to her.

The mainland wasn't the Aran Islands she could see from the cliffs, it transpired, but a fishing village on the coast of Galway Bay—all grey stone and green moss and hard sea, not too different from Hy-Brasil apart from the bustle of ships and carts and people. People most of all. The workers at the docks were the first strangers she had ever seen, and she stared at them with fear and fascination: their rugged faces, their grey stubble, their thick hands as they helped secure the boat.

"Can we look around?" she asked Rowan.

He shook his head shortly. "Not here. We have a train to get on. Besides, there's nothing to see."

Biddy had longed to travel by train since she had read *The Railway Children* six years ago, so she didn't argue. Besides, deep down she wasn't sure she wasn't relieved. The docks were unsettling. Everything was too close and too sharp, as if seen through a spyglass suddenly inverted, and she felt the curious eyes of the workers on her like a physical touch. It made her fidget and huddle deeper into her coat.

She didn't *want* to be scared. She had wanted to come here all her life. Now that at last she had, she wanted to be fearless and strong and meet all that came with shoulders squared and head held high, the way Rowan did. It was just that whenever she had thought of seeing the world, she had never realized what it would be like to have the world see her back.

The train at least was exactly how she had pictured it: a great black dragon, solid and muscular, breathing steam in a long shrilling exhale. It left the station in a great clatter, and she fought the urge to cling to the edge of her seat as the engine built up speed, faster than a run, faster than the boat, faster than she had ever been before. And yet very quickly she lost any sense of motion beyond the gentle rattle of the wheels. The landscape unfurled as if of its own accord: flat green-grey fields, wreathed in light drizzle; craggy hills dotted with stone walls and smoking houses; huge grey towns bustling with people and spiked with steeples and rooftops.

"We go by train as far as Dublin," Rowan said, after the first few

H. G. Parry

miles. It was a relief to hear him speak—not only because his silence was unnerving, but because she had been unsure how to ask without sounding naive or stupid. "We stay overnight there, then get the early-morning ferry to Liverpool, then another train to London."

She tried to fill that in on her mental atlas, the lines going from one city to another like the threads she had once used to plan journeys to other countries. But seeing it in real life had muddled the lines in her head. "What's in Dublin?"

"A lot of people trying to get somewhere else, mostly." He caught himself on her expression and found a rueful smile. "I didn't mean that. I've only been there a handful of times, to tell the truth, and most of those times I wasn't human. Tell you what, if the train makes good time, we'll go out after dinner and see."

"Please," she said, as firmly as she could. She could see that Rowan was concerned about the task they had ahead; she could see, less clearly, that being in the country where he had grown up was doing something to his feelings beyond her understanding. It was doing something to her own. She just didn't want any of that to stop her finally seeing the world.

But they didn't reach Dublin until after dark, and by that time it was teeming with rain and aglow with streetlamps. She couldn't tell if the people crowding the streets were trying to get somewhere else—most of them seemed to be trying to get home—but there were certainly a lot of them. Too many, if she were honest, and despite her resolve she found herself desperately wanting to go home herself.

They took a room at a boarding house run by a sour-faced old woman, with a single window that looked out to the crowded port. By that point, they were too late for any meals apart from bread and cheese, and the landlady insisted that candles had to be paid for separately. Rowan argued at first, then gave up in disgust and, once the door was closed behind them, pulled a tiny globe of light out of nowhere and sent it to rotate around the ceiling.

"Not that a dump like this isn't best left to the imagination," he snorted, as the globe illuminated a rotten chest of drawers and two sunken beds. Hutchincroft explored the sticky floor warily, back legs poised to run, head bobbing, neck and ears craning as far as they would go. "I don't think we'd better do any sightseeing outside tonight either. It's not the kind of place you explore after dark."

"That's all right," she said. Glimpses of the outside were drifting through the half-open window: the smashing of glass, raucous laughter, a smell like smoke and stale beer.

He looked at her more closely. "Are *you* all right?"

Biddy nodded, and wished she was as good as Rowan at smiling when she didn't mean it. "Yes. I'm fine. Just a little cold."

"It's always cold by the docks," Rowan agreed. He shrugged off his coat and wrapped it around her shoulders. "Here. We'll be gone in a few hours. The ferry leaves before dawn."

It would be warmer with the shutters closed, but Biddy didn't point that out. Rowan never closed windows if he could help it. Besides, the coat bore traces of woodsmoke and sea mist and the grass-after-a-thunderstorm smell that clung to the great oak, and that more than anything eased her chill. She sat on the bed closest to the door, and winced as it sagged and creaked beneath her.

"Nobody will give the rabbits vegetables tonight," she heard herself say.

"They'll be fine. More than fine. We'll be gone for days at least— I'd be amazed if they didn't get into the vegetable patch before we get back, even with all the spells I put around it."

His voice was absent, his thoughts clearly elsewhere. When he did move, he did so abruptly, as though getting something over with. He snatched the canvas bag in which Hutchincroft had been traveling off the bed, rummaged through, and pulled out a bundle of cloth.

"Here." He didn't quite look at her. "These are for you to wear tomorrow."

She took the bundle from him in surprise that quickly turned to dismay.

Her clothes at home were an eclectic mix of things Rowan had picked up from the mainland, sometimes under Hutchincroft's guidance, lately under her own. She had three dresses, in various states of repair; she had three shirts, a skirt, and a pair of boy's work trousers that she wore when there would be more climbing or gardening or exploring than she wanted to risk her good things on. Yesterday, she had put on her best dress to come out into the world—deep forest green, neat and tidy even after a few tumbles from trees and treks through muddy fields. None of her belongings had ever been new, or particularly fancy. But they had always been *nice*, well-made and warm and clean.

The clothes Rowan handed her now were not nice. The dress was black, made of cheap material, its skirts heavily mended in places and worn to near transparency in others. It was too large for her at the bodice, and yet the sleeves looked as though they would be painfully tight. The stockings and drawers and petticoats were the same: patched, threadbare, ill-fitting. The clothes of a young woman who had been sent out into the world with what she needed, and nothing more.

"Why?" she asked slowly. It wasn't only that the thought of appearing in London in that dress made her cheeks burn. She couldn't think what she might be doing that she would need something like it.

"Trust me, where you're going, it won't stand out," Rowan said. "And it'll be under your coat until you get there."

"Are you going to tell me where it is I'm to go?"

"Tomorrow," he said. "I promise. I'll explain on the crossing. Let's get some sleep, all right?"

It was all the answer she would get, she knew from long experience. From that same experience, she also noted one thing he had told her without meaning to.

Where you're *going*, he had said. Not *where* we're *going*.

She slept very little that night, and every time she turned over in the strange bed Rowan was still at the window, arms folded, looking out into the darkness that was so far from home.

London was every bit as Biddy had imagined. The trouble was, her imagination had never stretched far enough.

She had known there would be noise, buildings, people. She hadn't realized how much noise it was possible for seven million people to make: voices chattering, wheels clattering, horns blaring, whistles screeching, vendors shouting their wares. She hadn't realized the grandeur and scale of the buildings: as high as their castle, but everywhere, lining the streets in walls of grey and brown and dirty white. She hadn't realized the sheer heat and smell and press of the crowds. Leaving Euston Station and stepping out onto the swirl of the streets felt like being swallowed by something hot and hungry. She stuck close to Rowan, tried to keep her elbows tight to her sides, and barely remembered to breathe.

"Well?" Rowan asked, voice raised over the rattle of a passing carriage. "Do you like it?"

"Yes," she said—staunchly, not entirely truthfully. The city was wondrous, but it was frightening too. It seemed not to care if she lived or died. "Do you?"

"Bits and pieces." He rested his hands on his hips, heedless of the people pushing past them, and gave her a lopsided smile. "Tell you what, we have a few hours before we're expected. Is there anything you'd like to see?"

In the satchel over his shoulder, she heard the distinct thump and growl of Hutchincroft expressing his displeasure, but Rowan ignored him. Biddy, guiltily, did as well. She knew Hutch was worried—if Rowan was right, the magic in her heart had been singing out to the Council as soon as they had left Hy-Brasil. The trap could be sprung at any time.

But she didn't want to leave them so soon. Rowan had told her exactly where she was going now, as the ferry had lurched across the chopping waters between Dublin and Liverpool, and she had spent the rest of the day pushing it resolutely to the back of her mind. It would have been frightening no matter where he intended to put her, she supposed; she wasn't here for a holiday. She had promised to be brave. Just not yet. Not now, with London a sprawling forest of wonders and Rowan so close that she could feel the comforting press of his arm against her own.

"Can we see a shop?" she asked, and wasn't sure why Rowan laughed.

It turned out, they could see a *lot* of shops—what felt like hundreds of them. Huge department stores filled with clothes, bakery windows loaded with pastries and cakes, butchers and saddlers and stationers and booksellers. They walked down straight tree-lined streets, down cobbled lanes that twisted in on each other, past theaters pasted with old playbills and pubs beginning to fill with workmen looking for their dinners.

They came to Trafalgar Square as the sun was lowering in the sky, and the sheer scale of the enormous column and the city curving away in all directions took her breath away.

"It's beautiful," she said quietly, and forgot all about her shabby dress under her coat and the dangers in every direction. This was where she had wanted to come, and in that moment at least she was exactly where she wanted to be.

"I was here in the middle of a riot once," Rowan said. "In 1887. It wasn't quite so beautiful then." The satchel with Hutchincroft inside wriggled furiously, and he flinched. "Ow! Stop that. I never said I didn't *like* it."

Biddy smiled. "I know bad things happen in beautiful places," she said, to Hutch, but for Rowan's benefit. "Something bad must have happened to the people who lived on Hy-Brasil, after all."

"We don't know that," Rowan protested, as he always did. "They might have gone somewhere better. Speaking of, we need to get moving."

"You always say that when you want to stop talking." Biddy sighed, though she followed him willingly enough. "Even when there's nowhere to go."

On the steps down into the square, huddled so small that Biddy nearly tripped over him, was a shabby man with a woolen hat and a huge tattered coat. His head was bowed, and one hand rested, upturned and imploring, on his knee. Rowan must have seen her looking. He barely glanced at the man, but his hand reached out and brushed the top of the woolen hat, and Biddy knew a flash of magic had passed from his fingers.

"What will that do?"

He smiled ruefully. "Whatever it wants to," he said. "Something good, at least. Are you hungry?"

They ate chicken sandwiches and strawberry ice cream at a café by St. James's Park, and took the crusts to feed the ducks on the pond. Hutchincroft stretched his legs and nibbled the grass as they sat on a park bench, and the sun went down over the white towers of Horse Guards.

"I was twelve when I left my home," Rowan said, out of nowhere. "A little younger than you. I was alone by the sea, and a voice spoke into my head. The Council, of course—they could do that in those days, when they felt magic swirling about a new mage. The next day I sold my knife and my jacket to get to Dublin, made my way across the sea, and started my apprenticeship in York. I didn't go home again for another twenty years."

It was strange to think of Rowan being a child, of his features shrunk to child-sized. It was stranger yet to think of him without Hutchincroft. She couldn't help but think of them as lonely without each other. "Did you miss your home?"

"No," he said flatly. "It was a cold, hard rock in the middle of the sea, and everyone there already thought I was weird. I was too. It didn't cost me a second thought to leave. But I was going somewhere good, or at least I thought so. We're sending you somewhere terrible, Biddy. Just try to remember it'll only be for a while, and we'll be there the whole time." He hesitated. "And if something *does* go wrong, make your way back here. It's an easy place to find. I'll try to leave a message for you in this tree, and you can do the same. All right?"

She nodded, as nonchalantly as she could, while inside her stomach turned. *Terrible.* He had said it would be terrible.

"I'm not afraid," she said.

Rowan must have known it was a lie, but he said nothing about it. It crossed her mind that he did so as professional courtesy, from one pretender to another. Or perhaps he simply wanted to believe her. "Good," he said. "Because now we really do have to go."

Chapter Seven

*B*iddy had read about workhouses in *Oliver Twist*. She knew them to be harsh, cruel places where the poor were reluctantly given shelter and watery gruel in exchange for menial labor, and children were separated from their parents and apprenticed to horrible masters. The Rookwood Asylum for Destitute Girls was not a workhouse, exactly. It was an industrial school, Rowan said, one of many designed to take in poor children, educate them, and prepare them for a trade. And yet she couldn't help but think of Oliver and Mr. Bumble as they approached the iron fence that surrounded the school.

Many industrial schools were built on large estates out in the country, but this one was an ugly brick house on the edge of Whitechapel—a name that had meant nothing to Biddy a moment ago, and that she now knew as a grim labyrinth of back alleys where people in shabby clothes gutted fish on the side of the street or shouted at each other from pub doors or pushed past her without a word. They were only a few miles from the curve of Regent Street or the shade of St. James's Park, but they seemed in another world.

Biddy didn't know what Rowan had said or done or bespelled to earn her a position there, but when he showed up at the gates with her in tow, the matron, Miss Finchley, seemed to expect them.

"Is this our new teacher?" she asked, with the brisk, tired air of someone determined to check another item off a list.

Biddy studied Miss Finchley carefully, apprehension making her quiet. She was probably not very old, but her face was worn, and that and the streaks of grey in her hair made her seem part of the weathered buildings around her. She looked hard and uncompromising as the buildings too—as though wind and rain would lash against her and find no entry.

"This is my niece," Rowan replied, just as brisk. The soft edges had gone from his voice all at once, and he stood upright and rigid. "She's a good worker, and well educated. Mind you take care of her."

"We take care of all the young ladies here, staff and students alike," Miss Finchley said sternly. She looked Biddy up and down, and Biddy found herself standing a little straighter as well.

Rowan had taken her good coat away, replacing it with a grey shawl, and the memory of her worn black dress brought color to her cheeks. It was stupid, she knew. But after all her efforts to look nice on Hy-Brasil, where there was nobody to see her, it seemed wrong to look so shabby when she was meeting and being judged by a stranger for the first time in her life.

"She looks young," Miss Finchley said at last. "What's her age? Sixteen?"

"Seventeen," Rowan said—which might indeed have been true, for all they knew, but didn't feel it. The reason for her sudden growth by three months became clear when Miss Finchley replied.

"That's fine. Our oldest pupils are sixteen, but the most unruly tend to be gone by fourteen or so. She shouldn't have trouble keeping order." From that, Biddy understood that keeping order—whatever that entailed—was going to be impossible. Still, Miss Finchley was evidently satisfied, or at least resigned. "Very well. And you, young lady. I haven't heard your voice yet. Has your uncle explained to you what your duties will entail?"

"Yes. I mean—yes, Miss Finchley, he has explained." She stumbled, forgetting to reply in complete sentences, not sure if it was even a rule that she should reply in complete sentences—where had she read it, was it for ladies or for gentlemen, or was it invented entirely?—but Miss Finchley didn't remark. She said nothing at all, in fact, which prompted Biddy to speak again. "He said you were looking for a teacher."

"I am. He assured me you were competent in all the usual branches of a British education?"

"I am," she said, although she had no idea what this might mean. She could write and read anything, but her mathematics was shaky, and her knowledge of history and geography spotty at best. And she doubted there would be any call for knowing the medicinal attributes of plants, the ways of the tides, how to work a scrying glass, or the best method for climbing an oak.

"You've seen her certificate and references," Rowan said, which explained what at least some of the muttering and spellwork had been over the last few days. "Didn't they satisfy you?"

"I'll know soon enough, won't I?" Miss Finchley looked Biddy up and down one more time. "Very well. You can leave her with us now. Step inside, young lady. Welcome to Rookwood."

Biddy forgot all about her clothes, or Miss Finchley's disapproving gaze. This was it. Rowan and Hutch were really going to leave her in this dreadful place. She looked up at Rowan, and couldn't quite believe it.

He winked at her. She knew he was trying to remind her of his promise to remain nearby, and she did feel the icy grip about her heart lessen. But she was trembling as she returned his smile, and when he took her by the hand to say goodbye, it was all she could do to let him go.

"Be good," he said.

She nodded stiffly, rather than try to speak around the knot in her throat. If she opened her mouth, she might beg him to take her home again, and embarrassment curdled her stomach at the thought. Besides, what if she begged, and he refused? She would never have thought it possible before; he had said that the decision to come here was hers, and she was free to refuse. But that had been on Hy-Brasil. When he was talking to Miss Finchley, he had suddenly seemed a different person—harder, colder, as though she might bounce off him too.

Instead, she watched as Rowan inclined his head politely at Miss Finchley, then as he turned to walk away, bag with Hutchincroft inside slung over his shoulders. She wanted to keep watching him all the way down the dirty streets, just to see if he would look back. But Miss Finchley took her in a tight grip by the shoulder.

"Come on," she said. "No dawdling. The girls are just sitting down to supper."

⸺

There were sixty girls between four and sixteen at the Rookwood Asylum for Destitute Girls. Many were orphans, most had been taken from the slums, all had grown up in poverty and hunger skirting the edges of crime. The purpose of the asylum, Miss Finchley explained to Biddy as they swept through the school, was to educate the girls, to prepare them for work that befitted their stations.

"Most of them, we hope, will go into domestic service." She said it tiredly—the tone of someone treading a well-worn track for what she knew would not be the last time. "You'll be supervising them as they learn how to cook, clean, mend, and so forth, as well as teaching them their reading and writing and history. But to enter service they need to provide their own uniforms, and for that they need money of their own, so many will start out with lesser jobs cleaning or sewing until they can pay their own way. Many will go into factories. The important thing is they're kept off the streets and earning a decent living. Is that clear?"

"Yes, Miss Finchley," Biddy replied, though her head spun and her brain teemed with questions. She didn't know what it was safe to ask, what it would raise eyebrows for her not to know. Miss Finchley wasn't the enemy, and she had no reason to be suspicious of Biddy, but she was at least supposed to believe that Biddy had grown up in the world and not an enchanted island in the middle of the Atlantic.

She seemed satisfied with Biddy's lack of curiosity, at least. "Good. Stow your belongings upstairs, and then you can come back down and supervise the girls. Miss Belenky!"

This last was to a young woman—short, dark, perhaps a few years older than Biddy—who was coming down the stairs. The young woman turned to them with a quickness that reminded Biddy of a rabbit in the field: confident enough to hold its ground, ready for fight or flight.

"This is our new teacher," Miss Finchley said. "She'll be sharing your room, since Miss Burns left. Will you show her where it is and then instruct her in her duties? Miss Grey and Miss Prescott will supervise supper until you return, but don't be too late."

"Yes, Miss Finchley," the young woman said.

Miss Finchley left without further word, her mind already on the next task. Biddy was left alone with the first person of her own age she had ever met.

The young woman was thin, and her naturally dusky skin had taken on a greyish pallor—as though the place that had so weathered Miss Finchley was doing its best to whittle her down and turn her to stone. And yet she was very pretty, Biddy thought, with her thick eyebrows, curly black hair, and eyes that were so dark and expressive. It was difficult to look past those eyes, enormous in her elongated face. They grabbed at Biddy's own in a way that was part challenge, part wariness, part open curiosity.

The silence stretched. Was that all right, or should she be talking? Biddy had wanted to meet new people all her life. Now, though, she seemed to be outside her own body, looking at herself through a stranger's eyes standing awkward and uncertain in ill-fitting clothes. She couldn't find a way to get back into herself, and no idea what she should say if she did. In all her life, she'd never once had to think about how to make somebody like her.

"So you're the new teacher, are you?" the young woman said at last.

She nodded, and fumbled for her voice. "I just arrived."

It had seemed a safe thing to say, but the girl tilted her head critically. "Are you Irish? You sound a bit Irish. But you also sound a bit posh."

Biddy had never thought what her own voice sounded like. She knew only Hutchincroft's clear, precise tones, Rowan's gentler lilt. Her speech came from them, not from a country or a city. But now she could hear the other young woman's speech had the same rhythms as Miss Finchley's—clipped, jaunty, the consonants dropping in different places to Biddy's own. It was what Rowan's had hardened to match, she realized suddenly, when he had handed Biddy over at the gates. And when he had argued with the landlady in Dublin, his vowels had softened to meet the rolling pitch with which she had been denying them candles.

"I don't know," she said, and felt foolish. "I think my...my uncle was. Is."

"Well, what's your last name?"

It wouldn't help her. Rowan had asked what she wanted to be called the week before, and she had stolen a name from Sherlock Holmes because she liked the sound of it. (Rowan had forbidden her most of the good Dickens names on the basis that few people were really called things like Pocket and Pumblechook.)

"Adler," she said. "I'm Bridget Adler."

Even her first name, her real name, sounded strange to her. She could only remember being called Biddy.

"That sounds posh too," the young woman said knowingly. She was standing on the bottom stair; she took a step down to Biddy's level. "Was that your uncle I saw outside with Finchley, then? Why was he bringing you and not your parents?"

"My parents died at sea," Biddy said, on safe ground now. "My uncle raised me and had me educated, but when I turned seventeen he sent me here to fend for myself. I think he ran out of money."

It was the right thing to say. The young woman nodded, sympathetic, and the faint air of suspicion evaporated. "Probably drank it away."

"Probably," Biddy agreed. It served Rowan right, after all, for leaving her here. "And he never had real work."

She rubbed Biddy's arm comfortingly, and in a rush Biddy felt the warmth of acceptance. "Never mind. You're better off without him. I'm Anna Belenky. My parents died too. Consumption."

"I'm sorry," Biddy said.

"It was a long time ago," Anna said, with a shrug that was a little too careless. "I'm lucky that I ended up here, and that Finchley agreed to take me on as a teacher when I got old enough. I can read and write better than most here, which is good enough for her. They always need teachers. Most don't last long. They get married, or they find easier places to work. I don't expect I'll stay much longer myself."

It was a cold, matter-of-fact world she was describing, and it gave Biddy a surge of guilt at how readily Anna had accepted her lies about her own hardships. They were both orphans, that much was true; otherwise, Anna had grown up on the brink of an abyss and she had floated above it in a fairy story. "Where will you go?"

"Somewhere a long way away from here, anyhow." Anna caught herself with another shrug. "Anyway, there's food and board here in the meantime. Speaking of, I'll show you our room quick, then we'd better get back down. The girls have gone to supper—we need to be there to help supervise."

The room was upstairs on the first floor, and there was little enough of it to see—two narrow beds, a cracked washbasin, a window overlooking a barren courtyard. It was a matter of minutes to stow her old carpet bag under the bed, wash her face and hands, and follow Anna down to the dining hall.

There were so *many* of them. Rows and rows of girls, all different shapes and sizes and colors, all clad in the same grey dresses with their hair in the same long braids. All with the same bowls of a grey lumpy porridge, crust of bread, and glass of milk. All talking, giggling, complaining, so that entering the room was like walking into a high-pitched wall of sound. Her books hadn't prepared her for what being in the midst of people was like. She had to fight the urge to grab something and hold on, as she had in the train when the engine lurched forward.

"What are we supposed to do with them?" she heard herself ask.

"Now? Not a lot," Anna said dismissively. "They're under control. Not supposed to be talking, of course, but that doesn't matter much as long as Miss Finchley isn't here. We just need to sit at the foot of the table and keep order. This is the easy bit. Are you hungry?"

She should have been, she supposed. It was six o'clock, and the sandwiches at St. James's Park had been hours ago. And yet, sitting on a narrow chair that seemed to have hard bones within its wood, crushed between warm bodies, she found herself completely without appetite. The unappetizing mess in front of her didn't help.

Anna looked at her sideways. "Don't tell me you're one of those sorry cases who go off their food at the slightest worry?"

"I don't think so," Biddy said. "It's never happened before." She took a cautious spoonful of the grey porridge. Her throat closed at once, and Anna laughed at the look on her face.

"You *are* posh," she said, but fondly now. "You'd better get used to eating it. Under-teachers get fed the same as the girls, unless you want to buy your own food with your salary."

"Is it the same thing every day?" Biddy asked in dismay. It tasted like soggy paper, doused with salt water and half turned to paste.

"If you're lucky," Anna retorted. "Sometimes it's a lot worse."

Biddy took another spoonful, and tried to make it look like she'd eaten soggy saltwater paper every day of her life. Something crunched. She had the horrifying suspicion it was an insect.

"Well," she said, mimicking Anna's jaunty tone, "if this is the good bit, I can't wait to see what the work's like."

"You just stay with me," Anna said comfortingly. "I'll see you right."

Biddy's smile was real that time, although her heart ached for home. It wouldn't be forever, she knew. This would all be over soon. A mage would come for her—perhaps tomorrow, or the following day. Rowan and Hutchincroft would stop them. She only had to wait.

But she was here now, and the sun had set, and despite Anna by her side, the chatter of sixty girls like birdsong in her ears, and the city of millions around her, she had never felt more alone in her life.

＊＝＝＝＝＊

Supper finished quickly, as Miss Finchley had warned. Biddy endeared herself to the girls sitting near to her by not finishing— once they saw, her porridge vanished in a swarm of spoons. The children were directed upstairs for an hour and a half of sewing before bed, shepherded by the two older women whom Biddy hadn't met. Anna and Biddy were waved aside to take care, Anna said briskly, of the "little ones."

"The under-fours are in the nursery," Anna explained, seeing Biddy's confusion. Biddy suspected she was taking no small enjoyment in knowing the ropes of the place. "Poor little mites. Here, I'll show you."

The nursery was up the stairs, along the corridor from where Anna said they were to sleep themselves. It was a narrow room, with a single window at the end framed by long cheaply papered walls on each side. A fire flickered gamely in the grate, and yet cold seeped in from every corner. It was lined with cradles. One of them was empty; the other five were occupied by writhing, crying infants. Two of them looked almost old enough to talk or crawl, while the other three lay on their backs and kicked helplessly with their tiny legs.

"They're all orphans," Anna told her. "Like us. There's a nurse for them during the day, but she goes home before supper, so we check them before we go to bed. Just change them if they need to be changed, and all that."

"Who comes for them during the night?" Biddy asked.

Anna shrugged. Biddy was learning to recognize the gesture, as though something heavy was being tossed aside. "You can get up if you want. Our room's not too far, and the walls are thin, so you can hear them most nights. But Finchley says they need to learn to sleep the night through."

Biddy remembered her long, frightened wait in the dark for Rowan the week before, and felt sick.

"They shouldn't be here at all, really," Anna said, as an afterthought. "They should be in foster homes. They're not part of the school. The board takes them in for extra money."

The idea of money in connection with the tiny beings in their cribs made her flinch. "That's horrible."

"There are worse places they could be. For that matter, they could be dead."

"Well," Biddy pointed out, "anyone could be dead."

"Not the board," Anna snorted. "They'll live forever."

Anna was less dismissive than her words, Biddy couldn't help but notice. She tucked in the eldest girl, speaking quietly to her and tickling her until she giggled. Biddy found herself with one of the very small ones, who was crying a thin, hopeless wail. She seemed warm and dry enough, to Biddy's relief, but she wouldn't stop.

Biddy picked up the little girl, surprisingly solid and heavy in her arms, and rocked her awkwardly. "Shhh," she whispered. It didn't seem to help.

A dim memory came of Rowan singing to her softly when she was very young, and she had been sick or upset. The words were in the same lilting Irish he used for magic and she had never learned to speak, but a few came back to her, and she hummed the rest.

Anna watched her, unusually quiet. "What's that mean?" she asked, as the child's cries finally became disgruntled whimpers.

"I think it's a changeling song," Biddy said. "To keep the fairies from taking a child away." Rowan had always been vague on the details.

"They'd probably have a better time with the fairies than here," Anna said. She seemed tired now, and less jaunty than she had been downstairs. "But it's pretty. My mother used to sing to me in another language too. Before she died."

"Can you sing it for me?"

"Can't remember it." Anna stood abruptly, and laid the baby she was holding in its crib. "Come on. They'll be wanting us in the workroom. And then it's our job to put everyone else to bed."

Biddy and Anna, it turned out, were responsible for the wing housing the girls between ten and sixteen—much better, Anna assured her, than the under-tens, who from her description were basically feral. The children's room was the nursery made large: more beds, more children, more windows that showed only the cracked courtyard outside. Everywhere Biddy looked, adolescent girls were running and giggling and squabbling like the chickens coming to roost in the evening henhouse. Anna shooed the last of them into their beds, and Biddy, in imitation, did the same to one of the younger girls with whom she had shared her dinner. She hoped, vaguely, that she might have bought some authority with the gritty porridge.

"Come on," she said, as briskly as Anna. "You'll have a busy day tomorrow."

"I hate busy days," the girl complained, but she yawned and climbed into bed without further protest, so either the porridge really had worked or she was just very tired.

Anna and Biddy's own room adjoined the girls' dormitory, with only a door between them. The bed closest to the window had been left for her, and Biddy learned why as she slipped, shivering, beneath the one thin blanket. The glass gave off a chill like ice. It cut right through her plain white cotton nightdress, so that even her bones seemed frozen.

Anna was folding back the covers of the bed opposite. She glanced at Biddy, and for the first time she looked uncertain.

"Is this your first night away from home on your own?" she asked abruptly, in a low voice.

Biddy hesitated, wondering if this would give her away—Would a real orphan have left home before? Should going to live with her uncle count?—but Anna didn't seem suspicious. "Yes."

Anna nodded, a serious inclination of her head, as if considering a proposed strategy. "If you cry, just make sure you bury your head in the pillow, and the children won't hear you. I might hear, but I won't tell anyone. All right?"

"Thank you," Biddy said. "But I won't cry."

"Well, good." Anna blew out the candle between them, and her bed groaned as she settled back in it. "Lots of the little ones say that, though, and they do. And you're not much older than them."

She wondered if Anna had cried on her first night here, and if so whether she was trying to tell Biddy that or if she didn't want Biddy to guess. It seemed impolite to ask, either way.

"I won't," she repeated instead.

She thought she meant it, even though her insides were feeling shaky and her chest ached. After all, she wasn't like Anna or the poor girls on the other side of the wall. Rowan and Hutchincroft were out there, watching over her.

But without the light of the candle, with the room swallowed by darkness and the slow breathing of the woman in the other bed, Rowan and Hutch felt as impossibly far away as Hy-Brasil had the night before. It was almost impossible to believe in them at all. She had left Hy-Brasil only yesterday morning, and already she wondered if she had made it all up. The cold stones outside seemed so much more real than forests and castles and black rabbits and even than the room she had slept in all her life.

Why had Rowan brought her here? Surely the magic could call to the Council anywhere in the country. Why here?

Careful not to wake Anna with the creaking of the bed, Biddy sat up and looked out the window. Her eyes searched the courtyard: the cracked paving, the one spindly tree, the high wall. There was no sign of a raven anywhere, and no sign of a golden rabbit. If they were out there, they were hidden even from her.

She didn't cry, exactly. But she buried her face in the pillow anyway, just in case.

⤙⬩▸▪══════════▪◂⬩⤚

The next morning, she woke to the sound of Anna coughing. It was a terrible sound—harsh, painful, punctuated with desperate gasps as the other girl fought to catch her breath. Her head was muffled in the blankets, but the sound carried across the room into the dawn stillness.

Biddy was across the room at once. She put a hand to Anna's shoulder, and felt heat radiating through her nightdress. "Anna? Are you all right?"

"Don't you know?" It was a young girl standing at the door, looking on with interest. She had the build of a stick insect, thin and spindly with too many elbows and knees, and her wrists poked from her too-short nightdress. "She's got the consumption. She's going to die."

"Lizzie Thatcher!" Anna looked up, breathless and angry. "You hold your tongue or I'll have you whipped!"

"I didn't mean *now*," Lizzie protested, in the tone of one deeply wronged. "But you're going to die sometime."

"We're all going to die *sometime*," Anna said, before another bout of coughing seized her.

Biddy's heart twisted. She had read about consumption, many times. When she was ten, after her first reading of *Jane Eyre*, she'd been terrified every time Rowan had so much as a sore throat in case it foreshadowed the end. Her fears had eased as the seasons turned and he remained stubbornly healthy. But Anna's parents had died, Anna had told her last night, and there was no doubt that she was very sick.

"It's all right," she said to Anna gently, the way Rowan did when she was ill. She rubbed Anna's shoulder as she fought for breath, and cast an irritated glance at Lizzie Thatcher. "Well, you could at least get a glass of water!"

The girl stared at her, then was gone like a small flitting shadow. A second later, she reappeared, this time holding a cup in one hand and a pitcher in the other. It didn't look too clean, but Anna took it and gulped it down.

"Thanks," she said hoarsely. She sat up, looking more like the confident young woman of the day before. "Don't worry yourself. It's only bad on cold mornings. Come on. It's nearly six. You'd better start getting ready for prayers, or you'll be in trouble."

"Should I tell someone you're ill?"

Anna snorted. "Only if you want to get me in trouble too."

The girls on the other side of the wall were already getting dressed. Biddy put on her scratchy black dress, splashed her face with water, made her bed, and did her best to pin her hair the way it had been the day before. She'd half hoped last night that Anna might help, but there was no question of that now. The other girl moved slowly, painfully, and twice had to sit down to catch her breath.

Biddy was never sure afterward how she made it through that day. Miss Finchley led the school in prayers, a long and bewildering business during which fortunately nothing was expected of Biddy but that she stay silent and copy Anna as closely as possible. They went down to breakfast, which seemed a nightmarish echo of supper the night before—she wondered, in fact, if it might somehow have been the same porridge, an endless cauldron refilling itself twice a day like Penelope weaving and unweaving her funeral shroud. She tried to swallow the bread and boiled milk, telling herself she would need her strength, but in the end she gave most of it to Lizzie Thatcher. It wasn't just that the metallic taste turned her stomach: The little girl looked so lean and hungry, and Biddy had been eating ice cream a day ago.

They weren't rich on Hy-Brasil. They grew vegetables in the garden; they had the goats and the chickens to give them milk and eggs; there were wild berries and herbs and even an apple tree in the forest. Otherwise, Rowan went to the mainland, and Biddy had known for a long time that when he did that it was usually to steal what they needed. Hutchincroft had explained it to her when she was a little girl, and promised that Rowan took only from people who could spare it and made it up in any way he could. Even so, there were times when Biddy would go to the cupboard and find little there; when she was still hungry after supper and suspected

Rowan was even hungrier; when they ate nothing but boiled eggs and potatoes while winter storms kept the boat moored to the island. But she had never been allowed to starve. These children had, and even now they had food, they were haunted by the memory of starvation.

Miss Finchley came through the room as they ate, but didn't glance in their direction. She was in the company of an older man dressed in a suit that even to Biddy's unpracticed eye looked startingly well-made in this place. Miss Finchley talked to him in a low, nervous voice, but the man paid her little attention as he strode down the line between the tables. Biddy frowned.

"Anna," she whispered. "Who's that?"

Anna followed Biddy's nod—slowly, as though her head weighed a great deal and was unwieldy to turn. She had been subdued during prayers, and her own porridge was scarcely touched. "Him? No idea. Probably someone from the board, with a suit like that. They come to check on us every now and then."

"To see that you're being well treated?"

Anna gave a short, rusty laugh. "To see Finchley's not spending too much money on us."

Biddy watched the man leave Miss Finchley stuttering at the bottom of the stairs and ascend to the floor where the children had slept shivering in their beds last night; where the little ones lay miserable, earning him his pittance from the government. Hot, fierce anger kindled in her heart. She didn't let it show, but it burned all the hotter for that.

They had lessons all morning, four teachers and sixty girls all crowded into one schoolroom. They took a corner each, she and Anna and the two older women who didn't speak to her, and she was quickly surrounded by twenty or so girls clutching worn textbooks and looking at her with eyes that were half challenge, half hope. She had time in an excruciating second to try to remember everything about the scenes in *Anne of Avonlea* when Anne is a schoolteacher, to realize that she could only remember the one in which she straps a boy, to see that some of the girls were the same age as her and looked even older. Then, because she had to say something, she opened her mouth and heard herself say, "Open your books."

The teaching wasn't so difficult. The girls knew heartbreakingly little, even the older ones, so there was no danger after all of the gaps in her knowledge being exposed. She remembered that Anna had said teachers didn't last long here; clearly, most of them had left without leaving a mark. She heard their reading, corrected their sums, told them what she could remember about the French Revolution and, with more success, the story of Robin Hood and the silver arrow. She found herself channeling Anna's bravado mixed with the tone Rowan took with her when she pushed him too far, and though the girls were rowdy, they at least didn't actively rebel. By the time the bell rang for dinner at one, she was as exhausted and trembling as though she'd climbed every tree on Hy-Brasil, twice. There was some kind of meat and potato stew being served, although it did still look rather like porridge, and the girls' portions were gone in a flash of spoons.

The long afternoon was spent in what was called Industrial Employment. The older girls worked the laundry and mended clothes; some of the younger classes cooked the food for the rest of the school and cleaned the floors from the top of the house to the bottom. The youngest, under Biddy's supervision, were set to work in the courtyard picking oakum from old ropes. It was training in basic skills, but it also generated an income for the school—like the laundry, the mending, the children upstairs. The air outside was bitter cold under the slate-grey sky. The girls shivered in their thin dresses as they hunched over the ropes coiled like fat snakes at their feet.

"You just need to watch," Anna had told her in a hasty whisper as they had parted, "and pull them up if they stop working. They need to get it all done before they can go to supper."

And so she watched, chest aching, as their fingers rubbed against the fibers until they bled. Just once, she heard a rustle in the branches of the tree in the corner. Her head shot up. There, amid the grey-green leaves, was a large black bird. It tilted its head and looked at her, before taking off with a beat of its wings. Biddy bent back to her work, heart hammering, the rush of warmth to her chest making her feel as though she could breathe for the first time all day. Perhaps she wasn't so alone after all.

But it didn't help the other children, as the bell went and they filed in at last to their tasteless, cheerless supper. It didn't help the little ones upstairs, who lay in their cribs waiting to be tucked in and left alone all night. The infant Biddy had held last night quieted faster at the lullaby this time, and yet when Biddy put her back in the crib she started crying again and didn't stop.

Anna didn't have any comforting words that night. She climbed into her nightgown achingly slowly, as though every movement was an effort, and then fell into bed with her eyes already closed. The sound of her breathing was harsh and labored.

Biddy climbed into bed herself, berating herself for being so helpless. There ought to be something she could give Anna—a blanket, a hot drink, a comforting word of her own. But she had only one blanket, which Anna had refused when offered. And she could think of nothing to say.

This wasn't like the hardship in books. It wasn't just that characters in books weren't real and Anna and the children were—that part of it was obvious and expected. It was that the hardship in books was written. It had *purpose*. It was part of a story, and however bleak it looked for the people inside the pages, that only meant there were more pages left before the end—unless it was a tragedy, or something Russian. Even then, things would work out the way they ought. It wasn't true here. Pain was simply pain, and there was nothing to do about it except refuse to let it break you.

She thought she would never sleep, with her body and heart aching, but she did.

She dreamed of Hy-Brasil, twisted in the way that dreams

always twist places and faces. She stood in her room, but it was shot through with the trunks of trees and half-open to the sky outside. The air buzzed with crickets, as it did in the summer months, but when she looked closer she saw that the crickets were tiny dragons on clockwork wings.

"Hello, Biddy."

It was Rowan's voice, the familiar friendly lilt of her name, and when she turned he was standing in the door. Her heart, which had been beaten down all day, leapt. Without being able to say how, she knew that he was no dream. It was him.

Normally she would have run to him, demanded to know where he'd been, flooded him with a thousand questions. This time, inexplicably, she hesitated. She remembered him turning and leaving, with nothing more than a wink and a reminder to behave; she remembered the clipped, businesslike manner in which he had handed her over like a parcel. She remembered the children in the school, alone and shabby and cold. It wasn't that she blamed him for any of those things, exactly—that wouldn't be fair. But she had been looking at a very different world to any she had ever known, and now she looked back at Rowan, he seemed unfamiliar too.

His eyebrows drew together, puzzled and concerned. "Are you all right? What is it?"

She opened her mouth to say something—she hardly knew what. Instead, to her own surprise and embarrassment, hot tears rushed to her eyes.

"Hey." At once, his arms were around her, firm and wiry and comforting, and the sense of unfamiliarity melted away with his touch and the sound of his voice. She clung to him, as though she were still a child and he could protect her from anything in the world. "Hey, come on. What's wrong?"

"I'm sorry."

"Don't be daft. Did something happen?"

She shook her head against his shoulder. Amid a maelstrom of other feelings, it surprised her to find that she was almost as tall as him now. In a few years, they would look the same age, and then she would look older. "No. No, it's just... I didn't realize it would be like this. The world. I know I should have. You gave me the books. But—"

"Oh." His body stiffened, just for a moment; when his voice came again, it was very low and quiet. "Oh, I see. It's a mess, isn't it?"

Biddy took a deep breath, taking comfort in the smell of wood-smoke and sea salt that clung to his coat, and then forced herself to step back. She couldn't be a child now. If she had learned anything in the last day, it was that childhood was a luxury many her age had never known.

"I saw a raven in the trees." She tucked back a wisp of hair that had escaped her braid, discreetly wiping her eyes as she did so. "It was you, wasn't it?"

He winced. "That was a bit dangerous. For you, I mean—if you were being watched, they'd have seen me, and I don't pass as a raven to those with an ounce of magical talent. But I thought you'd like to see a friendly face. Especially after the way I left you, without a proper goodbye."

"I did," she said. "Thank you. Where's Hutch?"

"Right now? Watching over both of us while I'm in here. I'm using the dream ring, of course. I can hear him, he just can't come in. But he's been with you all day. We're both with you, all right? You're doing fine."

She nodded. Some of the fear in her stomach had settled. And yet it wasn't enough for her to know that she was being watched over, that she wouldn't have to stay much longer, that she could go home. Nobody was watching for the other girls. This was the only home they had.

"Where *are* you, though?" she pressed. "Where are you staying in London? Are you sure it's safe?"

"We're safe. Don't worry about us." A flash of movement distracted him. He laughed. "Was that really a tiny dragon? I ought to come here more often; it's much more interesting than *my* dreams..."

Biddy managed a very small smile. "Rowan?"

He looked at her, inquiring.

"The woman across the room from me—Anna. Her parents died. Now she's sick, and some of the girls are saying she'll die too. Can you help her?"

Rowan sighed, and she knew his answer before he spoke. "I'll do my best. When this is over, I'll scrape some magic to put under her pillow. But it'll be wild magic, and it won't be very much. I can't promise it'll heal her."

"You said magic always helps."

"It does. But the kind of help it gives isn't always what we want it to be. I can *ask* it to heal her. It might well ease her illness, as we hope. But it might just give her a night without pain, or a beautiful dream, or it might do something completely unexpected and upend her entire life."

"Can't you use a spell? Or an amulet?"

"A spell to cure illness, on request? There isn't one. If there was, do you think I would have let you be sick or hurt a day in your life?"

"Then what's the use of magic?" she demanded—bitterly, and she knew, unfairly. "What good does it do? What do *you* do, when you come into the world every night?"

"What I can," he said. "And I know it isn't enough. It's never enough. Even when the world was teeming with fairy tales, bad things still happened all the time. Hey," he added firmly, seeing her face fall. "Don't worry. Wild magic *does* heal, sometimes. Maybe it will for her. And it'll do something good, whatever it does. Magic is always good."

This time, that didn't comfort her. "Why did you send me here? I know I'm supposed to be bait for the Council. But why *here*?"

"I'll tell you everything later, Bid, I promise. For now, just trust me, all right? I wouldn't put you here if I didn't absolutely have to."

It wasn't good enough. The thought flashed into her mind before she could stop it, or perhaps before she wanted to. She *did* trust Rowan, truly. But trusting him didn't mean she had no right to know why she had been left as bait in a trap built from a poor school in the East End. It didn't mean she had no right to *question*.

It wasn't fair that he should tell her not to put herself in danger for his sake, and yet expect her to do so on nothing more than his word.

But he was looking at her, a soft, silent plea in his face, and finally she did as she always did and nodded, reluctant.

She was rewarded with a quick smile. "Thank you. Look, I can't stay long, but I'll be back tomorrow night."

"Do you promise?" she said, and didn't care this time that she sounded like a child.

"I swear." He gave her a one-armed hug and kiss on the forehead. "We're right by your side. Stay brave. This will all be over soon."

⇒■═══════════════●◄

The next day was both easier and harder. She knew what to expect now: the piercing cold in the mornings, the clammy taste of the food, the wary eyes staring at her in the schoolroom, the noise and the smells and the ache of homesickness. But that very repetition made it worse. It meant that this was what life was in this place, every day. Rise before dawn in the frost. Prayers and readings before porridge. Lessons all morning, crowded together in a dirty room. Dinner. Work all afternoon. Porridge for supper, more work, then back to a cold bed. Over and over, without reprieve or affection, until hopelessness was ingrained like dirt under their skin and they were thrown into an outside world that according to Anna was more hopeless yet.

She was starting to understand at last what Rowan meant when he talked about the days when there had been magic in the world— as he did sometimes, when he was in the right mood, which was usually "restless, fed up, might have had a bit to drink." There had been miracles then, he said. Sometimes, just often enough, families would go to sleep starving and wake up to a feast spread on their table; prison doors would unlock on the eve of executions and a dragon would be waiting to carry the prisoner away; orphans would open doors to find their families returned as if from the dead.

"Even books like that," Rowan had said once, with a nod at the volume in her hand. It might have been *A Tale of Two Cities*. "People say now the Victorian authors rely too much on coincidence, but it's because they grew up in a world where magic hadn't quite faded. Long-lost relations springing out of the woodwork, mysterious doubles, that sort of thing happened when the cracks in the world were open. It wasn't that things were better, exactly. Terrible things happened all the time. But there was always a *chance* of better."

This place—this world—desperately needed a chance of better.

That afternoon, she couldn't just watch the small heads bowed and the small fingers picking at tough bits of rope. The little girl next to her was sniffling, her nose frozen in the wind, and Biddy's heart flared again. Nobody had said, after all, that she had to please Miss Finchley. She wasn't part of this world; she didn't need to play by its rules.

She crouched down beside the girl and offered her a handkerchief. "Here," she said, and the girl stared at her for a startled, wary moment before taking it. She was perhaps eight or nine, with light brown hair and the wide dark eyes of a prey animal.

"What's your name, then?" Biddy asked, as gently as she could. She felt as though she was approaching a young rabbit in the field. (*Soft and careful,* Hutchincroft had always told her, *but direct. Rabbits don't like you if they think you're trying to trick them.*)

"Trotter," the girl said. "Elsie Trotter."

"Elsie." Biddy nodded to the rope at the girl's feet. "Can you show me what to do here?"

Cautiously at first, then with more surety as Biddy listened and didn't move, the girl showed her how to separate the threads, extract what was needed, discard the rest. Soon the rest of the circle was watching, a few joining in to correct or advise as Biddy picked up the rope and began to follow their lead. It was much harder work than it looked—the ropes resistant, the wind chill and quick to numb fingers, the bristles coarse and quick to rub skin raw. Within half an hour her neck ached, and soon her fingers were blistered and bleeding, but she didn't stop. Whatever she did, the girls wouldn't have to. It was all she could do.

She closed her eyes at once that night, willing herself to fall asleep so Rowan would come. She had to talk to him. There had to be something else.

＊＝＝＝＝＝＊

But Rowan didn't come.

She was woken by the chiming of the first bell, once again so early the sun hadn't even started to peek over the rooftops. It took her a few hazy moments to realize why her sleep had felt so empty. She could remember snatches of dreams, but she had dreamed alone.

Anna was already waking beside her, her hoarse, rattling coughs less desperate than the morning before.

"Come on," she said wearily. "You'll miss prayers."

"*Will* I miss them, though?" Biddy said, without thinking. It surprised a quick, unpracticed laugh from Anna.

"Well, you'll be missed by Finchley, and then she'd throw you out, and you'd miss your job."

Biddy sat up with a groan. "There have to be better jobs."

"Well." Anna was starting to sound less tired and more like herself. "You'd miss *me*."

Biddy found a laugh of her own, and got to her feet, trying not to think about Rowan. Perhaps she hadn't slept deeply enough, and the dream ring couldn't work. He'd get through that night. He never broke a promise.

But he didn't come that night either, or the night after that. Day by day, she looked for any sight or sound of a raven; her gaze drifted to every window, her heart leapt at the flap of every bird wing overhead. Not once did she see so much as a feather.

In some ways, her confidence grew over those days. Anna's bravado returned as her breathing improved, so that Biddy found it easier to match it. Their friendship took root when it could, in snatches ferrying the children between classes, in whispers before bed, in the infants' room putting the little ones to sleep. She became better acquainted with the two older teachers too: Agatha Grey, who was from Yorkshire and longing to return; Molly Prescott, the oldest at thirty-five and only teaching until her fiancé could afford to marry her. Her fears of saying the wrong thing blunted over time as sentence after sentence came out of her mouth without suspicion. Everyone at the school seemed to be from such different worlds, living in the overlap between them, not overly curious about anything outside it. The girls certainly never seemed to question her. To them, teachers came into being to supervise them and vanished when they weren't needed. They both liked and looked askance that she helped with their work when she could, her stories at the end of lessons were in favor, and they decided they could push her further than they dared push Anna but not all the way. Other than that, she could have been a Púca for all they knew or cared. If this truly had been her life, she could have felt secure at least that she could survive it.

But this wasn't her life. This was a trap Rowan had set, and now Rowan was nowhere to be seen. Something had happened to him. Despite all her efforts to keep it up, her heart began to sink, and cold dread settled at the bottom of her stomach.

By Thursday, she could no longer stand it.

"Are we ever allowed to leave the school?" Biddy asked Anna that night, as they settled the babies in their cribs. "I was hoping to go to the post office, but we always seem to be on duty."

"We're not *prisoners*," Anna said, then ruined her haughtiness with a yawn. Her eyes had been heavy and shadowed since that morning, and she had barely made it up the stairs to the nursery before needing to stop for breath. "Finchley will let you go to town if you give her a good reason, as long as you're not needed. I wouldn't say it was for the post office, though—she'd snoop. Think you were writing to a lover or something. Make up an errand."

"What sort of errand?"

"*I* don't know. Say you need to buy something. Your uncle left you with some money, didn't he?" She yawned again, not waiting for an answer, which was a relief. Rowan had left her money, just in case, but he'd also cautioned her not to let anyone know how much, and she would have hated to lie. "Saturday's best—there are no lessons in the afternoon, just extra prayers. They'll let you go after dinner as long as it isn't your turn to read. I can cover for you for everything else. Just don't be late back, or we'll both be in trouble."

"Thank you," Biddy said quietly.

We'll both be in trouble. Stupidly, it had never occurred to her until that moment that her being here could put Anna in real danger—not only for her job, as she had meant, but for her life. And not only Anna, but Miss Finchley, the other teachers, the girls, even the infants in the room upstairs. The whole school was a trap right now, and they had no idea. If Rowan really had been taken and the Council came for her, she doubted they would care about anyone who got in the way. She wondered whether it had occurred to Rowan, and how he could have ever brought himself to dismiss it from his mind if it had.

The tree in St. James's Park. Rowan had said that if something went very wrong, she could leave a message for him there. She didn't know if things were very wrong yet, but they certainly didn't seem right. And she couldn't be bait any longer without knowing for sure someone was there to spring the trap.

———————————————

St. James's Park was three miles from the orphanage. Biddy knew how to catch an electric tram from there to Whitechapel, because she had done so with Rowan to get there, but the thought of navigating the system in the opposite direction was intimidating. It was easier to walk, as she was used to—she had gone to Miss Finchley as Anna had said, and been given two hours before she was needed back. She could follow the Thames most of the way, and if she got lost, she reasoned there would be people to ask.

There were. Many people. She had been getting used to the students in the confines of the school, but the chaos outside hit her like a shout. It was late afternoon, grey and cool with occasional glimpses of sunlight through clouds, and the market by the docks was in full force. She had a bewildering array of streets to navigate before she even made it to the banks of the river, and the crush of people made it hard to see more than a few feet in front of her. Buildings stretched above her, cold and high and uncaring. She should have been braced against the longing to go home by now, but its attacks came in such different forms. At the asylum, it was a dull cudgel whose blows numbed over time. At the sight of the unfamiliar buildings, the longing struck her like a knife and was indistinguishable from fear.

Even a knife, though, couldn't keep its sharpness forever. Gradually her heart calmed. She started to look about her with interest, then with real pleasure. She bought a sticky bun from a bakery along the road, careful not to reveal how many coins were in her purse, and marveled at how fresh and sweet it was. As she followed the banks of the Thames, she found herself stopping to look at the great ships bringing in their cargo, the fishermen and women smoking their pipes on the muddy banks, the horses and carts and electric trams rattling through the streets, wary and yet fascinated. It was the way rabbits and mice and small creatures lived, she remembered Hutch telling her once. The world was filled with dangers, and yet they loved it. They wanted to know everything about it.

This, then, was the true outside world. She was standing in it alone, without Rowan or Hutch to protect her. If she were to keep walking, nobody or nothing would stop her. She had money in her pocket and clothes on her back. She could get on a train to Europe or a boat to China. She could go anywhere or be anything she wanted to be. In the midst of all her worries, she felt a treacherous thrill of rebellion.

It didn't last long, of course. If Rowan was right, then she wouldn't get far before someone from the Council found her and came after the spell. Besides, she didn't *want* to run away from Rowan and Hutch, and certainly not without knowing they were safe. She wanted to leave a message at the tree and go back to the orphanage; with any luck, Rowan would come to her that very night and apologize for worrying her. Well, not *apologize*—she'd never once heard Rowan say he was sorry—but make it up to her.

By the time the grimy streets had given way to the stony grandeur of Trafalgar Square, her feet ached from the unfamiliar cobbles, and the sun was lower in the sky than she'd thought it would be. People were starting to head home—shabby people like herself on foot or clinging to the trams, well-dressed ladies and gentlemen in private cabs, men and women alike pouring down into the stations, which she knew led to an underground train system. She hesitated in the middle of the square, trying to remember which way Rowan had taken her only a few days ago, wondering if anyone would listen if she tried to ask them the way.

In fact, near the foot of Nelson's Column, someone did seem to be looking at her. A tall man, clad in a suit like so many of the other men crossing the square, his face cast into shadow by his hat so that it was difficult to say how she knew his eyes were on her. Perhaps he was just looking at the square; perhaps she had drawn his attention because she didn't belong. It was what she had feared to be true the morning after Rowan's nightmare, as she had looked in the mirror and envied Morgaine—that in an ordinary street, she would be noticed.

She hurried past the gentleman, careful not to look in his direction again. She had remembered the way now anyway.

The park looked different in the shadowy twilight—softer, more dangerous, more like the forests at home where anything could happen after dark. She found the plane tree a short distance from the bench where they had sat to eat their ice creams, a bench that was now occupied by a middle-aged couple looking out at the ducks. She was about to slip her own message in a small hollow above eye height when she stopped short.

Up close, the tree was scored with long scratches. They looked like the marks of fingernails, or long thin claws. Made by an animal, perhaps, or some kind of gardening tool (she just didn't know what was *out* here). A cold trickle went down her back. Whatever they were they hadn't been there when Rowan had shown her the tree. She didn't like them.

There was no note in the tree for her, and she hesitated now whether to leave one of her own. In the end, she tucked it carefully into the lower branches of the tree. Rowan had told her it would be safe, and the note after all didn't say anything dangerous—only *I hope you're safe, please talk to me.* She had come too far now to leave nothing behind.

⊷⊷═══════════⊷⊷

The electric trams, it transpired, were more difficult to work out than she had hoped, just as the streets of Whitechapel had been. It was dark by the time she returned, and the children were in their rooms. Miss Finchley gave her a stern reprimand for being late, and a warning that if it happened again she would lose her job. That didn't trouble Biddy, and wouldn't have even had her head not been swimming with other worries. She did feel a stab of guilt when she returned to her room and saw Anna coming in from putting the girls to bed.

"I'm sorry I wasn't there," she said. "I got lost coming back."

"It's fine," Anna said with a too-careless shrug. "The little ones went down without a fuss. You owe me, though."

"I promise," Biddy said. "I'll put them all to bed tomorrow myself, if you need me to."

"I'm not likely to need you to, am I?" Anna retorted, and from the stiffness of her shoulders Biddy knew she'd said the wrong thing. She realized, too late, how tired Anna looked once again, and that there was a sheen of sweat across her brow. "*I* don't have anyone to post letters to. And I'm perfectly capable of doing all the work they throw at me, if that's what you meant."

"I never said you weren't!" She searched, with her patchy knowledge of social interaction, for a way to fix what she seemed to have broken. "I was just trying to make it up to you. I thought you might like a night off. You can have my porridge tomorrow instead, if you'd rather."

"Is that meant to be a reward or a threat?"

"All right, *I'll* have *your* porridge tomorrow!"

Anna chuckled, and the coolness had dissolved from her voice when she replied, "I'll hold you to one of those promises, and I'll leave you wondering all night which one."

Biddy smiled back, partly in relief. "I won't sleep a wink."

"Serves you right." Anna sat down on the bed with a heavy sigh. "I didn't mean to bite your head off," she added, without looking at Biddy. "I'm glad you've got someone to write to, whoever it is. And—I mean, I wouldn't *mind* you taking over for me tomorrow evening, if you're offering. I've been a bit under the weather lately. I could probably use an early night."

"Of course," Biddy said, as carelessly as she could. Her chest tightened. "Oh—I brought you these."

She handed over the extra buns she had brought to share, and Anna's face broke into a grin as she took one. "See, you should have said so to start with! I'd never have been cross at all."

In fact, when the buns had been eaten and the light put out, Biddy found she truly couldn't sleep a wink. The push and shove of the crowds outside had left her body exhausted yet her mind and heart racing. She could hear Anna's breathing ragged and painful opposite, the snuffling and snoring of the girls on the other side of the thin wall. She was angry with Rowan for putting them in danger, yet sick with worry about where he and Hutch might be. And, though she didn't want to admit it, alone in the dark she was scared for herself. Every time she closed her eyes, she could see the long scratches on the tree at St. James's Park.

Because of that, she was wide awake when she heard the noise from outside.

It was faint—a scratching, perhaps, or a scrabbling. At home, it would have been the branches of the closest oak tree against her window, on a windy night when the shutters were closed. But this wasn't home. There were no trees near the windows here. There was nothing but hard stone and grey sky and the stunted plane tree at the bottom of the courtyard, and yet now she could hear it even more clearly. It wasn't coming from her own window, which faced the courtyard, but from the girls' next door. The window that faced the street.

"Anna," Biddy whispered.

She didn't dare whisper any louder, but after a moment, the bed creaked as Anna stirred. "Mm?"

"Did you hear that?"

"Mm." It took her a moment to understand that this was not an affirmative: Anna had just turned over and gone back to sleep.

Biddy swung her legs out of bed, winced at the cold touch of the floor, and got to her feet quietly. The candle beside their bed had no real light left in it, so she didn't trouble to strike a match—there was moonlight to spare. Moving carefully, trying not to wake Anna, she made her way to the room where the girls slept. The scritching sound was getting louder now, less like branches and more like claws.

All looked quiet in the room when she opened the door. The rows of beds lined the room in their orderly lines; the girls slept, mostly one to a bed, although some of the youngest and the smallest were forced to share. Biddy was about to turn back to her own room—the air was frigid, and even her thin blanket was beginning to feel attractive—when she noticed something odd. Lizzie Thatcher wasn't lying down like the others. She was propped up on her elbow, staring at the far wall, very still.

Biddy picked her way through the beds toward her. "Lizzie?" she whispered. "What is it?"

Lizzie didn't look at her; her lips barely moved. "They're under the window."

She wasn't just still. She was rigid with fear.

"Who?"

Before Lizzie could answer, the scratching noise came again. It was unmistakable this time: like long fingernails, rasping against wood and brick. Biddy thought for a fleeting second of the time she had been certain there was a banshee under her window, when she had been younger than Lizzie. It had in fact turned out to be a rogue poltergeist, harmless. But she had known the sound of something supernatural then, and she knew it now.

"They're trying to get in," Lizzie said, in a very small voice.

Biddy shook off the paralyzing cold that had stolen into her blood. "Stay here," she said, just as quietly. "I'll go see what it wants."

Lizzie shook her head furiously. "No—"

The window juddered. The latch at its base shattered, tore loose, dropped to the floor. Slowly, in jerks and jolts, the window began to rise.

Afterward, Biddy cursed herself that she hadn't reacted sooner. She should have woken all the girls, shepherded them out of the room, slammed the door behind them. She should have run forward and pressed down on the window with all her strength. It might have made no difference—they were too strong. But at least she would have had the comfort that she had fought.

Instead she watched, frozen by dread like Lizzie, as the window opened an inch, two inches, four. She watched as long claws crept under the gap, made it wider, fought their way into the room. Not nails after all, but bone.

Bone wisps. The wisps that had come to the island, only those had been no larger than swallows or blackbirds, and these were the size of enormous herons or swans. Their heads rose to her shoulder; their legs were longer and thinner than those of any birds she had ever seen. Their spindly limbs gleamed in glimpses of white, but shadows covered them in a rustle of feathers. They took one slow, exaggerated step forward, their claws rising past their waists, their beaked heads tilting as if to discern shapes.

The Council had found her. They had not sent a mage after all, but the strongest forces at their disposal. And Rowan was nowhere to be found.

Lizzie Thatcher, tiny and wide-eyed, finally recovered her voice. Before Biddy could stop her, she screamed.

The scream shattered the quiet of the room like the breaking of a spell. The creatures' heads whipped in Lizzie's direction. Across the room, girls sat bolt upright in bed, and saw the monsters among them. More screams rent the air, fed off each other, layered.

"Don't be scared—move!" Biddy ordered them, at last. "Get outside, quickly!"

Elsie Trotter, the little girl from the yard, scrambled from her bed toward the door; one of the creatures leapt over her head, shadow wings spreading, and landed to block her path with a terrible shriek.

Across the room, Anna appeared in the doorframe, stumbling, still blinking awake. Her dark curls were in a cloud about her head.

"What the *hell* is going on?" she demanded, fierce and breathless. Then she saw.

For the first and only time since Biddy had met her, she was at a complete loss. Her face and limbs stilled; her mouth went slack; her eyes glazed in fear and disbelief. It was as though the house had at last turned her to stone. The nearest creature twisted its head to look at her.

Biddy felt the fear in her veins turn to white heat.

She barely knew what she was doing. She couldn't think clearly enough to know whether she was fighting, or giving herself up, or just furious. She pushed forward, between the wisps and her friend and the girls under her protection.

"That's *enough!*" she heard herself snap, as though the wisps were wayward children misbehaving and she was the only grown-up in the room.

The creatures turned to her. Their tiny bones clicked; their shadow feathers rustled like a whisper. The sound brought bile to her throat, but she didn't move. The other children stared at her, wide-eyed. In that one moment, she didn't have to remind herself to be brave.

"I'm the one you want. Leave them alone."

The wisps did not need telling twice. With a roar, they rushed upon her.

It was like being torn apart. Sharp fingernails dug into the soft flesh of her arm, her ankles, her waist; she struggled furiously, and found her feet leaving the floor. Shadow feathers rushed from the wisps' arms in a wave, leaving bleached white bone like driftwood beneath. The shadows crept up her arm, covered her as a swarm of insects covers a broken log, buzzing and fluttering. She felt the stabbing pinpricks on her skin, at once ice cold and burning. They were at her shoulder, her neck, coursing down her chest and up toward her chin.

The fury at her core melted then, and her bravery went with it. She cried out, just once, and the shadows closed over her head.

Chapter Eight

She woke to darkness, coughing and retching at the sensation of feathers clogging her nose and throat. For a heartbeat she panicked, still feeling the grip of the grotesque bird forms, knowing she couldn't see because her eyes were blinded by shadows. Then she sat up, and realized that where she was instead was even worse.

It was a square, high-ceilinged room, and it was made entirely of smooth grey stone. She lay on stone ground; a stone wall was at her back. There was no door at all. The only light filtered from far above her head, a tiny window crossed with an iron grill, and through it she could see no glimpse of sky. The place had a musty, underground smell of damp and dirt.

Biddy had grown up in a castle. She knew a dungeon when she saw one.

This was it, the very worst that could have happened. The Council had her. She had no idea where she was, or how anyone could ever find her. There was no way in or out of the room that she could see. Stories about oubliettes, dark chambers without doors where prisoners were thrown from above and left to be forgotten, flashed through her mind, and panic rose in her throat as thick and choking as the shadowy feathers only moments before. She tried to recapture the hot fury that had seized her when the wisps had come to the orphanage, but it was like trying to grab at smoke. That had come from her desire to protect her friend, her determination that the younger girls not be in danger because of her. There was nobody to protect anymore. She was all alone.

Stop it. She breathed in, trying to draw her thoughts about her. Rowan would tell her to stop and think. He always did when she was scared. As a little girl, she'd often freeze halfway up the trees he was teaching her to climb, frightened by the stirring of the branches in the wind. *You're all right*, he would say, lightly, confidently, as if it was an indisputable fact and not a reassurance. *Just think of what to do next. Don't worry about what might happen* to *you. What are* you *going to do next?*

There was nothing to be done yet, it was true. But the Council weren't actually going to leave her to be forgotten, surely. They had brought her here because they wanted her. That meant they would come back for her—probably soon, perhaps even as soon as they realized she was awake. All she had to do was wait, see what it was they wanted, and then she would have something to work with. She forced herself to stop thinking of oubliettes and think instead of Edmond Dantès in the Château d'If, Charles Darnay in the Bastille, all those princesses in all those towers. They all got out in the end. All she had to do was wait. Wait, hope, and plan.

She didn't wait very long. Her heart was only just beginning to calm when she heard the fall of heavy footsteps on the other side of the dungeon wall—the first sound she had heard since she had woken. She scrambled to her feet just in time to see the shadows on the blank stone wall opposite deepen, settle, resolve themselves into the shape of a door. The rock split open like the parting of a curtain. Beyond it, she could see flickering torchlight, a long stone corridor that disappeared into darkness. Standing in the doorway was a man.

At least, parts of him belonged to a man. A tall, broad-shouldered man, with a sallow strong-jawed face and dark hair roughly cut. He wore a long woolen coat, too heavy even for the chill of the dungeon, and leather gloves that disappeared into his sleeves. The effect was to render his body a great shadow, without texture or definition.

The rest of him, the parts that didn't fit, belonged to a bird. Enormous black-feathered wings extended from his back through slits in his coat—the weight of them hunched his shoulders, so that he moved with a faint limp. Above the high collar of his shirt his skin was split by a rash of tiny feathers, continuing in patches to his stubbled jawline. One eye was human and blue; the other was jet-black and without an iris. The same glistening dark of the ravenstone.

She realized with a shock where she had seen an effect like it before. He looked as she had glimpsed Rowan sometimes, for just a fraction of a second in the midpoint of a transformation into raven form. The feathers even quivered on the surface of his skin as if they were straining to change, to shift, to ripple into one shape or another. But he wasn't changing. This was who he was.

Biddy didn't let herself stare for more than a second. She scrambled to her feet, and lifted her chin. *Brave*, she reminded herself. *Clever, and brave.* Not scared and confused and about to cry.

The winged man gave her only a cursory glance too, head tilting to one side. "So you're awake, are you?" His voice was a rough, impatient growl. "Good. Come with me."

She kept her feet planted firmly on the ground. She thought of Anna regarding her on the stairs, and tried to match her friend's self-assurance. "Why? Where are we going?"

"You'll find out when you get there." He moved forward; she took a reflexive step back. "Come on."

"Where is this place?" Against her will, her voice cracked, and a sliver of fear escaped. "Please. Are we still in London?"

She didn't expect a response, but to her surprise he hesitated. "Below it," he said finally, and curtly. He folded his arms, and the giant wings hunched his shoulders. "This is the Undercastle."

"The Undercastle?" she repeated, stupidly. It sounded familiar, but she couldn't place it in the rush of new words that had swamped her in the last few weeks. She couldn't betray that knowledge now, anyway. She was supposed to be a young woman from the slums of the East End. She shouldn't know about magic at all. "And who are you? What's your name?"

The eyebrow above his human eye raised very slightly, as though startled by the question—which seemed a natural one to her, considering. "Storm," he said. "My name's Storm."

"Storm." She drew a deep breath. Once on the island she had watched a mouse building a nest, picking up and sifting through dried grass, rejecting what it couldn't use, stealing what it could, all at lightning speed. Her brain seemed to be doing the same thing now with questions and thoughts and half-formed plans, only it could find absolutely nothing of any use. "And what do you want with me? Please."

He gave a derisive sniff, but he answered. "We don't want you at all. We want Rowan O'Connell. I don't suppose you know where he is?"

It was all she could do not to flinch—perhaps she didn't even manage it. She tried to cover surprise with a frown.

"I don't know any Rowan O'Connell." It was even half true. She had always assumed that mages had no surnames.

The winged man's mouth twisted. "You'd better hope he knows you. If we can't get that spell out of your heart ourselves, then your only chance is for him to get it out for us. What was he thinking, anyway? Putting something that important inside a child."

She didn't have to pretend confusion this time. "Putting—?"

"The spell," he said, impatient. "The spell inside your heart."

It was all wrong. Nobody was supposed to know Rowan was involved. They were supposed to want the magic in her heart, and want it so much they didn't see him watching from the shadows. Instead, they seemed to think the magic in her heart was there *because* of Rowan. Because he had put it there.

"I don't know what you're talking about," she said, for lack of anything else to say.

"Really." The word dripped with flat disbelief. "Well, you can tell that to the Council. They're waiting for you." He jerked his head, summoning her forward. "Move."

She could tell from the edge that had crept back into his voice that she had lost him—he would give her nothing more. Perhaps he was even annoyed to have given her that much. Still, she made one last attempt. "Why? What do they—?"

With startling speed, he was across the room. Up close, he was a great mass of dark feathers and muscle; his fingers locked around her upper arm, so deep she felt them grate against her bones. Her heart spiked, not just at his strength but his sudden, terrifying fury, and her own powerlessness in the face of it. The eye that looked down at her was the black raven's eye, glittering and cold.

"Because the Servant of Magic asked me to bring you to him," he said, low and soft. His fingers tightened, and she bit her lip to keep from crying out. "Not to ask you questions, not to answer them. You're a package for me to fetch, nothing more. All right?"

Her body felt frozen and distant, but she managed a tight nod.

"Good. Now shut up, and *move*."

For a moment she couldn't move at all. It wasn't just that he had the power to hurt her, though he did: One twist of his fingers and her arm would snap. It was that she believed he would do it. His lunge forward had been as abrupt and unpredictable as his softening earlier. His moods were on a knife edge, and the slightest twitch from her might tip them over.

Then Storm yanked her forward, and she had to take a step or stumble. Her eyes were hot with anger and shame. She had been afraid before in her life. It was the first time in her life she had ever been forced to obey an order out of fear.

⟶•══════•⟵

Storm led her up crooked stairs, through tight passages lit by flaring torches, past wooden doors and stone archways. Through those doors she glimpsed sparsely decorated rooms with large fireplaces, mostly empty, though in one a tall shadow of a man sat at a table poring over a book by candlelight. He didn't look up; none of the occasional men (it was always men) they passed so much as glanced sideways as she was dragged along the corridors. She supposed it was possible that the sight of a disheveled girl in a nightdress was a common one, but it didn't seem likely. It was Storm. Whatever he was doing—whatever he did—they didn't want to know about it.

She tried not to think about what that might mean; she tried, too, not to notice the rustle of Storm's wings and the thud of his uneven footsteps, the grip of his fingers around her arm. She tried instead to memorize all the twists and turns of their path, as kidnapped heirs always seemed to do in adventure novels, even though she was unsure what use that would be in her case. She wasn't being taken to anywhere from where she might escape but, apparently, to the Council of Mages.

They had climbed some way up before Storm at last stopped before a wide door of polished oak. He knocked on it once, raised his voice. "I've brought the girl."

"So I assumed." A male voice, dry, even amused. The door gave an audible clunk. "Bring her in."

After the dungeon and the narrow corridors, the vast expanse on the other side of the door made Biddy's head spin. Their own Great Hall at Hy-Brasil was in the derelict part of the castle. The ceiling had fallen in, and centuries of rain had rotted the floors away and let ivy and wild grasses overtake the stone. This hall had all the splendor their own had lost: It was hung with tapestries, painted in red and gold, lit by luminescent globes that circled the hanging chandelier and bumped like dozy bumblebees against the high ceiling. In another time, she would have been fascinated. What held her attention instead was the large oval table, shaped like a horseshoe facing the door, and the thirteen people sitting at it watching her.

The Council of Mages.

Rowan had said the Council were old and wealthy and covered in dust. If that had changed during his time, it had changed back now. Only one or two were grey-haired—a wizened man with skin like paper, a rounder man with flushed red cheeks—but all looked old on some far deeper level. All were richly dressed, and all looked, if not exactly dusty, then certainly as though it had been a long time since anyone had given them a good shake.

There was only one woman. Biddy knew her at once, and her

breath hitched. Morgaine sat at the far left of the table, lace-gloved hands folded in front of her, face cool and impassive. It was the face from Rowan's dream, grown slightly older and paler; the same dark hair, though now it was caught up in soft curls and pinned in a knot at the back of her head. Her eyes flickered to Biddy just once, and then away again almost as quickly.

"Here's the girl," Storm said, and with that the rough fingers were gone from her arm and she was pushed toward the table. She stumbled in her bare feet before she caught herself.

"So I see." It was the same voice that had spoken before—soft, with a rolling accent, so courteous that it brought with it the suspicion of a joke—and it came from the man in the center of the table. He alone was looking Biddy full in the face, rather than glancing away uncomfortably as Morgaine and the others had done. Apart from his position at the curve of the horseshoe, there was nothing to mark him as anything more than another Council member. And yet this had to be him. Vaughan Carlisle, the mage who had taken the Council when magic began to fade.

A tiger in a business suit, Hutch had called Vaughan. Rowan had said he was clever, energetic, with a sense of humor. Biddy could see what both had meant. He was well-built and athletic-looking, perhaps Rowan's height but broader and better muscled. His eyes were a very light blue, his hair a grizzled blond, and his face was weathered with good-humored creases. But there was something coiled and powerful behind his eyes, in the set of his shoulders and his jaw, in the way he looked at her with open curiosity and kept looking.

And she knew, with her second shock of recognition in as many minutes, that she had felt those eyes on her before, and not in any dream this time. In the crowd, looking at her from across Trafalgar Square. And, even earlier, in the Rookwood Asylum, as he had been shown upstairs by Miss Finchley through the lines of girls in shabby, identical clothes.

"Good morning, young lady," Vaughan was saying to her. "Let me be the first to welcome you to the Undercastle—or so I suspect, given that Storm isn't known for his good manners. Do you know who I am?"

Biddy swallowed hard, thinking frantically before she replied. Vaughan's eyes looked the same, but one of them was glass, enchanted to see the deepest desires and resentments of those who looked into it. It didn't mean he could read her mind, Hutch had said—thankfully, or she would already be lost. But even her desires could give her away, if he read in them her need to protect Hy-Brasil, or to keep Rowan and Hutch safe, or any of the myriad longings she'd ever had about magic in the whole of her life. She tried to focus on the most innocuous as she raised her head to meet that blue gaze.

I want to go home, she thought. Not Hy-Brasil. Not Rowan and Hutch. Just home, in the vaguest and most abstract of terms. Surely if she flooded her mind with that, it would wash out anything else.

"Storm said the Servant of Magic had asked for me," she answered Vaughan. "I suppose that must be you."

"And did Rowan ever tell you what that title means?"

"I don't know anyone named Rowan," she said carefully.

I want to go home. I want to escape this place. I just want to go home.

"Of course." He smiled very slightly, a barely perceptible curve of the lips, and his eyes twinkled as though at a shared joke. "Well, this is the British Council of Mages. We watch over the magical community of Great Britain, and I have the honor of being appointed its head. The position is called 'the Servant' to remind us that we all, even the most powerful, should protect and serve the great magic with which we have been entrusted."

"Entrusted by whom?" she couldn't resist asking.

"The magic itself, I assume." He said this without irony that she could detect, only a certain dryness. But there was none of the respect and delight with which Rowan and Hutch always spoke of magic either. "You're familiar with magic, I take it?"

The Council were all staring at her now, their gazes curious and hungry, ready to pounce on a wrong answer and feed. Biddy had a horrible image of herself as she must appear to them: an awkward overgrown child in a ragged nightdress, hair coming loose from a braid, face streaked with dirt and tears. She knew then that she couldn't do this, that they were too old and too powerful, that she was too young and insignificant and not even a mage.

Stop it. She remembered, not Anna this time, but Rowan facing Miss Finchley, the way his back had straightened and his head lifted, the careless authority in his voice. She felt her own back straighten to match.

"How could I be familiar with it?" she said. "It isn't real."

"Yet you don't seem surprised to find yourself in an underground castle, having been abducted by creatures of bone. You don't seem very surprised by Storm, for that matter, and we generally consider him so surprising that we don't let him out in daylight."

Storm shifted, a rustle of feathers. "If there's nothing else, my lord—"

"No, wait there, Storm," Vaughan said, without looking at him. "We might need you to take her back soon."

Morgaine spoke up for the first time. Her voice had the same cool, firm inflections as it had in the dream, only a little quieter. "I can do that, if it's easier. I'm sure she'll be no trouble."

"Very kind, Morgaine, but I know how busy you are. Storm can afford to wait. Can't you, Storm?"

It seemed an innocuous enough comment, but Storm gritted his teeth. His voice was heavy with irony when he replied. "Of course, my lord."

Vaughan continued speaking to Biddy, as though there had been no interruption. "That was why I assumed, you see, that you'd seen at least a few surprising things in your time."

Her stomach coiled. She'd made a mistake there, clearly. She should have shown more horror, more disbelief—the way Anna or the girls would presumably act when faced with someone like Storm. But he was right. She had seen far too much magic to feign astonishment that it existed, and not enough of the real world to be able to tell what she should be taking for granted.

It was too late to do anything about it now. Besides, it didn't prove anything.

"I'm from Whitechapel," she said. "I'm not surprised by anything very much."

One of the mages at the table chuckled, and suppressed it with a cough.

Vaughan smiled too. "I'm from Salford," he said. "So I concede your point. Now you know who I am. Would you like to tell us who you are?"

"My name is Bridget," she said, and decided to take a risk. She didn't want Vaughan to think she was scared of him, just because she was. Besides, it felt like what Rowan would do. "Didn't Miss Finchley tell you that? You spoke with her at the school. We all saw you come in."

"Did you?" The lines around his mouth tightened. Then he leaned back, brushing it off. "Well. I like to look at a place before I send an army of wisps. It might not have been necessary."

"And you thought it was?" She clutched gratefully at the memory of the army of bone and darkness. Anger was so much better than fear. "There were children in that room! Nobody there was any danger to you."

"That's not quite true, though, is it?" Still his eyes didn't move from her face. It was starting to feel less like being looked at and more like being touched. She had to resist the urge to rub at her arms, as she would at the brush of an insect on her skin. "It was a trap. I know the ravenstone's magic—I should, we've had Storm fluttering about the corridors for decades. When I went to that school, I knew Rowan had been there. If I had sent a single mage to take you away, he would have been on them. It might have been worth it to draw him out, it's true. On the whole, though, I preferred to have you safe, given what was in your heart."

"What *is* in my heart?" Her confusion wasn't pretended. Storm seemed to think Rowan was responsible for the spell; Vaughan seemed to know what it was. Yet Rowan had said he had no idea. Beneath the immediate danger of her situation, it worried at her.

"You claim not to know, then?"

"I don't know anything!"

"Then how did you come to have a sixteen-year-old spell buried deep inside you? Why did you leave a note for Rowan at St. James's Park? And where have you been all this time, that we've only now learned that you exist?"

"I don't know anything about any spell!" Biddy pushed aside her doubts and made her eyes as wide and appealing as she could. "My name is Bridget Adler. My parents died when I was little, and I was raised by my uncle. He never liked me. When the money ran out, he said it was time I earned my own way, and sent me to teach at the orphanage. I left the note in the tree for a friend of mine—a gentleman friend, if you must know." She tried to give this the right mix of defiance and blush. "And then those monsters came, and they brought me here. You tell me there's magic in my heart? You're all mad. There's no such thing."

Strangely, she felt on safer ground with this. It was a mixture of stories she'd heard from the girls and read in books—the uncaring relative came straight from *Jane Eyre*. In a way, she was firmer on those than she was the circumstances of her own childhood. It must have seemed so to the mages as well, because a few of them exchanged uncertain glances.

"Perhaps she really doesn't know anything," one of the older ones ventured. "She would have been a baby when Rowan cast that spell. She might never have seen him afterward."

"Perhaps," Vaughan said thoughtfully. "But I doubt it. Listen to her. She sounds like him."

"That's merely touches of dialect. There are a good many Irish girls in East London. It doesn't mean she's even met Rowan."

"It isn't just dialect. What do you think, Morgaine?" For the first time since Biddy had entered the room, his eyes left her. They fixed on Morgaine, and they glittered just the way Hutchincroft had said. "You knew Rowan more intimately than the rest of us. Can you hear it?"

"It's been a long time since I've had conversation with Rowan," Morgaine said calmly, but her cheeks were too pale to hide a flush of color. "You should ask Storm. But it hardly makes any difference, does it? If you're right, Rowan set a trap for us with Bridget as bait. Surely he'll want her back. He'll come for her, and we can be waiting for him when he does."

"I'm not so certain of that," Vaughan said. "I'm sure he *will* want her back. It's just a question of how much. Until we know what that spell does, we can't know how important or unique it is. He may well decide she isn't worth the risk of capture."

It was nonsense. There was no risk Rowan wouldn't take for anyone. He broke into this place to steal magic for people he didn't even know. Of course he would come for her.

And yet, where *was* he? She had been afraid when he and Hutch had disappeared that their enemies had them, but that didn't seem to be the case. She was standing right in front of their enemies, and they had no idea where he was. If they hadn't snatched him away from her, who had?

Biddy should have kept quiet, but suddenly she couldn't bear to let them talk about her as though she wasn't in the room. As if she really were nothing, no more than the amulet they'd left to ensnare Rowan the last time. As if she were nothing to Rowan either.

"Excuse me." Heads turned to her in surprise. "I told you, I don't believe in magic or spells. But if you think there's something you need in my heart, I don't understand what the problem is or why you need this person. Can't you just take it and let me go?"

"We can't," Morgaine said, but gently. "It's almost impossible for anyone but the original enchanter to remove a spell, and yours has been in there a very long time. That's why we need Rowan."

Rowan had never said that the mage who had cast the spell might be able to remove it. It made sense. But that mage wasn't Rowan—it couldn't be.

"But why do you need it at *all*?" she persisted. "What do you think it is? Why is it so important?"

"There's no sense telling her," the older mage said impatiently, when Morgaine opened her mouth to reply. "Either she already knows, or it won't make any sense to her. She can't help us."

"I wonder," Vaughan mused. He folded his hands together and sat forward. There was no hint of irony in his face now. His voice, and his eyes, were deadly serious. "Bridget—if I may call you that. I know you've claimed to know nothing of Rowan or magic. Please allow me to speak to you as if you're being dishonest: as if, in fact, you are a very clever young woman who knows exactly why she's here. If I'm wrong—well, no harm done, no discourtesy meant, you go back to your cell and we'll say no more about it. Hm?"

Biddy said nothing. It seemed to satisfy him.

"We're not entirely sure of the nature of the spell in your heart," he said. "What we do know is this. Sixteen years ago—you would have been very young, I imagine, an infant—Rowan O'Connell found a schism in the world. The first to form in decades. He should have come at once to us. Instead, for reasons known only to himself, he chose to conceal it. When we captured him, he bore traces of particularly strong magic, wild magic, the kind that has recently come through from another world."

Rowan had said the Council had captured him once, she remembered suddenly. Shortly before she had come to the island. That had to be the time they meant.

"We asked him to tell us where the schism was," Vaughan continued. "Politely at first, and then with more force. He refused."

Biddy couldn't stay silent then. "I can't imagine why he wouldn't trust you, if you treated him as well as you've treated me."

"Oh, we treated him a good deal worse, in the end." The twinkle again, just a flash, as though he and Biddy were in on something together. "But he didn't have to trust me. Whatever personal disagreements Rowan and I have had, they mean nothing when it comes to the possibility of magic entering the world again. We need that schism, Bridget. In seventy years, nobody in the entire world has found a trace of any other. He could have named any terms he wanted—he could have asked to be named Servant in my place and for me to be thrown in the dungeon—and we would all have agreed. Instead, he chose to leave the world in darkness."

Rowan wouldn't do that. She swallowed back the words long

before they reached her tongue, pushing them down to where Vaughan's glass eye couldn't see. Rowan *wouldn't* do that, it was true. But then, Rowan had never found a schism—she was positive of that. He had told her there were no more to be found. Either the Council had made a mistake all those years ago, or—far more likely—they were lying to her. She just couldn't understand why.

"I don't see what this has to do with the thing in my heart," she said carefully.

Morgaine spoke this time. Her face was impossible to read. "We don't know how Rowan hid the schism from us," she said. "But we do know one thing. The spell in your heart was performed the same night he was captured. It might have been only minutes or hours before we took him. Whatever he did to conceal the schism we think you have the key to it."

"Please, Bridget." Vaughan cut in before she could process this. His eyes held hers, so pale and so blue they were like falling into the sky. She thought of Balor the legendary king and his evil eye, and understood for the first time how a person could die by being looked at. "We need you to tell us where Rowan is."

"I don't know," she said, and her throat tightened. It was the truth, after all.

"I'm sure you don't," Vaughan said. "He would have made very sure of that before he let you be caught by us. But you know where he might be, don't you? He's been hiding somewhere all these years, or we'd have found him long ago."

Hy-Brasil. It came to her in a rush like cold water. He was talking about Hy-Brasil. It was exactly what Rowan had been worried about, the day the skeleton wisps had come. Vaughan might not know Hy-Brasil existed, but that was what he was asking her to tell him. They wanted her to betray Rowan, and in doing so she would also betray her home.

Hy-Brasil protected itself. But if she told them where to find it, they might have a way of getting to it. They would strip it of its magic. And then they would find Rowan and Hutchincroft.

"I can promise not to hurt him, if that will put your mind at rest," the Servant said. It came so hard on the heels of her worries that she was certain all her resistance had been useless, and he had seen every last corner of her soul. "I don't *want* to hurt him, for God's sake. He was a respected member of this Council once. I was proud to call him a friend. All we want is magic back in the world."

"Whatever Rowan's told you about us, you can't trust him," Morgaine said. Biddy could hear no trace of the woman who had urged Rowan to run for safety in his nightmares. She sounded only disdainful, even contemptuous. "He means well, or he did once. But he's lost sight of why he fought us to begin with. In his head, we're at war, and all's fair in war. He'll go to any lengths to keep magic from us—even if that means preventing magic from coming back at all. He's dangerous."

This was the woman whom Rowan had loved; the woman who had killed her own familiar to stay alive. Biddy felt a welcome surge of disgust, and clung to it like a raft in the midst of her fears.

"I can't help you," she said, and let the smallest flash of defiance color her voice. "I keep telling you. I don't know anything about all of this. I don't know who Rowan is. I don't know where he hides. Please, just let me go."

She didn't need to focus on wanting to go home now. The image of her bedroom came to her, with its curved stone walls and wooden bed, and her chest ached. She would die before she betrayed it, she hoped. But she didn't want to die. *God, please don't let me die. Please let Rowan and Hutch come.*

The Servant of Magic sighed, and sat back in his chair. "Very well," he said. "If that's how you want to do things. I'm afraid you need to go back to the dungeons. But I'll see that Storm looks in on you and makes sure you're comfortable."

Chapter Nine

*H*utchincroft had told Biddy once about how mages got their familiars. Back when schisms split the world, there were a scattering that opened wide enough to admit a person. At the age of seventeen, in accordance with tradition, young mages would journey to one of those cracks and step through. Rowan had gone to one in Inverness, halfway up a mountain sheathed in mist.

It was very dangerous. On the other side of the schism was light and dark and chaos; it was pure magic, unable to be mapped or understood. It was where the spirits lurked, formless and nameless and strange, waiting to be caught and bound.

"Most mages trap the first spirit they find," Hutchincroft told her. "If a human stays too long outside their world, they start to fade, to forget themselves, and then they're lost forever. The safe thing is to snatch a spirit from the ether, bind it, and drag it into the world, where it takes a shape and becomes a familiar. But there are some that wait for a spirit to come to them—to willingly bind themselves and return with their mage. If none comes, then they must return with no familiar at all; if they wait too long, they'll fade. But the bond between a mage and a spirit who has chosen them is far, far stronger than one taken by force."

She had known already that Rowan and Hutch had chosen each other, and she was proud of it. But all the same, she had lain awake that night gripped by the horror of fading into pure magic, of losing form and sense and memory. It terrified her, as she had never been terrified by magic before. It terrified her particularly because it reminded her once again that she had no connection to magic—that she, in that world outside of time and place, would be lost at once.

The darkness of the dungeon reminded her of those long terror-filled hours. It was as though she'd slipped off the edge of the earth.

Vaughan had said *good morning* as she had entered the Council chamber, so the faint light that had come through the grate earlier must have been the beginnings of the day and not the end. And yet the sun must have been visible only at a particular hour, because when Storm pushed her in and the door was swallowed behind him it was as pitch-black as a night with no moon. She could see no sun or stars; she could see nothing but darkness, and that was the same as not seeing at all. The ground bit her bare skin, cold and unforgiving; if it weren't for that and the quick rasp of her breathing, she might not have had a body. She felt that if it went on too long, she wouldn't know who she was.

Don't be afraid. She tried to remember again Rowan's voice as she had clung to wind-tossed branches, high above the earth. *You're all right. What are you going to do next?*

But it was no use asking what to do next. There was nothing. Her plans and hopes were just shadows, and the throb of her arm where Storm had grabbed it, the cold of the dungeon, the lingering burn of Vaughan's eyes on her skin, were too solid and real. This wasn't a book, or if it was, it was a book for which she was too young and inexperienced, like when she'd tried to read *Les Misérables* at seven and didn't know what a revolution was.

And it was no use telling herself not to be afraid. She was, horribly.

She hadn't heard from Rowan and Hutch in days. They could be anywhere. They might not know where she was. They might be dead. And though she didn't believe for a moment that Rowan would ever abandon her, she couldn't silence the nagging whisper that he might indeed not have told her the whole truth. He had kept things from her most of her life. It was very possible that there had always been more to his plan than he had let her know about.

And though she didn't want to think it, however hard she screwed her eyes shut against it like a bad dream, Vaughan was right about one thing. Rowan had never told her where he and Hutch were in London, not even when she had asked. Why would he hide that, if he had never thought she would be taken? If the Council claimed they could tell so easily who had cast the spell and when, could Rowan really have no idea?

She tried to doze huddled on the stone floor, hoping against odds that Rowan would find her in her dreams this time. But cold and terror kept her awake, and the few scraps of sleep she managed to snatch were empty once again.

***

Hours might have passed, or longer. Her only sense of time progressing was the growing hunger gnawing her stomach—that, and the occasional soft footsteps outside that clenched her heart in fear. Once the door slid open with a burst of torchlight, and a wizened old man came with a pitcher and a metal plate, which he set down on the stone floor. He never looked at Biddy, and ignored her attempts to speak to him. After he left she forced herself to crawl to where the food had been left, fumbling by touch, almost knocking over the pitcher. The water was warm, with a metallic tang, and the bread on the plate was stale, but it was no worse than what had been at Rookwood Asylum. She swallowed it down, and tried to pretend she wasn't crying as she did so.

Please. The words went around and around in her head, like a pathetic ouroboros. *Please, Rowan, come and get me. Please don't leave me here.*

By the time the door appeared again, she had no more tears, and fear was alternating with boredom like the rise and crest of a tide.

She sat as before, wary, huddled against the wall, as the jailer came in with torchlight that pierced her eyes after so long in darkness.

This time, Storm was with him.

He stood in the doorway, a great hovering shadow, as the old man picked up the plates and replaced the toilet bucket in the corner. Biddy watched him, her eyes screwed up against the light, back to the wall as her heart hammered. She assumed Storm would go when the jailer did. The jailer seemed to think so too: He turned and waited for the winged man as he reached the door. Storm, however, hesitated.

"You go on," he said to the jailer abruptly. "I won't be a minute."

The old man looked surprised but left without a word. The door vanished behind him, and Storm remained. The flickering torchlight exaggerated his shadow on the wall behind them so that he seemed impossibly large, the quivering mound of muscle and feathers on his back elongated and strange.

"You know, you could make this easier on yourself," Storm said. His voice was deep and soft, almost kind. It sent a ripple of fear through her. She was painfully aware of how close he was to her, just the two of them, sealed in the bowels of the castle without even a door. "You heard the Servant. You just need to tell us where Rowan is, or at least how we can find him. The sooner we have the magic out of your heart, the sooner you can go."

Biddy hugged her knees, and clenched her fists in the folds of her nightdress. "I told you," she said. "I don't know Rowan."

It didn't matter how often she said it. Storm didn't believe her.

"Do you think he means to rescue you? I'd forget about that, if I were you. He wants you here. He set you up to be caught."

It wasn't true. Biddy repeated that to herself, over and over. It wasn't true.

"It's what he does." Bitterness crept in now. "Tricks you into betraying yourself. He's the reason I'm like this, you know. He's the reason I can't go among people anymore, the reason I've barely seen daylight for seventy years, the reason I'm a monster in body and soul. I bet he never told you that."

Rowan had never told her about Storm at all, but she didn't let that show either.

"And did you deserve it?" she asked, greatly daring.

"As it happened," Storm shot back, "I didn't. Not then. We were friends then—or I thought we were. Whatever we became afterward—whatever *I* became—is on him."

Whatever he became. Her eyes went to the great hunched wings on his back, the black raven's eye in a human face, the dark coat and gloves bundled over sharp feathers.

"Does it hurt?" she asked, on impulse. "The—your wings, I mean."

His head jerked back, startled, almost affronted. "No," he said, so defensively she knew he was lying.

Storm wasn't lying about Rowan, though, she was certain of that. Vaughan was too smooth, too plausible to be trusted. He could be lying to her—so could Morgaine, so could the entire Council. Storm had the cruel, unthinking honesty of a wild animal. If he said something, he believed it. He believed Rowan had hurt him; he believed Rowan had put the magic in her heart. Even if he was wrong, it was unsettling. It was too easy to see him as he saw himself, wronged and twisted and in pain.

"I was the one who caught Rowan that night," the winged man said, out of nowhere. "Sixteen years ago, the night he put the spell in you."

"He didn't put a spell in me." It seemed important to keep saying it, even though Storm wouldn't believe it.

"Is that what he told you?" He didn't wait for an answer. "How do you know? You're what, sixteen? Seventeen? You wouldn't remember."

Storm was right, of course. She didn't remember. She only had Rowan's word for it. She only had Rowan's word about anything. It had just never occurred to her to doubt it.

"Nobody thought I could do it," Storm was saying. It took Biddy a moment to remember what he was talking about. "They all thought he was too fast for me, too clever. But I knew him better than anyone, even Morgaine. I knew his weaknesses. So instead of going after him, I waited and laid a trap for his familiar. Once I had that, he gave himself to me in exchange without a second's hesitation. Nobody else thought to do that. It was me."

They had held him for a week before he escaped, Rowan said. He had never told her that he had given himself in exchange for Hutch's freedom. She had to swallow bile before speaking. "What did you do to him?"

"To Rowan?" The winged man's mouth twitched. "Not enough. Not that time. But I'll have him again soon."

"Why?" She knew it wasn't wise—she knew her best chance was to stay small and confused—but the thought of first Hutch and then Rowan in this enclosed place, alone and without each other, had flashed behind her eyes. It overwhelmed the small flicker of sympathy that had been kindling for Storm. "If you couldn't make him tell you all those years ago, I don't see why you think you can do it this time. Whoever he is," she added belatedly.

"It was the Council's fault. I could have made him tell me if they'd given me more magic. I could track him down and make him tell me now, if they'd only give me what I deserve."

"They didn't seem to think so in there," Biddy retorted. "As far as I could see, nobody except Vaughan even noticed you at all."

The twisted face darkened. Without warning, he stretched out his hand, and snapped something in a language she had never heard. Biddy felt something deep in her chest quiver; she flinched back, only to be stopped by the stone wall.

"What are you doing?" Her heart was beating rapid and painful. Some of it might have been fear. The rest was something else entirely. "Get off me!"

He didn't listen. His brow was furrowed—not in anger now, but in concentration. The tug came again, sharper this time.

He was trying to pull the magic from her heart by force. She could feel his touch like rough fingers inside her, careless and brutal. It tugged again, and it tore a cry of pain and shock from her even as she pressed back against the wall.

The Council had said that only the mage who cast a spell could easily remove it. Whoever that mage was, it wasn't Storm. He was going to kill her trying.

"Stop it!" Amid her fear, a flash of anger burst like a light in the dark. How *dare* he? She wasn't anything very much, it was true. She wasn't a mage, she had no power, she was a girl alone in the dark without even a pair of shoes. But whatever magic she had in her heart, however it had gotten there, it wasn't for him. "You can't have it. It's *mine*."

Her heart twisted and screamed in her chest.

The winged man fell back with a cry like a hawk.

And then, without warning, she was somewhere else entirely.

Chapter Ten

$\mathcal{I}$t was like entering Rowan's dream all over again.

Another fall.

Another plummet through the sky, stomach surging, lungs emptying in a rush.

Another crash that left her dazed, floating, sensation returning as her surroundings filtered through in watercolors around her.

Another new world.

She breathed in and out, gasping, barely noticing that the air smelled of smoke and stale beer and something cooking, that the light was so bright after her day in the dungeon that her eyes were blinded. All she cared about was that the terrible wrench in her chest had dulled, that Storm's presence had passed like a shadow. She didn't care what had happened, or where she was. It had stopped. Wherever she was, it had to be better.

This lasted only a minute or so, if that. Then she took hold of herself, forced her limbs to uncurl, and rose slowly to her feet. If she'd learned one thing about magic, it was that it could always get worse.

She was aboveground once more, with sunlight slanting, dust-speckled, through the windows. The light fell on a low-ceilinged room with a soot-blackened fireplace, a wide table, crooked floor-boards that shifted under her bare feet. The upstairs room of a public house, perhaps—Biddy had never been in one, unless she counted the guesthouse in Dublin, but she had read Dickens and *Tom Brown's School Days* and seen enough illustrations to recognize one now.

The windows looked down onto a crooked street, narrow and winding, the buildings high and close together and the roads cobbled. It looked ancient, medieval, and she thought for a dizzying moment that she had come very far back in time indeed. Then, as her brain cleared and the frantic drum of her heart slowed, she picked up other details—the clock on the mantel, the lampposts in the street, the top hats of the men and swishing dresses of the women outside. She remembered that plenty of streets in the world looked medieval, even now.

And yet she *was* back in time, at least a little way.

She wasn't alone in the room, as she had first thought. Two people sat at the table, a man and a woman. The woman, Biddy saw with a start, was Morgaine. She was the Morgaine of Rowan's nightmare again: Her dress, scarlet this time, was the same full-skirted style as the night the wisps had come, and her hair was back in its ringlets.

The man, too, she recognized. It was Storm.

She stumbled backward on reflex, adrenaline spiking, fumbling for something to use as a weapon. But it wasn't the Storm she knew. He was whole, human, no longer twisted into half-bird form or burdened with terrible useless wings. His hair was sleek black and fresh-cut; his face was startlingly and unexpectedly handsome, sculpted like polished marble, with strong eyebrows and a hawklike nose.

And there was something else. A grey wolf sat at Storm's side, slender and amber-eyed. His familiar. She glanced quickly at Morgaine and, yes, an owl was perched at the table beside her, golden-eyed, claws digging into the rough wood. Tilda, Morgaine had called her in Rowan's dream, with her death fresh on her soul.

It was another dream—another memory. It had to be. The world had the same faint, intangible quality of Rowan's nightmare;

Storm's clear blue eyes looked straight through Biddy without see-ing her. This was the time before magic had fled from the world, before the mages had harvested the power from their own familiars to survive.

The only question was how on earth she had gotten here.

"But it makes *sense*," Storm was saying—arguing, from his tone, the kind of argument that the participants had gone over many times. His voice was smoother, well-spoken, without the growl of the present day. "If magic is leaving the world, then we need to gather it up and save it for what's important. We can't know how long it will be before we get any more."

"And who decides what's important?" Morgaine retorted. Beside her, the owl ruffled its tawny wings. "Vaughan? Do you honestly think he'll make sure it goes where it's needed? It will go to peo-ple like him, and everyone else will be denied any chance to work magic at all. Where does that leave the hedgewitches, the apothe-caries, the mages who give away spells to the human world?"

"The important thing is to have it, isn't it? We can worry about logistics later."

A voice came from across the room, hard-edged with frustration. "And you don't think that's going to be too late?"

Biddy hadn't noticed the third figure standing by the far window until he spoke—perhaps, according to the rules of the memory, he hadn't been there before. But she knew the voice at once. She knew long before Rowan turned and came back to the table, Hutchincroft at his heels.

It wasn't like the dream trap. There, Rowan had looked the same as in the present day, with only his words and feelings echoed from the past. Here he was visibly younger, his face clean-shaven and overly angular. His shirt and waistcoat looked a little too big for him, as though he'd recently lost weight—he might have been get-ting over an illness, if it weren't for the fact that Biddy had never known him to be unwell. Besides, he didn't look fragile. He looked whittled down, concentrated into energy and muscle and magic, his frame taut with anger as he looked Storm in the eye. Hutchincroft, too, looked stronger, brighter in some way that went beyond the physical. Biddy should have been thrilled to see them, yet she found herself drawing back, unsure.

"What do you mean, too late?" Storm said to him. It was an innocent question, but his tone carried a touch of derision.

"You tell me, Storm." Rowan leaned forward on the table, lightly balanced, poised for a fight. "You've seen what's been happening the last few months. It's one thing to order all magic be handed over to the Council—I don't like that, I don't agree with it, but all right, it's an emergency measure meant in good faith. But the measures Vaughan's taking to enforce it are getting worse and worse. He's had three hedgewitches thrown in the dungeon in the last week just for giving away charms. And Morgaine's right. If he's like this now, what do you think he's going to be like once he has control of every scrap of magic left in the world?"

"He won't have control," Storm replied. "He has to answer to the Council."

"He owns the Council."

Storm snorted. "Well, you should know. You and Morgaine were the ones who gave it to him—and were happy enough to do it, as I recall."

Biddy frowned. She couldn't remember Rowan ever mentioning that. He had said the Council had granted emergency powers to Vaughan, she supposed, and Rowan had been on the Council. But...

"What are you after?" Rowan was asking, hotly. "Us to admit it was our fault?"

Morgaine interrupted. "It *was* our fault. Both of us—all of us. We thought Vaughan would make things better. But he's made them worse."

"I wouldn't be too hard on yourselves if I were you," Storm said dismissively. "Old Quirtle had no idea what to do when a crisis hit. Most of the Council was scared to act. Vaughan acted. Say what you like about him, he's a mage who gets things accomplished."

Rowan laughed then, softly, and his laugh had the same threat

Biddy had heard in the nightmare as he had taken the necklace from Morgaine's throat. She felt cold without knowing why.

"I should have guessed," he said. "He's promised you something, hasn't he? A place on the Council?"

Storm looked him the eye, defiant. "No."

"No? Then it's even worse. You're *hoping* he'll promise you something, as long as you stick to his side like a loyal little lapdog."

The wolf at Storm's side growled, either at the insult to Storm or at the mention of lapdogs. Morgaine sighed heavily. "For God's sake. Rowan—"

"I think he's the best mage for the job." Storm's voice was raised now. "But if he did offer me a place on the Council one day, what of it? At least I belong there."

"What's that supposed to mean?" Rowan demanded.

Storm's mouth tweaked in just a hint of a mocking smile. "Nothing."

"No, go on. Be brave for once in your life. What did you mean?"

"Will you two both stop this?" Morgaine's voice was exasperated now. "It's not helping."

"You're one to talk about being promised something," Storm said bluntly, without taking his eyes from Rowan. "The place on the Council you took should have been mine, and everyone knew it. The only reason they ever let you on the Council was because Vaughan put you there. And now you've done your job and got him into power, he doesn't need you anymore. That's what you can't stand, isn't it? You're an embarrassment to him, you and your crackpot ideas about why magic is draining from the world."

"And what if those ideas are right?" Rowan shot back. He had shown no visible reaction to the rest of Storm's accusations, but Hutchincroft was bristling. "What if we're the reason this is happening? What if we've used too much magic, too fast, and the cracks are closing because we haven't left enough to keep them open? Because if that *is* true, then everything Vaughan's done to gather the last scraps left is just making things worse. And you wonder why that's an embarrassment. Where does that leave him?"

"Exactly where he is," Storm retorted. "Because it's *not* true. Magic's not like gold or oil or…or bloody flour in the cupboard. We can't hurt it, and we can't help it. It's just there to be used, that's all."

"*Just there to be used?*" Rowan shook his head. "You lot really do think the world exists for your benefit, don't you?" He didn't wait for an answer. "All right. Explain to me one thing. If losing magic has nothing to do with us—if this is a natural phenomenon, no fault of ours at all—then why are the cracks closing faster and faster the more magic we take?"

"You can't prove they are," Storm returned. "It's just as likely that the cracks would close at the same rate whether we took their magic or not—which makes it all the more important to get as much as we can first."

"I didn't just pull that theory out of thin air, you know. It's been a school of thought for centuries. I saw one close with my own eyes, right when I was trying to harvest its power. And Morgaine agrees with it too."

"She does not!"

"I'm right here, you know!" Morgaine snapped. "And I honestly don't know what I believe. I don't think there's any way of telling yet. I'm more worried about how to curb the Servant's power before he's out of control."

Neither of them was listening to her. Her words were barely audible, as though even Storm's memory of them was muffled. The tension between Rowan and Storm was like heat, dizzying and stifling. It subsumed everything.

"If you really think we're breaking the world," Storm said, "then you're worse than the rest of us. How much magic has Vaughan given you to forge that stone of yours?"

"Shut up," Rowan said flatly. At his side, Hutch grunted a warning.

"Or what? You'll turn into a bird and fly away?" There was a note of triumph in his voice as his barb hit home. "From what I've heard, it hasn't been working too well."

"Oh, and you could do better, could you?"

"Why not?" Storm's lip curled. "At least I'm an English weather-mage of good family. Whoever heard of an Irish woodmage on the Council of Mages? It was ridiculous, and everybody knew it—even Vaughan. All those hours the two of you were off with your heads together talking about ravenstones and magic islands and fair folk, did you really think he was interested? He was flattering you until he had your vote and laughing at you behind your back. Years of him throwing magic at you, and no ravenstone in sight. And now your use to him has ended—"

"All right." Rowan's hand slipped into his pocket, lightning fast, and slammed something on the table. Biddy saw the flash of dark stone, and her heart started in recognition. It was on a silver chain, not the thread of leather she was used to, but it still gleamed hard and jet-black and dangerous. "Want to give it a try?"

Storm was thrown out of his carefully balanced contempt; his head tilted, and he blinked, confused. "What is that?"

"That's the ravenstone."

"But…" He shook his head, as though to set the world back in order. "Vaughan said you failed."

"Well, I wasn't going to tell him I'd succeeded, was I? Not the way things are going. It works."

"Barely!" Morgaine interjected. Her eyes had widened at the sight of the stone on the old wooden table. "You almost didn't come back from it."

"But I *did* come back," Rowan countered. "And as Storm says, why shouldn't he be able to do better than me? He's an English mage, after all. Aren't they supposed to be the finest in the world?"

Hutch's fur was still bristling, but there was an uncertain quality to it now. Storm's wolf had its tail between its legs.

"Is he telling the truth?" Storm turned to her. "Did he truly forge a ravenstone?"

Morgaine sighed. "We both did. A few days ago—we weren't going to tell the Council. Vaughan will only use it to his advantage in some dangerous way. And it needs taming. It's still too powerful."

"But he used it?"

"It's not safe, Storm. It would eat you alive."

"It didn't eat *him* alive."

Biddy's stomach was sinking; every nerve was screaming that this was a terrible idea, to stop now before it was too late. But she couldn't move. Besides, it would do no good. This was no dream; they couldn't be woken from it. This was history. It had already happened.

"He was lucky," Morgaine said firmly. "And he's been working on it for over a year. *I* haven't even tried it yet." She must have seen that she was getting nowhere, because she turned to Rowan, half-furious, half-appealing. "Rowan, for God's sake, don't be such an idiot!"

"I'm not doing anything." Rowan's voice was low, soft, but without a trace of gentleness. It didn't sound at all like the voice Biddy had known all her life. "If Storm thinks he can handle it, I'm not going to stop him. If he doesn't think he's up to it—"

Storm's eyes flashed. He stood to his full height, glowering and powerful, and Biddy shrank back instinctively. She was used to thinking of Rowan as tall, but Storm was taller, and much broader across his shoulders.

"Of course I'm up to it!" At his side, his wolf familiar gave an anxious whine. Storm ignored it. "I was always up to it!"

"Well," Rowan said lightly. "Now's your chance to prove it, isn't it? Who knows? If Vaughan hears about it, he might even let you on the Council at last. He'll need someone there, when he's arrested everyone else."

Morgaine was looking at Rowan; she didn't see Storm's jaw tighten, as Biddy did. She turned too late to stop his hand from snatching up the glittering ravenstone and setting it about his neck.

"No!" Biddy cried out, even though she knew it was useless, even as Morgaine turned and screamed the same thing.

It was too late.

Storm crumpled in on himself. His body was shuddering, flexing, skin rippling and muscles spasming. His legs went out from under him, the fingers gripping the table already twisting into claws.

Dimly, Biddy could hear Morgaine calling out, her words distorted. Rowan said nothing at all. She didn't even know where he was. The world was flashing white, then grey, streaked with swirling gashes of bloodred. This was Storm's memory, and it wasn't only his body that was being torn apart. It was his mind.

"Storm—"

The raven was there. Biddy could feel it all about them, wild and panicked and trapped, clawing its way from the stone through Storm's own body. One of Storm's eyes split open down the middle and clouded black. His mouth, still his own, worked for words, to call for help. Instead, a terrible cry rent the air—a bird's shriek, trailing to a scream of human agony.

"Storm!"

As if in answer, the pain in Biddy's chest flared. The spell in her heart gave a shuddering, convulsive tug; she gasped against her will, even as before her eyes Storm's back arched, hunched, as giant feathers erupted from his shoulders in a tearing of flesh.

Storm.

"Storm!"

It was a woman's voice, clear and brittle and angry. The surge of agony in Biddy's chest receded, and she sank, gasping, to the stone floor.

She was back in the dungeons. The memory of the tavern room was gone, but its pain and fear and confusion swam through her blood like a drug. Storm stood above her, flushed, feathers rippling, breathing heavily. Behind him, the walls of the cell had parted, and someone stood in the light from the corridor beyond.

It was Morgaine. Not a memory this time, neither Rowan's nor Storm's, but real and solid, her face drawn tight in fury. Biddy didn't think to feel surprise. It seemed inevitable that Morgaine would be there, as if she had stepped out of the memory with them. Only the familiars were missing, and Rowan.

Rowan. Rowan hard-edged and bitter and laughing, pushing Storm into the spell that had made him a monster.

"What do you think you're doing?" Morgaine demanded.

Storm raised his head. He looked defiant, but there was an edge of shame to his voice as he replied. "The Council need what's in her heart."

"They don't need you to try to tear it from her!" The door vanished behind Morgaine as she came forward. "You'll damage the spell beyond all repair that way. We need Rowan."

"It took them more than fifty years to catch Rowan the first time," Storm said. "And he escaped in a week. We don't need him. I know how his magic works."

"So do I. And I wouldn't try to disentangle it without him." Morgaine turned to Biddy. "Are you hurt?"

Biddy shook her head, not trusting herself to speak. She didn't want Storm to see she was still trembling.

"If the Servant hears you were down here—" Storm said, and Morgaine cut him off.

"He'll hear that you were endangering the spell because you wanted to be the one to draw it from her, in the hope of your own advancement. That was why you were doing it, weren't you? You want the Servant to reward you. If he hears about this, he won't do it. He might also remember how Rowan escaped last time."

Storm's feathers ruffled. He took a step toward Morgaine, and his voice lowered until Biddy could barely hear it.

"There might be a few things I could tell him about the night Rowan escaped last time."

Morgaine didn't flinch. "Storm, I'm telling you to stop for your own sake." Her voice was low too, but it was soft suddenly, cajoling. "You want to be on the Council. I want you there with us too. This isn't the way to do it. Now, leave the girl alone and let me see if she's in one piece." She held her ground, and slowly Storm stepped aside.

Morgaine dropped down to a crouch at Biddy's side, a hand

going to her shoulder. "Are you sure you're well? He didn't harm you?"

Biddy shook her head again, intensely aware of Storm standing only feet away; intensely aware, too, that this was the woman Rowan had been engaged to and betrayed by, the woman Hutchincroft had said was not to be trusted. The images of Storm's memories were fading, being pushed to the back of her brain, and she willed them to recede further. The tearing in her heart had settled to a dull, quiet throb.

"I'm fine."

Morgaine seemed oddly ill at ease too, now the first rush of concern had passed. "Good. Well. I was coming to make sure you were comfortable. I brought you some blankets, and a pillow."

Her movements were careful and deliberate, as though Biddy were a wild animal that might start away. It made Biddy careful, too, as she reached out and took the soft grey bundle.

"Thank you," she said, and meant it—not for the blankets, though she was freezing, but for intervening. She had no idea why she had found herself in Storm's memories, whether it had been intended on his part or a stage of removing the spell or something else entirely, but she was certain she had been in very grave danger.

"Don't thank me," Morgaine said. "I wish I could do more. Have you been given water to wash?"

Biddy shook her head again, and Morgaine sighed.

"Tomorrow morning, I promise. I'll do what I can."

"Come on, Morgaine," Storm said, impatient. "Are you even supposed to be down here?"

"I'm coming." Morgaine gave Biddy one final glance, a glance Biddy had no idea how to read, and stood.

This time, when the door vanished behind them, Biddy found she couldn't move. She curled up, shivering, clasping the blankets to her chest as though they were floating debris in icy water. Her mind teemed with the images of seventy years ago. Storm twisting, transforming, screaming. Morgaine's voice, angry, pleading, ordering them both to stop. Rowan. *Oh God, Rowan, what did you do?*

She tried to take a breath, to remind herself that she didn't have the full story. She didn't even know where Storm's memory had come from—how could she know if it was accurate? Even if it was, Storm had hardly been kind himself. She didn't know what history lay between them, what might have led Rowan to act so differently from the person she had always known. It was all true, or at least made sense. But she had been through too many uncertainties in the last few days, had seen the world change its shape around her too many times. This was once too many.

Besides, it wasn't only the feud with Storm. Storm had said, that day, that Rowan had gotten Vaughan into power in the first place—Rowan had made no move to deny it. Vaughan had said, only that morning, that he and Rowan had been friends; Storm had said Rowan was his friend too. What had Rowan been, in those days? What more hadn't he told her? Her heart quivered with every beat where Storm had torn at it, like the frightened flutters of a wounded bird.

Gradually, because she couldn't shiver forever, she stopped. Her breathing calmed, and with it her thoughts settled.

She didn't know where Rowan was. Perhaps he was on his way to find her, as she'd always believed. Perhaps he needed rescuing himself. Perhaps—she forced herself to think it—he really had never meant to come at all. Either way, she couldn't wait.

If she was going to get out of there, she would have to get herself out—now, before it was too late, and Storm tried again to take the spell from her heart. He would kill her the next time.

However Rowan had escaped was unlikely to help her. It would involve magic, and she had none of any kind. She was used to that, though. All it meant was that she would have to find another way.

Biddy got to her feet slowly, her muscles knotted and painful. The blanket was still in her arms; she unfurled it, shook it out, and wrapped it around her shoulders. It was then that something hard and shiny fell from it and landed with a clink on the stone floor.

Chapter Eleven

*H*er heart leapt. Forgetting her stiffness, she dropped to her knees. Her fingers met cobbles, and dirt, and then, at long last, something smooth.

Biddy's first thought when she had heard the clink had been a key—that Morgaine, on her side after all, had slipped her what she needed to get out. It wasn't a key. It was a mirror: a small, round, gilded mirror, no larger than her palm. Despite the pitch darkness, she could see the walls reflected in its surface. A spell, clearly, and probably a useful one for a fashionable lady looking to touch up their powder in the evening. Not very useful for her, though, surely? Biddy tilted it and saw her own face, pale and wide-eyed and surrounded by a messy halo of dark hair. She frowned, puzzled and disappointed, and the mirror reflected that too.

Think. She drew a deep breath, and searched her brain for everything she knew about mirrors and magic. Morgaine must have left it for a reason, after all. It had been a risk to bring her anything at all.

"Rowan of Hy-Brasil, please," she said out loud, as she would to the scrying glass at home, but wasn't surprised to receive no response. The mirror was tiny. Their own scrying glass was much larger, and Hutchincroft had always fretted that it was too small for the magic needed.

It showed a clear reflection in darkness. That had to be important somehow.

She tilted the glass again, to reflect the wall behind her. The stones looked different in the reflection: paler, smoother, the curves flattened.

"Mirrors show what's there," Rowan had told her once. It was after she'd read *Dracula* and wanted to know if it was true that vampires didn't have reflections. "I've never heard of anything *not* showing in one. More likely if a vampire looked in a mirror, he'd see himself as he truly was, fangs and wrinkles and whatever else. More's the pity. It would be nice to pretend mirrors lied when you look in them."

"You think you look wonderful in mirrors," Biddy had said to him sternly.

He laughed. "Only because I hardly ever look in them."

The last time she had used the scrying glass had been the night of the dream trap, nearly two weeks ago.

Her heart quickened.

The dream trap.

When they had been in the dream trap, Rowan said that mages always built doors in case they were trapped in their own spells. The door to the dungeon was an enchantment too, one that could only be opened from the outside. But what if somebody was trapped inside by mistake? What if there was another door, one that could only be found by someone who knew where it was?

Or by someone with a mirror. A mirror that showed what was there.

Biddy had searched most of the room with the mirror, pushing back against rising panic, knowing Storm could be back at any moment and she could be wasting time on completely the wrong idea, when the reflection at last caught something it shouldn't. Just a glint of light at first, in a corner where there was no light. She tilted the mirror, holding her breath. And then, as if it had been there all along, there was a door reflected in the glass—an old, cracked wooden door, startlingly warm and homelike against the rest of the dungeon.

There had been no door all the long hours Biddy had spent in the dungeon. The walls had been smooth and impenetrable, even in the place where the rock parted to let in Storm. And yet when Biddy turned to the spot now, heart pounding, the door was there.

It stayed there as she moved toward it, and when she reached out a trembling hand the iron doorknob stayed there for her to grip. It was real. The only question was why she had been allowed to find it.

Morgaine had rescued her from Storm's magic; now she had given her the means to escape. There were only two possible explanations. Either she really was working against the Council from the inside, as she had told Rowan she would all those decades ago, without ever once getting word to him about it...

Or this was a trap. It would be the easiest thing in the world, after all, for the Council to slip Biddy the mirror, let her get out, and then follow her wherever she went. They wanted Rowan—they could well think that Biddy would lead them to him.

The irony was, she had no idea where he was. She didn't have any means of getting in touch with him, or even getting home to Hy-Brasil. If anyone tried to follow her after letting her escape the Undercastle, they'd all be going in circles. She had to bite down on a laugh at the thought, before it escalated into tears.

Just think. Just think of what to do next.

It didn't matter if it was a trap. She had no other means of getting out, and nothing to be gained by staying where she was. She was already caught. It could get no worse. At the very least, she wouldn't be in the dungeon for Storm to return to that night. She'd be away from his anger, and the rough fist of his magic about her heart, and the memories that turned everything she knew to ash.

Biddy turned the handle, and the door opened easily.

———————————————

Footsteps.

Biddy heard them before she had a chance to take in her

surroundings. Not Storm's heavy tread, no whisper of crumpled wings, but more than one of them, and moving fast.

She looked about her quickly, trying to get her bearings. A corridor, small and narrow enough that it was almost a tunnel. The floor was cold, and the walls were lit by the barest flicker of torches. It could have been anywhere in the lowest level of the Undercastle. She had no idea how to reach the surface.

Without the footsteps, she would have despaired which way to go. As it was, they gave her only one choice. She had no time to think—or rather, she had time for only one thought. The footsteps were coming behind her, so she had to go forward, and quickly.

Luck was with her, to a point. Only a few yards down was a door in the stone wall, and it opened to her touch. What lay beyond it was startlingly familiar: a small, shabby room, very like the kitchen on Hy-Brasil, with its worn table and wide, high fireplace built to accommodate an oven. The table was littered with a set of playing cards and old unwashed glasses, and the room smelled faintly of ale and old socks. A guardroom, perhaps, which meant she'd come out not too far from the dungeon after all.

Unfortunately, there was no second door. The only way out was back the way she had come. And the footsteps were getting louder and closer.

The fireplace. Her eyes, scrambling about the room for a place to hide, landed on it. It was unlit, with grey ash piled against its hearth. When the shadows had closed in on Rowan, the night she had seen in his nightmares, he had turned into a raven and flown up the chimney. She was no raven, but she was small for her age even if she wasn't particularly thin, and the fireplace looked wide enough to take her.

And she had been taught all her life how to climb.

It was a tighter fit than she had hoped. She wouldn't have made it had it not been for a set of iron rungs inside the chimney. One desperate jump, and her fingertips brushed the lowest rung; another, and she found a firm grip. The muscles in her arms screamed in protest, but panic gave her strength. She pulled herself up bodily, wriggling and scuffling, her feet scrabbling for purchase as ash fell in her face and choked her. Her toes found purchase just as she heard the door open in the room below.

She was only just in time. Sounds drifted up the chimney: the door swinging shut first, then mumblings, a cough, soft thuds, the clink of a bottle against glass, the splash of liquid. She rested her hot forehead against the stone wall, fighting to stifle gasps, and strained her ears to distinguish the voices.

"This is going to be a long night," she heard from down below. A male voice, gruff, with yet another accent she couldn't identify. "Storm's mad. Rowan isn't coming within a mile of this place. He knows we'll be waiting."

"He was up in Yorkshire last night." The scrape of a chair, and the thud of boots on a table. At least two men, then. But of course there could be many more sitting and drinking in silence. "Augustus and I nearly caught him."

The reply was inaudible—something about wisps, or possibly chips. It was the first part that hit her. *A long night.* They would be there all night.

She couldn't do it. The iron rungs were biting her hands; her back and arms were aflame; she was already so exhausted by the long day of fear and cold she could have burst into tears then and there. There was no way she could cling to the side of the wall in the darkness for hour after hour. At any moment, they could hear her—a slip of her foot could give her away, or a sneeze.

They could light the fire.

The thought chilled her. She remembered books where witches were burned at the stake, words that spun thick black smoke and the sharp licking tongues of flame, and her spirit quavered. And even if they didn't, if she didn't give herself away or slip and fall, when the dawn came they would find the dungeon empty and search for her in earnest. However it happened, she was trapped. She tightened her grip on the metal, closed her eyes, and tried not to even breathe.

Please, she thought, to anything, to any fragment of a miracle left in the world. *Please.*

She remembered that moment afterward, a still point in a frantic night. Because it was at that very moment a shout went up from down below.

At first, ludicrously, all she could think was that someone had seen a spider, or a snake. The sudden flurry of movement was like that of birds taking flight at a predator in their midst. Chairs scraped; boots hit the floor; someone swore at the smashing of glass. But mages weren't startled by predators. The people in the guardroom were running toward something, not away.

Someone had found the dungeon empty. It had to be. They knew she was missing, and they had been called to search for her. It surely wouldn't take them long to look up the chimney—it seemed so obvious to her that she couldn't believe they hadn't looked at once. This was what she had dreaded.

And yet—she grabbed at the thought—it was also her chance.

The room would be empty again. She had to get down and out of there as soon as possible. The thought made her sick, but she forced herself to face it. Get down, stay out of sight, try to make her way to the surface. There had to be a way out. Rowan had managed it, after all, long ago.

The noises receded. She heard the sharp thud of the door closing. Soon. She would go down soon. If there was anybody still in there, she was out of luck anyway. She couldn't stay in the chimney forever.

Out of nowhere, something struck her lightly on the back of her neck. She looked up, and it came again, right between her eyes. Something cold and wet. Drops of water. As though, somewhere, it was raining.

Her heart quickened.

She was deep underground—Storm had told her as much, if she'd had any doubts. Hutchincroft had told her all about tunnels underground, the ones the black rabbits dug. The most important thing about them was that they needed to be well ventilated. Surely this chimney had to reach the surface at some point, to vent smoke; for that matter, there had to be shafts to send down air. There was a window sending down daylight to the dungeons, after all, and she'd seen more along the way to the Council chamber.

All was still below now. The guardroom was probably clear if she wanted to go down. She would have far preferred it, despite her fear—the chimney was tight, and from the way the stone scraped her head as she looked up it would only get tighter.

But if rain was coming down the chimney, then there had to be an opening to the surface not far away. All she had to do was follow the direction of the wind. This, after all, could be her way out. At the very least, she would be unlikely to be caught doing something so dangerous.

Biddy turned her face toward the faint rush of air, drew a deep breath, and started to climb.

------◆◆◆================◆◆◆------

It wasn't as simple as it seemed.

The rain was falling straight down, it was true, but soon the chimney tapered into a point too narrow for her to continue through. It branched off into a wider, horizontal shaft to her right, and she was forced to follow it or go back. She was grateful for this in one aspect, as the ache between her shoulders was sharpening to the point of agony, but it also worried her. She needed to go up, and yet she had no choice. There was an entire castle beneath the ground, and the chimneys formed an impossible labyrinth through its walls.

Keep heading up when you can. Surely, as long as she kept heading up, she would come out somewhere.

She crawled a very long way—so long and so far that she started to fear the place was enchanted, she was going in circles, and she would be caught after daybreak crawling back into her own cell. Often she could indeed climb again, as massive chimneys cut across her way, but they always inevitably branched out again to the side. Once, horribly, a blocked shaft meant she had to go *down*, and the fear of squeezing herself headfirst down the small gap entwined with the certainty that she was lost behind walls of stone and would die the next time someone lit a fire. Claustrophobia seized her then, and she froze, motionless with terror, for some time before she got a grip on herself.

She was grateful that she had been taken in her nightdress—she had climbed in a corset once or twice, and it was often enough to know that she would never have been able to wriggle through the dark labyrinth of stone in one. And yet the thin fabric snagged on rough shards of brick and tore; her knees were soon bruised and bleeding, and the palms of her hands were so raw she had to bite back a whimper every time she put weight on them. Sweat dried on her skin, and she was chilled to the bone.

At times strange noises drifted up from the fireplaces she passed: a rustle of feathers, a hiss like a snake or escaping steam, the sound of a cauldron bubbling and low voices chanting. Once she heard the low moan of someone crying, but when she dared to crawl down to see if anybody needed help, she found only an empty room and a cold like death. After she scrambled back up the chimney she had her second bout of shaking, and it was even longer this time before she set her chin and kept going. The occasional drafts of rain-speckled air were teasing her now. They seemed to be coming from nowhere at all.

And then, in a place that felt very far from anywhere, she saw a flicker of light through a gap between stones. It was so unexpected in the eternal darkness that she stopped, twisted toward it as much as the cramped space would allow, and peered through.

The gap looked out almost to the ceiling of a high room—or rather, she corrected herself, a room that plunged deep into the earth. The room was curved, wide, and empty except for one enormous rock in the center. Easily twice Biddy's height, it glowed with faint green-gold shimmers beneath its smooth surface.

She had seen that light before. Flashes of it in the old oak, when Rowan drew magic through the skin of the tree. And once, in the scrying glass, as a glow on the wall illuminating Rowan as he lay in enchanted sleep in an underground room.

This was it, the room where Rowan had come to steal magic on the night he had nearly never come home. The vault, he had called it. The place where the Council hoarded its wealth like fairy gold.

A suspicion came to her, and she dug her fingernails into the gap through which she was looking. The stone came away easily in her fingers; she put it back quickly, but it was enough to tell her that someone had loosened it deliberately, to make a hole in the wall. Not large enough for a person to get through, even a child. But large enough for a raven.

Hope, which had been dying, flickered once again. If this was how Rowan entered the vault, then he had been in this passage too, many times. The surface couldn't be too far away.

It wasn't.

———————

It was still raining outside. A spear of light plunged through the roof ahead, and in it the fine droplets glittered like sandflies. Biddy was so deadened by exhaustion that she was halfway to it before she realized what that light meant. She crawled forward as fast as she could, the pain of her scraped hands and knees forgotten, her breath hitching in her throat.

The tunnel widened out as she drew nearer the light, so that she could crane her neck and see the two-foot shaft straight up. The rain was coming through a narrow opening in the side—small, but not too small to take her, she thought. She didn't care if it was. She'd widen it with her own nails and teeth if she had to. What frightened her was the silhouette of rusted bars across it. If they were bolted tight, then she'd come all this way for nothing. She didn't have time to find another escape route. It might be morning already. The light seemed too bright to be the stars.

In fact, when she wriggled her face close to the grill, she could see that the light was neither the stars nor the sun, but a street-light spilling across cobbles. Beyond it, London lay abandoned and gleaming wetly in the early hours before dawn. She was at gutter level, peering through an opening that would probably be taken for a drain of some kind. Nobody would notice, as she had cause to, that though rain fell lightly through the grill not an ounce of water was sluicing through from the pavement and gutters themselves.

Even better, when she frantically pushed at the grate, it buckled once, and then fell to the ground outside with a clatter.

The opening was large enough to take her, but barely. She had thought herself already bruised and scraped from hours of tunnels. This last push bent her very bones out of their shape like the most fashionable of corsets. For several agonizing minutes her hips wedged half in and half out, and she clawed frantically at the cobbles, rain streaming down the back of her neck. Then, with a final push and a sound of tearing fabric, she was free. The glowing face of Big Ben was in front of her; the Thames snaked to her right into the distance. She was outside, and she was free.

She lay there on the ground, exhausted, muscles burning, chest aching. Rain pelted her head, her back, her shredded nightgown, and it was the most welcome thing she had ever felt. She wanted nothing more than to close her eyes and sink against the wet pavement. Her limbs seemed very far away, and so stiff and heavy she was sure they could never move. Escape was all that had kept her in motion, and now she had escaped. It wasn't fair that there should be more after that. She was in the air again. She was no longer enclosed by stone. It was enough.

With effort, she forced herself to raise her head.

Not yet. She was free, but that was nothing. She could so easily be caught again. She had to be *safe.*

Biddy had barely gotten to her feet when something caught her.

Her first panicked thoughts were that it was a rope. It wrapped tight around her, pinning her arms to her sides and binding her ankles. When she glanced down, frantic, she could see nothing. And yet something was there. She stumbled forward, twisting her shoulders to free herself. Her breath came in tight gasps, not in fear so much as fury. Not here. Not now. Not when she was so *close* . . .

She shouldn't have stopped to rest. If only she hadn't stopped—

"Stop!" Arms were around her, holding her tight alongside the invisible rope. "Stop, please, it's only me. I gave you the mirror, remember? I want to help you."

Morgaine.

Biddy stopped struggling. Partly she was just surprised into stillness; partly she realized that Morgaine would only hold her tighter the harder she tried to get away.

Morgaine heaved a sigh of relief, and shot a quick glance at the entrance behind her as she released her. The invisible ropes untangled. Biddy could have run then, but she didn't. She wouldn't get far.

"I was so afraid you'd escaped too well. I gave you the mirror so you could come out of the secret door behind the dungeon, but I had to deal with Storm, and then by the time I'd lost him and got back down there you had gone. You should be safe until morning, but you never can tell with Storm."

So Storm didn't know she was missing. Biddy wondered briefly what the commotion had been in the guardroom, if it hadn't been her disappearance. It was too much to think about now.

"We don't have much time," Morgaine was saying. "As soon as Storm finds an empty cell, wisps will be scouring the streets, and that magic in your heart will call them like a foghorn."

Biddy found her voice then. "Foghorns don't call people. They're a warning to stay away."

A startled laugh. "No matter. Wisps don't understand warnings. And they'll never leave you alone."

She had barely thought of the wisps in the chimney. All her fears had been of Storm. Now the memory of those terrible shadow feathers crawled across her skin. "I'll hide this time. I won't let them get me again."

"Exactly." Morgaine's voice was low and urgent. The rain was dampening her hair, gently plastering wet tendrils to her face. "That's why I wanted to find you. You can hide with me."

She blinked. "With you?"

"Yes. My flat is hidden to them—they won't see you unless they come to search it in person. You'll be safe there. I promise."

She wanted it to be true, badly. She was desperately alone, and she needed help. But this was exactly what Morgaine would say if the mirror had been a trap all along.

"I'm not an enemy, Bridget, I swear. We've met before, you and I. Do you remember? Your dreams?"

At first, confused, all Biddy could think of was Rowan's dream: the flat, small and dark, the glass-grinding shriek of the wisps, Rowan's terrible shock.

"When you were very little," Morgaine pressed. "Three or four. Some nights you would have dreams, and a woman would come into them. She probably seemed very old to you. You played games together."

Of course. Morgaine had looked different inside Rowan's dream—younger, harder—or she might have recognized her earlier. Even as it was, she had always known Morgaine was familiar.

"That was you," she said slowly.

Morgaine smiled, bright with relief. "That's right. We were friends, I thought."

They had been.

The lady in her dreams had come for the first time when she was four, and a handful of times shortly after. There was no rhyme or reason to when she would come—she came in summer and in autumn, in dreams good or bad or boring, on cold nights and warm. The first time she had seemed surprised to see Biddy, but after that she had come on purpose to visit her, and to play with her.

"I thought I imagined you," Biddy said. "You disappeared when I turned five. I thought . . . well. I thought I imagined you because—"

"Because why?"

Biddy looked down, cheeks burning. She wasn't going to tell this woman that she used to pretend she was a mother, or an older sister. "Nothing."

It could still be a trick. This was Morgaine, after all. She had killed her familiar to save herself. She had betrayed Rowan. He hated her.

But she had also been engaged to Rowan. She had tried to warn him that the wisps were coming, almost too late. And her face now, looking at Biddy's, showed nothing but anxious concern.

"It's across London," Morgaine said into the silence. "I've a cab waiting. Please, I know you have no reason to trust me, but will you come?"

Strangely, it was the thought of that cab that convinced her. She had nowhere to go, and nowhere to hide. She was trembling with exhaustion and soaked to her skin. She barely knew where she was. A cab would take her *somewhere*. Surely even a trap was better than a return to the dungeon.

She nodded, just once, and Morgaine gripped her hand.

"Thank you." Her face was soft with relief. "Follow me. Just a short ride, and then we'll be safe."

Chapter Twelve

*B*iddy had grown up in a falling-down castle with a rabbit and a mage who lived on cold mugs of tea and never brushed his hair. She had never in her life been in anything so soft and clean and pretty as Morgaine's townhouse.

The sitting room to which she was taken looked as though it had been designed afresh only moments ago for their benefit. The walls were pure white; the warm oak floor, the dove-colored armchairs, and the pale blue curtains were bright and without stains. When Morgaine turned on the electric lights, the effect was like being inside a winter sunbeam. Even the books lining the shelves around the fireplace were new, with soft covers in sea blue and forest green and lilac grey. The books in the library at Hy-Brasil were a mismatch of worn leather, and whenever Biddy opened them, loose yellow papers fell from them like confetti. It made her feel shy all of a sudden, as though she were leaving smudgy fingerprints just by looking.

"The bathroom's just across the corridor," Morgaine said. She lit the fire with a whispered word and a flick of her finger, as Rowan did only when he was being very lazy or extravagant. Clearly, Council members at least had magic to spare. "You must be exhausted. I'll heat a bath for you and find you something clean to wear, and I'll have some supper for you when you come out."

Biddy hesitated, torn between her longing to be warm and dry and her determination to stay on her guard, which she suspected shouldn't involve hot baths and supper. And yet she had been completely within Morgaine's power already, right outside the entrance to the Undercastle. Surely whatever she had planned, she hadn't brought her all the way across London only to have her taken back again?

"Thank you," she said.

Morgaine was already on her way out of the room, the idea of Biddy refusing her having evidently never crossed her mind. "Would you like some tea? Or coffee?"

She didn't want either of those things. She wanted Rowan to come in and laugh at her for having been so worried; she wanted Hutchincroft to leap into her arms and nestle his lithe, soft body against her chest. She wanted things to be back the way they had always been. But that wasn't offered.

"Do you have cocoa?" she asked instead.

Morgaine smiled. "I think I might manage that."

The bathroom, too, was wondrous: glittering with white marble and ceramic and gold plating, its claw-footed tub perched like a benevolent dragon in the center. Hot water gushed from the taps, which she knew wasn't magic but might as well have been. At home they had a tin tub for special occasions, but the stream to fill it was some distance from the castle, so she usually stripped and washed in a basin in her room as quickly as possible. This one immersed her, stinging her scrapes and bruises then soothing them to nothing. Against her will, her throbbing muscles relaxed as the grime of the past few days soaked from her skin. A deep yawn engulfed her. She was so tired—not just in body, but of being alert, watching herself constantly for any missteps, not knowing whom to trust. It was an effort to stir from the water finally, to dry herself with fluffy lavender towels, dress in the soft nightgown Morgaine had left, and make her way back out to the sitting room where the woman who might be her enemy was waiting.

There was a little table by the fire now, and Morgaine had laid out a silver tray like the one that had brought their tea at the restaurant at St. James's Park. It was spread with hot buttered toast, tiny cupcakes iced in pink and white, and dishes of different jams with a flat silver knife beside them. A cup of cocoa sat in a saucer; Morgaine heated it through in a burst of magic as she handed it over, exactly the way Rowan always did.

"There," she said, with satisfaction. "Drink up. You must be exhausted."

Biddy took an obedient sip, and was immediately flooded with warmth and sweetness. Her eyes closed involuntarily, and the flicker of the fire at her side cast the room into sleepy shadows. She forced herself to sit up, to stay alert.

"It's very good," she said. "Thank you."

"Is there enough?" Morgaine asked. "It's been so long since anyone came to this place, especially a young person. We don't have young mages anymore. And of course I gave the maids the night and tomorrow off, once I knew you were coming, so the kitchen's a bit of a mystery. I could get you a boiled egg if you like. I *do* know how to boil an egg."

Maids. She hadn't thought of mages having servants, although the house from outside had looked very tall and Morgaine didn't seem the type to do any housework herself, even by magic. Biddy looked at the spotless surfaces with new eyes, and the thought of the young girls in the orphanage saving their money to go into service was like a breath of cold air through an open window. She was still tired, but her senses sharpened.

"No, please. This is fine." She hesitated, torn between not wishing to reveal how little she knew and not knowing how to find out any other way. "Where *is* this place?"

"My townhouse." Morgaine sat neatly in the chair opposite her. She was anxious, Biddy realized with surprise—perhaps as much so as Biddy. She hid it well, but her hands flexed on her lap before folding, taking all the nerves she wouldn't show on her face. "In Primrose Hill."

"That was where Rowan lived."

"Yes." A tiny beat, as if startled. "Yes, he did. You *do* know Rowan then?"

"He raised me." She had already decided that there was no point pretending otherwise to Morgaine. Nobody believed her when she lied anyway. "Since I was a baby. He and Hutchincroft."

Morgaine's laugh was equal parts bitter and delighted. "Rowan and Hutch, raising a young girl? Oh, I would have loved to have seen that."

"You will." Her eyes stung with unwelcome tears, and she tightened her grip on her cup so they didn't fall. The porcelain felt paper-thin, as though it might crumple at the pressure. "If I stay here. They promised they would come for me."

It sounded childish to her, as though she were claiming Father Christmas would be here, and the softening of Morgaine's face confirmed it. "I'm sorry. I shouldn't have laughed. If those two said they would come for you, they will. Do you have a way to get a message to them?"

"No." It was true, after all. Plainly the tree at St. James's Park was no longer safe. Rowan in theory had a means of getting in touch with *her*, but she wasn't about to mention the dream ring to Morgaine. Not yet.

"I see." Morgaine asked no questions, though the look she gave her was skeptical. "Well, we'll work something out. Don't worry. I don't think I ever told you my name, did I? I'm Morgaine Trevelyan."

"I know. Rowan told me all about you. So did Hutch."

"Did they? What did they say?"

"That you were on the Council. That you and Rowan used to be engaged to be married." She hesitated, not sure how far she should push. And yet she wanted to see what Morgaine would say. "They told me that you killed your familiar."

"Oh, I'm sure they did." Morgaine tucked a stray wisp of hair behind one ear, a frustrated, helpless movement. Something angry and bitter flashed behind her eyes. "I know what they think of me for that, and for everything I did after. But they never understood. I had no choice. Sometimes the world changes underneath you, and you have to find your footing as best you can."

The last sentence had a rehearsed quality, as though she had repeated it often. It came to Biddy that Morgaine was a good deal like her sitting room—luminous, beautiful, but the beauty was cultivated with the precision of a glass cutter or a watchmaker, and the luminosity was designed to conceal more than it revealed. Everything important was tucked away where nobody was supposed to look.

"I *am* on the Council," Morgaine said. Her hair and her voice had been smoothed back now. "That much is true, as you know. But I don't agree with everything they do. I try to change their minds when I can. When I can't—sometimes I have to take matters into my own hands."

"How?"

Morgaine's mouth twitched very slightly at one corner. In that movement was a shadow of someone who might have once agreed to marry Rowan. "Well. You're here, aren't you?"

"I don't know why," Biddy said honestly. "What do you want from me?"

"Nothing," Morgaine said firmly. "I promise. I only want to help. I couldn't have left you in that dungeon, at Storm's mercy—or lack thereof."

The mention of Storm was like a cold finger on the back of her neck. "Thank you," she said. "I thought he was going to kill me."

"He almost certainly would have." She said it matter-of-factly, but her hands gave their telltale flex. "People die in that dungeon all the time these days—mages who are supposed to be only detained on suspicion of illegal possession of magic, hedgewitches guilty of minor spellcraft. Everyone pretends not to notice, because they're never sure if Vaughan orders it or if Storm simply…loses control. The latter, probably, but if it didn't suit Vaughan, he wouldn't let it go on."

Biddy thought of the flash that had come over Storm's face before he had lunged for the spell in her heart, the sharp, birdlike twist of his neck. She shivered despite the heat of the fire.

She also, though, noticed one thing. Morgaine had said people died in the dungeon all the time. That meant she didn't usually save them.

"Why do you stay with them and watch all this happen, if you don't agree with it?" she asked. "Rowan wanted you to run away with him and fight back."

Morgaine made a sound that might have been a snort or a bark of disgust. "Oh, that's what Rowan imagines he's been doing all these decades, is it? Fighting back. By breaking into the vault, stealing magic from us a handful at a time, and throwing it back out into the world. He always did like the idea of himself as a hero."

"He gives magic to people that need it, he says."

"But Vaughan clamps down harder on it as a result," Morgaine countered. "I'm trying to persuade the Council to relax the laws, to allow leftover magic to be given exactly where Rowan wants it, but there isn't a hope with Rowan scraping our supplies dry. He may be helping individuals; the system remains unchanged. And in the meantime, any mage suspected of helping him gets punished. He's a danger to himself and others, and he won't see it."

A danger. Biddy had been trying not to think about Storm's memory, about Rowan's cruelty and Storm's agony and fear—to shut it out, as she might a moth beating against a lit window. Now that window cracked; the sound of Storm's inhuman screams as the ravenstone tore apart his flesh from the inside made it through. She put down her cup carefully, trying to hide the shaking of her hands.

"That's what you said in the Council," she said, as normally as she could. "That Rowan was dangerous, and I shouldn't trust him. That he had lost sight of why he was fighting you and that he was using me to do it. Did you mean it?"

"I honestly don't know." Morgaine straightened a little self-consciously, remembering herself or something else. "I haven't spoken to Rowan in seventy years. For what it's worth, I *do* understand why he won't tell Vaughan where this schism is. He never trusted the Council even when he was a part of it; there's no way he'd hand over a rare source of magic to Vaughan now. But I can't understand why he would keep hiding it for so long once he was free—and I truly don't understand why he would endanger you with the key to it. The Rowan I used to know wouldn't have done that."

"But he *didn't*." The protest tumbled out of her. It might have been what Morgaine was trying to get from her all along; it might all be a trick. She didn't care. She had to know that Rowan was who she thought he was, which meant she needed Morgaine to concede it too. "Not in the way you mean. I *was* meant as bait, just as Vaughan said. But just to lure in a mage that he could question. He wanted to find out why the Council have been trying so hard to catch him recently, and why they have so much more magic to do it. I said I would help. He never found a schism, and he never put any spell in me. It's all a lie."

Morgaine shook her head, more in confusion than denial. "It isn't, Bridget—I swear. I was there when they brought Rowan in sixteen years ago. He had definitely been near a schism. And I saw the spell in your heart when the wisps brought you in last night. It was Rowan's spellmark, cast the night we caught him. If he told you anything else, *that* was a lie."

"Why would he lie?"

She'd meant it as a challenge, but Morgaine took it as a serious question. "I don't know. I'm sorry." She paused. "As to why we're trying to catch him—we're not, any more than usual, as far as I know. Certainly no new magic has been allocated to it. Storm would love to mount a hunt, if Vaughan would let him, but he's hardly ever allotted magic these days. It's a sore point with him." Her mouth twisted wryly. "One of many."

Biddy took another sip of her cocoa to hide her disquiet. It was cooling now, but so familiar it made her heart ache. If she closed her eyes again, she could imagine herself back in the castle kitchen, feeding Hutchincroft the crusts of her morning toast under the table while Rowan leaned against the kitchen bench with his fingers wrapped around his mug and his eyes twinkling. She kept her eyes open.

It couldn't be true. It couldn't. Even if Rowan had hurt Storm, even if Morgaine was right and his actions were dangerous and misguided as well as heroic—*instead* of heroic—he would never have used her. He would never have lied to her.

"It's almost dawn," Morgaine said into the silence. She rose to her feet, smoothing out her skirt on reflex. "I'll make up a bed for you. We can see about finding Rowan when it—"

Biddy interrupted her. An idea had come to her in a welcome flash, and she seized it. Of course. "Rowan couldn't have put that spell in my heart," she said. "Not if you think he found and hid the schism the night you captured him. He didn't know me then."

The Council did catch me once, a few months before you came, Rowan had said. *You've always been safe, I promise.*

Morgaine, frowning, sat back down. "That can't be true."

"Why not? You said you hadn't spoken to him for seventy years."

"I haven't. But—" Morgaine bit her lip, hesitating, and Biddy saw the same calculation of what to tell and how that she had seen behind Rowan's eyes many times. She saw the moment the resolve snapped into place, the decision to tell everything. "Bridget. Have you ever known Rowan to own a locket made of silver, with a tree engraved on the outside?"

"Rowan's never owned anything like that," Biddy said. "He made me a locket for my birthday once, from the wood of the old oak tree, because I had read about lockets in a book and I wanted one. He said he'd never had one."

"I'm sure he said that," Morgaine said carefully. "But he did own this one. I took it from him when he handed himself in sixteen years ago."

Suddenly, she wasn't at all sure she wanted to hear this story. The flare of hope, so bright, was fading without her quite knowing why. "You were there?"

"I was part of the team that brought him in." Her head raised proudly, but her cheeks had flushed. "I asked to be part of it. I thought I could at least keep him from being hurt."

"Could you?"

"No. He fought too hard—it was idiotic, you can't fight wisps. But I did get the two amulets he was carrying from him before anyone else searched him. The first was the ravenstone—I knew it very well. I should have handed it over, but I didn't want Storm or the Council to have it. I thought it might come in useful."

"*Oh.*" A piece locked into place with a snap. Storm, in the frightening haze after she had come out of his mind. *There might be a few things I could tell him about the night Rowan escaped last time.* "You got the ravenstone back to him, didn't you? That's how he escaped."

"I did. It took me a week. When they brought him back unconscious to the dungeons one night, I dropped it where he could find it. He never even knew I'd been there. He got out through that tiny window in there, you saw it? It didn't have the grate over it then. Everyone assumed that Storm had missed it when he captured him. But the other amulet was a locket. I could see the magic clinging to it, but I didn't know what it was for. There was a lock of hair inside it. Have you finished your cocoa? Would you like some more toast?"

Biddy shook her head, even though her cocoa was just powder in the bottom of her mug and she hadn't touched the food on the tray. "No, thank you. What was the locket for?"

"I still don't know. But I kept it because—well, because I thought the hair in it belonged to Rowan. It *should* have. It was clearly part of a spell; when a spell uses blood or hair, it's usually from the mage in question. Magic doesn't give you credit for somebody else's sacrifice. And...do you know how a dream ring works?"

"I've used one," she said, very slowly.

"Then you'll know you need something of the person you intend to visit. I thought I could use it to enter his dreams and find him, after he escaped. I wasn't trying to hunt him down," she added quickly, as though Biddy had accused her. "I just wanted to talk to him. I wanted him to know—" She broke off.

"Know what?"

"Oh, I don't know." She huffed a sigh, and looked away. "I wanted him to know I hadn't meant things to go the way they did between us all those years ago. I wanted him to know I was working against the Council too, and perhaps we could help each other. But when I tried to use it, I found you instead. Your hair *is* a similar shade, now I've seen you. It was more so then. I suppose it darkened as you grew up."

Her mouth felt dry. "Where was I? Was I with Rowan?"

"Not that first time. I found you in a nightmare of cobwebs and screaming lights. You were very small—not yet able to talk. But you didn't know who Rowan was. I could tell that through the dream. You had nobody. I stayed with you and comforted you until you woke up. I couldn't understand what it meant."

Before she had anybody. Before she was in Hy-Brasil, before the shipwreck, when she wasn't yet old enough to talk. But if she hadn't known who Rowan was, if he had been captured before she came to the island, then how could her hair possibly have been in a locket around Rowan's neck?

Oh God. No, please no.

"I remember when you came again." She could hear her own voice, too calm and precise. "I was four."

"I know." Morgaine smiled, but it was a sad smile. "You told me. You were in a good dream that time, a dream of trees and black rabbits. I asked you for your name and where you were, but you told me Rowan had said never give your name and home to a stranger in case they were one of the fair folk. And then I knew I had found Rowan after all."

Rowan *had* said that, when she was little. She had forgotten after a while, because she had never met any strangers. They all had her name now, Storm and Morgaine and Miss Finchley and Anna, who was probably going to die now because Biddy had been taken before Rowan could help her. Besides, she was no longer certain that Rowan could help anybody.

He always did like the idea of himself as a hero, Morgaine had said.

"I never understood what you were doing there with him, wherever he was," Morgaine was saying. "And you would never tell me. I didn't ask you after that first time. I just liked to see you, and to see that you were happy. I visited you a few times, then I stopped. You were starting to ask questions yourself, and I was worried you would take them to Rowan."

"But I wasn't with him the first time." The words felt pulled from her—not from her heart, as the spell had been, but from somewhere even deeper and more painful. "Was I?"

Morgaine shook her head. "You were alone, somewhere dark. I wished I could find you."

"And the locket was on Rowan when he was captured. You're certain of that?"

"Of course. I couldn't have gotten it from him any other way. So, you see, he must have at least known you before, even if you weren't yet living with him." She seemed, belatedly, to notice Biddy's growing horror. "Perhaps that was what he meant, and you misunderstood."

"I didn't misunderstand." She felt sick, the cocoa churning her stomach. "He said that I came to him in a shipwreck, a few months after he'd escaped the Undercastle. He said he found me with the spell already inside me. But he already had my hair in a locket when he was taken."

Morgaine had visited her dreams when she was little. It was something Biddy knew indisputably to be true, amid all the hearsay and promises and stories. She could not have done that without Biddy's hair. It was possible she was lying about the locket, that she had gained Biddy's hair some other way, in some other time. But it was too unlikely a lie, too small a piece to try to reshape to fit the picture Biddy had always been given. It felt true.

Which meant that what Rowan had told her was not.

"Storm was right, wasn't he?" she said. "You all were. He put that spell in my heart that night."

"Well," Morgaine said carefully. "I agree it means he lied about when you came to him. It doesn't need to mean he put the spell in your heart."

"But you think he did." It wasn't a question.

"Yes. I'm sorry, but I just can't see another reason why that spell would bear his mark. Or why that locket would have your hair, if it wasn't part of some strong magic."

"He lied to me." That was the part that kept repeating in her head, like the chorus of a terrible song. "He does that, doesn't he?"

"Yes," Morgaine agreed. The bitterness was back in her voice. "When he thinks he has to, he does lie."

Biddy sat very still. Nothing Storm had done had made her heart feel like this. Something deep within it was cracking, and any movement would break it apart.

How do you know? Storm had asked her, when she had insisted that Rowan had put no spell in her. *You wouldn't remember.* He was right. All her life, she had only ever had Rowan's word about anything, and she had believed it without hesitation. Because she loved him, because he was brave and laughing and kind and wonderful, because he was the only human soul she had in all the world.

But he had never told her about the spell in her heart until he needed her to know it. He had never told her about the Council, or Vaughan, or Morgaine, or Storm. He had kept things from her all her life, and now she was finding that some of the things he had told her weren't even true. When it came to it, she couldn't believe anything he said. She couldn't believe anything he was, or had ever been to her. She couldn't believe, after all, that when he had put her in the orphanage last week he really hadn't meant to abandon her there to be taken. She didn't know what his plans really were.

Morgaine seemed to remember she was there. "Bridget," she said, more softly. "God knows I don't want to stand up for Rowan. But if it helps, whatever his faults may be, he'd never willingly hurt anybody. For one thing, Hutch wouldn't let him."

Hutch. The thought of him made it so much worse. Even when she had been unsure of Rowan over the last few days, she had never doubted Hutchincroft. But Rowan couldn't do anything without Hutch knowing. If Rowan had lied to her, so had Hutch.

"He hurt Storm," Biddy heard herself say. "He made him a monster, didn't he? That's why Storm hates him so much."

I'm not doing anything. The light, soft note of cruelty as he had goaded Storm into his own destruction. She had told herself it sounded nothing like Rowan, that Storm might have imagined it, but it wasn't true. She had heard it herself, just once, when Rowan had taken the key from dream-Morgaine's neck.

It's what he does. Tricks you into betraying yourself.

"Bridget—"

"I think if I slept now, Rowan might be able to find me," she interrupted. She knew that whatever Morgaine was about to say would be to make her feel better, and suddenly she couldn't bear to hear it. "He had a dream ring before. He might be able to use it again."

He hadn't come to her the last few nights, it was true. But if the others were right, and he had meant her to be captured by the Council, then surely he would come to see where she had gone now.

Morgaine nodded. Her eyes were searching Biddy's face, worried. "Good. And I'm sure you could use the rest. Would you mind if I put you in the back bedroom? It's small, and it hasn't been properly aired for a guest, but all the other rooms are in the front of the house. I wouldn't want you to be seen from the street."

Biddy started to laugh, and bit down on it before it could unravel into tears. She had been in a dungeon that night, and in an orphanage the night before. Whatever the back bedroom was, it would probably be more comfortable than anything she had ever seen in her life. And yet she couldn't imagine ever sleeping again.

It was beautiful, of course. The room was on the floor above, across the stairwell from a larger bedroom that must have been Morgaine's. It was darker and more worn than the rooms downstairs, in an out-of-sight sort of way—the dark wood furniture was probably older pieces that had been moved from other rooms once they were replaced, giving it a mismatched, cluttered look. But the wallpaper was a delicate blue grey, the bed enormous and strewn with pale cream cushions. The bedcovers were a soft green that would have reminded her of the forest moss at home, if they weren't so rich, so luxurious, so obviously the product of an expensive London shop.

"You can borrow some of my clothes tomorrow," Morgaine said, as Biddy settled under the sheets. "They'll fit quite well, I think."

It was exactly what she had longed for, with almost comical precision, the morning she had looked at herself critically in the glass on Hy-Brasil and judged herself against Morgaine's effortless style. It didn't seem so important now.

"Thank you," she said, because Morgaine was being kind, and anything else sounded like self-pity.

"You're very welcome." Morgaine's hand made a small, aborted gesture, as though about to reach out and stroke Biddy's hair or squeeze her shoulder. In the end, though, she just turned off the gas lamp by the bed. "Sleep well. I'll be downstairs if you want anything."

Morgaine had been right: She did need the rest. Her muscles throbbed against the softness of the bed, and her eyes ached to close. But her thoughts were churning like the sea in the grip of a storm. Whenever she tried to settle, they threw images to the surface, as she had once been thrown to the shores of Hy-Brasil. Morgaine seated at the Council table, not to be trusted; the sympathy in her eyes before she had turned off the lamp. Rowan telling her stories soft and quiet by the light of the fire; the edge to his voice as he had goaded Storm. The children at the asylum, eating gruel in their identical rows. Storm's screams. Vaughan's eye scouring her soul.

The clock on the mantelpiece ticked over many times before her breathing slowed and she drifted into dreams.

She dreamed of London streets, hard and unforgiving and wreathed in cruel fog. She dreamed that someone was searching for her, and she was searching for them, but she didn't know what they looked like. In her sleep, she frowned and twisted under the covers.

She didn't see Rowan this time. But at last, from very far away, she heard him call her name.

"Biddy? Biddy, can you hear me?"

His voice, so familiar in the midst of her unfamiliar doubts, struck her like a blow. She had to fight past a lump in her throat to reply. "I'm here!"

"Biddy." The word was a sigh of relief. "Thank God. We've been looking for you everywhere. Hutch said you'd have to fall asleep sometime, but... Where are you?"

"Morgaine's flat." Biddy kept her own voice neutral. Tears were pricking her eyes, and she wasn't sure if they were relief or anger.

Part of her had been hoping she wouldn't find him at all. If he could talk to her in her sleep now, then where had he been the last few days? Why would he come now, when she had already escaped her captors?

"Morgaine?" She could see the way his brows would draw together, considering. "What are you—? Are you safe?"

"Yes. She helped me get out of the Undercastle. She's hiding me here." She hesitated, loyalty pricking her conscience. "It might be a trap."

If Rowan had any doubts, he didn't show them. "Never mind that. I love walking into traps. I don't suppose she gave this one an address?"

"Primrose Hill."

"Whereabouts in Primrose Hill? Wait. Can you picture it for me?"

Biddy did her best. The hard stone streets around them flickered, and resolved into the front of the house, then the drawing room with its white walls and pale blue curtains and ornate fireplace, then the bedroom with its heavier wood furnishings.

Rowan muttered something that she wasn't sure she was supposed to hear. "I thought so. What's she done to it? All right, I definitely know where that is. We'll be right there. Just wait for us."

He was gone before she could answer.

The streets came back, cold and lonely. She wandered them for a long time.

Biddy woke to the sound of voices, muffled and angry. There was no confusion, no gradual return to awareness—she knew exactly where she was, why the bed was so soft and her nightclothes so warm and silken, what had happened the night before. She knew to whom the voices belonged. And part of her, the same part that had wished Rowan would stay away forever, wanted nothing more than to turn back over, curl up in the bedcovers, and hide.

Instead, she threw back the blankets and sat up, wincing as her stiff muscles protested. Her knees and her back ached as though the hours in those chimneys had aged her a hundred years. The curtains were drawn tight, but the sliver of light spilling under the door was enough to let her squint at the clock on the mantel. Not quite eight o'clock. They would have missed her at the Undercastle by now.

The voices grew clearer as she followed them down the stairs to the sitting room. Morgaine's first, biting and poised as if they were meeting in a ballroom. "You found us, then?"

"You didn't exactly make it difficult for us." Rowan. She could hear the roll of his eyes. "This is my flat."

"It was Vaughan's name on the lease, as I recall. Besides, that was seventy years ago. It was very clear you weren't coming back."

"You did your best to make sure of that, didn't you? Or did I imagine you there helping Storm to bring me in sixteen years ago?"

"Oh, grow up, Rowan! Obviously I was trying to protect you."

"Well, you did a wonderful job of it. I still have the scars." His voice softened. "Morgaine, I didn't come to fight you. Where is she?"

Biddy pushed open the door to the sitting room.

Rowan and Morgaine stood almost nose to nose by the cold embers of the fire, as Biddy had seen them face each other in Rowan's enchanted nightmare. Hutchincroft was bristling at Rowan's feet, ears back and tail raised; Rowan, disheveled and streaked with soot, had his hands on his hips. Morgaine was in her clothes from the night before, and her hair was tumbling from its pins as though she'd been awakened from sleep. Biddy took them in at a glance, oddly frozen, a tableau against the drawn curtains. Then Hutchincroft saw her, and the spell was broken.

His ears shot forward, and he was across the room in a flash. He bounded toward her, and she couldn't help but scoop him up, hold him tightly, bury her face in his soft fur as he buried himself desperately into her shoulder. Whatever Rowan had done, Hutch's love was a warm, fierce, protective thing in her arms. She had missed him so much.

Then she heard Rowan's laugh, joyful and relieved, and her heart hardened.

"*There* you are! Where have you been? Are you all right?"

"Don't come near me!" she snapped—he had taken a step forward, and she knew in a moment he would have held her as she was holding Hutchincroft. And if that happened, she wasn't sure she could stay as angry as she wanted to be. He looked exactly the same—no longer Storm's Rowan, or even Morgaine's, but her own. It threatened the phantom version of him she had started to build out of doubts and suspicions, and she couldn't afford to let it go. "Not another step. You lied to me."

"What?" Rowan stopped, bewildered. "What did I lie about?"

"Everything!" Hutchincroft was pulling back, confused; she deposited him on the ground and folded her arms tightly against them both. "For starters, you told me the wisps wouldn't come to the school. You told me it would be one mage, you'd be watching me the whole time, and when they came you'd stop them from taking me."

Rowan's face was grave now. "I meant to, I swear. I made a mistake—a big one. I had no idea they would come for you in force like that."

"Then where *were* you? After the first day, you just went away."

"I know." She watched him glance away quickly, gather himself, then look back at her once more. "After the first day, we started seeing wisps on the street. Vaughan's, we think. Just glints at first, on rooftops, scurrying up walls, catching the streetlights around our lodgings. We stopped using magic entirely so as not to attract their attention, which is why we couldn't talk to you at nights anymore or go near the school. I left you a note in the tree at St. James's Park, nothing incriminating, just in case you grew worried enough to come look, but the same night the wisps swarmed the tree and took it. That was when I knew we were in real trouble."

The claw marks on the tree. Vaughan's eyes across the square, watching her leave a note of her own. Her anger didn't fade, but it quieted, enough to listen.

"They were getting closer," Rowan continued. "I thought if I could draw them away from you, then double back, I could lose them. We let them get close one sunset, then took them all the way to York. I was sure they'd send a mage for you in daylight, if they sent one at all, and I knew I could be back by then. It was a mistake. They must have guessed you were a trap, though I don't see how. Did they say anything to you?"

She laughed, bitterly. It hurt. "Did they *say* anything to me? They had me for a whole day! Storm tried to tear the spell from me by force."

Something hard and dark flickered in his eyes, and in it Biddy saw the Rowan of Storm's memories, the version she had feared to come downstairs and find. "I'll kill him."

"Never mind him! Why didn't you come get me out of the Undercastle?"

She had changed the subject as much to bring Rowan back as to get answers, and it worked on both counts. The anger flickered away again like a candle going out. "We did—or we tried. You must have beaten us to it. We broke in after dark, by the front entrance. It took me that long to reach you and come up with a plan. I've broken into the vault many times, but nobody's ever gotten out from the Undercastle dungeons."

"Except you," Biddy pointed out.

"Except me," he agreed, quietly, as if admitting a fault. "By the time we got there, the dungeon was empty. They nearly caught us."

That gave Biddy pause. She remembered the commotion in the corridors as she had clung to the inside of the chimney; the sudden call to arms that had sent the guards fleeing the room. She had assumed her absence had been discovered, but Morgaine hadn't known anything about it. It was entirely possible that she and Rowan and Hutch had missed each other by that little, in that dark underground labyrinth.

"I know I let you down," Rowan said into the silence. "I know it's my fault you were taken, when I promised you wouldn't be. Of course you're angry. But you can't honestly think we *meant* for it to happen? That it was the *plan*?"

She had, in her darkest moments, when her memories of him had twisted into something alien and unknown. Now that he was standing in front of her, in the light of day, she wasn't so certain. It even seemed childish, part of an old belief that Rowan was infallible and things always happened as he intended. The cold grip around her heart loosened, but not enough. It wasn't the worst of it.

"You still lied to me about where I came from," she said. "The Council told me."

"How could they—?" He heaved a weary sigh before she could answer. "It doesn't matter. Yeah. All right. That I did lie about, and it was wrong."

Deep down, she must have had one last, faint hope she'd been wrong about that as well, because hearing it from him ripped that hope out at the roots. "You didn't find me with magic sealed inside. You put it there yourself."

"What—? No!" The bewilderment was back on his face. "That magic was there when I found you. It was why I took you, to keep you safe."

Morgaine spoke up for the first time, her voice dripping acid. "If you wanted to keep her safe, perhaps you shouldn't have buried magic in her heart and sent her to be captured by the Council."

"Don't you *dare* talk to me about how to keep anyone safe." Rowan turned a glare on her. "Not after what you did to keep safe yourself. I didn't bury anything in her heart. I told the truth about that—I did, Biddy, I swear. I found you with that spell in place. I only lied about *where* I found you. You didn't come to the island on your own."

The shipwreck. The waves bringing her to shore. She should have known—now she had been in the world, she knew it didn't sound true. It sounded like something in a book. But all her life, all she'd had were books. She hadn't been able to tell.

The next question lodged in her throat. She swallowed several times before she could spit it out, knowing that when she did everything really would change.

"How did I come to Hy-Brasil?"

"I found you," Rowan said. "In London. I found you one night when I was looking for magic, a few months after Storm captured me. I brought you to the island."

It wasn't what she had braced herself for, all that long night. It was a different lie, and so it caught her entirely off guard. She balled her hands into fists, tightly, until it hurt.

"Where did you take me from?" she said, and managed to keep her voice from trembling. "Did you take me from my parents?"

"*No.*" He started forward as if to touch her, but she flinched away, and he stopped. "No, I took you from the same place I returned you to a few nights ago."

"The school?"

"The school. The Rookwood Asylum for Destitute Girls. You were around a year old—they didn't know exactly when you were born. Your mother had brought you there and disappeared without a trace. Nobody else had claimed you. But I didn't know any of this at the time. All I knew was that I was crossing Spitalfields in the dark hours before dawn, and the spell cried out. It was so sharp and so sudden, like the swoop and cry of a hawk in the air, and it sank its talons into me. I've never felt anything like it. I thought it was an amulet, or just a particularly powerful fragment of magic. When I realized I'd followed it to you, I couldn't believe it. Magic doesn't bury itself in the human heart by chance. Someone must have done that to you, but I had no idea who. I still don't."

"If that's true," Morgaine said, "why does it have your spellmark on it?"

"It doesn't," he snapped. "Or if it does, it's probably because I've tried so many times over the years to get it out. I *told* her that. I tried the night I found her. It was locked in too tight. That's why I had to make a decision." He turned back to Biddy. "I could have left you there. But the call of that magic was very strong—it was only a matter of time before the Council found you. They would certainly take you, and I didn't know what they would do to you. Or I could take you with me, try to keep you safe. I thought I might be able to free the magic, and then I could return you to the mainland— somewhere better than that place. But I never could."

"*We* never could." Hutchincroft stepped forward, in human form. He had melted into it so softly she hadn't seen. "I told Rowan to take you. If you hate him, Biddy, you should hate me too. But he's telling the truth, I promise. The magic was there when we came."

"I don't hate you." It was hard to talk around the lump in her throat. "So that was why you put me in the Rookwood Asylum?"

"It was where you started," Hutchincroft confirmed. "It was where you stood the greatest chance of being found quickly— where the magic would give the strongest signal. We wanted it to be over as soon as possible, for all our sakes."

"He means *I* did," Rowan added. "It was my plan, and it was stupid. I should have thought more about the risks to the school, as well as to you."

"But—" She pinched the bridge of her nose, trying to hold the spinning fragments of her new story together. "The Council said that you'd found a rift in the world. A crack where magic could enter. They said you'd hidden the key to it in my heart."

Rowan made a peculiar sound, something that wanted to be a laugh but lodged halfway. "Jesus, not that again. They kept on at me about rifts the whole time I was there last time. Hutch and I were looking for one when he was first caught—there had been things happening in the East End, the sort of storybook miracles that you get around a new schism. But that was months before I met you, I told you. And I *hadn't* found one. If I had, don't you think I would have used it since then?" He shook his head, frustrated. "Forget that—Morgaine, you know what Storm did to me to get me to talk. If I'd actually had the secret he wanted, do you really think I would have been brave enough not to tell him?"

"Yes," she said, as if startled. "Of course I do."

An odd flash passed between them, almost of recognition.

"But I wasn't," Rowan said. "I didn't find anything."

"Are you *sure*?"

His laugh this time was done better. "Pretty sure, yeah. It's the sort of thing I'd remember."

Remember. Perhaps it was simply because Biddy had been trying so hard not to dwell on the memory of Rowan in Storm's head, but the word resonated inside her, like the strange echoes in the ruins by the shore.

"When Storm tried to get the spell out of my heart," she said slowly, "I resisted him. And I found myself in one of Storm's memories instead—one from before magic left the world. Why would that happen?"

"I don't know." Rowan turned, surprised. "What sort of spell was he using?"

"Just a summoning word," Morgaine answered for her. "I was there. That shouldn't cause any kind of shift of memories. Are you sure that's what it was, Bridget?"

The unfamiliar sound of her full name was almost enough to make her doubt herself. After all, she wasn't a mage. She knew nothing about magic. She pushed that doubt aside. "Of course I'm sure. It isn't something I'd imagine, is it?"

Hutchincroft's eyes, which never truly stopped being those of a rabbit, widened. "Rowan. The crack in the world. What if you did find it, and you *don't* remember? What if you don't remember because a memory is precisely what you planted in Biddy's heart?"

There was a very long silence.

"I couldn't have," Rowan said, but he didn't sound at all certain. He leaned back against the wall beside the fireplace, arms folded, as if suddenly a little less sure of his footing. "I'd know. *You'd* know."

"I wasn't with you. I'd already been captured myself. It's the one day, in all our days together, I don't know what you did. And it would explain why, when Storm tried to remove it, it rebounded back on him and triggered a memory of his in return. Memory spells do that sometimes."

"It never did that when *I* tried to remove it."

"Well, of course not," Hutch said reasonably. "Not if the memory you were trying to remove was already yours. It would explain why you couldn't find a spellmark either. You would take it for your own magic reflected back."

Rowan shook his head without conviction. "No."

"We *were* looking for a rift. We were close. You might have found it. And right before they took you, you might have taken the knowledge from your mind and hidden it, so they could never torture it from you."

"In the heart of a *child*? You couldn't possibly believe I'd do that."

"You might not have had a choice." Hutchincroft's voice was becoming more certain. "A memory that important—that would be a very powerful spell. You couldn't store that in a stone or a tree—it would need to be within a living soul. We don't know where Biddy was at that time, or how she came to be at the Rookwood Asylum those months afterward. Her heart might have been the only safe place. It's possible."

"You would have had time," Morgaine said slowly. "Just. And the Council let Hutch go in exchange for you. He wasn't in the dungeons when you were brought in, to notice what you'd done."

"He'd have noticed after I escaped! Hutch, if a piece of my mind was missing, surely when I got back to the island you would—"

"Master, your mind was *broken*," Hutchincroft said. It was the first time Biddy had ever heard him use the traditional address between familiar and mages. "You'd been in the Undercastle for seven days. They'd taken every ounce of magic you had in your blood, and they'd hurt you terribly, and flying five hundred miles as a raven took everything you had left. By the time you got home, you could barely remember *me*. You made it through the window in the turret, you transformed back at least most of the way, and that was *it*. You just lay there on the floor and shivered. I didn't know what to do. You were so cold, and so ill, and I didn't have any magic of my own to help you. I couldn't even turn human."

"Hey. You did fine." His voice gentled. "I remember that much. You looked after me. You probably saved my life. I didn't need you to be human."

"You did," he corrected. "You were bleeding, and I couldn't stop it. You were thirsty, and I couldn't bring you water. I could drag you blankets with my stupid teeth, but I couldn't get you to a bed, and I couldn't get you warm. It was the worst time of my life."

"I was all right in the end."

"Yes, you were. And that was all I cared about. So no, I didn't notice if a few shards of your memories were missing when they finally pulled back together. I would have thought nothing of it had I done so. I was so happy to have you back. I just wanted you better."

"But why didn't *I* notice?" He straightened from the wall, restless and frustrated. "If you're right, and I hid my memory in an infant girl, I must have meant to go back and retrieve it from her! I must have. I wouldn't just leave her in danger. I wouldn't just *forget*. I would have left myself something to trigger the memory, after it was safe. Did they take something from me, in the dungeon?"

Hutch shook his head, in confusion rather than denial. "I don't know! I told you! All I thought of was you."

"Morgaine took something," Biddy spoke up. Her head was still spinning, but she felt curiously calm. The spinning was bringing things into place, the way she always imagined a carousel ride winding down. "She took a locket from you. And it had my hair in it, months before you said you met me."

It was Morgaine's turn to grow quiet.

"If I were trapped, and the Council was coming for me," Rowan said slowly. "If I knew where a crack in the world was to be found, and I didn't want the Council to know it, and I removed the knowledge from my mind before they could reach me and buried it in the safest place I could find... Then that's what I would do. I would have something that would unlock the memory, so that I could go back to it and get it out. Like a locket with a child's hair in it. I would have tried to hide it somewhere on me, and hoped nobody would find it."

"It was in the secret pocket of your coat," Morgaine said. Her scorn had drained away all at once; beneath, she looked faintly sick. "I knew where you hid things you didn't want people to take. And I took it from you."

"It wasn't your fault," Rowan said, more gently than Biddy had yet seen them speak to each other. "If you hadn't, the Council likely would have. It was better in your hands than theirs."

"It *is* my fault," she corrected him. "Because I didn't give it back. I slipped you the ravenstone so you could escape. I could have given you back the locket at the same time. But I kept it. And as it was— you might never have found Biddy at all."

"Oh, I found her," he said ironically. "That explains why the Council never noticed the magic in her heart calling out. It was asleep until I came near her again, months later, and awakened it. It was calling to *me*, as it was supposed to do. Only I didn't know what it was. I couldn't even recognize it. But why? Of all the places I could hide magic, surely I could have done better than an innocent little girl."

"We don't know for certain any of this happened," Hutchincroft said—perhaps because he liked certainties, and always had, but Biddy suspected he just hated to see Rowan so horrified.

"We know," Rowan said. "It's the only thing that makes sense. Besides, I can feel the memory missing now. The way you cut yourself and you don't notice until you look down and see blood. I don't know what I did the day before I was taken, and I should know that."

"What do we do?" Biddy asked, into the silence that followed. They looked at her, startled, as though they had forgotten she was there. It gave her a welcome burst of irritation. "Well? There has to be something we can do. You always say that working out the problem is half the solution."

Rowan laughed, very softly. "God, do I? That sounds unbearable."

"We need to get the locket," Hutchincroft said. "If we get that, we can unlock the memory in Biddy's heart. We'll know what happened. And then . . . and then we'll know what to do next."

"If you did find a schism," Morgaine said to Rowan, "then perhaps it hasn't quite closed. Perhaps there *is* a way of opening it further, the way we were working on all those years ago."

"Maybe." Rowan's brow was furrowed, and his eyes were dark. He shook himself out before he could get too deep into thought, and turned to Morgaine. "We'll see. Do you have the locket?"

"Not here, obviously," she said. "I wasn't going to have your magic in this house when the Council came to call! But it's safe."

"Safe where?"

For the first time, she didn't quite meet his eyes. "The Undercastle."

"What—?" His eyebrows shot up, somewhere between incredulous and exasperated. "What's it doing there?"

"I had to keep it somewhere, didn't I?" It might have sounded reasonable, had she not been so clearly flustered. "It's in my desk there—it has been for years."

"Nice to know you just left the key to my memories lying about with the spare pens."

"Oh, for God's sake. It's locked up safe, obviously. Don't be such a child. I can bring it here."

"Then that's what we'll do," Rowan said, with a nod at Hutch. "The most important thing is to unlock that memory. This is going to be all right, Biddy. I promise."

She said nothing. She knew now that he could promise nothing of the kind.

Chapter Thirteen

*B*iddy felt as though she had been trapped within walls for a thousand years already. She had never thought of herself as an outdoors person particularly. Unlike Rowan, she liked curling up in the library by the fire when the skies threatened and closing the shutters against the snow; she had always been more entranced by stories of bustling streets and close-packed buildings than of wide-open spaces. But she was starting to realize that the castle at Hy-Brasil, with its ruined walls and wind and rain whistling through eternally open windows, was not a true measure of what it meant to be inside. Even in the library, the only truly watertight room, there was always a breeze to be found. Morgaine's house, with the curtains drawn too tightly to see even the smoggy London sky, was too much like being deep in the walls of the Undercastle. If she couldn't be home, then she longed to at least step out the door, just for a moment, to stand with the sunlight on her face and space around her and a thousand sights and sounds in her eyes and ears. She knew it would be dangerous, with the magic in her heart calling all the mages in the city to her, but she couldn't feel it. Her terrors were all of the dark, of being confined in a tiny space with the rustle of Storm's wings and the creeping cold of stone.

But it wasn't possible. She accepted this with only a stifled sigh. Rowan was complaining enough for both of them.

"I still think I ought to go with you," he said, as Morgaine pulled on her gloves.

In the light of day, on the other side of last night's misery, Biddy could find it in herself to be interested anew in Morgaine's clothes. They had changed with the fashions from what Biddy had seen in Rowan's dream, yet they had the same heady aura of glamour, of beauty, of letting their wearer walk across a street and *belong* in a way that Biddy couldn't imagine. Oh, she was wearing them herself now, technically: Morgaine had found her a white lace dress, only a little too loose in places, with long petticoats that drifted with her like shreds of cloud. It wasn't the same. She felt stiff in it, unfamiliar, as though the clothes were wearing her and finding her too small. Morgaine wore hers effortlessly, without thought, as a second skin. She had a suit today, pinstriped grey with black trim, and her hair was piled on her head to frame her face in soft tendrils—what Morgaine had told her, seeing Biddy watching her pin it up earlier, was called a pompadour. She'd offered to do Biddy's hair just like it, but Biddy had declined regretfully on the grounds that it seemed to take a long time and Rowan would probably implode.

"Oh really?" Morgaine returned. "And what logic do you have to justify that?"

"It's my memory. It's my magic."

"Well, this is your house, isn't it, according to you?" She didn't wait for a reply. "You know you can't come, Rowan. It's too dangerous—for you, for Hutchincroft, and most of all for Bridget. I'll only be an hour or two."

"And how do we know you won't come back with Storm?"

Morgaine raised her eyebrows. "You *are* in a mood, aren't you? I bet you haven't had a cup of tea this morning."

"Of course I haven't! I've been trying to break into the Undercastle all night—I wasn't going to stop for tea before coming here, was I? And I'm not in a mood," he added, somewhat belatedly. "I'm trying to avoid being betrayed again."

"By asking if I *plan to betray you*? Does that usually work for you?" She selected a wide-brimmed hat, white with a cream ribbon. "I don't, if that makes you feel any better. There's breakfast in the kitchen. Stay in this room as much as you can, away from the windows. You should be safe, unless you were followed. I suppose you *weren't* followed?" She looked Rowan up and down. "What did you do to your hand?"

"Burned it," he said briefly, with a glance at the bandage. "They set a trap for me with an amulet a week or so ago."

"I suppose you also know that once you'd touched it, there was a spell buried in it to track you wherever you went?"

He rolled his eyes. "Of course I did! That's why I burned it."

"You said the amulet burned you!" Biddy protested. It shouldn't have stung particularly, in the swarm of all the other lies and half-truths, but it did.

"I said the burn was where the amulet had touched me," he corrected, not quite looking at her. "It was. It left a spellmark. I scorched it off before I came home. It's safe now."

"Is it?"

"Well, it had better be! It hurt like mad. I'd hate to think I'd done that for nothing."

"All the same," Morgaine said skeptically, "I doubt we'll be safe here for long. As it is, I'd better make sure I visit Storm while I'm there, just to keep him happy."

Rowan raised his eyebrows. "Oh, had you? And how exactly are you going to keep him happy?"

Morgaine made a small growl of frustration, almost like Hutchincroft. "I'm trying to help you! What does it matter what I might have to do?"

"You tell me. What does it matter?"

"For your information, I intend to call on him, let him see that I haven't disappeared suspiciously along with the prisoner, and see if he has any leads on where Bridget has escaped to. Is that acceptable? Or would you prefer it if I slept with him?"

He shrugged. "I don't see that I get any say in it. You stopped listening to me seventy years ago."

"Oh, just shut up, Rowan!" Morgaine jabbed the last pin in her hat, so furiously Biddy feared it would go straight through her head.

Just before she reached the door, Morgaine stopped and turned back.

"Has it ever occurred to you," she said, with great dignity, "that you missed being caught that morning seventy years ago by pure chance? That if you and Hutch had been home just a little earlier, they would have come for you and forced you to prove your allegiance then and there? What would you have done? Refused? Died fighting?" She didn't wait for an answer. "Some did. And I understand why they did, their consciences are clear, but it was no help to us, was it? Dead mages can't make anything better."

He gave an almost-laugh, a sharp intake of breath. Perhaps he recognized it, as Biddy did, as being almost word for word what she had said seventy years ago. "Oh, and you have, have you?"

"I got you out of the Servant's dungeons and away from Storm! I got Bridget out last night!"

"I know, I know." His voice softened. "And I'm grateful for that, truly. But that isn't what you usually do, is it?"

"I try to improve things from inside the system."

"From inside your comfortable house, while being paid a comfortable sum for a comfortable position on the Council, I see."

Her eyes flashed. "*Comfortable?* Do you think I've enjoyed myself all these years, living with a piece of my soul missing, constantly watched, constantly watching the Council suck the last dregs of magic from the world?"

"Oh, do you think *we've* enjoyed ourselves?" Hutchincroft bristled at his side. "And just so you know, the answer to your first question is yes. I would have died."

"Well, it's a good thing that I was caught and not you, then." Her voice was acid, but Biddy wondered if some of the brightness in her eyes was tears. "Since you so clearly need the help of someone on the inside now. Just try not to get Bridget captured again before I get back."

Rowan struck the mantelpiece with his fist as the door closed behind her, his face such a mixture of frustration and fury that Biddy almost smiled.

"I know," he said to Hutch, whose nose was twitching indignantly. "She's unbelievable."

"She *did* rescue me," Biddy pointed out. She couldn't help it. Whatever Morgaine had done, whether she was right or wrong to do so, her loneliness and regret were so piercing that she was amazed Rowan couldn't feel them. "I think she's sorry about her familiar, whatever she says. And about you. She stole the locket in the first place because she was trying to find you."

"I bet she was." He leaned against the mantel with a faint sigh, and rubbed his brow. "You didn't tell her about Hy-Brasil, did you?"

"Of course not! She didn't want to find where you were hiding, anyway. She just wanted to talk to you. There's no need to be so grumpy." She looked at him more closely. "Are you all right?"

"Me? Always." Biddy gave him a look, and his smile turned a little rueful. "Bit of a headache, I suppose."

"You don't get headaches."

"Well, I haven't had to deal with Morgaine for seventy years." He met her eyes more seriously then. "I truly didn't mean to lie to you about where you came from, you know."

She wasn't sure what to say. It was the sort of thing Rowan often said in lieu of an apology—so often, in fact, that she'd wondered if he didn't even realize that not meaning to do something wasn't the same as being sorry for doing it. She could accept it, when it came to forgetting to buy something on the mainland or leaving the oven burning or getting caught up in his own work and missing her childhood bedtimes. Not this. He *had* lied to her; she couldn't see how that could be done by accident. And she couldn't forgive him when he hadn't asked for forgiveness.

He exhaled slowly, as though she had responded after all, and sank down into the armchair by the fire. "Go on, then," he said. His face was level with hers, but the room was dim enough with the curtains drawn that she couldn't see its expression clearly. "Anything you're still wondering, just ask."

Only days ago, she would have given anything to hear that. Now, even though she could tell he meant it, it felt too late. "Do you know who my parents are?" she asked. "Truly."

"No," he said. "Truly, I don't."

"Did you ever try to find them?"

"For years. We had nothing to go on. You were a foundling: That was it."

She swallowed hard. "Do you still think they were mages?"

"We thought that because of the spell in your heart. If I was the one who put it there and not them…" He shrugged, and for once it looked more helpless than careless. "It's possible, I suppose. Perhaps they helped find the rift, and Vaughan tracked them down. I just don't know, Bid. London's a big city, and Whitechapel…Well, all sorts of people drift into the docks there and disappear without a trace."

It was true. She had seen it firsthand, the maelstrom of humanity congregating in the East End. In a way, it wasn't far from the shipwreck story. She could have come from anywhere.

"How hard did you look?" Despite her best efforts, a bitter note of recrimination crept into her voice.

"Hard," he said firmly. "Believe me."

She did. The trouble was, she had believed him when he had said she had washed up in a shipwreck as well. "But even if you'd found my family, and they'd wanted me, you wouldn't have given me back to them. You couldn't. The spell was still in my heart."

"No," he conceded. "But I would have let them know you were safe. I would have told you who they were. I was always trying to get that spell out, you know. That's what I meant when I told you that you'd go to the mainland someday. I thought we'd have done it by now, and you could have gone back to your family or anywhere else you wanted to go."

That gave her a confused pang of hurt. As angry as she was at how she had come to be on the island, she wasn't sure how she felt about the idea that Rowan had been working to send her away either. But she couldn't say so, when she'd just been accusing him of not trying hard enough to do exactly that.

She looked up the ceiling—white, with molding in the corners and a many-globed chandelier in its center. Morgaine's house, she had been thinking of it as, wealthy and self-assured and too pristine to be trusted. And yet it had been Rowan's once. And, Morgaine had said, Vaughan's name had been on the lease.

"Were you only on the Council because of Vaughan?" she asked.

That question startled him, though it might have been only the abrupt change in subject. "Who said that?"

"Doesn't matter. You said to ask anything I wanted. Is it true?"

He shifted in the armchair, in the way he did when he was very uncomfortable and thought he wasn't showing it. "In a way, yeah. So was Morgaine. Vaughan pulled strings and found us seats when older members left. I told you, we would never normally have gotten near the Council."

The *I told you* felt like some kind of final straw. Anger flared brief but bright in her chest. "You told me you made it to the Council. You never told me you got there because of Vaughan Carlisle. You never told me you made a deal with him in exchange for your support. And you *definitely* never told me that your support was what let him become Servant of Magic in the first place."

"I did!" He did, at least, sound genuinely bewildered. "Or at least...I didn't mean to *not* tell you. I didn't think all of that mattered."

"You didn't think it *mattered*?" She had meant to be very cool, but her voice rose without her consent. "Vaughan is in power because of you!"

"That's right," he agreed, and she suspected he wasn't sounding quite as cool as he'd intended either. "He is. He's in power because a handful of us were young and stupid and ambitious, and because that eye of his read our every desire to change the world and made full use of it."

"Is that supposed to be an excuse?"

"Oh, come on, Biddy, you know me better than that!" He stood in one movement, his habitual restlessness at last getting the better of him. "Of course it's not an excuse. I should have known better.

I could see what he was doing, building a Council filled with loyal up-and-coming mages who owed him everything. But I liked him. I spent hours talking about different projects to him, ones nobody else believed in, and he listened. Or I thought he did, at least."

Did you really think he was interested? Storm had jeered. *He was flattering you until he had your vote and laughing at you behind your back.*

She'd never imagined anyone in the world could deceive Rowan. The thought that Vaughan had was almost worse than if Rowan had made a deal on purpose.

"And he bought you this lovely house," she said flatly.

"Vaughan bought me," Rowan said. He had clearly taken her point. "Is that what you want to hear? It's true. He bought all of us. I don't just mean with money and houses and things. Vaughan sees people that others don't. If you're one of those people who are used to not being seen, that's difficult to resist."

She kept her voice under control this time. "And did he buy Storm too?"

"Storm..." Something in his face closed off, veiled, like a curtain coming down. "Storm he bought by *not* seeing him—or pretending not to, at least. Storm had everything going for him—money, looks, class. He was used to being given things. Vaughan kept them just out of his reach, knowing that under those circumstances he'd do anything for them. Still does, for all I know. Why are you asking about Storm?"

Until that moment, she hadn't known if she would ever tell him what she had seen. She had been burning to ask about it, but just as afraid that it would send everything up in flames. It was too late now. "I told you I saw Storm's memory when he tried to take the spell from my heart," she said. "It was a memory of you."

"Was it?" He sounded indifferent, but his shoulders stiffened. "Which one?"

"The day he transformed." She saw the look dart across the surface of his face before he forced it back under, and knew he needed no elaboration. "The three of you were in a pub somewhere—not in the Undercastle. I could see the sky outside. The streets looked old, and sort of crooked."

"York." It came out absently, on reflex, the way he'd identify a song she half remembered or a book she'd read when she was much younger. "Marney's place. There used to be lots of little pockets like that, before. You couldn't get into them without magic—like the Undercastle. There were charms on the door, so anyone without magic stored in their blood would see a blank wall."

She would have been interested in that at any other time. "You were different."

"Well, it was about seventy years ago." She didn't say anything, and he relented. "Different how?"

She grasped for words. Harder, angrier, crueler. "Your accent was stronger," she said feebly. She couldn't help but think that a few days ago she hadn't even been aware that Rowan had an accent. Now she knew it shifted depending on whom he was talking to, and what she thought of as his real voice might just be the one he used with her.

"All right," he said cautiously. "Well. That might have been Storm's memory playing tricks. Or, if I'm honest, I might have been playing it up a bit on purpose. Morgaine said I used to do that when I wanted to get Storm's back up."

"Why would you want to get Storm's back up?"

He sighed. "Can we just leave it, Bid? It was a long time ago, and everything was a mess. I can't remember the exact details of what was going on between Storm and Morgaine and myself."

"Storm can remember everything."

"Storm is stuck there. I can't do anything about that."

"Do you want to?"

His laugh had no humor in it. "Last time Storm and I met he spent a good deal of time rearranging my insides. You'll forgive me if his emotional well-being isn't the *first* thing on my mind." Her look must have been skeptical, because he shook his head, frustrated. "What do you want me to say, Biddy?"

"I don't know!" She wanted it never to have happened. She

wanted never to have seen it. She wanted to go back to the world she had lived in mere weeks ago, when Rowan was her frustrating but wonderful guardian who loved her and nothing more. That wasn't possible; she knew that. She even understood that it wasn't fair. Rowan hadn't pretended to be perfect. But she couldn't help but think he had pretended to be better.

"I want you to tell me that Storm remembered it wrong," she said at last.

"I'm sure he did," Rowan said, and she knew that he didn't understand. "I'm sure I remember it wrong too. But if you want me to come out looking better in my own memories than I did in Storm's, you'll be disappointed. I wasn't always the kindest person back then. Is that all?"

Of course it wasn't. There was so much more—a vast ocean more. But she didn't know how to put those feelings into questions, even for herself. They were like the magic beyond the cracks in the world, unseen and unknowable and beyond her understanding.

Besides, he wasn't going to tell her. She had felt the change in his voice, seen him get to his feet, and knew from bitter experience that she had lost him again. Trying to pin down any answers now would be like trying to catch a will-o'-the-wisp in a high wind.

"That's all," she said. "Except for the question of why you put a spell in my heart and left me in that place. And you can't answer that, can you?"

"No," he said quietly. "I can't."

A dark, corrosive taste filled her mouth. It took her a moment to realize what it was. In all their years together, she had been annoyed with Rowan, afraid for him, frequently puzzled by him—for a few sickening hours last night, she had even felt that she couldn't trust him at all. But she had never before been disappointed in him. Now she was, and that disappointment was the worst betrayal of all.

It wasn't fair. She could see he was trying his best; she could even see, as she wouldn't have mere days ago, that he was tired and worried and genuinely shaken by the gap in his own past. But he owed her answers. He had all but admitted as much. She had done everything he had asked of her, and nearly died for it. And yet when it came to what she really needed to understand, he had nothing to give her.

***

Hutchincroft, of course, alerted them first. Biddy was curled up on the bed with one of the books from above the mantelpiece, pretending to read—in part, she had to admit, to avoid talking to Rowan. As far as that went, she needn't have worried. Rowan wasn't pretending to do anything, and he was well past talking. He had barely touched the tea Morgaine had left, and had shaken his head at the array of sausages and eggs and assorted baked goods. (Rowan, Biddy was starting to realize, was one of those irritating people Anna had mentioned who lost their appetites at the slightest worry. She was anxious and unhappy too, but she saw no reason to let that ruin a perfectly good blueberry muffin.) For the last twenty minutes he had been leaning against the covered window, tilting his head to watch between the curtains, biting his fingers absent-mindedly as he did when he was thinking very hard. Hutch dozed beside her, content enough as long as they were together and safe. As Biddy turned a page, however, he sat bolt upright. His ears were up, and his body was rigid.

Rowan was upright himself in an instant. "Are they coming?"

Hutch didn't nod his head as he would for Biddy, but he must have answered, judging by Rowan's reaction. Biddy had never heard him swear before.

"Is it Vaughan?" she asked.

"No. Not this time. It's Storm."

As he spoke, there was a roar of wind, and a sudden thrash of rain against the walls. In the living room, with its exposed glass, it would have been deafening—as it was, a cold gust funneled down the chimney, speckled with icy droplets. Biddy looked up at Rowan. He had turned absolutely white.

Rowan was always a little on edge around storms. Hy-Brasil

was battered by them often in winter and the tempestuous spring months, and Biddy had always loved the lash of the wind, the low rumble of thunder, the dash through the quickening rain to herd the chickens into the old fort and drag the goats inside. The three of them would curl up by the fire with biscuits and hot milk and a solid pile of gothic novels, and stay there reading and giggling over the scary bits until it passed. Often, if the storm raged all night, she would fall asleep on the cushions with Hutch at her side and wake to bright sunshine and the world made new. She thought of those nights as safe nights—the wind was too high for a raven to fly or a ship to sail, so nobody was going anywhere. It had only been in recent months that she had noticed how Rowan's fingers tightened around his mug when the wind roared, how he would take a breath and release it after a particularly loud clash of lightning, how comfortingly close Hutch would press to him as the rain struck the shutters.

This was what the two of them had been fearing. Whatever shared terror they had locked her out of, she was now in the middle of it.

"What do we do?" she asked.

It was the right question. Rowan blinked as though coming out of a dream. "Well, we're not getting out the windows. Let's try the cellar. Quick!"

She hadn't known the townhouse had a cellar, but of course Rowan and Hutchincroft knew the house inside out. Hutch leapt from the bed, and Biddy almost fell after him.

The cellar was at the bottom of a stairwell, on the other side of a green door that she would have assumed was a pantry. It jammed at first; Rowan pushed the handle up, hard, and it opened.

"She never fixed it either," he said, with a shake of his head. "All those years she went on at me."

Biddy managed a tight smile.

Through the door was a cool, dim room, its walls and floor made of rusted red brick. It was tiny, not much bigger than the pantry she had taken it for and half-filled with coal, but a small window at street level glimmered above. She started inside, only to have Rowan catch her by the arm.

"Back!" His grip was tight enough to hurt. "Upstairs. Now!"

"Why—?"

The words caught in her throat. In the corner ceiling, where the cellar met the ground outside, water was trickling through a crack. A leak in the roof, she would have said, like the many they had in the castle back home. Hutchincroft was always complaining about them. But where the water fell, something was rising from the ground—something sharp-edged and frost-white, long-limbed and unformed, wreathed in glittering droplets.

Wisps. Wisps formed from rain, fledged in water and cold. These belonged to Storm.

With a tiny cry that she hoped wasn't a scream, she scrambled back up the stairs.

Hutch was already there waiting for them both, whiskers quivering in agitation. Rowan let her arm go as she passed and grabbed the wooden stairwell instead. He whispered a few words, eyes fixed on the emerging rain forms; the stairs creaked and flexed weakly, and six tiny wooden wisps, their wings sharp as splinters, flaked off from the banisters. They were sluggish and small compared to the yew tree wisps that had battled the bone wisps on the island, more insect than bird, but they flew at the rippling creatures of rain with feathers buzzing furiously, voices raised in creaking battle cries. Rowan slammed the door shut behind him.

"Well, that should hold them for a few minutes," he said, breathless. He climbed the stairs two at a time and pushed Biddy forward. From behind the closed door, the buzzing and creaking had mingled with a terrible gargling shriek and the crash of hail. "Come on. Sitting room."

Biddy ran, Hutchincroft swift at her side. They couldn't get out through the sitting room—the rain was lashing those high windows, every drop ready to come to life. But Rowan had to have a plan. He always had a plan.

He did. When they reached the sitting room, he stopped. The

bright room was dim now with the storm clouds outside, and filled with shadows.

"Here." Rowan threw something, and she caught it on instinct.

It was the ravenstone. It sat in her palm, sharp-edged and glistening black. She looked at Rowan, shocked, and he gave her a smile.

"You always wanted to try it."

"But..." Beside her, Hutch thumped loudly. "There's only one stone."

"And it's for you—well, you and Hutch. You can get up the chimney here. It's a tight fit, but we only came down it a few hours ago. Don't worry about flying, the raven knows how to fly. The trick is to remember who you are, all right? Hutch will remind you."

She shook her head, unable to speak.

"I know what you saw happen to Storm." Perhaps he genuinely misunderstood her reluctance; more likely he pretended to. "I promise it won't happen to you. The stone was young and wild then—it's a lot quieter now. You can do this. Once you're free, fly back to Hy-Brasil. It's the only place you'll be safe. Stay hidden, and stay free. I'll join you when I can."

"No!" Her protest was a whisper, fierce and furious as a shout. "I won't leave you."

"Yes, you will." There was no trace of a smile on his face now. "And so will you, Hutchincroft, so stop it. I'll be all right. When I fight them off, I'll follow you."

"And what if you can't?"

"Well, that's not much of a vote of confidence, is it?" She said nothing. They all knew he couldn't. "I've done this before, remember? They took me to the same place they took you. I got out last time."

Morgaine had helped him last time. He didn't mention her, and Biddy knew why. He thought she had betrayed them. She had left the house, and now Storm and his army were converging upon it.

"Hutch, come here." Hutch was already there, his front feet on Rowan's boots, ears back and eyes imploring. Rowan scooped him up, held him tightly for just a moment, then kissed his forehead and released him. "There. That's most of the magic I've got left. I'll keep some to try to hold them off, but there's no point in me saving anything. If I get caught, they'll only take it off me once I get to the Undercastle."

"I'm not going," Biddy repeated. Her eyes were burning with tears.

"You are," Rowan countered. "If you don't, then Hutch doesn't get away. He needs you to fly. And Hutch, if you don't look after Biddy, she won't go, or she'll go and be lost on her own. You need each other. Biddy," he added, and his voice was very low and soft, "I promise I'll see you again. Please. Please, both of you, for me, just go."

She couldn't go. She couldn't. They had argued the last time they had spoken. She had spent the last hour in a haze of shimmering resentment. That couldn't be the last words they ever spoke, the last time they ever had. But against her will, she placed the ravenstone around her neck. It was heavier than she expected, and it quivered against her chest like the rapid-fire beating of a second heart.

Rowan nodded. His shoulders lightened with relief. "Thank you."

The room was darkening now, and the rain against the windows had the force of bullets. The glass buckled and cracked under it. Hutchincroft stood where Rowan had put him, anguished, but when Biddy scooped him up he lay flat against her and didn't resist.

She had meant to ask how to use the ravenstone to transform, but she had no need to. The magic was there, fluttering, aching to be used. She had never felt anything like it before. The effort was in *not* turning into a bird. The slightest nudge of her thoughts, and her skin began to prickle, her body to shrink in on itself. It would have been terrifying, if she hadn't known what to expect. Even as it was, a flash of Storm's transformation split her head—the twisting limbs, the ghastly cleaving of his brain, the screams torn from shrinking lungs—and she nearly flinched back from it in horror. If she had, mid-transformation, it might have been disastrous. But she had seen Rowan transform many times, and Hutchincroft was already soothing the raven within her, and so her fear was softened by pure wonder even as her arms elongated into wings, her feet sprouted claws, her flesh burst into feathers, even when Hutchincroft's soft body melted from her grasp and he folded into her heart. And then she was a raven, on the floor of a giant human room, and a storm was coming.

Up the chimney, Biddy. It was Hutchincroft's voice in her head. That of all things startled her—she hadn't expected to be able to hear him as Rowan always heard him. His voice was tight with grief, but firm and strong. *I'm here. I'm with you. Just let the raven fly.*

Rowan was right. The raven knew how to fly. She spread her wings, flapped once, and took off straight up the chimney.

Her first thought was that she was going to die. This was nothing like the underground chimneys she had traversed the night before. It was tight and pitch-black, the air so thick with soot and darkness that she couldn't tell which was which. The raven part of her mind was panicking, wings beating painfully against the enclosed space, and grit caked its feathers and stung its eyes. Its fear joined hers and overwhelmed her. She couldn't breathe. She couldn't see.

You can do it, Hutchincroft said. *Just head for the light.*

And there *was* light, above their heads. She could see it, a tiny circle like a sliver of a moon on a dark night, and she gritted teeth the raven didn't have and pushed forward up the chimney. Her claws scraped the brick, desperate.

There was no light behind her anymore. The room she had left was utterly dark, though it was the full light of day. Behind her she could hear the burst of rain on the walls, then, terribly, the crash of breaking glass. In her mind, she felt Hutchincroft stiffen.

"Where is she?" It was Storm's voice—the deep growl that had dominated her long day in the castle dungeons. It fixed her in place like a pin through a butterfly.

She heard Rowan laugh, clear and low and threatening. "It's nice to see you again too. Especially out in daylight. Congratulations."

There was a clash then, as though of metal against metal, and the fireplace beneath her sparked with green-gold light.

Go! Hutchincroft urged, and she went. One final push of her wings, a scrabbling of her claws, and she was out and over the rim of the chimney. Rain hit her like ice, the grey sky was unbearably bright and cold, her feathers were caked with soot, and everything hurt. She beat her wings furiously, frantically, and then she was in the air.

Something hit her from the side. Sharp claws, a rush of cold— not bone this time, but ice and rain. A wisp. The raven shrieked, struggling, wings flapping as the claws of frost dug into its warm feathers. Biddy grabbed at it, trying to get its fear and rage under control.

Fight! she ordered. She never knew if it was her or the raven, but together they twisted about in midair, so they were face to face with the wisp. Its face was transparent, its beak a shard of ice. The raven sank its talons into the watery chest and pushed it back—once, twice, the third time with a burst of frantic strength. The wisp's claws tore from the raven's feathers, and it shattered into rain.

They were free, spiraling through the sky, first in rain and then, all at once, in sunlight. London wheeled underneath her, dizzying and glorious.

She was in the city, and she was flying. The two things she had always wanted most in the world, and she didn't care. There was a battle going on behind her, and Rowan couldn't win it, and she was supposed to leave and let him lose. She would have sobbed, but the raven couldn't cry.

Don't stop. Hutchincroft's voice, fierce and clear and beautiful, anchored her. *I'm not going to lose you too. Keep flying.*

She kept flying and, with every beat of the raven's wings, left Rowan farther behind.

She didn't know where she was, or where she was going. Without Hutchincroft, she would have been lost, and her mind would have been lost too. She understood now why Rowan had never let her use the ravenstone, why it had torn Storm apart when it was raw-forged and wild. It was beautiful magic, but it was powerful—almost too powerful for her to bear. When her thoughts drifted, worn out by grief and exertion, she would find herself sinking into the raven's body as she might beneath the surface of a pond, and only Hutch's voice pulled her out and kept her afloat. She felt it happen more and more often as the sun rose and set around them and the sky turned to grey, as the ground beneath them passed from city to flat green country.

Keep heading west, Hutchincroft said. *Follow the sun. We're going to Hy-Brasil, Biddy. Keep holding it in your mind. You have to remember who you are and where you're going.*

Hy-Brasil. She could remember Hy-Brasil. She knew every inch of it, perhaps even better than Rowan did, because she had lived there almost her whole life, and he only a fragment of his. She knew its trees, its rocks, its scraggly grass. She knew her bedroom with its collection of shells and pebbles and leaves, her favorite reading spot in the fields out of the wind where the rabbits would graze around her, the best places to swim and climb and dream.

She had thought the island had chosen her. That it had saved her from the deadly seas when she was a child, because her parents had been someone special, or because she was, or because there was a great destiny to fulfill. She had built her whole idea of herself around that: that the island had saved her for a reason. But it hadn't. Whatever the true story was, whatever Rowan had done, Hy-Brasil had not wanted her. She shouldn't care about that when so much else was at stake, but she did, desperately.

She didn't know who she was anymore.

No. Hutch's voice was firm, with just a trace of panic. *No, you need to do better than that. Please, Biddy, stay with me.*

She was so tired. Her wings ached, and so did her soul. It seemed they had been flying forever, and they would never stop. She didn't know how far Hy-Brasil was.

It's around four hundred and fifty miles, Hutch said. Until then, she hadn't realized he could hear her. *A true raven would take all day and half the night to fly there, if it could make it at all. But this isn't a true raven. It can go at speeds that no true bird could manage, and it won't tire. The only one who will tire is you. I'm sorry this is so hard, I am. I wish it could be hard for me and not for you. But you have to keep going.*

There was ocean beneath her now, black and hard and glinting. The raven couldn't see well in the dark. The wind was bitterly cold, and pushing them back away from home.

She kept going.

⟶•══════•⟵

It hurt to come out of raven form, as it hadn't going in. She had to fight her way back, and she screamed as her limbs twisted and her feathers dissolved. But when it was all over, she was curled up on a dusty wooden floor, and Hutchincroft was a rabbit in her arms again, nudging her worriedly. She tore the ravenstone from around her neck, shaking, and its fluttering ceased.

"I'm all right," she told Hutch, as soon as she found her voice. She didn't feel it at all. She was shuddering horribly, her flesh chilled and her bones like ice, and the floor bit her through her clothes. None of her limbs felt her own. But she was safe, for now. Her mind was clear again. She tucked the ravenstone into her pocket, and managed to sit up.

She was on the floor of Rowan's study. The raven had taken her on the journey Rowan made every night, across the water and through the open window, fighting to get in before dawn. It had brought her home.

"Where is he?" she asked Hutch. Her throat was raspy, and her words came in a hoarse whisper. "Did he escape?"

She wasn't surprised when Hutch shook his head, but it hurt all the same. It had really happened. Rowan had fallen into the hands of his enemies, and however long she waited, this time he would never come home. He was gone.

She had never, in all her life, imagined that she would be on Hy-Brasil without Rowan for longer than a single night. Leaving the island, yes—she had imagined that a thousand times. But Rowan and Hy-Brasil had always been entwined in her mind.

"Can you see him?" When she received a miserable headshake, she laid a comforting hand on his ears. Tears burned in her eyes, but she refused to let them fall. "It'll be all right. He might get out. He said he would, after all. We'll wait for him. He'll come back."

She was saying it for Hutchincroft, not for herself, trying to reassure him as though he really were a tiny golden rabbit in need of comfort and not an immortal being of pure magic. He moved closer to her, but he didn't relax.

Her shivers were passing, and in their wake came deathly exhaustion. She lay back down on the hard floor, drawing her knees up to her chest, her hand resting on Hutch. She knew her bed would be downstairs, exactly as she had left it; she didn't want to try to get to it, even if she could. Moving felt like giving up, somehow. She lay still, and wished for Rowan's safety with all her heart.

———————⟡———————

In the thin grey hours before dawn, she started awake to a terrible sound: a high, piercing shriek that chilled her heart. It was a rabbit's scream. She had heard it before, just once, when one of the young black rabbits near the castle had been set upon by a hawk. This time was worse. It was Hutchincroft screaming, not blind panic but a high note of rage and terror and grief.

"Hutch!" She reached for him in the darkness and wrapped him in her arms, trying to soothe him. His small round body was trembling so hard he vibrated. "Hutch, have they killed him? Hutch, please stop. Please. Tell me. Is Rowan dead?"

He silenced, though he was trembling as hard as ever. To her relief, he shook his head in a swish of ears. The relief was short-lived, though.

"They're hurting him, aren't they?" Her stomach surged; she dug her fingernails into her palm as her head spun. "Hutch?"

He buried his head in the crook of her arm, quivering miserably, and she held him even tighter.

It was a very long night.

Chapter Fourteen

$\mathcal{B}$iddy woke to thin, early-morning light and the faint tang of smoke. When she sat up, wincing, rubbing the grit from her eyes, it was to see Hutchincroft in human form standing over a fire that flickered blue flames. He looked smaller than usual, his soft face tired and troubled. His eyes warmed when he saw her, but he wasn't practiced enough at human expression to give her a smile he didn't feel.

"I'm sorry," Hutch said quietly. "I didn't mean to scare you last night."

"I would have cried out too." Perhaps she had. Her eyes were tired and swollen as though with tears.

"Are you feeling better?" Hutch asked. "Can I get you anything?"

"I'm all right," she said, and it was a little more true than it had been. There were two blankets over her now, and a pillow at her head—Hutch's doing, presumably, along with the bowl of stewed apple cooling on the floor beside her. She ached all over, and she was deathly cold, but she found she could clamber to her feet stiffly and with Hutch's help even walk a few hobbling steps to the armchair by the fire. He gave her a one-armed hug, the human kind he had learned from Rowan, and she leaned into him gratefully before twisting around to face him.

"What about Rowan?" She held her hands over the warm glow

of the fire and rubbed them briskly, trying not only to warm them but in some strange way to remember them. The raven was a feathered shadow across her mind. "Is he safe?"

"I don't know," Hutch said. "He's hidden from me in those dungeons."

"Why could you see him last night?"

"They wanted me to." His voice was very, very calm. She didn't know Hutch's spoken voice well, but she knew his moods, and this one made her shiver. "They lifted the spells of protection so that I could hear him scream for me in his heart. They want me to bring you back to them in exchange. They know I would see the last magic go out of the world in a heartbeat, myself with it, to stop him hurting like that."

She had to close her eyes against a wave of nausea. "Did he scream for you?"

"Yes," Hutch said, in the same calm tone. "Yes, of course he did. You can't help what your heart does. But he also told me, in the breaths between the hurt, not to listen. And I told him we were safe, and he wasn't to worry. And he said to tell you that he loves you very much."

Biddy knew Rowan loved her. She understood now that she had always known it, even in her darkest moments when she doubted everything else about him. It had been in every touch of his hand, every crinkle at the corners of his eyes, every softening of his smile when he looked at her. But he never said it. The fact he had done so now chilled her to the depths of her heart.

"*Do* you want to take me back?" she asked Hutch, and knew the answer before it came.

"Never." His blue eyes were fierce. "They don't understand, the Council. The only thing in this world I love as much as Rowan is you. I would deliver them anything, but not you. And the more they hurt Rowan, the more determined I am that they will never, ever lay a sliver of magic on you again."

She folded her arms tightly across her chest. "Rowan always said that magic was good. He said it couldn't hurt."

"It can't, on its own. People can." Hutch shook his head. "When we knew Storm, he had a stone that could heal broken bones. Morgaine made it for him; she was always the stonemage. Good magic, very useful and kind. When he imprisoned Rowan last time, Storm broke every bone in his body, and then he healed them, and then he broke them, shattering and mending, over and over again. People find ways to make anything hurt."

Last time Storm and I met he spent a good deal of time rearranging my insides, Rowan had said. It had flown past her; if she had thought about it at all, she would have assumed it was figurative. Now she remembered Storm looming in the impenetrable doorway of the dungeon, his sudden surge of anger, the rough grasp of his magic about her heart, and bile rose in her throat.

"Is that what they're doing to him now?"

"I don't know. Probably. Storm doesn't have a great deal of imagination." She saw Hutch stop and gather his optimism, deliberately, as though it were a cloak he was pulling about himself out of knowledge that humans thought it bad to be naked. "But as long as they need him, they'll keep him alive. In the meantime, you're safe, and—"

"No."

With effort, perhaps the greatest effort of her life, she raised her head and set her jaw. That couldn't be it. It just couldn't be. It wasn't that she was brave, exactly, unless hopelessness brought its own kind of courage. It was just that a wild creature pursued by a predator that would never stop sooner or later has to either turn and fight or die of fear. The Council would never stop. She had been terrified all night; one way or another, she had been terrified ever since she had woken to find herself in the dungeons of the Undercastle. She couldn't be afraid anymore. She had to turn. And the fact that she didn't know how, the fact that the thought filled her with dread, the fact that part of her would rather die—none of that mattered.

"They want Rowan and me because they think that together we can guide them to the schism, don't they?" she asked.

"Yes," Hutch said cautiously. "But...you can't give yourself in, if that's what you're suggesting. There's no real certainty they'll ever let you go, even once they've taken the spell from your heart. And certainly Storm won't want to give up Rowan."

"But what if we gave them the schism itself?" She hated the words even as she said them. She said them anyway, because it was the only way. "What if we find it, and offer it to them in exchange for Rowan's freedom?"

Hutch blinked. "Let them have the schism?"

"It's what they want most. Vaughan said that they would have agreed to any demands Rowan made for it, when he first found it. Storm won't like it, but they don't listen to Storm. And if they have their rift in the world, they don't need Rowan or the spell in my heart."

Hutch shook his head; the quick, slightly exaggerated headshake of a being used to having ears to swish. "Rowan would hate that. He would rather die than let magic fall into the Council's hands."

"Then he should have thought of that sixteen years ago when he planted the schism's location in me for safekeeping and forgot about it!"

She stopped to collect herself, as she had seen Morgaine do the night before, clenching her fists and steeling her face into calm. Hutch was watching her with worried eyes.

"I know he doesn't want the Council to have control of the schism," she said. "I know he wants to use it for good. But it's not doing any good now, is it? Nobody knows where it is. What's the worst that could happen if the Council get their hands on it?"

"They'll drain it of whatever magic they can," Hutch said promptly. "They'll be even more powerful, and nobody else will see a spell of it. And, assuming Rowan's theories were correct, if they take too much from it, it might close again forever."

"The Council already hold all the magic they can get their hands on," Biddy said, unmoved. "A little more won't hurt. And if it closes forever, we'll be no worse off than we were before."

"We will," Hutch corrected. "We'll have lost the chance to fill the world with magic again. That's what Rowan truly hoped, all these years. If we have just one schism, we can use it to open the others."

Morgaine had mentioned that, back at the house. There had been so much to take in that Biddy hadn't asked what she meant. "Can that be done?"

"Well...Nobody knows," Hutch admitted. "But Rowan believed it was possible."

"Rowan believes a lot of things are possible, Hutch! It doesn't make much difference if he doesn't know how to bring them about."

"I believe it to be possible too," Hutch said stoutly.

"Good!" She got to her feet in a burst of frustration, shrugging off the blanket. "Then there'll be other chances to do it, won't there? With another schism, or with this one if the Council doesn't close it after all."

"Rowan said—"

"I'm not Rowan!" It came out in a burst of hurt. The hope of magic in the world hit too close to her tenderest dreams, from when she had been a child who believed, like a fool, that Hy-Brasil had rescued her from the waves for a reason. "I didn't get into this to restore magic. I agreed to go into the world because I wanted to keep this island and all three of us safe. I can't stay here and hide, knowing they'll never stop hunting me and that if they find me they find Hy-Brasil. I can't let them torture Rowan to death—and believe me, Hutch, whether Vaughan wants him kept alive or not, sooner or later Storm *will* kill him."

"I have no intention of letting Storm kill him." This time the conviction in Hutch's voice was real. "I will get him out, if it takes every last scrap of magic I have. But he wouldn't want us to give his enemies the key to more power. He wouldn't want us to risk the schism. And most of all he wouldn't want to risk you."

"He *did* risk me," she said. "He risked me when I was a baby. He risked me when he put me in that school as bait for his enemies."

"Not to save his own life," Hutch said firmly. "I'm certain of that." He hesitated, with the wary side-eye of a rabbit in the field watching the approach of a stranger. "Are you very angry with him?"

She sighed heavily, trying to breathe out something that couldn't be exhaled.

"Yes," she said honestly. "I'm very angry with him. But no matter what he's done, I love him too. I won't leave him in that dungeon. I can live without a world filled with magic if that's what it takes."

"Well…" Hutch shifted, wavering. He was fighting a battle he didn't want to win, and they both knew it. He felt a duty to argue for Rowan's wishes; if left to act on his own, though, he would sacrifice not only magic but the rest of the world to keep Rowan safe. "How do you intend to find the schism?"

She rubbed her temples, against which thoughts and worries were beating a frantic drum. "The Council are wrong about one thing. We don't need Rowan to unlock the spell. We need that locket. We need to find Morgaine and get it from her."

Hutch laughed, high with disbelief. "Morgaine betrayed us! She is the last person we need."

"We don't know for certain she betrayed us." It sounded unconvincing to her own ears. Morgaine had left the flat to see Storm, and less than an hour later Storm had been at their window. Of course she had betrayed them. "But even if she did, it doesn't matter. She wasn't lying about one thing, at least: She *did* visit me when I was a child. To do that, she must have had the locket with my hair. Either she still has it, or the Council took it from her. One way or another, she'll know where it is."

"And you think she'll tell us where it is?" Hutch's eyebrows were raised almost to his hairline. "I saw her last night, Biddy."

That startled her, despite her resolve. "Last night?"

"When they were…When I saw through Rowan's eyes. Storm was inflicting the pain, of course, but Morgaine stood beside him. She watched. And she did nothing."

Another image she didn't want: Morgaine at Storm's side, her face and her hair smoothed into precise lines, while Storm cracked human bones like a fox tearing open a chicken. She couldn't fit Rowan into the image, not because she couldn't bear to, but because she'd never seen him betray pain beyond a flinch. She didn't know what it would look like on his face, or what it would sound like if he screamed.

"I suppose she could have been pretending," she said, when she could manage to speak again.

"Rowan was sure she wasn't. I could feel it hurting him, mixed up with everything else. He still loves her, you know."

She knew he did. She had seen it when she had walked in on them both the morning before, face to face with each other for the first time in decades, disheveled and glaring and fragile. She had heard it as they fought, the bitter quarreling of two people who had hurt each other very deeply and were trying to fight about anything other than that hurt. But she was learning through the confusion of her own feelings that love didn't mean you saw a person clearly.

And yet if Morgaine hadn't betrayed them, then surely no amount of pretending would have kept Vaughan's trust after Rowan had been found in her house. Surely she wouldn't have been standing alongside Storm, but thrown to the ground as a prisoner beside Rowan. And if she hadn't—if she had been watching someone she loved be torn apart, and for the sake of her own safety pretended so well not to care that she had convinced both Vaughan and Rowan himself—then that was almost worse than betrayal. That was grotesque.

She thought of Morgaine's face soft in the firelight over the silver tray, of the arrested motion of her hand as she'd gone to touch Biddy before turning out the light.

"I'm sure she did betray us," she forced herself to say, and told herself it was stupid for those words to sting coming out. She wasn't Rowan, who had loved Morgaine for God knows how long. She barely knew her. Just a few half memories of the woman in her dreams who had played games with her, and a night when Morgaine had saved her and it hadn't felt like a lie. If she'd started to think of her as a friend, someone whom one day she could talk to, then that was her fault, wasn't it?

"I didn't mean that we should trust her," she said. "The plan from the start was to capture a member of the Council, remember?

That's what we need to do. Only this time, we won't wait for someone to come to me. We'll go to them."

"You can't mean to trap *Morgaine*. She's a very powerful mage. You can't even make a trap circle."

"Then I need to find out what magic I *can* do." It seemed strange to her now that in all the years she had been on Hy-Brasil, she had never thought of it in quite those terms. "I can work magic through anything already bespelled, after all. There's a room full of things like that here—amulets and scrying glasses and oddments Rowan's brought home. There are spellbooks and notebooks and a whole library through that door. Not being a mage doesn't mean I'm shut out from all magic."

"I never said it did!" The words were indignant, but she suspected it came from sheer surprise. "How could you think that? I *am* magic. This entire island is magic. We would never shut you out."

She *had* felt shut out, it was true, many times when Rowan's office door was closed to her or her questions went unanswered, and not that long ago she might have lashed out and said so. Now, in the cold light of day after the worst night of her life, she knew it was unfair. Rowan had always shown her spells, and let her try the artifacts he thought she could handle; Hutch had never hesitated to tell her about the mysteries of the island, as long as he had a voice to do so. It was the adult world they had shut her out from, with all its dangers and secrets and lies. She had shut herself off from magic, because she had felt it hadn't wanted her. Well, too bad.

"I just mean that I have to try," she said. "I can't afford to be powerless anymore, and I can't afford to be kept safe. I have to do something. Rowan would do it, whether he had magic or not. You know he would."

Hutch obviously agreed, or perhaps the thought of Rowan in the Undercastle was simply more than he could withstand. He sighed.

"I will help you all I can. But I fear it won't be much. Spells and amulets are closed to me. And I can't stay human for much longer, Biddy. I want to. I want you to be able to hear me. But it's taking too much magic."

A frightening thought came to her. "Hutch. Does...If Rowan isn't here to give you magic, does that mean you'll fade when it's used up?"

He hesitated, then nodded.

"How soon?"

"A few weeks, perhaps," he said, as offhandedly as he could. "Longer if I use as little as possible."

"Then turn back to yourself!" she ordered. "Quickly! I can't lose you too."

"You won't," he said. "I promise. I'll hold on as long as I possibly can. But I don't like you to feel alone."

"I never feel alone when you're here," she said. "I promise."

───────── ⊷⊷ ─────────

But she did feel alone, often.

The nights were the worst. She'd fall into bed, exhausted, only to twist all night in memories of the dungeon's cold and the raven's terror and Hutchincroft's screams. Grief and fear came in jagged waves. At times she was numb, and it seemed impossible that she would ever cry again. The next she saw the walls in a tight circle about her, shadowed and impenetrable; she felt the lightning crackle of Storm's anger and his sudden terrible closeness; she'd remember anew that Rowan was there at that very moment being broken and mended and broken again, and she would lie racked with sobs in the dark. Hutchincroft would bury himself tight under her chin, and she would cling to his soft fur, but it wasn't the same as it was when she was a child. She was very aware that she was comforting him as much as he was comforting her, and neither was truly comforted.

In the day, at least, she could keep her mind busy. It was a fraught and time-consuming business just to stay alive. The island was different without Rowan—not hostile, but wild, even wary. The rabbits were on edge, shying away as she approached, casting her suspicious looks from the corners of their dark eyes. The vegetable garden was far more overgrown than seemed realistic for the few days they had been away, and the rabbits had, as Rowan had predicted, broken in and devoured most of the cabbages and the tops of the carrots. The goats were headstrong after their brief freedom from human interference, and the chickens had either laid few eggs or hidden them well.

The supplies from the mainland were all but gone. She lived on boiled potatoes and wrinkled apples and the last of the tins of sardines; she made soup out of what vegetables the rabbits left and what she could find in the forest that was safe to eat. She was constantly rubbing against the knife edge of hunger, made sharper by her fear that soon she would have nothing at all. Winter was coming, and Hy-Brasil was harsh in winter at the best of times.

She wouldn't be here alone in winter. She told herself that, over and over. Either she would have Rowan back, or she wouldn't be back herself.

Any time she had left over was spent as Rowan often spent it: locked in his study, his notebooks spread out in an overlapping palimpsest, trying to break into the world of magic. There were frustratingly few points of entry for her. Rowan had taken the most useful amulets with him, along with the dream ring—presumably they were now in the hands of the Undercastle. There were a few objects from the ruins, some strikingly powerful—a cup that purified all water, a broken sword whose shards could cut through any barrier. But Rowan had always warned against using those, and she didn't want to purify water anyway. The silver amulet from the Undercastle vault, the one left as bait to enchant him, sat on the desk, but she didn't know what it did. That left mostly trinkets: a candle that stayed alight in any weather, but left her feeling cold whenever she managed to coax it to life; a key that could open any door, but would be unlikely to work against the stronger magic of the Undercastle; a knife that turned jam into butter, which she couldn't help but think must have been meant the other way around. Even those seemed to fight her when she used them, as she couldn't remember them doing before.

"Stop it!" she snapped once, at the end of a long day when the candle refused to light. "I can't help it if I'm not Rowan. I can't help it if I'm not anybody."

The candle remained stubbornly dark. She couldn't help but suspect it wasn't the candle's fault, but her own. Magic needed conviction. It asked for your whole heart, and promised nothing back. Her own heart was too divided, and too full of fears and doubts. It was all very well to say, as she had to Hutchincroft, that she didn't care if magic wanted her. She *did* care. She had always wanted it to invite her in, and now she knew that it never had. The only one who had chosen her was Rowan, and even he didn't know why.

The best weapon she held was the ravenstone, and she forced herself to practice with it every evening. Their boat was still moored on the mainland. If she was going to return to London, it would have to be the same way she had left. Hutch would come with her, reluctantly, concerned for her mind. She was concerned for her own mind, at first. The raven was not happy with a new partner. Its fear and rage scrabbled at her thoughts the way its claws had raked the chimney, and it was all she could do to hold on as she guided it in slow, swooping circles over Hy-Brasil. Its heart was struggle and flight, and weathering it left her shaken. She started to understand why Rowan had looked so lean and worn and on edge in Storm's memory, when the ravenstone was new-forged and wild.

And yet, slowly, it did calm. She learned how to hold on to herself while focusing on soothing and gently guiding its flight. She started being able to relax enough to realize that she was *flying*, to feel the thrill of joy as she plunged down to skim the tops of the trees or up over the cliffs. She loved the feel of the raven's feathers rippling in the wind, the clean cut of its beak through the air, the constant whisper of Hutch's voice in her mind, as though he really were her familiar. This last thought she tried to repress as much as possible. It felt, in a guilt-stricken way, like wishing Rowan gone.

You're getting it, Hutch said to her, as they flew over the forests as the sun set. *You're listening to each other.*

If she had a mouth, she would have smiled.

It isn't enough, though, she said. It was only recently she had been able to extract her thoughts from the raven's enough to reply to Hutchincroft's conversations while they flew. It still felt like a victory at times; it would have now, had what she'd been saying not been so undeniably true. *None of this is enough. I'm going against mages who have been practicing for hundreds of years, and I have a butter knife and a candle that doesn't like me.*

The candle likes you better now. It lights almost every time.

That's nice, but I can't find the schism by lighting a candle at it. I need a way to capture Morgaine on her own ground, without the Council knowing. Are you sure you don't know any magic that might help?

She knew the answer as she asked it. Hutchincroft, as he had warned, wasn't able to help very much. It wasn't only that he was a rabbit almost all the time now. He was a familiar. To him, magic was like the air around them—he would notice if it wasn't there, but he couldn't explain it when it was, and he couldn't explain how to breathe to someone without lungs.

I've never exactly done *magic,* Hutch said, sure enough. *Not spells, and certainly not amulets. Those are for human mages. Rowan needed all this to talk to the otherworld. I only needed the fractures between worlds. Didn't he leave notes? He wrote things down all the time.*

He did. I've spent hours on his notes. But he was writing to himself, and I have no idea what he was on about. The Council's silver amulet, for instance. He seemed to have had some kind of breakthrough on that the night before we left, but the notebook just says "yes," underlined three times. What does that mean?

It means he asked himself a question, Hutch said. *And the answer was yes. Underlined three times.*

But what was the question? You were there.

I was, Hutchincroft conceded. *But most of the time I was napping. Or thinking about dinner.*

She had to laugh, because she was sick of crying.

The raven spread its wings, catching the updraft, and she let it do so. They were flying high above the cliffs now, almost out to sea, and the waves glittered hard and bright under the grey sky. More and more often, now the raven's fear had calmed, she could feel glimpses of other things beneath it—curiosity, mischief, a playful and glittering intelligence. There was a strange joy in losing herself through the raven's eyes, as if her own worst thoughts and worries and tensions were sinking to the bottom of a river and she was swimming through clear water.

The ruins were dotted with black rabbits; one of them raised its head to look at her, and she saw with a start that even at this distance its eyes glinted gold.

Be careful, Hutch warned.

It took her a moment to find words this time. *Why? What was I doing wrong?*

Nothing. That was almost what I meant. When Rowan came back from the Undercastle last time, when he was so unwell, he used to spend hours as a raven. Not just all night, like he does now—all day as well, sometimes days on end. Sometimes when I talked to him, he stopped hearing me. It's dangerous to use magic as a way to be something else.

I'm not doing that. She wasn't so sure it was true. At the very least, it was startling to hear the impulses she had barely recognized put into words, and realize they had belonged to somebody else. *At least—I didn't realize. I'll stay in control. Hutch?*

What is it?

She could see no trace of the gold-eyed rabbit now, even as she circled back. Perhaps it had never been there at all, but she doubted it. It wasn't the first time she had seen the glint of gold at dusk since she had returned.

What about the Púca? she asked.

She couldn't see Hutchincroft, but she felt him stiffen, as a rabbit does sensing danger. *What about it?*

It's a being of pure magic too, but it's lived in this world a long time—since before people came, Rowan said. *It's played tricks for thousands of years. It might know a spell to trap a mage.*

If it does, Hutchincroft said, *then it won't share it with us.*

I'm not so sure. I've seen it around lately, more than usual. Even before I returned—it was there the day Vaughan's wisps came. I think it might want to tell me something.

It wants you. *Those things live to play tricks on humans.*

But they do make deals at times, in the old stories. Has Rowan ever spoken to it?

Rowan does deal with the Púca on occasion, Hutchincroft conceded reluctantly. *He tries to get information from it. But to do so, he has to give it secrets of his own. It's dangerous.*

Dangerous for Rowan?

Hutchincroft snorted. *Rowan doesn't care about that sort of danger. Dangerous for the world. A mage can't trust a Púca. They're creatures of mischief. They're always trying to get a mage's secrets, and who knows what havoc they'll wreak with them?*

Then I'll be safe, Biddy said. *I'm not a mage. I don't have any secrets.*

You won't *be safe! Nothing about those things is safe. They're... they're not like us.* He struggled for words to explain. *Mages follow rules. So do familiars, once they're bound. Things like the Púca and the good folk and Hy-Brasil—they're old magic. They're on nobody's side but their own, and they'll do anything they like.*

That doesn't mean that what they like needs to be dangerous. Perhaps in this case, it might be more fun to help. It can't be fond of the Council, surely.

Rowan said you should stay away from it.

Rowan said a lot of things that turned out not to be true, didn't he? she said before she could stop herself. She was trying not to think about the lies at the core of her life, or at least not to resent them. It seemed childish when Rowan was miles away, in terrible pain and terrible danger, and he'd put himself there to save her. But it hurt. Sometimes she wondered if trying not to think about it made it hurt worse than ever.

It wouldn't help if you did have a way to trap Morgaine, Hutch pointed out. If he had felt the undercurrents of her thoughts, he showed no sign. *You'd still need a way to do it without the Council seeing. Her house will be watched.*

Perhaps it will be able to help with that too, she said, though with less conviction. It seemed less likely, somehow—the sort of thing that needed more than a spell or a trick.

You can't trust it, Hutch said firmly. He must have sensed her wavering. *Please. Promise me you won't talk to it.*

She sighed. *All right*, she said. *I won't.*

It wasn't a promise.

—————————⊷═══════════⊶—————————

Biddy had been on the island for seven days when she saw Morgaine first disappear. She was watching her in the scrying glass with half an eye, trying to decipher one of Rowan's scrawled notebooks at the same time (this one had a large tea stain across two pages, just to make it worse). Morgaine had been walking in the park at Primrose Hill in the late afternoon, alone under a grey sky. Biddy glanced up idly, only to see that in the few seconds she had looked away Morgaine had simply vanished.

Biddy had spent a good deal of time at the scrying glass over the last few days. It was one magical artifact she had always been able to manage, and now there was nobody to stop her from trying it whenever she wanted. When she asked for Rowan, it would show nothing but the thin white mist that hid the dungeon. Storm's name never yielded any images, presumably because he was always in the dungeon too; Vaughan she saw once in the street, but his eyes snapped at once so precisely to meet hers through the surface of the mirror that she flinched back, afraid to look further. She had no doubt that he had known he was being looked at, and she didn't trust that cursed eye of his not to see her in return.

Morgaine's flat, too, was veiled to the mirror—not even the outside of the building would appear for the asking. Morgaine herself, though, was another story. Biddy saw Morgaine often: riding in the back of a cab, drinking tea in cafés, or just walking through wide, flat gardens, arms folded and head cast down. She couldn't read her expression—guilt at her betrayal? Worry at her discovery?—and couldn't guess at what lay behind it. She had started to watch her more and more, learning the times when Morgaine was likely to be visible, trying to track her movements. It was a matter of strategy. It made sense to know where she was going, and where she was likely to be. And yet if it had made less sense, she would have done it anyway. Morgaine fascinated and troubled her on a level she couldn't explain.

Hutch was never very pleased to see Morgaine's image in the glass. Biddy assumed he couldn't bear to see the woman who had betrayed them. Once, though, it occurred to her to wonder if Rowan had ever watched Morgaine through the scrying mirror, in his office on his own.

Hutch was by the fire when Morgaine vanished from sight; Biddy's sharp exclamation brought him to her side. The mirror was showing only a veil of silver mist. Morgaine had gone somewhere hidden, clearly. But it was impossible to tell where.

He watched the mirror for three hours, ears rigid, eyes fixed, while Biddy tried to finish off the notebook and most of an apple. In the end, she watched too, frustrated but unable to concentrate on anything else. It was dark when Morgaine at last jumped back into view of the scrying glass, and Biddy's heart sank. The view was the same as when Morgaine had gone away, except that Morgaine was now walking back in the opposite direction: the slopes of a hill, the wide paths, the clumps of tall trees. It told her nothing.

Hutchincroft, on the other hand, flicked his ears joyfully and jumped off the desk. He was human as soon as he hit the floor, words tumbling from his mouth before his face had lost its rabbit softness.

"I know where that is!" he declared. "*That* is a library."

Biddy frowned. "A library?"

"Their library. Rowan and Morgaine's." He pushed his fair hair back from his forehead and pointed at the glass. "That's right about the crest of Primrose Hill. They built a library there years ago, a secret one. Rowan goes back there sometimes, even though I tell him it isn't safe—well." Hutch broke off, his exuberance fading. "He *did*."

She tried to steer him away from that line of thought. She'd spent too much time there herself. "And this library—you think the Council doesn't know about it?"

"I feared they did, in fact. That's why I warned Rowan away. Morgaine knew, after all, and if she wanted to help the Council, she would have told them about it. But if Morgaine is sneaking there on her own, very much as if she doesn't want to be seen..."

A place Morgaine might be, and that the Council might not know of. It was something. It was the closest they had come to a plan in days.

"There's still no way to trap her," Hutchincroft reminded her. His eyes were on her face, wary.

"No," she agreed. "But I know how to find one."

He knew at once what she meant. It couldn't have escaped his attention that she had never promised. He opened his mouth to protest, but she cut him off.

"Hutch," she said, as calmly as she could. "Why might Morgaine be going to that library now? Rowan clearly never saw her there, so she doesn't do it often."

"It could be any number of reasons!" he protested. "Perhaps she just wants to think. Perhaps she's looking for something."

She waited.

"Or perhaps," he conceded, "she's trying to cover her tracks. Perhaps she wants to make sure any association she has with Rowan is gone, now they've finally caught him. She might be about to unmake that library very soon."

"Exactly." She hadn't known enough to think of it in those terms, but her thoughts had been on similar lines. "It means we can't afford to wait."

And they couldn't. Hutch knew this better than she did, she suspected. Rowan had been a week in Storm's hands. Hutch had never made a sound since that first night, and had always maintained staunchly that the Council had never allowed him a glimpse of Rowan again. But at times he would shudder, or his ears would go flat against his head, and Biddy knew that something sharp and painful had slipped through the spell of the Undercastle dungeons. And he himself was losing magic every day. Rabbits were good at hiding their weaknesses, but she could see it more clearly in his human face: the tired lines about his eyes, the faint pallor to his skin, the slump of his round shoulders. They couldn't afford to wait.

"Rowan wouldn't want it," Hutch said, but without heat. Rowan wouldn't want her to do anything she was now doing.

"Rowan isn't here," Biddy said firmly. "I am."

The mist was thick that evening. It cast the island into shades of silver—against it, the black rabbits grazing looked like specks of midnight. When Biddy walked up to them softly and crouched down in their midst, they ignored her.

"Please," she said, very quietly. One raised his head eyes large and liquid, a tuft of grass poking from its mouth. It looked at her, the enigmatic gaze of a rabbit who could be listening to you or to a tiny noise miles away. "If you see the Púca, will you tell it I want to speak with it?"

Chapter Fifteen

She was by the old oak when it finally came, three days after she had told the rabbits in the fields to find it for her. The light was fading in the sky, and she was worn and hungry after a frustrating morning in the library and a long flight in the afternoon. The flight at least had gone well, but that was its own source of frustration: Her skill with the ravenstone had plateaued, and she knew she had it under as much control as she ever would with only short flights around Hy-Brasil. It was ready for her to leave the island. She was desperate to leave, despite her fear. But she still had too little magic, and no plan. It didn't help that she had woken from broken sleep half-entangled in nightmares of dungeons and screaming, and been fighting both despair and a splitting headache all day.

Biddy was focusing so hard on that battle that she almost missed the slow hush that descended over the clearing, as though the call of each bird and the rustle of each tree was being put out like a candle one by one. Her eyes were on the great tree, examining it for any signs of decay or damage after so long without new magic stored in its branches. She looked back, only half-aware of what had caught her attention, and saw with a start that Hutchincroft was nowhere to be found.

"Hutch?" she called, and heard her voice echo oddly in the silence. She took a step forward, and even her footfall sounded muffled. Her grip tightened around the ravenstone in her pocket. "Where are you?"

A branch cracked, sharp and deliberate, and she turned.

Biddy saw the Púca often at twilight. It usually took the form of a black rabbit, as it had that day in the ruins. Once, walking with Rowan, they had seen it as a black stag with towering antlers; another time, looking out her bedroom window, she had seen a black pony gallop across the hills. Both times, even from a distance, she had recognized its eyes.

It was a rabbit this time, larger than Hutchincroft or even the ones that inhabited the fields, glossy and deep black flecked with silver. It came through the forest, picking its way through the undergrowth with exaggerated care.

"Hello, Bridget Hutchincroft-O'Connell," the Púca said. Its voice was high and lilting, neither male nor female. "I've been waiting for you to come to me for a long time."

"I know." She stood as straight and calm as she could, heart hammering. "I used to see you out my window, and watching me in the fields. You were there the day the wisps came."

"I'm always here. Don't take it too personally."

That made her smile, despite herself. "I don't. But Hutch said Púca like to play tricks on people. It must be boring for you here."

"Not as boring as everywhere else," it said. "It's become a grey, bleak world without magic. And cruel, which is worse than boring."

"Where *is* Hutch?" Biddy dared to ask. "What have you done with him?"

The black rabbit shifted on its haunches. "He's safe. I thought we should talk alone. What exactly do you think I can do for you?"

She couldn't worry about Hutch now—though she did, desperately. Now she was standing nose to nose with the Púca, she could see what Hutch had meant. It wasn't malevolent, but it was *other*. None of the rules about how a conversation was conducted between two living beings applied to it. It might answer her questions, or stop talking altogether. It might lie, or tell the truth, or help her, or harm her, and it would do so for no reason except what would amuse it the most at the time.

"The Council have Rowan. I'm trying to rescue him." She said it as formally as she could, as though she were speaking of a business matter and not the inmost need of her heart.

"Even though he lied to you?" It didn't wait for an answer. "I don't know how to rescue him. What mages do to each other isn't my concern."

"I think I know how. But I need to entrap another mage. I hoped you might know how to do that, as you're so powerful."

"Don't flatter me, child. I'm a Púca, not a common dragon. Rowan showed you how to trap a mage."

She didn't even think to question how the Púca knew that. It seemed insulting to think it wouldn't, somehow. "He showed me how he meant to do it. The trap circle. But I can't do that. I'm not a mage."

"Neither am I. I told you, it's no business of mine what they do to each other. If you want me to help you on your quest, you'll need a better one than that."

"Such as?"

It looked at her with its golden eyes, as if cataloging her inch by inch. "Bridget Hutchincroft-O'Connell," it said at last. "The girl with the spell in her heart. You should have come with me that day when we first met, you know. When you were four years old, and I was a black pony offering you a ride on my back. I would have told Rowan about the memory and what it held, once I'd had my fun with you."

The words hit like a rush of cold rain. "You knew about it?"

"Of course I knew. I can recognize Rowan's spellmark even when he doesn't recognize it himself. I knew from the first time I saw you."

"Why didn't you tell him?"

"He never asked. He just wanted to know how to open the schisms between this world and what lies beyond. And yet, it's interesting... When it came to it, he didn't want to know enough."

"Are you telling me that *you* know?" Without thinking, against every rule she knew, she took a step closer. "You know how to bring magic back to the world?"

"I've seen it done."

Her breath caught. "How? I mean—by whom?"

These were two different questions; it answered the latter. "By them. The old ones—the ones who used to live on this island."

"The people who left the ruins? The—the Tuatha Dé Danann?" She stumbled a little over the name, which she had only heard Rowan say a handful of times. "When was this?"

"A long, long time ago. Hundreds of years—thousands, it must be. I was young then, and I haven't been young for a very long time." It paused. "They nearly stole all the magic from the world too, at the last. Only they put it right."

"How? How did they put it right?"

"And why do you want to know?" There was no accusation in the question, only something soft and shadowed she couldn't read. "Is it your quest then to bring magic back to the world?"

"How could it be?" The excitement that had been building in her chest dissolved at once, like salt in water. It left a bitter residue on her tongue. "I told you, I'm not a mage. I can't do anything about magic."

The Púca didn't blink. "That isn't what I asked."

"No." She drew a deep breath, blinking back the hot tears that threatened her eyes. Neither she nor Rowan had ever had any patience with self-pity; she couldn't imagine the Púca would. "No, it wasn't."

The Púca waited. It clearly wasn't going to move without an answer, and yet she wondered if the wrong one would send it away. She didn't know what answer it might be looking for, or why.

"I used to think I could be the one to return magic to the world," she said at last. It felt like a confession. She had never said anything of the kind before, not even to Hutchincroft, not even when she was very young. It had sounded arrogant in her own head; it sounded downright stupid now, when she had seen the world and her own insignificance in it. A flush came to her cheeks, but she went on. "I used to think that—even though I wasn't a mage, I thought I'd washed up on the island for a reason. That I had a destiny, the sort you find in legends. But I don't, do I?"

"No," the Púca agreed. "You don't. Legends are the correct environment for destinies. They take very careful curating; it's rare to find a wild one outside them."

"And I'm not..." She paused to arrange the words carefully before she handed them over. "I'm not the child of anybody special. Not a mage, or a queen, or...?"

"You're simply a human creature, born of two other human creatures," it interrupted. "No different to any other of your kind."

Somehow it didn't hurt to hear it as she had thought it would. If it was what she had feared, it was also no more than she expected. "Well, then. I want to get Rowan out of the Undercastle. I want us all to be safe. If I can do that, it's more than I ever hoped."

It didn't answer, and she understood why. What she said wasn't true. Deep down, she had always hated the idea of handing over the schism to Vaughan. It felt like a betrayal of something deeper than principle. He was a cruel person, and helping cruel people to grow stronger couldn't be good. It was just too big for her to think about right now. She was barely holding together as it was.

And yet.

"If I *did* find a schism," she said slowly, "and it was alive and well—could I do it? Could it be used to open all the others?"

"Not alone," the Púca said. "Not by you. But yes. It could be done. I could show you. But I would ask for something in return. A secret bargain."

That was unexpected, and distracted her momentarily. "What is it?"

"That's the secret. I won't tell you."

Its eyes glinted with something that wasn't quite malicious, but was definitely mischievous. It sparked a small flare of irritation. "That's not fair. You can't expect me to make a bargain without knowing what it is."

"I expect nothing." The mischief was unmistakable now. "I only offer. Rowan said much the same as you when I offered to him, if you want to know."

"No wonder. Hutch said he was worried you would take knowledge of magic you shouldn't have."

"That was the case at first, when he was new to this island," the Púca agreed. "He thought he could find the answer on his own. In the last few years, when he grew more desperate, I think he might not have minded giving me forbidden knowledge so much. But by then, of course, he was afraid that I would ask for you instead."

That startled her more than the deal itself—more, in some ways, than the Púca's claim to have watched the original inhabitants of Hy-Brasil bring magic back. "Me? Why would you want me?"

"You? I'm a Púca. I want nothing except trouble. Rowan understood that perfectly well. That's why there were some risks even he wouldn't take."

She smiled, though her heart clenched. She had thought over the last few days that there were no risks Rowan wouldn't take, with her life as well as his. She had thought that he wanted to bring magic back to the world more than anything at all, even her.

"And what about you, Bridget Hutchincroft-O'Connell?" the Púca asked softly, as though she had spoken aloud. "What do you want?"

She had meant what she had said before. If she could choose one thing, out of all the world, it would be to have Rowan safe and well—whatever he had done to her, or lied about. Deep down, so deep she didn't even want to admit it to herself, she wanted things to be back the way they had been only weeks ago: the three of them on the island, the outside world a formless blur on the horizon with a safe wild sea between it and them. She wouldn't care how bored and frustrated she felt, wouldn't care where Rowan went every night, she wouldn't even care that many of the things she believed to be true were wrong. What did it matter, as long as she never found out the truth? She'd lived all her life in stories, after all.

But it didn't work like that. She *had* left the island. She had seen the children cold and miserable in a Whitechapel school, spared from even worse on the streets; she had seen Anna sickening in a thin, hard bed and an old man hunched on the steps of the National Gallery; she had seen the Council in their kingdom under the earth, hoarding anything that had the power to help so it could help them instead. She had seen the world, and the world *needed* magic. Whatever Rowan had lied about, knowingly or otherwise, he was right about that. She knew that now, perhaps even more surely than he did, because she was precisely one of those ordinary human creatures who would never normally have known magic existed and yet missed it desperately. Knowing that made it her responsibility to help if she could.

And there was something else. If magic came back, not just a trickle but wholly and entirely, then Vaughan's iron grip on the Council would be weakened. He would no longer be able to hoard the last scratches of power for himself. There would be thousands of mages with years' worth of pent-up spells at their fingertips, and they may not be pleased with him. There was a chance, however slim, that his term of office might finally be at an end. He might grow more powerful, of course; he might kill Rowan in retribution. And yet there was a *chance*. That, Rowan had told her once, was what magic meant. A chance of something better.

Biddy, like Hutchincroft, didn't like risks. She had never liked setting her weight on a branch she wasn't sure would hold her, never liked jumping off a cliff without being sure of the waves beneath, she always took a jacket with her when she went out for the day in case of rain. Even Rowan, for all his recklessness, had taught her to be clever as well as brave. This was a great risk—so was making a bargain with a Púca, a risk not only to her but to others as well. The enormity of it terrified her. But that was no reason not to do it.

"I won't make your secret bargain," she said slowly. Thoughts were taking shape in her head, and for the first time in days, they were starting to look something like a plan.

The Púca inclined its rabbit head. "Then we have nothing more to say to each other. Not until next time, at least."

"I'm not finished," Biddy said, before it could turn. She swallowed hard. "Instead, I'll make *this* bargain. If you show me how to open the schisms and restore magic to the world, I will do everything in my power to bring it about."

It went still, as only a rabbit can. "Why would I accept that?"

"Because you said you wanted nothing but trouble, but I don't think that's quite true. I think you want magic restored, perhaps even more than we do. You said it yourself: The world is so dull without it." The words came tumbling out now, too fast to take back. "You've been watching me ever since I came to the island, knowing what the spell in my heart meant. You said that if Rowan had only made a deal with you, you would have told him everything. I think you've been looking for an excuse to help him, and hoping all this time we would give you one. Well, here it is. I'm promising you a world brimming with magic. Whatever you were planning to take from me, it can't have been as important as that. I'm not a mage. I have no magic, no knowledge, no tricks."

"Don't be so certain." The Púca sat back on its haunches, nose twitching. "Well done. It's been a long time since anybody surprised me."

"Does that mean you'll agree?"

It didn't answer for a while, or directly when it spoke again. "The rabbits like you," the Púca said. "Just as they like Rowan, and for the same reason. In all the years you've been here, you've never hunted them."

"Of course not," she said, surprised. "Why would we?"

"Because you could. Because the winters are cold here, and their flesh can be eaten. Because they eat the food you wanted for yourself. Because they are wild and joyful and belong to nobody but themselves, and some people couldn't bear that."

Biddy felt a little uncomfortable. It wasn't, after all, as if they never ate the flesh of animals at all. Even had such a thing occurred to her, she could never have persuaded Hutchincroft to give up bacon.

"Even in the worst winter, we would never hunt on Hy-Brasil," she said truthfully. "It doesn't belong to us. And the other reasons aren't reasons at all."

"Perhaps not to you."

This time, the silence was even longer, and Biddy caught herself wondering if perhaps time meant nothing to a Púca—if, perhaps, it was perfectly capable of sitting in thoughtful silence all night or even for many nights, and thinking nothing of it. She wondered if perhaps this wasn't silence to the Púca at all, if its gold eyes could see things she couldn't and it was even now thumbing through her mind like the pages of a book. She had time to remember, anew, that she had been about to go home for dinner and she was still hungry. She wondered if she was brave enough to do this after all. She hoped that Hutch really was safe.

"Very well," it said at last.

She frowned, cautious. "What does that mean?"

"It means very well." The black rabbit stretched, arching its back, then bounded forward. In midair its body twisted; by the time its front feet touched the ground again, they were no longer paws but hooves, and they belonged to a wild pony with tangled mane and shaggy jet-black coat. The Púca's gold eyes gleamed out of its head. "Climb on my back."

Biddy laughed. "No."

"Why not?"

"I'm not stupid! This is what you do to unsuspecting travelers. You persuade them to climb on your back, and you take off with them and terrify the living daylights out of them and then deposit them in a patch of thorns and stinging nettles when you're done. Rowan told me all about it when I was little and you nearly did the same to me."

She had been three or four that day, just before Morgaine had visited her in her dreams. She remembered it more as a story than as a fact, apart from a few glimpses: a warm summer evening, prickly grass against her small bare feet, the arch of a pony's neck and the glint of golden eyes, the wiry grip of horsehair in her fist just before a raven's call split the skies.

It was the Púca's turn to laugh, the high, strange laugh of a creature who doesn't draw breath. "Rowan was so angry with me. You didn't see; Hutchincroft took you away. He swore that if I ever did anything of the kind again, he wouldn't rest until he'd banished me from the island. I don't know if he could have done it. He should have known better than to threaten it. But I never tried again. In every fairy tale ever told, it's a bad idea to tangle with a magician's daughter."

Nobody, not Hutch, not Rowan, not even herself, had ever referred to her in those terms before. And yet hearing it made her relationship with Rowan so clear and so bright that it hurt. She still didn't know who he was, or why he had done so many of the things he had done. But she knew who he had raised her to be. If he wasn't her father, then she at least was his daughter.

"Is that why you're trying it now?" She willed everything but confidence from her eyes. "Because he's gone?"

"No." The Púca's own gold eyes held nothing at all. "You know exactly what happens to unsuspecting travelers who climb on my back, Bridget Hutchincroft-O'Connell. It was what would have happened to you as a young child, seduced by a beautiful black horse met in the fields of a summer twilight. But you are no unsuspecting traveler now. You are not being tricked. You know exactly what you're doing, and you do it willingly. That makes a difference. Besides, we have a bargain."

She didn't even know if the Púca kept bargains. "How do I know this isn't a trick in itself?"

"You don't. There are never any sureties with magic. You can never know what will happen. All you can do is throw yourself in with your whole heart, and expect nothing more than a wild ride."

Biddy drew a deep breath. This was, after all, what she had been waiting for. She had been scrabbling at the surface of the island's magic, trying to find cracks and weaknesses that could let her through. If nothing else, this was a way to plunge into the depths, and see what lay there.

She had to do something. This was what there was to do.

And the Púca had said it was a bad idea to tangle with a magician's daughter.

She reached out, as she had that evening as a child, and gripped the Púca's wiry black mane. To her surprise, it sank immediately down onto its knees, and she swung her leg over its side and sat on it with no more difficulty than she might have climbing up on the old walls by the ruins. It was surprisingly hard and round, like mounting a barrel of solid muscle.

That was the last coherent thought she had. The Púca rose to its feet, shook its head once, and began to run.

＊＊＝＝＝＝＝＝＝＝＊＊

Biddy had never ridden a horse—longing to do so was part of what had nearly driven her to the Púca's back as a child. But she had seen pictures and watched the carriages trot past in London, and she knew that this was no horse. It had the body of a pony, but it moved with the impossibly swift bound of a rabbit. Its back arched and flexed beneath her as muscles bunched and back legs kicked. She tried to move with it at first, locking with her knees, keeping her back ramrod straight like she had read how to do. That was for the first few paces, when it was only moving the same speed as a fast gallop. Then it really started to run, and there was no chance of doing anything at all but winding her hands tight about its mane and clinging on with all her strength.

The forest streamed past her, faster and faster. The trees were a long streak of color, and then there was no color at all. Wind whipped her face with such force that she couldn't breathe, couldn't move, couldn't tell it from the physical impact of the branches flying past her face. The landscape she had known all her life was dizzying, unfamiliar, nonsensical. The Púca's neck was in front of her; everything else was a swirl of chaos. If she came off, she would be lost.

Stop it. She tried to ignore the tears stinging her eyes, the agony of the wiry horsehair cutting her into her hand, the wild terror trying to claw itself from her chest. *The Púca doesn't kill. It plays tricks. You're not going to die.*

She couldn't believe it. Death, after all, was nothing if not a terrible trick, the worst life can play. And there was very little that the Púca wouldn't do.

Wind.

Leaves.

Darkness.

And then, a burst of light.

The forest was gone. They were rising toward the highest cliffs, across the fields where the rabbits grazed, and the Púca was slowing. The light was moonlight, silvering the grass, clear and low and bright, though the sun had been setting when the Púca had come and it should have been only a thin quarter moon that night. She barely had time to wonder before the top of the hill came into view and she understood everything.

The ruins were no longer ruins. On the cliffs, at the highest point of the island, white towers rose to breathtaking points. As they thundered up the slope, the rest was revealed: a vast fortress, almost a citadel, its jumble of solid buildings and soaring parapets ringed by pale walls. It was clean and shining and new-made, entwined with climbing plants and trees and dark moss. In the darkness it glowed with a hundred hanging lights.

She was seeing the island as it had been thousands of years ago, under an ancient moon. This was the lost civilization of Hy-Brasil.

"Hold tight," the Púca said, as though in all the swirling maelstrom of the past few minutes Biddy had been relaxing with her hands in the air. The Púca swerved sharply to one side, so that Biddy lunged forward with an undignified yelp, and sprinted toward the fortress. A black rabbit grazing in the field looked up, startled, as they passed.

The gates were closed, and yet the Púca ran straight at them, and before Biddy could blink they were on the other side of the stone walls. Beyond, in the center of a great circular courtyard, stood the great yew tree. It was a young tree now, smooth and graceful. The courtyard around it was filled with people. Or, Biddy realized with a start, *beings*. Good folk, Hutch might have called them, or even gods. Whatever they were, they were not human.

They looked human enough from a distance, or should have.

They were tall and strong, it was true, clad in armor and woolen cloaks, the men and women alike standing seven or eight feet high and all with long braided hair. Their skin was ghost white, the color of marble or chalk, almost blue in the moonlight. But Biddy had seen so few people compared to how many there were in the world, and those she had seen had been all colors and sizes. It was possible that in other parts of the world, people were taller and paler than the ones she knew.

Their faces, though, were not mortal faces. They were too sharp, their cheekbones too high and their chins too pointed, as though the skull beneath was a very different shape. Their eyes were green gold, the flicker of light through trees, and had the remote look Biddy recognized on Hutchincroft when he was listening to something far away.

"They don't live here," the Púca said, as though she had asked a question. "This was a fortress, an outpost. They established it during the first war, the war to take the land."

"The war with the Fomorians." Rowan had told her those stories.

The Púca carried on as if she hadn't spoken. "They brought the rabbits with them to hunt if they were cut off from the coast. They wove the island with spells, and when they won their war, they kept it so that in the case of another war they could retreat here at the very last. This isn't the very last yet. Almost. Your kind have taken the mainland."

"Have they come to fight back?"

"The fighting is over. Soon they'll be forced underground, little more than stories. They're here for the schism."

"There's a schism on this island?"

"Not anymore. It closed with all the others. But there was once. There was."

The Púca was still moving beneath her, the wind was rushing in Biddy's face, but they had stopped moving forward. It was a strange sensation: She glanced down at the ground disappearing beneath the Púca's feet, then forced herself to look up as her stomach rebelled at trying to make sense of it. She fixed her eyes on the courtyard ahead of her, at the crowd standing in a half circle to face a bare white wall. A woman, bronze-armored with a coil of black hair, stepped forward.

The schism. The fracture. The crack in the world.

Biddy couldn't see magic; she knew that for the most part the fractures between one world and another would have been invisible to her too. But she could see this one, the schism the fair folk had come for. It *glowed*, gold and green like the eyes of the Tuatha Dé Danann, a crack across the stone wall through which light from another world gleamed. The woman pressed her fingertips to the wall, head lowered, green light highlighting the sharp planes of her face.

The schism grew.

Four years ago, Hy-Brasil had been gripped by a black, viciously cold winter, the kind that whipped the sea into a frenzy and blew snow and sleet against the castle walls. Now, she knew it could easily have turned deadly: The blizzard prevented them from reaching the mainland by boat or by wing, food and firewood and soon even magic was running low, and they spent most of the time freezing in the library pretending not to be hungry. Then, she was just young enough to believe Rowan that it was all a fun adventure, if she tried very hard, and she did. For the first time in Biddy's memory the stream in the woods had frozen to ice. She had thought, one unusually quiet morning when the sun had peeked out enough to leave the castle, that she might be able to skate on it. When she had set her foot on it, though, there was a sharp crack, and a barely visible fracture beneath her boot spidered out to the far bank. She just had time to throw herself back in a panic before the ice parted.

That was what the opening of the schism reminded her of now. The woman's fingers put pressure on the tiny crack, and the wall splintered open, a great glittering fracture across the white stone. But it wasn't the pressure that had done it. The woman was whispering, a low steady stream of words in another tongue, the rise and fall of a spell.

"What are they doing?" Biddy whispered.

Her voice was too quiet to carry over the keening of the wind, but the Púca answered anyway. "They took too much, trying to hold the land for themselves. They're giving back what they've taken."

It was what Storm and Rowan and Morgaine had been arguing about the day of Storm's memory, before the ravenstone had been laid on the table and everything had twisted out of control. Rowan had believed that magic was leaving the world because the mages had used too much of it, too fast—so much that the schisms were unable to stay open. Biddy had seen the theory in some of the oldest spellbooks in Rowan's office she had sat up at night reading. Morgaine had believed it too, Rowan had said, and so had many of the others the Servant had murdered upon taking power.

"It's that simple?" she asked. "They just give it back?"

"It was simple for them. They saw it happening, and they acted. They didn't leave it until all the world was so grey and cold that returning it to life would take everything."

"But when did they—?"

"Hush. This isn't a history lesson. Knowledge has a price. This is what you paid for."

"I didn't pay anything."

"You got on my back, and you rode with me through time and magic. You're a different person now, a person who has seen past the veil. Do you truly think that isn't a price?" It didn't wait for an answer. "Besides, you made me a promise. A promise to give everything to restore the world."

The woman had dropped her hand now. She threw back her head with a high, wild cry, wordless and thrilling, almost a note of music. It made the leaves stir in the young yew tree and the hairs rise on Biddy's neck. The cobbled ground beneath her feet cracked and split, a sharp fault line that shot out from the base of the schism to the roots of the yew. The crowd didn't move, didn't start. It must have been meant to happen—a sign, perhaps, that the work was done.

The woman lowered her head once more. Her face was glowing,

flushed not pink but silver. Her eyes glinted in the moonlight. Then, astonishingly, they met Biddy's. The look was like a shock of salt spray, unexpected and stinging and ice cold. The wild eyes held her, and the lips curled into a very slight smile. Biddy inclined her head, stiffly, heart pounding, and the smile deepened. She had no idea what it meant, only that she would never be the same again.

"Time to go," the Púca said.

***

It had dumped her in a bramble bush.

When awareness came back to her—a strange feeling, her senses not awakening but quieting, the world around her settling into something that could be seen and felt—the first thing that made sense was the thorns digging into her arm. She hissed, more in annoyance than in pain, and struggled upright. Branches snagged on her hair and her shirt; her bones ached where she had hit the earth.

"You didn't have to do that," she complained, breathless, and heard a high laugh on the wind in response.

"You got what you wanted, didn't you?" the laugh said, in words she could understand without hearing. "You should thank me."

"I do!" she retorted, and then more quietly, she repeated, "I do. Thank you."

Because it had helped her, after all. It had given the key she needed to do what she had to do, and in its own way it had done so willingly. She wasn't foolish enough to think she could have tricked a being of pure magic who didn't want to be tricked.

But still. It *hurt*.

"Good luck on your quest, magician's daughter," the Púca's voice came. "From the little I know of Morgaine, she has a battle ahead of her with you."

"You could at least tell me how to trap her," Biddy said, without rancor this time.

The laugh was softer now, farther away. "I did."

Biddy frowned, and then the memory blossomed. It had. Of course it had. She laughed herself at the simplicity of it.

The soft scrabble of running feet across foliage cut into her thoughts, followed by the welcome sight of a small gold rabbit bursting through the thicket. Her heart flooded with relief, even as Hutch's lithe rabbit body twisted and burst into his human form.

"Unbelievable!" Hutch's voice blazed with fury, and Biddy had rarely been more happy to hear anything. "It turned me into a spider! Or it forced me to turn myself, I'm not too sure, but either way!"

"The Púca?"

"A common trickster spirit, and I'm a *familiar*. If my mage had been here, it would never have dared. I heard you talking but you have *no idea* what it's like being a spider. They hear through their *legs*. And they may have eight eyes, but those eyes are *terrible*, I could barely see you. I couldn't see that creature at all until it changed into something bigger. And then you were gone with it, and I had no way to follow. What were you *thinking*? Did it hurt you?"

"I'm fine," she said, and found she was smiling. "I'm so glad you're safe."

"Me? It couldn't do anything to me. It's you I worried about. If it had wanted to harm you..."

"It didn't," she interrupted. "It didn't harm me. It helped. And we need to get moving. We have a long journey to make."

"A long journey? Where? When?"

"We're going to London," she said. "Now. Tonight. As soon as we can be ready."

"Now?" He looked at her with a rabbit's startled eyes. They cleared when he saw her face, as though they had seen something more beyond it. "What did it show you?"

"Everything." She pulled a thorn gingerly from her hair, wincing. "I know how to open the schisms. But we need Morgaine."

Hutch knew better than to insist Morgaine couldn't be trusted.

"We always needed Morgaine," he protested instead. "The trouble is, we don't know how to make her help us. Be careful, those are stinging nettles."

She pulled her hand back quickly from the nettles, probably far too late, and scrambled to her feet. "I've had an idea about that," she said. Her knee was still throbbing where she'd landed, but her head was fizzing with half-made plans. "I need to check Rowan's office."

Chapter Sixteen

Primrose Hill in the light of early morning looked very different from the last time Biddy had seen it through human eyes, when the cab had pulled up in the pouring rain before dawn and Morgaine had held an umbrella over her as they got out. The sun was warm for autumn, without a breeze to cool it. When Biddy twisted out of raven form and rose unsteadily from the cluster of trees, brushing leaves from her skirt, the parkland around her looked green and grey and quiet. By London standards it was all but deserted: a man in a thick tweed overcoat walking a dog in the distance, a tired-looking young woman pushing a pram. Neither so much as glanced in her direction. She could see no sign of mages, and Hutchincroft seemed unconcerned. He periscoped just once, nose twitching, then loped forward.

Biddy knew the trees as soon as Hutchincroft led her to them: three of them in a triangle, each slender and white-limbed, leaves turning gold brown and bristling with red berries. Rowan trees.

"There?" she asked Hutch, and he gave a firm, decisive nod. His ears were poised for danger.

The raven had known the way to Primrose Hill, at least. The flight over had been nothing like the long, nightmarish flight back to Hy-Brasil. Biddy had been out of her own mind with terror and grief then, and the raven had been a wild thing determined to fight her or consume her. This time, she burned with purpose; they cut through skies with the ease of a fish through water, and the ocean and fields and buildings beneath her rolled by at times too fast for even the raven's eyes to see. She trusted the raven's guidance—Hutch had been right, Rowan had definitely been back to the mysterious library recently—but she also urged it on, trying to match the speeds it could reach with a more experienced mage until Hutch warned her to slow down or lose control.

She was more prepared for this journey too. Last time, she'd left with nothing but Hutch and clothes that weren't even her own. This time, she'd found an old leather satchel in Rowan's study (he'd taken his good one, so she'd had to patch it) and packed it full of all she needed. She took his old brown coat too, because her own coat had been left somewhere in East London the day she had gone to Rookwood. She'd cleaned Morgaine's white dress, because it was much nicer than her own, and brushed her hair—wild and tangled from her breathless ride on the Púca's back—into the long plait that was the only hairstyle she could reliably fix on her own. She thought, looking in the glass, that she looked like some strange hybrid of Hy-Brasil and London, childhood and adulthood, fairy tale and novel. She thought she looked ready. She hoped it would be enough.

The trouble was, now she was standing in front of the three rowan trees, she had no idea of how they could become a library. Hutch had been vague on matters, in the way he often was when magic was concerned. All he could tell her, mildly puzzled, was that it *was* a library, and she'd see it when she got there.

"I can't see anything," she said aloud. She looked at the creamy trunk in front of her, then laid an uncertain hand upon it. The bark was rough and solid. She could see nothing but a tree. It *was* nothing but a tree, surely. And yet Hutchincroft had said it was more.

Hutchincroft nudged her once, sharply, and a wave of irritation washed over her.

"Stop it!" She didn't mean to snap, but her confidence had, horribly, wavered. She'd felt, on the rush of the ride on the Púca and the raven's flight, that magic had let her in. Now it seemed that she was locked out once more. "I don't know how to get in. You might have told me on the way here."

He looked at her, wide-eyed, and she sighed and scrubbed at her tired eyes with her sleeve. There was no way he could transform again to talk to her. The last burst, after the Púca had taken her, had burned his magic to the merest scrapings. Even as they had flown here, he had been unusually quiet. Without Rowan, he didn't have long left in the world.

"I'm sorry." She forced herself to think. "Something would happen for Rowan, wouldn't it? But probably only for him, or it wouldn't have stayed safe all these years. And you can't open it, because you can't work spells."

He nudged her more gently this time.

Light dawned then. "Will it work like the dream ring? If I hold you, will it recognize you as part of Rowan?"

Biddy didn't wait for an answer. She bent down and scooped him up in her arms, then pressed her hand once more to the bark. It might have been her imagination that it warmed slightly.

"Please," she whispered. "Please, it's us. Let us in."

She couldn't explain what happened next. Perhaps she melted into the tree; perhaps the tree reached out and enfolded her. Perhaps neither, or both. But the world around her grew dim, then faded. The sounds of early-morning London traffic were gone, and so were the sounds of birds. She was dissolving into sunlight and shadow and the whisper of leaves. It was good magic, beautiful magic, and she wasn't afraid. She closed her eyes, and let it take her.

⋯⋯⋯⋯⋯⋯⋯⋯⋯⋯⋯⋯⋯

Her eyes opened at the touch of light. It was slanting light, golden and shimmering with dust, the kind that filtered through the forests on Hy-Brasil in the late afternoon. And yet when she stepped forward, she found she was no longer amid the trees but inside, at the center of a circular tower that extended up for as far as her eyes could stretch. The walls were the white of polished marble, and the floor beneath her feet was polished wood partially covered by a thick red rug. There was a fireplace with two worn armchairs, and a desk fitted to the curve of the room and strewn with papers. Everything else, every inch of towering wall, was filled with bookshelves. They went all the way up to the high ceiling, at least seven stories, connected by ladders and balconies and ledges. The place had the old-paper smell of Rowan's study at the castle. Biddy stared, barely noticing as Hutchincroft jumped from her arms.

"It's a library," she said out loud, in wonder. "It's a library inside a tree."

Hutchincroft's snort expressed, very clearly, that he'd told her so.

She resisted the impulse to look around, to trace the spines of the books with her fingertips and breathe in the leather-and-paper smell. There was no time. Morgaine might come in at any moment. Instead, she dropped to a crouch and opened her satchel.

In the end, she had taken very few things with her. The raven-stone was around her neck still—she put it away, and felt the absence of its frantic brain like a rush of calm. She had wanted to bring a shard of the god-sword from the ruins, but she hadn't been able to work out how to carry it when it cut through any material she tried to wrap it in. Perhaps Rowan had found the same problem, and that was why it stayed put. Otherwise, there was the inextinguishable candle, which she set unlit on the floor by the armchair for future use; the key, just in case; and the butter knife, because why not? There was the silver amulet that had trapped Rowan the night he had disappeared—she thought she knew what that was for now, though she still wasn't sure it was safe to use. There was food too: an apple, going soft; a water bottle; the last two oat biscuits from the cupboard.

Last of all, and most important, was a square of dirty rug, which she had cut carefully with her pocketknife only the night before. Biddy unfurled it, holding a breath. She released it in a sigh when she saw that the chalk circle, which she feared would be smudged on the journey, was whole and unbroken. She spread it out, and it stared up at the ceiling like a roughly drawn eye.

It was the thought that had come to her the night she had ridden the Púca, the flash that had felt like the final piece of a puzzle.

Rowan showed you how that might be done, the Púca had said.

She couldn't draw a trap circle herself. But Rowan could, and he had, just before they had left for the mainland. He had drawn it on a rug in his office, and then, in true Rowan fashion, he had rolled up the rug out of the way rather than go to the trouble of washing it clean. It had been there all the time they had been away, all the time she had sat in his armchair poring over books and watching the scrying mirror and despairing. When Biddy had unrolled it, hands trembling, the circle was there in faded chalk. When she had cut it out, to her unpracticed eye it still radiated magic.

He had said it was a good one.

It was too obvious out in the open, she could tell at once— Morgaine would have to be very preoccupied indeed not to see it. But the rug under her foot stretched almost to the entrance; she lifted the edge and slid the square beneath it, careful not to blur the chalk line. Hutch had assured her the magic should work through a thin layer of carpet. Once back in place, only the slightest bump in the rug showed. Morgaine usually came late, when the room would be dim. It would just have to be good enough.

The library was cold after the sun outside, but she couldn't light the fire without giving her presence away. Instead, she curled up on the chair facing away from the door, out of sight of anyone coming in, nestled into the cushions, and waited.

She ate the apple and the oat biscuits first, hungry after her long night, and washed them down with water from her canteen. Then she tried to sleep while she could. It should have been easy: She had been flying all night after a very strange day, and even with all her practice she was worn to the bone with the raven's efforts and her own. The library felt safe, somehow, in the way that Rowan's study always did, and Hutchincroft was far more alert to every sound and movement than she could ever be. And yet she felt restless, mind on edge, body fighting to move of its own accord as though it was a thing like a ravenstone outside her control. She wondered if this was how Rowan felt when he frustrated her with his inability to be still. It must be exhausting.

After an hour or so the thought came to her, unwelcome, that it might be days before Morgaine returned to the tree, if she came back at all. She pushed it away. They didn't have days. Morgaine would just have to come, that was all.

And she did.

<hr/>

At some point Biddy had managed to slip into a thin grey doze, threaded with snatches of noise from the human world outside the tree and flickers of light as the sun slipped between the branches that made the ceiling. It was dark when she woke with a start. The tree was moving. The massive trunk that enclosed her creaked and groaned; the floor trembled; the books shifted on the shelves with a rustle like leaves. She sat upright, silent and still, and felt Hutchincroft in her lap do likewise. Just in case, knowing rabbits' tendency to bolt, she laid a warning hand on his shoulders. If Hutchincroft was right, there were only two people who could enter the library, and one was locked deep under the earth. This was it.

The trap circle gave no sign of its spell. Morgaine would never have known she had stepped into it. All Biddy heard was a small, soft cry as she tried to step out, and found she couldn't.

Morgaine barely struggled—she was too experienced a mage not to know what had caught her and how impossible it was to escape. When Biddy risked a careful look around the back of the seat, she could see her figure in the darkness standing tall and firm. One flare of light flickered between her fingers and hit the edge of the circle at her command; Biddy held her breath, but it shattered into sparks. Morgaine raised her head with the blaze of defiance Biddy remembered well from her own time in the dungeon—the kind that only came with defeat.

"Well, then." Morgaine's voice barely trembled. "You have me, and if you've found this place, you know everything I've been doing these last few decades. You might as well show yourself."

Somehow, in all her planning, it had never occurred to Biddy that Morgaine would have no idea who had caught her—that she would be expecting a practiced magician to emerge from the shadows. The lines of conflict were so clearly drawn in her own head that she had forgotten that, in Morgaine's, Biddy was only a scared young girl in a cotton nightdress. Perhaps there was a way she could have turned this to her advantage. Rowan would have found one. She didn't want to. Instead, she lit the candle on the floor in front of her, lifted it to her face, and stood.

"Hello, Morgaine," she said.

Perhaps surprise was its own advantage. Morgaine's mouth fell open in pure shock.

"Bridget! How did you . . . ?" She let the end of the question drop, as though it were too big to carry. It was the first time Biddy had ever seen her truly taken aback. "I heard how you escaped. I thought you were dead."

"You didn't think Hutchincroft and I could manage the ravenstone?"

"I helped forge that ravenstone. I saw what happened to Storm all those years ago when he tried. I was sure you couldn't."

The two of them regarded each other in careful silence. Morgaine looked to Biddy as she always had: poised, meticulous, her dark hair a coil of artful curls under her sweeping hat, and her dress (a deep blue this time) perfectly arranged. She wondered how she looked to Morgaine.

Morgaine was the first to move. She smiled, despite the puzzled knot between her eyes and the still-wary tilt of her head. "I'm glad I was wrong. But what are you doing here? And how did you cast a trap circle?"

"I didn't," she said, ignoring the first question. "Rowan did, before he left home for the last time."

She was encouraged to see Morgaine bite her lip and look down. Whatever she had done, she at least cared.

"Where is he, Morgaine?" she asked, before the other woman could recover. "Is he alive?"

"He's in the dungeons. I've never seen the place under such a tight guard. Storm barely leaves the room. Although I wouldn't call that a guard, exactly. More of an obsession."

"He's torturing him, isn't he?" Biddy said it as flatly as possible, determined to keep the flare of pain in her chest from reaching her voice. "Storm. He let us see it, the first night."

"Yes." Morgaine's own voice was just as carefully controlled, but it was trembling on the brink of something less so. Her hands had curled into fists. For the first time, Biddy saw the dark smudges under her eyes, the tight lines at the corner of her mouth. Perhaps, after all, the precision of her hair and clothes wasn't callousness or even pretense, but a way of keeping herself from falling apart at the seams. "I can't stop him anymore—he won't listen to me. It's even worse than last time. I don't think even Vaughan could curb him now. And when he's not hurting him, he's down there just *talking* to him."

Biddy had a sudden flash of Storm's visits to the dungeon—his low, threatening growl, the silhouette of his painful, useless wings, the suffocating anger that filled the room like the heat before a cloudburst—and had to swallow hard.

"I'm sorry," Morgaine said. She was watching Biddy closely. "You know I'd get him out again if I could. Listen, Bridget, you need to release me from this. Vaughan's wisps have been following me for days. If I stay out of their sight too long—"

"Did you betray us?" Biddy asked bluntly. Beside her, Hutchin-croft stiffened. "Did you tell Storm we were at your house?"

"No." Morgaine's answer was firm, but tinged with weariness, the tone of someone who no longer expected to be believed. "I swear. I don't know how they found you. If I had to guess, I'd say it was the spellmark on Rowan's hand. Those things are very difficult to scorch off—if you aren't fast enough, they go right to the bone."

Hutch's ear twitched beside her, just once, but not in denial. It *was* possible. It would explain why Rowan had been troubled by it in ways he wouldn't mention, why the wisps had been coming for him as soon as she'd been installed in the school.

"When I arrived at the Undercastle," Morgaine continued, "I looked for Storm as I said I would. The dungeons were all but empty. Crag was there—the jailer, you must remember him, the old mage who brought you food—and I asked him where Storm had gone. He said that Storm had been sent to Camden, and he had been told to prepare the dungeon for you and Rowan. I knew at once he was going to my house."

"If that's true," Biddy said, and let Morgaine hear every ounce of skepticism, "why didn't you warn us?"

"I couldn't. There would have been no way to reach you in time. It was all I could do not to be arrested myself on suspicion of helping you."

"Why *weren't* you arrested?" Biddy heard her voice rise in anger. "We were at your house! How did they not suspect you?"

"They did!" Morgaine's voice had risen too, defensive. "If I'd gone straight to my office pretending I didn't know where you were, as I'd planned, they would have arrested me. Even now, I don't know how I wasn't thrown in the dungeons with Rowan. As soon as Crag told me Storm was at my house, I went straight to Vaughan and told him that I had come to the Undercastle at the first opportunity to betray the three of you. I looked right into that horrible eye of his and I told him I had caught you escaping last night, and rather than call the guards I brought you to my house to lure Rowan there. I told him that Storm needed to be careful, Rowan was very dangerous, perhaps Vaughan should go himself, should I go maybe and help...Oh, all that nonsense. I made it as convincing as I could. He believed me. Or at least, he pretended to. I never know with him."

"And is it the truth? Did you take me to your house as a trap?"

"*No.*" A flare of real defiance broke through. "Bridget, I helped you escape in the first place, remember? If the Servant knew that..."

"He must know! Storm knew you had visited the dungeons just before I escaped. Surely he's not that stupid."

"Oh, Storm." She shook her head, dismissive. "Rowan's not the only one who can play about with memories. Why do you think it took me so long to come find you after you escaped? Storm has no idea I was there."

"You stole his memory?" She had no idea that could be done, and it startled her despite herself.

"Just my own part in it." Morgaine carefully didn't meet Biddy's eyes. "It's difficult magic and absolutely forbidden for one mage to do to another. It also needs very close physical contact, and it isn't easy trying to find a reason why I would want to be close to Storm under the circumstances. But I managed it. Everyone thinks you had a sliver of mirror hidden about your person that Storm missed."

It was possible she was telling the truth. It was, after all, what she had done when Rowan had been captured all those years ago: helped so far, and not further. It was what Biddy had hoped—what she needed to be true for her plan to work. Somehow, though, it was more infuriating than if Morgaine had meant them harm all along. When it came to it, while Storm had been at their door, while Rowan had been handing himself over so she and Hutch could escape, Morgaine had been in the Undercastle urging the Servant to send reinforcements.

"So Storm takes the blame again," she said, with more bitterness than was probably fair and certainly more than she felt on Storm's behalf.

"Does that matter?"

"It might to Rowan," Biddy retorted, "if Storm's taking it out on him right now!"

"I didn't have a choice, Bridget!" Morgaine's face had flushed, and her eyes glittered. "I didn't have a choice about any of it. I had to do the best I could."

"You mean you had to do what you could to keep yourself out of danger and in a position on the Council." Her fury lashed out like a whip, unbidden. All she could see was the look on Rowan's face as he'd thrown her the ravenstone and told her to go. "Don't tell me you had no choice. You always had a choice. You made it seventy years ago, and every day since."

"Oh, not you too! Very well, then, let's say I did make a choice. Are you honestly telling me you wouldn't have made the same one in my place? How could I have helped you if I had been jailed alongside you?"

"How were you planning to help us now?" she countered. "You thought Hutch and I were dead. Rowan's being tortured to death under your office. Were you just going to stand by and let it happen?"

"If I had to, yes! I have to pick my battles."

"And what battles have you won in all these decades that were worth the life of your familiar?"

It was a cruel thing to say, and she knew it. To her credit, Morgaine met it without flinching.

"Nothing was worth her death. Nothing could ever have been. But at least I've tried to make it all worth *something*. I've stayed on the Council, despite everyone who wants me gone. I've argued for the rights of lesser mages. Last summer I helped acquit a hedge-witch of using excess magic to save the life of her lady friend. Vaughan agreed only last month to consider donating a portion of magic to help the mortal world. It's been a long game, I know, but things have been getting better. They trust me—or they did, until you three were found in my apartment." She brushed her hand over her eyes as though to chase away tears, although Biddy could see no trace of any on her face. "God, why does Rowan always have to *ruin* everything?"

"Nobody *made* you help us," Biddy said hotly. "If you wanted to keep pretending, you could have left me in that dungeon."

"I didn't mean that! I'm glad I helped *you*. But you never would have been there if Rowan hadn't put you in danger. You admitted that yourself."

Had she? Possibly, but she wasn't willing to yield that ground now. "I put myself in danger. I'm not a child."

"Not now, perhaps. But you were a child sixteen years ago, when your paths first crossed—less than a child. He certainly put you in danger then."

"I don't know why he did that!" The words came in a torrent of frustration, not at Morgaine but at the whole world. "I don't know the first thing about him lately. I don't know what I would have done in his place or yours or anybody else's; I don't know whether I want to defend him or condemn him or forgive him. I just know that he's locked up, and you're free and safe, and that *can't* be right. It can't be because he liked to think of himself as a hero, or because he was stupid, or because he was reckless. I was there, and he was none of those things. He let Storm take him so Hutch and I could get away. You stayed in the Undercastle. You did nothing, just as you did seventy years ago. And now you tell me you're *sorry*."

Morgaine opened her mouth to reply, then closed it again. Her face was white and quiet, and otherwise impossible to read.

"I know you helped me escape," Biddy said, into the silence. "And I'm grateful. I'm free now because of it. But that might have been a plan to draw Rowan out, as you told Vaughan."

"It wasn't." The fight had gone from her, as Biddy had seen just once before: back in her house, when she had admitted that taking the locket had been her fault. "I don't know how to convince you, except to tell you that I saw what they did to Rowan last time they caught him. I heard it. And I knew then I'd done the wrong thing helping them bring him in. I'd thought I could keep him safe as long as I was there. I'd known Storm hated him—I was there, that day with the ravenstone. But I didn't believe, until then, how deep that hatred ran. I didn't realize how much I'd been lying to myself about what Storm had become."

Biddy remembered Storm's bitterness when he had spoken to her about Rowan. It had turned her cold then. It was worse now.

"I saw what happened with the ravenstone," she said. "But I'm not sure I understood it."

It was the closest she could come to what she really needed to know. She couldn't quite bring herself to ask if Storm's transformation had been Rowan's fault.

"I've thought about that day for seventy years." Perhaps Morgaine had guessed the memory Biddy had seen from the first, because she showed no surprise. "And I'm not sure I do either. It all went so wrong so quickly. I do blame myself, in part. I insisted we meet with Storm that day. The world was falling apart; I wanted to bring us together. I should have realized that Rowan was worn to raw nerves and ready for a fight, and that Storm had been looking to give him one for years."

"But Storm said that he and Rowan were friends."

"Oh yes." It was clearly meant to sound careless, but carelessness didn't suit Morgaine. It only sounded tired, a borrowed robe too old and threadbare to cover her. "We grew up together, the three of us—did Rowan ever tell you that?"

"No." She tried to say it without resentment. There were too many things Rowan hadn't told her.

"We did. We came into magic around the same time, when we were thirteen, and we were all apprenticed together in York. It was the happiest time of my life." Her face softened, and for once she seemed to be speaking without carefully considering every word. "I don't know if you understand what it was like growing up as a young girl in society. It's still difficult, no doubt; a hundred years ago it was like being a lamb fattened for slaughter. I was luckier than many— my father was a reasonably well-off wine merchant in Sussex, I was never forced to work in a factory or go into service to survive—but even so, my childhood was a narrow corridor of deportment and music lessons and fine stitchwork. There was one door out, marriage and children, and God help you if the wrong person opened it. And then, all of a sudden, another door opened, a secret one, and it was mine. I was an apprentice mage. There was the whole world at my fingertips, all for me to explore. And Rowan and Storm were there to explore it with me, like ready-made brothers and best friends in one. I hadn't realized, until I had them, how lonely I had been." She caught herself. "But you didn't ask about me."

"I want to know about you too," Biddy said, and meant it with all her heart. It was why she had watched her for so many hours at the scrying glass, trying to puzzle out her movements and her face. Morgaine was a mystery to her—a collection of dream figures, Rowan's and Storm's and her own from four years old. Her own memory was vague; Rowan's was tinted with hurt; Storm's relegated her to the shadows while the rivalry between the two men blazed bright. She needed to understand Morgaine, so she knew if she could trust her. More than that, she *wanted* to understand her. She was the only female mage Biddy had ever met; she was the only adult woman she could remember from her childhood. She wanted to know who she was. "And I do understand what you mean, about being lonely. I have been too, the last few years. Although I could never have been a mage."

"Don't let anybody tell you that," Morgaine said quickly, almost fiercely. "They tried to tell me I couldn't be a mage too—not a real one. Girls were taught magic; grown women were supposed to use it only for safe, domestic purposes, exactly like every other lesson I learned as a child. I wanted to do research, real research, in the Undercastle. I wanted to be on the Council, to help change laws that hadn't been touched since the Salem witch trials. Rowan wanted that too. We were going to sweep the dust away, to tear down the curtains and let in some light. And we did. For a few years, right up until the world changed, we did." She looked Biddy directly in the face, her chin lifting as though meeting an execution head-on. "I know what you think of me staying with the Council all this time. But I'd fought so hard to be there, and I was making a difference. I couldn't—I just couldn't bear to give it up. To be powerless again, trying to resist from the outside. I'd sworn I'd never do that, no matter how hard they tried to force me out."

She fell silent. Biddy wondered if she had noticed that she had begun to speak of her decisions in the past tense. It didn't necessarily mean she'd changed her mind, but it gave Biddy a kindling of hope. Questions were crowding her tongue, but this time she pushed them back. She sensed that Morgaine was on the brink of something, that years' worth of caution and turning aside had pushed her at last to the edge, and anything Biddy said was as likely to pull her back as move her forward. She needed to jump on her own.

"You asked about Rowan and Storm," Morgaine said at last. "They *were* friends, truly. But it's also true that even when the three of us were inseparable, those two never quite saw eye to eye. I told you, Rowan and I wanted to change things, always. Storm, though...He was one of the chosen ones, exactly the kind of mage the Council hoped to find. Edward Sturm, younger son of the Earl of Something-or-other, English, male, wellborn, handsome and talented enough to pass for clever. The Council's stories were written to suit him, and he couldn't understand why they needed rewriting—why magic needed to be treated as a living thing and not a tool, why it mattered if only some had use of it provided they were the *right* people. He and Rowan started to argue about it more and more. And when that story began to change, when Storm was jealous and hurt at being locked out of the Council when we had been let in, Rowan had no problem with using that to provoke him. He *did*, Hutch," she added, as Hutchincroft next to Biddy gave a tiny growl. "Maybe Storm deserved it, but Rowan was always very...uncompromising with people who didn't live up to his ideals. He made Storm worse. They brought out the worst in each other, really. And Vaughan made it worse than ever. He was the one who seeded the idea in Storm's head that Rowan had taken *his* place on the Council, the place that should be his by right."

"Why would he say that?" Biddy asked.

"It's what Vaughan does to people he uses. He tries to isolate you, to play on old fears and resentments, to make sure your support is coming from him and nowhere else. I saw through it, even then. I used him and I let him use me, but I never liked him."

"Rowan liked him." He had told her so, back in Hy-Brasil. She hadn't realized then that he had meant it as a confession.

"Yes. Storm still likes him, even though he's never had anything but humiliation at his hands. Men are easily impressed by other men." Morgaine shifted her feet within the circle, perhaps remembering for the first time it existed. "He never used to be like this, you know. Storm. I think he's gone a bit mad since he was stuck. Part of his mind is trapped as a raven's, all fury and flight. And he's turned all that on Rowan."

Biddy's fingers closed over the stone in her pocket, recalling its first frantic scrabble to fly, to fight, to be free. She tried to keep her voice steady, but it probably shook. This was it.

"Then we need to get him out before it's too late. Morgaine, I know you've helped us already. If I gave you the chance to help us again, even if it was a risk, would you?"

"Yes," she said, with far more certainty than she had before. "I know you have no reason to believe me, but I would. I will."

Biddy had little reason to believe her, it was true. But not none. She had seen the guilt in Morgaine's eyes when she defended herself, the flashes of anger and bitterness and pain when she spoke of Vaughan. Biddy thought she understood the reasons why Morgaine had chosen to stay with the Council, and even if they were misguided, they weren't wrong.

And she needed to trust her. If Morgaine couldn't be trusted, then she had no plan at all.

"We need to bring magic back into the world."

Morgaine wasn't quite past surprise after all—her head snapped up, and her face stilled as her feelings sorted themselves behind it. "It isn't possible."

"It is. But I need you."

"But..." She shook herself. "What do you need from me?"

"Two things. First, the locket. The one with my hair inside it. Where is it?"

"In my office, the same as before. I never dared to touch it, in case it was found. But I can get it for you, if it would help. What's the other thing?"

"Magic." She tilted her head to meet Morgaine square in the eyes, hoping to overcome any disbelief with sheer conviction. "It's happened before, the schisms starting to close. Thousands of years ago, the fair folk did the same thing as you—drew too much magic too fast, until there wasn't enough magic for the schisms to stay open. But if we flood the schisms with magic, with the right words and at the right time, they can open again. Magic can come back. If Rowan did find a schism, then that's the next step. For a mage to go to that schism, and return all the magic they have."

"But—" Morgaine shook her head. "Bridget, I have barely any magic. Even as a Council member, I'm only given a very small amount each week. Most mages are given none at all."

Her heart sank; she pulled it resolutely back to the surface. She'd known, after all, that Vaughan controlled magic strictly. "There *must* be some, or else all this has been for nothing."

Morgaine almost laughed. "That doesn't mean that there must be some! Believe me, most things are for nothing. I should know. It's been decades since magic flowed into the world. There's nothing left."

Biddy caught herself before she fell into despair. She'd had a lot of practice at that in the last few weeks.

"That can't be true," she said. "All this started because the Council were trying harder than ever to capture Rowan. I know you said they weren't," she added, as Morgaine opened her mouth. "But I saw the wisps myself. I had to pull him out of their trap. They are. And he said they were getting more and more powerful."

"We aren't. At least—" Morgaine looked away, struck by a thought.

"What?" It came to Biddy before Morgaine could answer. "At least most of you aren't. Vaughan is, isn't he? You think he's hoarding magic for himself."

"We've suspected it for years," Morgaine conceded. "We seem to get so little back for what we give. Vaughan blames the lack on Rowan stealing it, of course. But nobody can get into the vault to be sure, and nobody dares question him outright. Mages have died for far less."

"Well, then." Biddy looked at Hutch, who gave her a firm nod in response—as though they really were mage and familiar, and he agreed with her before she needed to speak. "That's the answer. Rowan hasn't been stealing from the vaults in the last week or so, at least. I think we need to see just what Vaughan has in there."

Morgaine's eyebrows shot up. "You want to break into the vault?"

"If he's hiding magic anywhere, that's where it will be, won't it? And we need it. It can't be too hard. Rowan breaks into that vault all the time."

"That doesn't mean it isn't hard, Bridget!"

"But it means it's *possible*," Biddy insisted. "That's all we need."

Morgaine made a strangled sound of disbelief. "You really were raised by Rowan, weren't you?"

"I was raised not to give up." She swallowed down that thought along with the lump in her throat. There wasn't time to remember now, and definitely not to feel. "I saw the hole in the chimneys where he got in, and I have the ravenstone now. I can get in the same way. I'll let you in—it must be possible to get out from the inside. You can bring the locket. And then, if we're right, we'll have everything we need."

"And we unlock the memory in your heart and take the magic back to the schism."

Biddy nodded. "Exactly."

It sounded clear enough to her, but something in Morgaine's face worried her. Biddy saw her square her shoulders, as though bracing herself against a wind or a wave.

"Morgaine?"

"It isn't that simple. If all goes well, we get the locket out and there *is* enough magic to put things right...Once the memory awakens, Rowan will have it too. And that will put him in exactly the situation he wanted to avoid—captured, with the knowledge of a crack in the world right where it could be tortured from him. If he tells them—"

"He wouldn't!"

"He might. He feared he might. And he didn't want that. At whatever cost, he wanted to keep it out of Vaughan's hands."

"So what do you want to do instead? Just leave things as they are?"

"Not forever. But for a little while, perhaps. Until they stop looking so closely. As long as you and the locket stay hidden, they can't touch the schism."

"And what about Rowan?" Morgaine looked away. Biddy didn't need to see Hutch's ears go back to read her face. "No. No, we aren't leaving him in there. They'll kill him. They're *hurting* him."

"Do you think I don't know that?" The calm in her voice broke all at once, and pain brimmed through the cracks. "I've seen it first-hand. They find excuses to make me watch, just so they can see my reaction, and I have to pretend not to care. I have to ask how it's *going* as though all I want is for him to break. I have to see the look in his eyes when I enter the room. I would give almost anything to stop it. But he wouldn't want us to risk the only chance we might have to bring magic back."

Somehow, impossibly, Biddy heard herself laugh. "Yes, he would! Have you met Rowan? He never met a risk he didn't want to take."

"If we fail—"

"We won't fail." She hoped she sounded as firm and as confident as she didn't feel. In a flash, like seeing a page of a book illuminated by a strike of lightning, she understood why Rowan always refused to admit that things might go wrong. "We'll unlock the memory. Rowan won't give it up, I know he won't. And then we'll split the world wide open."

Morgaine started to shake her head, to argue. Biddy didn't let her.

"Morgaine, please," she said, and she wasn't trying to persuade her now. She was just asking, with her whole heart. She needed her. She needed a mage. As far as she had managed to come she could go no further without one. "He can't die in there. Not in that dungeon. Rowan hates being locked up. He can't even sleep with the window closed."

For some reason, that made Morgaine laugh, though her eyes were suddenly bright with tears. "He can't, can he? We always used to fight about that."

Biddy felt the shift in her, like a sudden crack that heralded ice melting. Perhaps Hutch did too, because he put his front paws on the chair leg and looked up at her, eyes enormous and imploring.

She pressed her advantage. "Please. He's in there because of me. Do you know what that feels like?"

"I do." Morgaine drew a deep, serious breath. Biddy realized she was holding a breath of her own, and didn't release it until Morgaine spoke again. "Very well. Let's see about getting that locket first."

Chapter Seventeen

*B*iddy knew almost nothing about the London Underground. Rowan had told her that trains moved underneath the city, but it had all been built since he had fled the Council and she suspected he avoided them because he found them rather bewildering. She had always liked the idea of it, like a great rabbit warren beneath the feet of the millions passing through the city, humming with activity down deep where nobody could see. She would never, in a thousand years, have expected Morgaine to shepherd her toward its entrance on their way to the Undercastle.

"It was the Servant's innovation," Morgaine said, as they descended the stairs. "He actually nudged the entire Undercastle sideways to better link up to the District line. It was the closest he came to encountering opposition from the Council in decades—it took a year's worth of magic—but he argued it would save more in the long run by giving us an easier route in from across the city without rune doors. In the end he did what he wanted, as always. We change at Charing Cross."

Biddy was going to ask about rune doors, which she had never heard of before, but then they reached the foot of the stairs. The sight of the Underground took her breath away and her questions with it.

Until that moment, she hadn't realized that she had been

picturing it *too* much like a rabbit warren, all twists and turns. The tunnel she found herself in was perfectly round and perfectly straight, like looking down a very long tin can. She had seen nothing like it on Hy-Brasil, or even in the London aboveground. It was eerie, a piece of precision engineering papered with signage that vanished into darkness at each end. It fascinated and repelled her in equal measure.

There were a few people on the wooden platform, only one of whom—an elderly man reading a newspaper—bothered to look up as she and Morgaine came down. She fought against self-consciousness. Hutchincroft was hidden in the satchel slung over her shoulder; apart from that satchel itself, which nobody would give a second glance, she looked no different from any of them.

In fact, she barely recognized herself. It turned out many of Morgaine's clothes fit her well, with slight magical alterations: a white cotton shirtwaist, a dark tie, black stockings, a dark blue woolen skirt and coat that would help her easily pass for a clerk or a secretary. Her hair was now arranged in something Morgaine called a Psyche knot, which made her head feel oddly heavy and her neck exposed. When she'd looked in the mirror, she'd been startled at how her tangles and half curls had been teased into something that looked deliberate, purposeful, even elegant. Her shoulders had straightened in some unconscious attempt to keep her hair from toppling, and her eyes looked dark and serious, almost the same color as the ravenstone around her neck, as though they knew something she didn't.

"You're lovely," Morgaine said, looking her over with an air of satisfaction.

"I've never known how to dress properly," Biddy admitted. "I've always wanted to. I've only had what Rowan brought back from the mainland."

Morgaine gave her a rare, genuine smile. "If we survive all this, I'll take you shopping in London. I'm sure Rowan did well, but everything he knows about dresses and corsets he learned from me, and it was in 1842."

"I don't suppose it matters how I dress," she said, out of some faint sense of loyalty to Hy-Brasil or her own wardrobe.

"You might find that it does," Morgaine said. "The right clothes can be a kind of armor, if you wear them right."

Biddy understood that when the long metal train arrived with a rumble and a squeal, and she stepped inside and into a crush of people nudging and elbowing and murmuring apologies. Scarcely anyone glanced up at them. There were several young ladies in the same carriage; one of them caught her eye, and looked away quickly with a smile so brief it only half existed. It wasn't just that Biddy looked like them. She looked like *one of them*. Nobody thought to question her right to be there. It was exactly what she had envied in Morgaine, what she had tried clumsily to emulate before the mirror at Hy-Brasil. Yet it was uncomfortable, somehow. It wasn't fair that a clean skirt should make such a difference. She thought of the girls in the children's home, with their patched uniforms and long braids, and mingled guilt and injustice burned like the touch of a brand in her chest.

Their final stop, after a brief change of trains and a few minutes lurching and rattling through the darkness, was at a station that looked no different to any other. Instead of following their fellow passengers up to the surface, however, Morgaine guided her down a tiny side tunnel. It was very short, and ended in a wall of solid brick.

"Here's the door," she said quietly. "Do you have the amulet?"

Biddy took the Council's silver amulet from her satchel and clasped it in the palm of her hand. The enchanted sleep and the tracking spells were gone from it, Morgaine had said; it was perfectly safe, and it would get her across the threshold of the Undercastle undetected. It was one of the few things that would—even going through the chimneys as a raven wouldn't have worked. Rowan had presumably used spells of his own, but Biddy didn't know them, and wouldn't have been able to perform them if she had. She still didn't like to use it. The memory of it in Rowan's hand as he had lain in the dark of the vault was difficult to shake. And she couldn't help but be aware that he had chosen to leave it behind, even after working out what it was. It didn't seem a good idea to be less cautious than Rowan.

Morgaine was oblivious to this. "Good. I'll take you through and straight to my office. There's a fireplace in there—the raven can go up and find its way to the vault. Ready?"

Biddy was about to ask where the door was, when the memory of Storm's transformation came back to her. They had been in a pub, a pub closed to the outside world.

There used to be lots of little pockets like that, before. You couldn't get into them without magic—like the Undercastle. There were charms on the door, so anyone without any magic stored in their blood would see a blank wall.

This was obviously the same kind of door, or something similar. That was simple enough. The frightening part was on the other side. She slipped her free hand into her satchel and buried her fingers in Hutch's soft fur, fighting for calm.

"Are you all right?" Morgaine asked, just as quietly.

Biddy nodded, and tried to smile. "Fine. Just a bit sick from the train. Shall we go?"

Morgaine slipped her hand around Biddy's wrist. Her fingers were cold. "You really are such a lot like Rowan. Very well, then. Deep breath."

And she stepped forward and pulled Biddy through the wall, before Biddy could tell her that she wasn't anything like Rowan at all, not even slightly. She'd been pretending her whole life, and now she wasn't even sure who she was pretending to be.

———◆———◆———

When Biddy had last been in the Undercastle, it had been a place of stone and darkness and horrors, of cold and dirt and pain far below the earth. It had been Storm's Undercastle, where Rowan was trapped even now.

Morgaine's Undercastle, the Undercastle of the members of the Council, was very different. The wall opened to a wide courtyard, the castle entrance ahead illuminated by the same hovering globes from the Great Hall. If it weren't for the curved stone ceiling overhead they could have been outdoors at night, under a particularly low and cloudy sky. The guards at the door wore ordinary clothes, and they barely looked up when Morgaine swept past with her head held high.

They didn't see Biddy at all, for one very simple reason. When Morgaine had told her to take a deep breath, she had done so. She still held that breath, all the while clutching the silver amulet so tight its edges bit into her palm. As long as she did so, she was invisible.

Biddy had discovered the amulet's properties in a very mundane way. Sitting in Rowan's study, turning it over in her palm as she had seen Rowan do, she had heaved a deep, disconsolate sigh, the soul-scraping kind of small children and adults trying not to cry. As she had drawn breath, she had blinked out of sight. It had surprised Hutch only minimally—smell and sound are more important to rabbits anyway. He couldn't even recall if Rowan had ever done anything similar. But judging by the single word underlined in his notebook, he had, on his very last night on Hy-Brasil. In that moment, she had a flash of being very close to him. She wondered what he had been sighing about.

Even Morgaine hadn't known if it would work through the threshold spell of the Undercastle; whether the fact the amulet came from the vault in the first place would pose a problem. But it had worked. It really had.

Yes, she thought, and underlined it three times.

Her elation didn't last long. She hadn't liked to practice with the amulet too much, wary of it as she was. She had tried it again before Morgaine had taken her to the Underground, but only briefly. It hadn't prepared her for how difficult it would be.

This wasn't the safety of home or the hidden library. It wasn't even the cold seas around Hy-Brasil, where she had learned to hold her breath swimming. It was enemy territory, right in the midst of mages who wanted to tear a memory from her heart. Her pulse throbbed at double speed; her chest tightened in panic; her lungs felt squeezed in a giant fist. She had crossed the threshold, it was true, but she couldn't simply blink into existence in midair. The great open courtyard was overlaid in a pale grey-white stone—glacial, silent, eerily beautiful, and horribly exposing.

And then there were the people. Morgaine had told her that there would be other mages there but had also said, optimistically, that they wouldn't be many.

"It's mostly scholars who come to the Undercastle, when the Council isn't in session," Morgaine had said as she'd brushed Biddy's hair. "There's very little practical study now, unless the Servant approves the magic, but there are books and scrolls and artifacts. Nobody in this section will have seen you in the dungeon, and unless they're concentrating, they won't feel the spell in your heart with all the other scraps of magic drifting around to confuse it. Once you get inside, we can let the spell go, and you can just walk with me and try to look like you belong."

There seemed a great many to Biddy—worn, pale-skinned men, a few women dressed more like Biddy than Morgaine. They held rushed, busy expressions that seemed practiced, as though walking fast and looking worried had become a habit. A man with grey whiskers and a hooked nose came perilously close to brushing her arm, and it was all she could do not to gasp. Her chest spasmed painfully.

God. There were stairs leading to the main castle, steep ones. The air was shimmering in front of her; her heart pounded in her ears. She didn't see how she could do it.

"Not much farther," Morgaine murmured, almost too low to be heard. Biddy saw the tension in her shoulders, and had a confused flash of what this must feel like to the other woman. She had let Biddy's wrist drop as she had entered the courtyard, and was walking without knowing for certain Biddy was even behind her, like some twisted Orpheus going deeper into the underworld.

She did make it up the stairs, step by step, hugging the satchel with Hutch inside it close to her hip so as not to lose contact. She made it into the vast entrance hall of the castle—so like the one at home on Hy-Brasil, but where that extended up into a tower, this one was inverted, with the staircases plunging down into the earth. Not far now. There were corridors here. All they needed was a fraction of empty space, a moment when nobody was passing. They were *there*.

And then—

"Ah, Morgaine!"

A hard body cannoned into her shoulder. The breath rushed from her lungs; she caught herself, doubled over, gasping. Her own body came into view—her boots, her dress, her satchel, against which Hutchincroft's claws scrabbled indignantly for purchase. The relief of the air to her chest was so great it almost swamped the sinking of her stomach. That was it. She had been found.

"Hello, Algie," Morgaine's voice said, so calmly that Biddy felt a flicker of hope. She straightened, and looked more closely at the man who had bumped her. He was a small, pale, wizened creature, bent over to pick up both a book and a monocle from the floor. He fitted the monocle into his eye and squinted at Biddy.

"Oh, I'm sorry. I didn't see you," he said vaguely. "I was reading and walking—bad habit. Have we met?"

Biddy kept her face carefully blank, though her heart was racing. Surely, surely he had realized that she hadn't been visible to see? Surely he would notice, now, that there was something strange about her? There were so few mages left, and none that looked as young as she did. Right now she had never felt younger in her life.

Morgaine didn't blink. "This is Sophie, Algie," she said, somewhere between fond and exasperated. The tone implied it was something Algie should already know. "From Devon. She's assisting with the new translations of Agrippa."

"We met last week," Biddy said, greatly daring, but she could tell at once it was the right tactic. The old man's face relaxed into completely artificial recognition.

"Of course, of course. Lovely to see you both. Morgaine, I was wondering if you'd had any word from the Servant—about whether any magic could be spared for my work on transmutation theory?"

"I'm afraid changing mice into badgers isn't a strong priority at the present time," Morgaine said sympathetically. "But I'll bring it up with him at the next meeting."

"Thank you." The man looked disappointed. "Yes, do. Well, don't let me keep you. We must have tea sometime."

"We must," Morgaine agreed and, smiling, turned Biddy away. Her eyes were twinkling as they walked quickly down the nearest stairwell.

"Did that work?" Biddy asked in a whisper, as soon as it felt safe.

"Perfect." There was a laugh bubbling under her words. "He won't give you a second thought. Silly old duffer. It took him fifty years to learn *my* name, and he still thinks I'm somebody's assistant half the time."

"Why would he think that?"

"Why do you think?" She didn't wait for an answer. "God, Rowan would have loved that. Algie wasn't much better with him—he used to call him 'that Irish woodmage, the one with the rabbit.' Rowan started to give him a different name each time just to see if he'd notice."

The term tugged some faint strand of memory. "What's a woodmage?"

"What?" Morgaine shook herself. "Oh—a mage who works best with trees and living things. The way a stonemage like me works best with amulets and gems, and a bonemage like Vaughan works best with—"

"Dead things." Vaughan's wisps had been made of bone, and Rowan's had taken flight from the trees. "I didn't know it worked that way."

"Well, it's not a science, just an affinity. Anyone can learn any spell. It started as a medieval theory about the way magic is channeled through the humors, and turned into a way to discriminate, like any other. Women are supposed to have more of a bent toward plants and trees, men are supposed to forge stone."

"You and Rowan were the other way around."

"And he was looked down on for his magic, and I was repeatedly locked out of mine. It's nonsense. It's all nonsense." Any trace of laughter had faded. "I hate this place sometimes, I really do."

Biddy's heart was still hammering and her lungs heaving for breath, but she had a chance now to look about her—at the ancient stone corridors, the winding downward staircases, the archways opening out into great chambers filled with mages poring over books. She pictured Morgaine walking these same corridors seventy years ago with Rowan and Storm, when the air was crackling with magic and familiars dogged the heels of their mages. It would have been a wonderful place, ancient and steeped in history, and yet the image of Rowan and Hutchincroft there jarred somewhat. For all its grandeur, it had a faint air of decay, of stateliness, of mold and rot lurking in crevices that was completely at odds with the energy the two of them always brought with them. They must have been like a cold gust from the west, threatening to unsettle the dust and bring the building down with it. Morgaine too—she had shaped herself to fit, the way a corset shaped a body and could be both armor and support, but this place hadn't been built for her either. No wonder they had found each other.

Morgaine's office was a small room, little more than a desk and a set of shelves and freezing cold despite the fire flickering in the small fireplace. Morgaine put that out at once with a word and a flash of magic, and turned to Biddy.

"You'll have to go up this one as a raven, I'm afraid—it's not as wide as the main rooms. We're right above the dungeons now. Can you find the way?"

"Hutch will help," Biddy said. He had been in the Undercastle before, after all, and rabbits had a very good sense of direction in tunnels. "Where's the locket?"

Morgaine opened her mouth to reply, right as a sharp knock came at her door. They froze as one, wide-eyed and stricken.

"Go now!" Morgaine hissed. "Quickly. I'll meet you at the door to the vault."

grim corner, no different from any of the others, that it became clear why.

He's there. Hutch's voice across her thoughts was taut with misery and longing.

Something sharp and painful and deep-buried leapt, and she stopped at once. *Where? Can you hear him again?*

No. I should have been able to as soon as we passed through the walls of the Undercastle, but there must be more than one spell. They're being very careful. But I can feel the void where he should be now. The dungeons are just below our feet.

Below their feet. The fireplace came out in the guardroom. She had been there before; she could get there again. They were so close.

And yet...

There was still a great impenetrable door between the guardroom and the dungeon. Even if they could find a way into that dark room, Morgaine had said there was always someone there with him. Storm. Storm was always with him.

We can't, she said, as though Hutch had made the suggestion. And he had, in a way. She had been an idiot not to realize that Hutch had all along been hoping to hear Rowan once more as soon as they passed through the barrier; not to realize that for Hutch, deep down, this plan had always been about finding some miraculous opportunity for breaking Rowan free. No wonder he had let Biddy take the risk of coming in the end, though he'd never admit that was what he had done, even to himself. *It will never work.*

Hutch might have argued further, but he froze, and a second later Biddy did too.

Footsteps. Not the first they had heard while traversing the walls, but it had been quiet as they drew near the lowest levels. These had a peculiar heaviness that Biddy's heart recognized before her head. It plummeted.

Storm, Hutch said quietly, and with loathing.

Coming up from the dungeons. The thought turned her stomach.

The raven must have picked up on her disgust, or perhaps,

though she hated to admit it, her fear. It hopped once on the spot before she could stop it, and ruffled its feathers uncomfortably.

Most mages passing probably would have thought nothing of it. A sound in the walls could be anything. Even if they recognized the flutter of a bird's wings, they would assume a bird had come down from the outside and been stuck somehow—birds came into the castle all the time on Hy-Brasil. Once a seagull had even fallen down the chimney in a dramatic crash of feathers and scream of a sharp beak, and the three of them had all been scratched and pecked to ribbons trying to get it out. Even in the Undercastle, things like that must happen.

But this was Storm. Storm, of all people, knew the sound of a raven when he heard one. The footsteps paused.

Oh no, Biddy whispered, her voice in her head so quiet it was little more than a thought.

The scrape of a boot as the owner of the footsteps turned.

Biddy pressed close to the stone on instinct, holding her breath, trying to burrow down and disappear. Surely he wouldn't see them. They were on the other side of a wall. Surely. She heard Storm mutter something, his voice low and deep. It sounded like Latin, perhaps Greek.

The wall exploded.

It was instantaneous: One moment she was enclosed by solid stone, the next there was a shower of dust and a crack like a pistol, and a hole the size of a fist gaped in the wall. Light poured through—sharp, sudden, exposing. The raven's wings beat in alarm, and Biddy barely managed to clamp down its tongue before it cried out.

If the hole had been a few inches back, she would have been in plain view of the room beyond; a few inches more, and she might have been crushed into feathers and bone. But Storm had been guessing, and the magic was imprecise. The dust from the blast tickled the raven's beak as it shrank back into the stone, but she was in the shadows. He hadn't seen her.

And yet she could see him. Through the gap in the wall, a

mound of black moved, impossibly clear through the raven's eyes. He was looking for her.

Biddy... Hutch's voice warned in her head, high and panicked. She didn't dare reply.

Fight or flight. The insistent pull of the raven's brain tugged at her, over and over. Try to scrabble backward into the shadows, or launch herself at Storm with claws and wings flying. Neither sounded good, or possible. If he heard her move again, he would be on her before she could blink. As for clawing at him, stabbing with her sharp beak—it was what she most wanted to do in the world, but it couldn't work in the end. He was too strong.

He was coming closer.

Fight or flight.

Fight or flight.

Fight—

"Storm!"

Morgaine's voice cut across the silence as it had in the dungeon, and like then Biddy flinched. This time, though, her voice wasn't sharp with command, but light, pleased, the tone of someone coming across an unexpected friend in a crowd.

"*There* you are," she said. "What on earth are you doing?"

There was a pause, during which Biddy hardly dared breathe, before Storm responded. "I thought I heard something in the walls."

"Really? That's odd." The implication was that it was not odd at all, or at least not interesting. Biddy dared to lean forward to peek out the hole in the wall just in time to see Morgaine catch Storm by the arm and turn him deftly aside. "I was coming to see you. I thought you'd be in the dungeons."

All Biddy could see of Morgaine was the back of her head and the curve of her shoulder, but most of Storm's face was in three-quarter profile as he faced Morgaine. His head tilted, birdlike, and his blue-black eyes narrowed in suspicion. "Why were you coming to see me?"

"You've been down there since yesterday. I wanted to see if you needed anything."

"You mean you wanted to see if Rowan was still alive."

"What is that supposed to mean?"

A short, harsh chuckle. "Nothing." He paused, and his eyes flickered briefly back to where the raven sat huddled. Evidently, though, he dismissed it from his mind. "He is, if you were worried by the silence. We just can't keep him awake very long anymore. Fixing bones isn't everything. I told the Servant if we didn't leave him alone for an hour or two, he soon won't be able to talk to us even if he wanted to."

"And he listened to you?" Not a waver of her voice betrayed that she cared beyond that. Biddy no longer found her ability to pretend grotesque, but it was uncanny. "That's a good sign. You were worried he was ignoring you lately."

"I don't think he much cares what we do to Rowan. He's more interested in finding that girl."

Biddy's heart missed a beat, and her hearing went with it. It came back just in time to hear Morgaine ask innocently, "Has there been any sign of her?"

"None." Storm's voice lowered abruptly. He had forgotten about the sound in the walls now; his attention was entirely on Morgaine. It was what she had intended, and yet it suddenly felt dangerous. "I didn't miss any mirror in her pocket when she was here, you know. She had no mirror. She was wearing a nightgown, for God's sake; she didn't even have pockets. And Rowan didn't have that raven-stone when I captured him sixteen years ago. Of all the things to miss, I would never have missed that."

"Then how do you think they escaped the dungeons?"

"I don't know. How did they end up in your apartment?"

An edge crept into Morgaine's words. "I told the Servant how that happened. He was satisfied."

"That's because he doesn't know that you visited the girl alone after everybody else."

"What?" Biddy saw Morgaine's shoulders tense. "Who said they saw me do that?"

"Nobody. And that's how I know you did. I know you. She was

a human girl in a dungeon, practically a child—there's no way you wouldn't have come to see she'd been fed, that she had a blanket, that she was being treated well. The fact that nobody remembers you doing it tells me that you had reason to make sure they forgot. I'm right, aren't I?"

"That would take very difficult magic," Morgaine said carefully. "Forbidden too."

"You're more than capable of it, in every sense. We grew up together, remember? You always were good with memories." His voice changed—it was softer, suddenly, clearer, more like the young mage from his own memory. "Was it me who let you in? You might as well tell me. I think I can remember everything about that evening, but there's one thing that doesn't make sense. I tried to get that memory out of the girl's heart. I don't know why I stopped."

"Why would I—?"

Storm continued as if she hadn't spoken. "A memory stone needs close contact. Prolonged contact—the length of an embrace, or a kiss. How close were we exactly, Morgaine?"

The tone of the conversation had changed. It had twisted outside Morgaine's control—or perhaps it had never been within her control to begin with. Biddy watched, heart in her throat, as Morgaine raised her head and tried to wrest it back.

"I suppose you think I helped Rowan escape all those years ago too?"

"Oh, I've always known you did that. You're not going to this time, though. There are three guards with him at all times. You can't steal memories from all of them."

"Storm—"

"Don't." The word was harsh, painful, like a blow delivered or taken. "I protected you when Rowan escaped. I protected you again when the girl escaped. Don't insult me by lying. I'm not stupid."

"I never thought you were," Morgaine said, very quietly. She was silent for a long time. Biddy, behind the wall, didn't dare move, even though the raven's wings were cramping and there was a sharp edge of rock digging into its chest.

"Storm," Morgaine said at last. "I won't tell you that I set Rowan free all those years ago, and I won't lie to you either. But what if we did it now? What if you let me into that dungeon, dismissed the guards, and we got him out, together?"

Storm's brow creased. "Why in God's name would I do that?"

"Whatever deal he made you, Vaughan is never going to put you on the Council. You're far more use to him as you are, willing to do whatever he says because you'll never give up hoping he'll reward you."

"That's not true. But even if it were, why would that mean I let Rowan go?"

"Because what you're doing to him is monstrous. You must see that. Whatever else passed between you, we were all friends once. Surely you can't want him hurt like this."

"Him? Hurt? I'm in pain *every day* because of him." The words rasped in Biddy's ears like gravel against sandstone. "I've spent the last seventy years cleaved in two, trapped underground, barely seeing the light of day. I want him to know what that feels like."

"You've been tormenting him for days. He must know by now."

"Because I've broken a few bones?" Storm laughed. "That's nothing. He doesn't *like* it, but it doesn't really touch him. You know how I know?"

Morgaine didn't answer. Perhaps she shook her head, the movement too small to be seen from behind.

"When I was twisting into *this*, I would have given anything for it to stop. You, Rowan, all the magic left in the world. Anything. When the Servant told me that he would fix me when he had enough magic, I jumped at the chance. That was the deal he made me, by the way. Not a place on the Council, just the chance to be myself again. I took it without a second thought. I gave him my familiar, I gave him my allegiance, I gave him everything I had, because I want it all to *stop*. But Rowan—" The black eye glinted in the dark. "Rowan could stop what I'm doing to him any time he likes, just by telling us where the girl is hiding. And he won't give us a thing. Whatever I do to him, there's something that matters more, something that he still believes in. I don't have that, not anymore. *That's* what I want him to feel. I want him to break, to know that he's given away everything he had, and that in the end it meant nothing. I want him to feel what it is to be me, now, forever."

"Storm." Morgaine's voice was clear and precise, carefully under control. "I gave the Servant everything I had too. I know what it feels like. Why in the world would you want anybody else to feel like that?"

"Because *he is not better than me*." The words came out in a low hiss, and the twisted black feathers bristled. "He always thought he was. You both did. Even when we were children, you two were always off together, always laughing, always clever, always planning to change the world. I saw the way your faces would open for each other and close when I came in the room. I saw the scorn in Rowan's eyes and the pity in yours. But you did what Vaughan said when it came to it, exactly the same as me. And Rowan—he's a common criminal who put a spell in the heart of a little girl. He'll see that in the end. Everyone will."

Storm drew a deep breath. When he spoke again, he was calm, but ludicrously so, a parody of a person who was not seething with rage.

"Don't worry," he said, as though replying to something Morgaine hadn't said. "He'll break soon. He'll tell us where to find the girl, and it will be because of me. We'll find the schism, and the first thing the Servant will do will be to reward me by restoring me to what I was. I'll earn a place on the Council myself then. I'll be able to leave the Undercastle in daylight. I'll have everything I was supposed to have. We could even marry, if you wanted to."

Morgaine actually laughed—an involuntary sound, like a choke. "What?"

"Why not? It should have been me you were engaged to, not Rowan. You told me you weren't sure about marrying him."

"I didn't want to marry anyone! I didn't want to lose everything I had built for myself by becoming somebody's wife. That doesn't mean I was going to marry you instead! And I certainly wouldn't now."

"Not now, no. But when I'm whole again—"

"It has nothing to do with the ravenstone. I know it hurt you, and I'm sorry, I truly am, but it didn't break you. You broke yourself when you agreed to follow Vaughan because it was so much easier than fighting back. I don't blame you—I did the same thing." She hesitated, then raised her head and went on. "If you want to be whole again, then help me put it right. Let's leave here, the three of us. Together."

"You really don't know me at all, do you?" Storm shook his head. "Well. Think about it, at least. You're good at making decisions in your own best interests."

Morgaine didn't speak again. Storm held her gaze for a moment longer, both eyes blazing, light and dark. Then he turned and left the room. He had forgotten about checking the walls, at least. Somehow it didn't feel like a victory. Biddy sat there, frozen and trembling and yet oddly calm. She felt as though she had brushed against the edge of some abyss large and dark and teeming with monsters she could barely understand.

We have to get him out. Hutch's voice was low and trembling with rage and grief. It raised the raven's feathers.

We can't. It was the hardest thing she had ever said. *You heard Storm—there are three guards in the room with him. Even if we got in, how would we get him out?*

Had he been a rabbit, his hackles would have risen. *Watch me.*

I don't want to watch you die! And you would. We both would. I can't bear leaving him either, but we have to. She felt his anger abating. She'd meant it, but it broke her heart. *We'll come back for him. I promise.*

"Biddy?" Morgaine's voice, very low, at the wall. Biddy had almost forgotten she was still in the room. "Are you safe? Did he hurt you?"

Biddy couldn't speak to her with the raven's voice, but she fluttered her wings, and hoped Morgaine would understand.

She seemed to—at least, her shuddering sigh might have been relief. "The vault's not far from here, and the corridor's clear. Move quickly. I'll be right outside."

She said nothing about Storm. She didn't have to.

The raven knew the gap in the rock over the vault. The oppressing weight of fear and uncertainty lifted from its breast as they drew close, long before Biddy saw the flicker of light in the darkness that had alerted her to the opening many days ago; its head twisted to one side with a spark of mischief. Somewhere in its mind, Biddy smiled.

She had forgotten how high in the wall the gap was: at least twelve feet, right near the ceiling. The stone was the only thing in the room, and it stood in the center: enormous, impossible, faintly shimmering. Biddy flapped down with stiff wings, shifting back to herself as soon as she hit the floor. The air was cold against her bare human skin. She stretched, as she had often seen Rowan do after many hours in raven form, not to relieve cramped muscles but to rid herself of the raven's lingering tension—and, perhaps, to settle back into her own body.

Hutch was already running for the door. Biddy followed.

It was a simple door considering the vastness of the room, and when she saw it, she breathed her first sigh of relief since she had entered the Undercastle—perhaps her first since Rowan's capture. Morgaine hadn't been able to tell her what spells were guarding the vault, and she had been terrified that she would get this far only to be unable to open the door. But it was only a rune lock. She knew about rune locks—Rowan had used them all the time when she was younger, to keep her from poking around in his study when he wasn't there. It was simple, effective magic: You drew a design in chalk on the inside of a door, along with the right words, and then the door could only be opened by someone tracing the same design on the outside. This design looked particularly intricate, and Biddy couldn't begin to work out how to replicate it. It didn't matter. She didn't need to open it from the outside, after all. She reached into her satchel, where her charms lay in a jumble at the bottom, and pulled out her canteen. She wet the hem of her dress with the last of the water, and scrubbed at the chalk. It rubbed out easily.

Morgaine was waiting on the other side of the door, pacing, her hands balled into fists at her side. She flinched as the door clicked open, then her shoulders sagged in relief.

"The locket." The words came tumbling from Biddy before Morgaine was even in the room. "Did you get it?"

Morgaine pressed a finger to her lips, then nodded. She closed the door behind them and pulled from her pocket a tiny bundle wrapped in a lace handkerchief.

Biddy didn't have to wonder what it was. The magic in her heart knew. It tugged, sharp, the exquisite ache of longing for a place she had never been. Long before Morgaine had unwrapped it, she was staring at it in wonder.

It was a silver locket, shaped like a teardrop, and on it was engraved a silvery tree—an oak, like the one in the forest at Hy-Brasil, with outstretched branches.

"This is it," Morgaine said. "There's a lock of your hair inside. Take it, and let's go, quickly. Don't put it on!" she added quickly. "If it touches your heart, the spell will awaken."

Biddy tried not to sound annoyed. "I grew up with magic, you know."

"Of course you did." Morgaine sighed. "Forgive me. It's been too long since I've done anything like this. That knock at the door in my office was only someone looking to borrow a pen, can you believe it? Why do they always think I have pens? I almost died."

"Me too," Biddy agreed. She pushed the locket into her satchel without daring to look at it again. Morgaine's caution had made her wary of it, as though even its touch might cause her heart to break open and memories to come spilling out into the cold dark of the vault.

"There's no going back." Biddy looked up at the sound of Morgaine's voice, startled, and saw belatedly how shaken the other woman looked. Her hand trembled as she tucked an imaginary strand of hair behind her ear. "I can't believe I said that to Storm. He could go straight to the Servant. It's enough to have me arrested."

"He might not tell him. He's suspected you for years and never done anything."

She wasn't consoled. "I haven't been honest with him for seven decades, and *this* was the moment I chose. God, I was a fool. I just...had to give him a chance."

"He doesn't deserve one," Biddy said. "Not now."

I told the Servant if we didn't leave him alone for an hour or two, he soon won't be able to talk to us even if he wanted to.

"Perhaps not." Morgaine must have read something in Biddy's face, because she reached out suddenly and rubbed her shoulder. "It'll be all right, Bridget. Rowan's very hard to break."

"They don't need to break him to kill him. They can do that whenever they want." It was sinking in against her will, like the raven's talons into stone. Rowan was so close, perhaps only the distance of a few corridors away, and he had no idea they were there. She would never see him again. He was *dying*. And she had just fought with all her might to leave him there. "Hutch was right. I don't know what I was thinking. We should have gone to get him out right then, while Storm was with you."

"You couldn't. You can't." Morgaine was calm again—not her usual forced composure, or even resignation, but something deeper and sadder and infinitely sympathetic. "Believe me, nobody knows that better than I do." She gave Biddy's shoulder one last squeeze, then looked over at the obelisk in the center of the room with purpose. "Very well. I'd better do this quickly. In theory, Vaughan shouldn't be here until morning, but if he *is* dipping into magic on the sly, then he could come at any time. Especially if Storm tells him I wanted to break Rowan free."

The stone glowed as Morgaine approached, as though it knew her and was waiting.

Morgaine lay her hand flat against it, and her eyebrows shot up. "Dear God."

Her tone distracted Biddy from her worry. "What is it?"

She took a moment to reply. It was as though she had opened a door to a shallow step, and instead found herself fighting for balance on the brink of a precipice. "You were right."

Biddy didn't need to make it a question. "There's more magic than expected."

"So much more. More than Vaughan claims we've had in years. Rowan stole from here only—what was it, perhaps a month ago? It's *brimming* with magic. Vaughan's been lying to us. I don't know for how long, but it doesn't matter. Too long." Her fingers curled against the rock in a spasm of anger. "He told me we'd put things right if there was ever enough magic. I *believed* him. All this time I've been waiting, biding my time, and he had this all along. We could have given this to every mage in the country; we could have let it find the people without magic who need a miracle. I hate him. I hate everything he's made us into."

Biddy had every sympathy for this, but she was also painfully aware of the mirror in the corner, and the footsteps outside the door. Real or imagined, she could hear them coming closer. Hutchincroft evidently felt the same: He thumped sharply, and Morgaine shook herself.

"Of course," she said, as though Hutch had spoken. She drew a deep breath, as Biddy had seen Rowan do so often at the great oak; as then, the cold, stifled room under the earth whispered with the rush of an impossible breeze. This was not the faint rustle of the trees at Hy-Brasil, though. It was a surge like the wind from the sea, clear and cold and smelling of far-away horizons. It fluttered Biddy's hair from its knot and stirred the spell in her heart. It felt like the first step of an adventure.

Morgaine's eyes glimmered as they opened.

"Done," she said—matter-of-factly, but the word trembled with suppressed excitement. She brushed her hands on her skirt as though wiping off the last traces of dust, and the movement had the same restless, too-vibrant quality that Rowan's always had when he was brimming with magic. "I took everything. I hope it's enough. Now, quickly. You need to get out the way you did last time. I'll stay on here a while longer to allay suspicion. Wait for me at the library— and don't put the locket around your neck without me! It could be very dangerous without a mage to guide the two parts of the spell."

"You'll be back soon?" Biddy checked. The ravenstone around her neck was already fighting to fly.

"Oh yes." Morgaine's face was determined. The magic had given her more than energy, or perhaps it was the encounter with Storm after all. There was a new purpose to her, clear and sharp-edged and full of light. "Whatever that locket shows us, we're going there tonight."

Chapter Eighteen

$\mathcal{M}$orgaine didn't return to the library for over an hour, and it was the longest of Biddy's life. Her mind was teeming with too many things, things she hadn't imagined she could feel all at once—anticipation of Morgaine's return, anxiety for her safety, exhilaration, impatience, overwhelming fear. They had done it. They were ready. But it might still be too late. If Morgaine was captured and locked in the dungeon with Rowan, there would have been no point to any of it. She tried to distract herself by looking at the books that surrounded her, trying to guess which might be Rowan's and which Morgaine's. They were an eclectic mix, like the library at home—books of magic, but also fairy tales, legends, histories, the occasional novel. One, a volume of Shakespeare, was inscribed from Rowan to Morgaine on their engagement, which she found both interesting and a little strange.

The locket burned in her hand, where she held it clenched like a talisman. It took all her self-control not to put it around her neck. Not yet. Soon.

Hutch didn't seem his usual self. He had been far too quiet on the flight back; now he sank down in front of the fire, not in his typical contented flop but with the hunched, tense stance of a rabbit in pain, and barely responded when she crouched down beside him and rubbed his cheek. It had been over a week now since Rowan had given him the last of his magic, and he had taken human form yet again on their last night on the island.

"Stay with me," she whispered. "Please."

He straightened at her voice, and flicked his ears briskly. It made her smile.

"I'm glad I saw this place, whatever happens," Biddy said to him, more for something to say than anything else. She looked up at the books around them. "Trust Rowan to put a library inside a tree."

"I wanted it inside a theater," Morgaine's voice came from the entrance. She found a wan smile when Biddy flinched. "We used to go to plays at Drury Lane all the time. I thought a tree could be too easily cut down, and then we'd lose the door. But Rowan thought trees lasted longer than buildings, and we fought about it, and eventually I threw my hands up and gave in. He let me have my way about the interior, to make up for it."

"Well, he was right," Biddy said, getting to her feet. "The tree's still standing."

"The theater's still standing as well," Morgaine said. "So we have yet to see who was right. But I do like the tree."

Rowan loved trees. It was something she'd never thought of in quite that light—she'd just taken it for granted that trees were good. But she saw now that she only thought that because he had taught her, because he knew the ways of every tree in the forest on Hy-Brasil. She thought perhaps she might cry after all.

"I stopped by the dungeons before I left," Morgaine said, hesitant. "I didn't care what anyone thought. I can't go back to the Undercastle again anyway, not once they find the magic gone from the vault tonight, and if this works, I won't have to."

Biddy turned to her quickly, and Hutch did the same. "Is he—?"

"He's alive, don't worry." She didn't quite meet either of their eyes. "I insisted the guards let me give him a blanket—at least stealing Storm's memories means they have no idea I've pulled that trick before—and when I got close enough I whispered to him that you were both safe and he'd see you soon. I hope it'll help him to hold out a little longer."

"You mean hold *on* a little longer," Biddy said flatly. "Don't you?"

"I hope not. But yes, I suppose I do. He'll die before he gives you away, I'm sure of that. And Storm—well, he'll make a token effort to keep him alive until he has permission to kill him, because he wants Vaughan's favor. But there's only so many times you can break and mend someone, even with magic, and have them come back the same. You lose a little every time. I don't think Rowan has a lot left to lose. At least Storm wasn't there when I went down."

Biddy hesitated. "Did you know Storm wanted to marry you?"

"He doesn't," Morgaine said flatly. "Not in the way he thinks. He wants to put me back in my place, just as he wants to do to Rowan. He's trying to prove that he's still the hero, the chosen one, that I'm the woman that should have been his, that Rowan's the best friend turned enemy. And the worst part is that he doesn't even understand the point he's trying to make to himself." She looked at Biddy. "I never kissed him, by the way. The night I helped you escape, and stole his memories. I took him by the arm and I led him away, and then I clasped the stone in my pocket with one hand and wrapped my fingers around his wrist as it took effect. I want you to know that."

Biddy wasn't sure what to say. "I'm sure Rowan would have understood if you had," she said at last.

"Oh, Rowan." It wasn't dismissive this time, somehow. "He would understand perfectly, and what's more he wouldn't care. I want *you* to know that. If you're out in the world for any length of time, there are going to be people who will accuse you of using sex as a weapon just because they're afraid it would work on them if you did. It *is* a weapon, if you want to use it. But it isn't the best or the only one you have, and you shouldn't ever let them make you feel it is."

She still didn't know what to say, but now for an entirely different reason. It was too strange a thought that anyone might ever look at her and accuse her of any such thing. She put the advice away for later, unable to imagine a time when she would need to bring it out, knowing it might indeed come.

"Do you think Storm will turn you in?"

"I think his feelings about me and Rowan are complicated enough that he might do anything now. But I meant what I said: I don't care anymore. I'm sick of hiding in the shadows."

I am half sick of shadows, said the Lady of Shalott. The line flitted across Biddy's mind in Rowan's softest lilt, along with a flicker of firelight in the castle library, the sound of rain lashing outside, a cold draft through the half-open window that seemed to bring with it the promise of adventure. She had been perhaps six or seven, hearing the poem read to her for the first time. It had thrilled and spellbound her: the woman in the tower, longing for life and experience, the bold knight outside, the ebb and flow of the rhyme as relentless and inevitable as a river. She felt a pang of longing as sudden and fierce as the thrust of a dagger—not just for Hy-Brasil, but for her childhood, which it seemed had been hers only a few weeks ago and now was lost forever.

That was the real reason she was nervous about unlocking the memory in her heart, now she had the locket. At long last, she would see the night Rowan had planted the spell in the first place, the memory that even Rowan and Hutch had been unable to explain. She would know the truth, when she had spent so long on the island trying to convince herself that she didn't care about the truth. She told herself, over and over, that as long as Rowan could be safe she would forgive him anything, and she meant it. She just didn't want that put to the test. She didn't want to lose more of him than she already had. Deep down, she didn't want to know.

But this wasn't about her. It couldn't be. And even if it was, Morgaine was right. She couldn't hide forever.

"I think you'd better sit down," Morgaine said, "if we're truly going to do this."

The chair by the fire was old and squashed; when Biddy sat on it, she sank through the cushion almost to the floor. Hutchincroft jumped into her lap, and she entwined her fingers in his fur gratefully.

"Will it hurt?" she couldn't help asking, as Morgaine bent down beside her with the locket in her hands.

"I don't know," Morgaine said. At least that was honest. "I've never done magic like this before. It will certainly be very strange. Are you sure you want to go through with it?"

Biddy nodded firmly. "I don't care if it hurts. I just wanted to know."

It was a lie. Of course she cared. But there were so many worse things than pain.

"Very well, then." Still, Morgaine hesitated. The locket gleamed in the firelight, like a threat or a promise. "Bridget, if they *do* force him to tell them…"

"He won't." She wasn't lying this time. She was as sure of that as she could be of anything. "You said he wouldn't, and I think so too."

Morgaine nodded, and put the locket around Biddy's neck.

Biddy's heart opened wide.

The library was gone, swallowed up in a shimmer of light. She was soaring above the sea in a raven's body, Hutchincroft's solid, luminous presence in her mind, the moon glinting on the waves as they raced them to shore. Her hopes and fears tugged at her heart like a child tugging at a sleeve, urging her onward, faster and faster.

She was in the chimney. Everything was soot-dark and choking; the raven's terror clawed at her brain as its feet clawed at the brick, but each movement showered them with soot and blackened the world further. It was in her eyes and in her throat and in her lungs, nothing but darkness swallowing up everything.

She was in the dungeons, and Storm's magic sank into her chest and clawed at the spell. She screamed at the pain and shock of it, but also with rage. That magic was hers. It hadn't just been planted in her, it had been *entrusted* to her. He had no *right*. The ground beneath her was so cold, and when she pressed against the wall the stone dug into her shoulders like points of ice.

She was breaking apart. Her heart was unfurling like a flower awakening to sunlight, her ribs expanding, her head splitting open like that of Zeus when Athena sprang full-formed. She couldn't scream this time, because she had no breath, no lungs, no tongue. The kernel of magic inside her had opened, and it was flooding her body like salt water or light.

In a chair in the library inside a tree, her eyes closed.

On the floor of a filthy dungeon far beneath the earth, Rowan's opened.

She was standing in the dining hall of the Rookwood Asylum for Destitute Girls in Whitechapel. She knew it at once: the long dirty tables laid out in rows, the filthy windows looking out into the courtyard, the same high ceiling and redbrick walls. The only difference was that it was the dead of night, and she had never seen the room outside the strict mealtimes.

This wasn't her memory.

Biddy rose shakily to her feet, and only then realized that she had a body and it had been crouching on the ground. She brushed at her dress with a shudder, less to clean it from dust—it was, after all, only the memory of dust—than to reassure herself she was solid once more, at least to herself. Her skin prickled as though with cold or fear, and yet she felt neither.

This was it.

The children's home was quiet in the dark, the children and wardens alike asleep upstairs. Only one person stood in the center of the room, a thin shadow against the faint moonlight. As Biddy watched, he held up his hand, whispered something into the palm, and a tiny ball of light rose to illuminate the ground before him. Biddy had seen that spell hundreds of times: when they had been out walking late in the evening, and the sun had gone down before they could reach home; when they stood on the open turret late at night to watch the stars; when she'd been very small and afraid to sleep alone in the dark.

"Rowan," she whispered.

It was the strangest feeling, not at all like the other memories she had found herself in. She was herself, standing apart from Rowan, but she also *was* Rowan. She could feel his thoughts and sensations beneath her own skin: his breathing rapid and fast, his heart pounding, the perspiration turning ice cold on his forehead. Most of it was from exertion—she noticed the dull throb of exhausted muscles, the hollow ache between the eyes from lack of sleep—but not all of it. He was scared. There were people coming, and things coming with them, and they were almost here.

Hutch was in danger. That was the thought that burned in his heart, in his brain, in the part of his soul where his magic lived. Storm had captured Hutch, and he would destroy him unless Rowan gave himself up in exchange. He had to save him. He had so little time.

And yet he was so close. They had been looking for so long, and he was so close.

"Are you looking for the crack in the world?" Biddy asked. He couldn't hear her, but it didn't matter. She knew, in a way that wasn't quite hearing his thoughts. He was.

It was here. Here, in the place where Rowan had found her all those years ago, he had also found the schism. She had been right here only days ago, and none of them had ever known. Why had they not known? If the schism was here, why had Rowan never found it again?

She barely had time to think about it. Rowan was moving forward, purposeful. She started to follow him, but there was no need. This was Rowan's memory—she couldn't part from him. When he moved, she moved with him, like a ghost tethered by an insubstantial string.

Together, they moved through the corridors that Biddy had walked herself, climbed the rickety stairs to the second floor, down yet more corridors. He moved quietly, as he usually did. Even so, there must have been magic to hide him, because when he opened the last door on the left, not one of the infants in the room stirred at his presence.

It was the nursery, the room where the very youngest abandoned or orphaned girls slept—six of them this time, three on each side. Not one of them was over two years old, Biddy knew from her own time in the children's home, but even the toddlers were so small and sickly that they seemed much younger. Some of them slept, some lay awake and stared. One of them was crying—the low, thin wail of a child who did not expect comfort, but was too upset to stop calling out for it. The sound caught Biddy's heart painfully, like a barb sinking into flesh.

Rowan obviously felt something similar, because his step faltered next to that child's crib, then stopped. He glanced around quickly, as though expecting to see someone else, and when nobody was evident, he bent down over her.

"Come on," he said—soft, smiling, the way he always had when Biddy had been very young and upset. He tweaked the child lightly on the nose. "Don't cry."

When the child still wailed, Rowan reached into the crib, scooped her up, and nestled her against his hip as though he had done it a thousand times. She was a scrawny little girl with tufts of chestnut-colored curls, red-faced from distress, with eyes screwed shut. Biddy's heart tugged again, but this time all the breath rushed from her lungs. She knew who that child was.

The little girl's crying quieted slowly, warmed and distracted by the novelty of being held. Rowan rocked her gently, humming something low and soft. Biddy, watching, felt herself smile. She remembered Rowan singing that to her, when she was very, very little, the snatches of words in the lilting language she didn't understand.

"I know, I know, you're cold and hungry and lonely, aren't you?" Biddy could feel his heart beating quick and rapid, but he kept his voice light. "I'm a bit that way myself. Do you want to see into another world?"

Still humming, he carried the little girl to the far wall. It was the same stained, crumbling brick it had been when Biddy had seen it last week, though she knew she was watching something that had happened sixteen years ago. She could see nothing special about it now. It was only when Rowan brushed it with his fingertips and scattered some of the dust that she saw, to her surprise, a glint of something green. It was like a seam of moss, or a glimpse of forest through a gap in the castle stones. For some reason she couldn't fully understand, her own heart quickened to match Rowan's.

"Wish me luck," Rowan whispered to the child, whose cries had subsided into whimpers.

Rowan drew a deep breath, and pushed against the wall. Biddy felt the magic shiver under his skin and through his fingertips, and the schism in the wall glowed in response. Something was trickling through from the other side—not quite light, not quite substance, like the glint of dust motes dancing in a sunbeam with no sunbeam and no dust. The air about them stirred, and Biddy's heart caught.

She was *seeing* magic. In all her life, she had only had it described to her, and felt the movement of it in the air. Now, in Rowan's memory, it shimmered the gentle green gold of sunlight through leaves.

"It's beautiful," she whispered, even though she knew Rowan couldn't hear her. She felt something spill down her cheek, and only then realized she was crying.

Rowan's own eyes glinted with tears. At first she thought they were of joy, and some of them were, but when she looked closer, she could see that there was more darkness on his face than light. She hadn't looked at his face properly since she had come here, and it startled her. She had seen him in his dreams of Morgaine, young and open and hurting; she knew him in the present day, quicksilver and laughing and brave. He was neither here. He was tired and alone and scared and doing everything he could to keep going, and for some reason that burst of magic had broken him.

"It's not enough," he said to the child in his arms. She could hear the despair underlying his soft voice, but she knew the child couldn't. All she knew was a low, comforting murmur in the dark, and a tickle of wind from another world. "It's too small. There's a bit of magic coming through, more than there's been in decades, but it's not strong enough to make a difference, and now I've found it the Council will come and suck it dry just like all the others. And I won't be here to stop them. I'm not even sure I'll be alive." The child reached out toward the light, eyes wide, tears dried by interest, and Rowan managed a shaky laugh. "Still. Pretty, isn't it?"

A roar of wind lashed against the window, rattling the pane, and Biddy jumped at the same time as Rowan turned sharply. Thunder rumbled, and a howl tore across the night. The stars disappeared behind rolling clouds.

"It's all right, my love," Rowan whispered, as the child's face crumpled. A couple of the others had begun to whimper in their beds. "Hush. That storm's for me, not you. It's time."

She wasn't sure when the idea came to him. She couldn't see enough of his thoughts for that, and she couldn't read what flickered across his face. But she saw him reach across and brush his hand over the schism, and whisper something that made it disappear from view. She saw him pause, more still and quiet than she had ever seen him, for what seemed a very long time. She saw him walk the child who was Biddy to the crib and set her down.

"This won't hurt," he said to her. "I promise. And I'll come back as soon as I can. This isn't the end—I won't let it be." The child looked up at him with wide eyes filled with trust, and he sighed. "I swear, I would do this differently if I could. I wish there was time to find somebody else willing to hold it safe. But I'm about to walk into the hands of some very bad people, and whatever happens they can't be able to torture it out of me. They can't."

Biddy knew what was coming next. He pulled out the knife at his waist and gently cut a lock of the child's hair. He put the hair into the locket he wore at his neck and locked the clasp. And then he laid his hand on the child's head, drew a deep, shivering breath, and closed his eyes.

The room split in two. There was a noise like the tear of paper and a shatter of glass, and blinding white light filled her eyes. The room stood frozen, bright, overexposed. Biddy stood in the center of it, the only color in a world of overlit shadows. The memory of Rowan and the child who was herself was quiet now. The only movement was the rise and fall of Rowan's shoulders as he breathed, and a faint breeze from the storm waiting outside.

"My memories start again a few moments later." She turned, her heart pounding. Rowan—another Rowan, her Rowan—stood beside her, arms folded, staring contemplatively at the ghostlike figures in front of them. "Didn't even notice the gap. Maybe there was a jolt, like when you nearly trip over in the dark. I was a raven flying in a storm, and I thought I was going to my death."

It took her a moment to find her voice. "Is this—? Are you really here?"

"Morgaine said you were safe and we'd see each other again," Rowan said. "I'm glad she was right."

"What are you doing here?"

"This is my memory. Where else should I be? You can't leave a memory behind without leaving part of yourself with it." He shook his head, smiling a little. "No wonder I forget to do the washing up every now and then. My mind's been in pieces for years! Tell Hutch that, so he'll feel guilty about telling me off."

"Nobody's going to feel guilty about telling you off," Biddy informed him. There was a lump in her throat. "Not as long as you only ever forget to do the things you don't like."

His smile deepened briefly, then faded. "I'm sorry," he said quietly.

Biddy had never in her life heard Rowan apologize for anything. A few weeks ago, she would have been pleased and satisfied to hear an apology from him. Now, it filled her with a nameless dread. "For what?"

He laughed shortly, and looked away. "Everything. I'm sorry I put you in danger. I knew it was wrong—Hutch would never have let me, if he'd been here. I lost my nerve, simple as that. I'd spent over fifty years since the world broke trying to do the right thing—year after year, day after day. I'd never, when we first ran away, thought it would be as long as that. On that night I was all alone for the first time since I found Hutchincroft, I was tired and scared and sure I was going to die, and I didn't trust myself to be brave at the end. So I put the burden on you. I meant to set it right if I lived, but I failed, and I'm sorry for that too. And I'm sorry I took you, when I came back a year later with no idea who you were. I thought I was keeping you safe. If I'd had any idea what I'd done—"

"*I'm* not sorry you took me." She thought of the orphanage, its stones and its grime and the cold that went to its bones. She thought of Hy-Brasil, green and grey and wild. She thought, too, of Rowan reading her stories by the light of the fire and teaching her to climb trees and making her laugh when she was sick, of Hutchincroft sleeping by her side on storm-racked nights and running with her through the grass and fussing over her socks. "I'll never, ever be sorry. I'm not sorry you hid a memory in my heart either. I understand that now. I'm only sorry that you lied to me about where you found me."

"Well, that one I've been sorry about for years."

"Why did you do it?"

He shrugged. "It was a mistake, honestly. You started asking questions earlier than I expected, and I didn't know how to explain to a three-year-old about orphanages, or the outside world, or that she was in danger. I wasn't ready. So I invented something easier, and then every year it became harder to tell you otherwise. You seemed to like the story so much. Sounds a bit stupid, doesn't it?"

"Not stupid," she said. "But you could have told me the truth. Or that you'd tell me when I was older."

"I'll keep that in mind for next time." He laughed again, but very softly. "I really didn't know what I was doing, Bid. I always liked children, but I didn't know how to look after a little girl. I didn't know how to look after anything in those days, including myself. It was all a bit of a mess. I just did my best, and was very glad for Hutchincroft. That's my life, come to think of it."

She smiled.

"I said I'd put this right," he added. "But I can't just at the moment. Are you with Morgaine?"

"Yes. She gave me the locket. She's on our side, truly."

"I hope so. It looks like we're going to have to trust her. She needs to go back to the children's home, and she needs to make sure that fracture's safe. It's still hidden, clearly—that's why I never found it again. But it needs to be kept safe until we can find a way to open it."

"I know how to open it now," Biddy said. "You were right. The cracks closed because they didn't have enough magic to stay open. If we push through as much magic as we can, they'll come back."

He didn't ask how she knew this, only nodded quickly. "Then Morgaine needs to make sure she has enough magic, whatever it takes. She *needs* to do this, Biddy. Don't let her talk herself out of it. She's better and stronger than she thinks."

Biddy nodded seriously. "She'll do it. I'll take her there myself."

"You need to go back to Hy-Brasil." His voice was uncompromising. "Unlocking the memory doesn't mean the magic's no longer in your heart. As long as you're in the world, the Council can find you. I put you in danger once already. You're not to go back into it again. Especially when I'm not there to protect you."

"You didn't protect me last time!"

"I know. That's all the more reason that you get home, and stay there until this is over. Let Morgaine handle it. All right?"

Biddy didn't answer directly. There was no sense in arguing. Rowan couldn't stop her. "And what about after that? If it works? Do we come and rescue you then?"

He hesitated. "Maybe. If it's safe." She knew that tone well, from the rare occasions when he didn't intend to let her do something but didn't want to fight about it. She folded her arms and raised a skeptical eyebrow. "You might not have to. I told you, I'll get myself out!"

The room had almost faded now. In the crib, Biddy could just make out the face of her younger self, Rowan's hand resting on her chest. Soon, he would twist into a raven and fly to his fate, leaving her with just the lingering comfort of his smile and a shard of magic in her heart. She wouldn't see him again for months, and neither would remember each other.

What if she had been asleep that night? What if another child had cried? Rowan believed that magic found its way to where it was most needed, but she didn't see that her need was any greater than that of any other child there. It could have been any one of them with a memory planted in her heart that night.

"Rowan?" she asked, hesitant.

He was looking at the fading room too. "Mm?"

"Were you really sorry you took me? I mean, for your sake."

"Never," he said immediately. "Not for a moment."

It was all he said, but it was enough.

"Are you safe and well?" she asked. "The real you, I mean, the one that Storm has."

He started to answer, then stopped. "Not so very well, if I'm honest," he said reluctantly. "It might be a while before I make it back to you."

"You don't have to," she said firmly. "We're coming for you."

Chapter Nineteen

Whitechapel at night was not a kind place.

Even in the most genteel parts of London, the parts that Rowan had shown Biddy in an effort to ease her gradually into the real world, there had been poverty creeping through. There had been glimpses through cracks in a beautiful stone facade: a man hunched on the steps of Trafalgar Square, the worn face of a woman trudging home in a maid's uniform, a girl with no shoes holding out flowers for sale. The dark alleys by the docks were the other side of that crack. It was well after midnight now, but the streets teemed with life. Drunken laughter and shrieks cut the air; children with pitifully sharp faces curled up in alleys trying to steal rest; women dressed in bedraggled finery waited, bored, on street corners. The place had a wary, exhausted air of never having a good night's rest.

Biddy had seen it in the daylight, and it had fascinated and repelled her in equal measures. She had hurt for its inhabitants, and longed to make it better. Now she knew she was one of those inhabitants—or would have been, if not for an accident of magic. It was where she had been born, where the mother and father she had never known had lived. They could be any one of the older people she and Morgaine and Hutchincroft passed, or they could be buried in paupers' graves in the nearest shabby church. Any of the younger ones could be brothers or sisters she had never met. She would have known these streets the way she knew the forests and cliffs of Hy-Brasil; her accent would be the clipped, jaunty rhythm of Anna and the others; and her own country wouldn't care if she lived or died. She didn't feel sorry now. Anger and purpose filled her like cool liquid in a vial. They needed to split the world open. These people deserved every scrap of magic they could get.

The Rookwood Asylum for Destitute Girls was one of the few buildings on the street that was quiet. This made sense, since Morgaine had touched it with a gentle spell earlier that evening, while Biddy waited for nightfall in the library. Its inhabitants would sleep peacefully all night, Morgaine had assured her, and stay asleep no matter what happened—the same sleep from which Biddy had rescued Rowan before all this had started, only with far softer dreams. Biddy had imagined the magic creeping over the old building like Sleeping Beauty's vines, coiling around the girls in their cold beds, around Miss Finchley as she sat in her rooms working out how to stretch money to feed her charges, around the infants in their cribs.

"Are the girls still in the school, though?" she had asked. "The last I saw, the wisps—"

"The wisps didn't touch anyone but you," Morgaine said. "They never do, once they have what they've been sent to find. They vanish like smoke, and leave behind nothing but bad memories and ash. All that the warden of that place found in the morning was a group of terrified children filled with stories about shadows with claws that nobody believed."

"But I had vanished too. Where did they think I was?"

"They would have said you ran away, if anybody outside the school had asked," Morgaine said. "Teachers never stay long in schools like that. In this area, though, most people wouldn't ask. They remember the Ripper murders here twenty years ago, and many more since. You wouldn't be the first young woman to be taken out an unlatched poorhouse window in the middle of the night and the body found along the Thames." She said it gently, as though she really was giving Biddy news of her death.

It did feel like that, somehow. Biddy wondered if any of the girls had been upset by her loss. They were used to death, even death by violence. But then, they were used to lies as well. Perhaps they didn't believe she was gone for good. She felt sure that Anna wouldn't.

"I'll leave a note for Anna. I'll let her know I'm safe."

"Best not," Morgaine advised, not without sympathy. "It's better for them if they never know we were there. If all goes well, you can come back and see your friend anytime."

If all went well. If all went well, the world could be very different after that night.

Morgaine was crouching down now; when she stood again, she had left a small polished stone at the entrance of the door.

"A seeing stone," she explained, and Biddy remembered the small grey pebble Rowan had put on top of the castle after Vaughan's skeleton wisps had screamed from the sky. "I'll know if anything tries to follow us in."

"Surely the building's being watched. I was found here."

"Storm wanted to watch it," Morgaine conceded. "He was over-ruled. The Servant said there was no point, now we had taken you. Anyway, I don't care if it is. If there is a schism, then we only need a matter of minutes. Once we've opened it, there's nothing in the world that can stop us walking out."

Her head was raised and her face flushed as she spoke, and in that flash of defiance Biddy saw suddenly what she must have been like with a familiar at her side, when the world shimmered with magic and she and Rowan had been in love.

Nobody stopped them as Morgaine unlocked the gate with a touch of a spell, or as they pushed open the worn door and let it close softly behind them. Enchanted sleep lay heavy in the entrance hall; Biddy felt its tendrils pressing the edge of her senses, and forced it back quickly before it could take hold. The last thing she needed was to doze off herself. Hutchincroft moved silently, wary, periscoping in the entrance hall as Biddy and Morgaine joined him.

"The room is just upstairs and along the corridor," Biddy said, mostly to break the thick silence.

"It's a horrible place," Morgaine said, almost to herself. Her arms were folded tightly across her chest, as though trying to keep out cold, or keep in something else. "No wonder a schism opened. It was needed."

"Is that true, then?" she asked, interested despite her worry. "Do cracks really open where they're needed?"

"It was a theory, long ago. Rowan believed it. I'm never sure if I do. But in places like this, I want to."

Biddy understood this perfectly, as she couldn't have weeks earlier. Rowan's ideas about magic were beginning to seem overly hopeful to her now she had seen more of life outside Hy-Brasil: If magic worked as he thought, there were simply too many places that would call to it. The world would shatter with the tides of magic breaking through. And yet as they made their way upstairs, past the sleeping girls and into the narrow room with its threadbare rug lined with cradles, it did feel as though the sadness of the place was strong enough to call beyond the bounds of the earth. The five infants slept their enchanted sleep, tiny chests rising and falling.

Morgaine cast her hand into the air, whispered something, and tilted her head as if waiting for a reply. "I can't see anything," she said, after a fraught pause. "Are you certain it was here?"

"*Yes.*" Biddy fought her rising impatience, which she knew was mostly borne of fear. The quiet of the room was eerie, oppressive with the weight of enchanted sleep and the dread of what might be coming for them right now. She had been hiding so carefully. It was hard to believe they could be safe here, at the heart of everything. "I told you, it was on the far wall, just under the window. Of course you can't see it—Rowan hid it so well he couldn't find it himself. You have to look for it."

"I *am* looking—oh, stop it, Hutch!" she added, as Hutchin-croft gave her the full brunt of a rabbit's glare. "I believe you, I do. I thought that spell would work, that's all. Just let me..."

She put her hand to the wall by the door, then followed the edges of the room, picking her way past the cradles. Biddy moved with her, casting an anguished glance at the window. It would be there, she knew it, and nowhere else. But plainly Morgaine needed to search in her own way, and interrupting the spells involved would just take longer.

A few minutes, Morgaine had said. Those minutes ticked away, then they ticked away again. They were under the window now, and still Morgaine's hands found no purchase on the wall. She went to the wall, then back to the window again. Her movements were quiet, unhurried, but Biddy knew Morgaine better now, and could see that her calm was like Rowan's carelessness. It was an armor, one that was growing increasingly brittle as the corners of her mouth pressed tighter and tighter.

This was the same window against which rain had lashed, all those years ago, when she was only a child and Storm had been on his way. The darkness outside was quiet now. Biddy imagined a sudden dash of rain against the dirty glass, and knew, with a certainty that was almost cheerful, that if it happened she would probably just die.

And then—

"It's here," Morgaine said abruptly.

Her frown smoothed into wonder.

"I have the corner of it now. It's really here. I can feel it."

Morgaine was crouched down under the window; Biddy dropped down to join her, so close and eager she nearly overbalanced. She could see nothing under Morgaine's fingertips, but she didn't expect to, and what's more she didn't care. She had already seen it through Rowan's eyes, glistening with power. "Can you open it?"

"Let me take the spell from it first." Biddy saw no difference before and after Morgaine's fingers rubbed across the wall, but Hutchincroft was suddenly quivering with eagerness. "There! God, it's so *small*. I can't imagine how Rowan found this in the first place..."

"Can you open it up?"

"I don't know." Morgaine sat back on her heels with a sigh. "You've seen this done before; I haven't. It's a lot smaller than I imagined. I wish I hadn't put this house to sleep now—even that spell might have made all the difference. But I'll try. I promise you, I'll try."

Biddy had given her the words back at the house, and done her best to answer every one of Morgaine's questions, even the ones that risked betraying that she had been on Hy-Brasil. Now Morgaine closed her eyes, and the air around them began to stir.

A whisper like the rustle of leaves overhead went through the room, and the hairs on the back of her neck rose. Morgaine pressed her hand to the wall so hard that the tips of her fingers paled, and a frown line appeared between her eyes.

"Please," Biddy heard her whisper. "Please."

Beneath Morgaine's fingers a green line flickered, then caught. Biddy could see it this time—whether because the spell itself was revealing it or as some lingering gift of the Púca's wild ride. A crack spidered out across the wallpaper, as it had across Hy-Brasil many thousands of years ago. It reached the edges of the wall, and then it widened like the opening of a crooked mouth. The schism was the width of Biddy's hand, then wider, the width of her body, more. The air was so thick with magic she could barely breathe.

This was it. It was really it.

The light gleamed green gold, the colors of the forest in summer.

And then Morgaine dropped her hand with a cry.

"It isn't enough," she said huskily. There were tears in her eyes, as there had been in Rowan's, and she looked utterly drained.

"It is!" Biddy protested. She gestured, as if Morgaine could somehow have missed the great tear across the wall. "Look. I can see it!"

"It won't stay open. That was everything I had. And it's already closing."

It was. Even as Biddy watched, the edges were bleeding shut once more. The light was dimming, slowly but certainly. It was like watching a wound heal at impossible speed.

Morgaine hit the wall with a balled fist, hard. "We're so *close*! Just a little more and it would hold, I'm sure it would. But I don't have it."

"I have the ravenstone. If I threw it in ...?"

"Objects won't work. It has to be living magic, held in a living soul. I'm sorry." She drew a deep breath. "It's open now. We're simply going to have to trust it won't be seen, gather what further magic we can, and come back."

"No!" Hy-Brasil. There was magic on Hy-Brasil. But that was so far away, even if she gave Morgaine the ravenstone to get there. Rowan could be dead by the time they got back. "There has to be more. Hutch, do you—?"

Biddy turned to Hutchincroft just in time to see his eyes widen. All at once, he was eerily still, as though turned to stone. Her heart froze with him.

"Hutchincroft!" Biddy sank down and drew the rabbit spirit into her arms. He was freezing cold, and his muscles were rigid and trembling. She stroked his ears frantically, trying to warm him. "Hutch, what is it?"

"Something's happened to Rowan," Morgaine said slowly. "Something terrible."

Biddy opened her mouth, on instinct, to protest—it couldn't be true, not when they were so close. Except that of course it could. Every book in the castle library had taught her that, even before the outside world had.

Before she could speak, something caught her eye.

Down on the floor, where her shoe had overturned the rug as she had crouched beside Hutch. A scraping of powdery white on the floor, curved. A chalk line. She turned up the rug a little more, and saw the line extend.

A circle. Drawn on the floor, in the aisle where under any other circumstances they would have walked.

Oh no. God, no, *no*.

"We need to get out of here." She scooped Hutch in her arms; he thrashed once, weakly, on reflex. She didn't even feel it. Her heart was thrumming too fast. "Morgaine!"

"What is it?" Morgaine glanced down herself, and her eyes widened. "But how—?"

"It doesn't matter. Watch where you stand, and *move*."

It was too late.

There was no slow creep of shadows this time, no rumble of a storm outside. The door through which they had come simply burst open. Splinters of wood flew through the air; Biddy was knocked back, as though an unseen hand had pushed its way through wood and plaster and punched her to the ground. She lost her grip on Hutch as she hit the floor, and her breath was knocked from her lungs.

Morgaine threw herself in front of Biddy, arms flung wide. "Stay there!" she called over her shoulder. Her face was set, and her eyes were blazing.

But all her stolen magic had been poured into the hungry schism in the wall. Through the open door, tiny bird skeletons swarmed like insects over rotten wood. The barest glimmer of flame sparked from Morgaine's fingers, useless, and then the flurry of beaks and bones caught her and flung her aside like a broken doll. Her body slammed against the wall next to the schism, and she fell to the ground with a terrible cry. Biddy heard a snap, then nothing at all.

"Morgaine!" Without thinking, without caring, she scrambled to her feet. Morgaine lay sprawled on the floor across the room, eyes closed, her breath coming in jagged gasps.

Biddy made it two paces before sharp talons dug into her arms. Her feet left the ground as more wisps grabbed her shirt, her hair, her shoulder. She thrashed and struggled, heedless of the burrowing pain at the points of their claws. Then she was falling—not against the wall like Morgaine, but straight down feetfirst, her knees hitting the floor in the middle of the room with a crack that sent hot agony blazing to her waist. She curled up on the rug, stunned, unable to move.

In the exact center of the trap circle.

"I'm sorry for the violence," a voice said. "If you'd stepped in on your own, you could have been spared. But you weren't to know."

She knew that voice. With effort, she looked toward the door.

Vaughan Carlisle, the Servant of Magic, stood in the frame. The wisps surrounded him in a swooping cloud—the wisps made of dead things, the same wisps he had sent to Hy-Brasil the day Biddy had stood by the ruins.

He couldn't be here. Her head whirled, tried to grasp at impossibilities. Morgaine had put the stone behind them. It was supposed to see if anyone followed them. Morgaine was the stonemage who had helped forge the ravenstone; there was no way the spell had been broken. He couldn't have come in behind them. Besides, that trap circle had been waiting for them. It had been drawn after the babies had been put to bed—none of the teachers had been caught in it as they gave them their final checks. As Morgaine and Biddy and Hutch had been making their way toward the asylum, Vaughan had been drawing a circle where he hoped they would stand.

Which meant only one thing.

"You didn't follow us." The pain of impact was settling to a dull throb. "You were already here, waiting for us. How did you know where to come?"

"It's obvious, isn't it?" His shoulders rose and fell in the slightest shrug. "Rowan must have told me where the schism was. I wouldn't blame him. Storm was very enthusiastic about his work."

For a moment she believed it. For the space of a single heartbeat, she believed that Rowan had broken down and betrayed them, and she didn't blame him at all, because she had seen the depths of Storm's hate and understood exactly why Rowan had been so scared to face it. Then a glint in the Servant's eyes caught her. It was too playful, too interested in her reaction for someone who was telling the truth. In the light of the schism she could see for the first time the glassy sheen of his right eye, and she knew the magic in it was working.

He could see her desires, her resentments, her darkest fears. He knew that the answer she feared most in the world was what he had given her.

"No," she said. "He wouldn't. Not when he knew Hutch and Morgaine and I would be coming here too. He'd die first." The answer came as though someone had whispered in her ear. "You already found the schism, didn't you? You found it years ago."

This was why there had been too much magic in the stone, far more than there should be; why Rowan had been certain his enemies were more powerful than they had any right to be. Vaughan had been drawing it from here all along.

"Of course I found it." His lips curved in a quick smile, but there was a touch of bitterness at its edges. "I taught Rowan most of the tricks he knows. Did you honestly think he could hide it so well in half a second that I wouldn't find it for a hundred years? It took me nearly ten, mind. I found it six years ago. Just in time too. This school was about to shut down. Lack of funds. It always comes to funds in the end, doesn't it?"

Biddy tried, surreptitiously, to get to her feet, and fell back with a grunt of pain and frustration mingled. Pain crunched like shards of shattered glass in her right ankle, and her left knee throbbed. Besides, it would make no difference. She could feel the shadow of resistance pushing at her mind at the edge of the chalk. It couldn't be stepped over, not even by a mage.

She was trapped.

"But then—" Morgaine spoke up from across the room. Each word was a gasp, but the sound of her voice brought Biddy a wash of relief. She was very white, and blood darkened her hair at the temple. "You didn't need Rowan to tell you where it is."

"No. In fact, Rowan didn't know where it was himself until today. That's right, isn't it?" He was looking at Biddy now. "I talked with him sixteen years ago, and I couldn't find anything about the schism in his thoughts at all. I thought at the time he'd hidden the memory for safekeeping. When I saw you, I knew it. The only thing I don't understand is why he kept you all those years and never took it back."

"He didn't know," Biddy heard herself say. "He lost the key, and even when he found me, he never remembered he cast the spell."

"Did he?" The smile surprised from him was absolutely genuine, even fond. "Oh, Rowan. I should have guessed. Even when he was on the Council, he always did tend to succeed too well. If I'd known that, we might have worked together after all." He didn't wait for Biddy to answer that. "Never mind. He can't cause any more trouble now."

"What do you mean?" Biddy's anger turned cold. "Where is he?"

"Dead," the Servant said bluntly.

Her head spun; there was a roaring in her ears, as though something inside her was screaming. She clenched her jaw and blinked hot tears from her eyes. It wasn't true. It couldn't be. Surely, even through every barrier they could raise, Hutch would have known if Rowan was dead. And Hutch showed no sign of knowing. He was standing at Biddy's side, teeth bared, fur bristling with fury, and he had not given up.

Yet he looked so very faint and weak now. And Morgaine had said, only moments ago, that something terrible had happened to Rowan.

"It's your own fault," Vaughan was saying, as if from a great distance. "Once you awakened that memory, he knew where the schism was. When I came to see him this evening, I saw his fears for you had shifted, and guessed what must have happened. I couldn't let him live then. He might have broken and told Storm where it was. I told Storm to dispose of him, and came here to wait for you. That was about an hour ago. Knowing Storm, he took his time."

Morgaine said you were safe and we'd see each other again, Rowan had said, only hours ago, in a sixteen-year-old memory. *I'm glad she was right.* He'd known they were seeing each other for the last time.

"I don't believe you." She forced defiance into her voice, let it raise her head. "If you wanted to kill Rowan, you'd have done it at once. You said yourself, you didn't need him."

"I didn't need him to tell me where the schism was," Vaughan corrected. "I was looking for something different. I asked you about it before, you might remember. In the Council chambers."

And she did. That was the worst thing. The memory was like a lightning strike, and in its afterglow everything, suddenly, was horribly clear. "You asked me to tell you where Rowan was hiding."

"Hy-Brasil." The words sounded strange in the Servant's voice, or perhaps it was the Servant's voice itself which was strange. For the first time, reverence had stolen into it.

All those hours the two of you were off with your heads together talking about ravenstones and magic islands and fair folk, Storm had jeered, the day he became a monster, *did you really think he was interested?*

I spent hours talking about different projects to him, ones nobody else believed in, Rowan had told her, *and he listened.*

Rowan had seen Hy-Brasil for the first time when he was a child. He had thought that nobody believed him, and perhaps for a long time nobody had. English gentlemen mages, after all, weren't interested in myth and superstition. But he had told Vaughan about it— he had told Vaughan everything. And Vaughan had believed in the ravenstone enough to pour scarce magic into creating it. It stood to reason that he might have believed other stories too.

Rowan had worried that Vaughan might find Hy-Brasil through hunting him. It had been the other way around. Vaughan had been hunting Rowan to find Hy-Brasil.

"Rowan thought nobody on the Council believed in Hy-Brasil," she said carefully.

"They didn't," Vaughan agreed. "Even I didn't, for a long time. I was interested in a good many things that the old Council dismissed, but magic islands were too far even for me. I believed Rowan had seen *something* when he was young, some phantom from the past; I didn't think it was anything that could be colonized and used."

He stepped closer, and, horribly, crouched level in front of her. He must have been on the edge of the circle, but from her perspective he was only an arm's length away, with nothing between them, not even the table that had been there in the Council room. She flinched back, only to hit the invisible barrier. In the light of the fading schism, she could see every line on his forehead, every pockmark on his skin, his fine blond eyelashes framing his pale eyes.

"And then we caught him sixteen years ago." The words were soft, almost kind. "I looked into his soul, trying to find a sign that he had found a schism. I couldn't find one, despite the spell he'd just cast and the new magic lingering in his blood. For a long time I could see nothing useful at all. Rowan knew how to mask his darkest fears from me very well; torture, oddly enough, helps with that. It's very easy for someone in terrible pain to focus only on the desire for it to stop, and block out anything more incriminating. But then, after days of being broken and put back together, he started to lose focus. Things started to slip through. And that was when I glimpsed Hy-Brasil—his longing to be back there, his dread that I would learn of it through him. I realized then why he had been so impossible to capture, why sometimes he seemed to drop out of mortal sight entirely. He had found it."

Morgaine laughed, a short breath of disbelief. Biddy couldn't tell if it was genuine, or if she was trying to help. "You're insane. Hy-Brasil doesn't exist. It's not even a myth—it's a cartographical error, a blot on a map. Rowan was always looking for it, and he never found a trace."

Vaughan ignored her. His eyes were fixed on Biddy, and mingled in their blue was something far stranger even than reverence. It was envy. "It must have been a wonderful place to grow up, even for someone like you. I came from a factory town. No stories there— no miracles, just a lot of toil and dust. But Hy-Brasil...So many secrets, so much ancient magic wild in the forests. It must have been like living in a myth. Wasn't it?"

Biddy met his glass eye, and tried with all her soul to give nothing away, to think of nothing but how much she hated him. In that moment, it wasn't difficult. "What makes you think I know anything about it?"

"Because I saw it in you too, the first day we met." Her face must have shown something, or her heart, because his lips twisted. "I know you tried to hide it—and for what it's worth, you hid your *desires* very well. I didn't see Rowan or Hy-Brasil at all in them. But your resentments you never hid from me. Perhaps you had hidden them too well from yourself. And both were blazing there bright as day. How much you hated that island at times, how stifling you found it. How much you hated Rowan too, for keeping you there."

"I don't hate Rowan," she said. "I never hated him."

"Don't feel badly about it. If you knew half of what I've seen in people's hearts..."

He said nothing more, but it made her wonder for the first time what it might be like to know the very worst of human desires and resentments before knowing the people to whom they belonged. She thought of the jealousy and anger she had seen in Rowan for the first time in Storm's memory, and how long it had taken her to accept that those impulses could live in the heart of the person who had loved and protected her since she was a child, who was also brave and clever and kind. She wondered if seeing those things, over time, might change a person, might turn curiosity into disgust and knowledge into cynicism, might cause him to give up on everything but his own self-interest. She didn't let herself wonder for long—the last thing she wanted was to understand Vaughan Carlisle—but she put it away for later.

He was so close. It was frightening, her skin was prickling as if in proximity to a nest of scorpions, but she forced herself to wonder if she could use it. If she could convince him to reach in, perhaps, and she could grab his hand and pull herself out.

The wisps would throw her back in again. Her ankle had settled to a quiet throb—enough to stand, probably, but not to run. She had nowhere to go. But still...

"Rowan thought you had started trying to capture him in earnest a few months ago," she said. If she could only keep him talking, there might be a chance. "Was that about Hy-Brasil?"

"I was always trying to capture him," Vaughan said. "And it was always about Hy-Brasil of late. But certainly I grew more desperate in the last few months. Far less discreet. I'm not surprised he noticed. I came close to the island once or twice, didn't I?"

"Why? What's been different about the last few months?"

Vaughan laughed. "Didn't you teach mathematics at my school?"

She might have got it then, but he went on before she could.

"Hy-Brasil can be found and reached every seven years," he said. "I know Rowan saw it the winter before he was apprenticed. That would have been 1821. I know it was seen again the year magic faded, in 1842. Which means, according to calculations, the next time it will be present will be this year. This is the first chance I've had to see it for myself."

For the moment, she forgot about trying to escape the circle. She even forgot her fears for Rowan and Hutch and Morgaine. She stared at him in mingled horror and scorn.

"Not just anyone can see it. It won't show itself to *you.*"

"It won't have to," he said, "if you take me to it."

It was her turn to laugh—a Rowan laugh, defiant and reckless and brimming with danger. "I'll die first."

"That's what Rowan said—well, that's what he did." Vaughan rose to his feet and stepped back to look at her appraisingly. She knew then that he would never pull her out of the circle by mistake, and her own lack of disappointment told her that she had known that already. "But he was trying to keep *you* safe. He thought you and his familiar were there, and if he told me where it was he would be betraying you. You have nothing left to betray. Rowan is already dead."

"That was your mistake," Biddy said. "If you hadn't killed him, we might have bargained for his life."

She shouldn't have meant that. She'd abandoned that idea long ago. She'd promised the Púca. But in that moment, she would have given the whole world and every atom of magic that had ever been in it to have Rowan safe.

"I couldn't have offered that, I'm afraid," Vaughan said. "But I'm willing to bargain for your own. I can tear you to pieces here and now, and nobody who found you in the morning would know who you had ever been. But if you take me to Hy-Brasil, I'll let you go free, and what's more I'll give you money and passage anywhere you like. The Council will never hunt you again. You can live an ordinary life—or an extraordinary one, if you prefer. You never need to think about magic again."

"I love magic," Biddy said. It was what she had been unable to explain to Rowan, when he had asked her to leave Hy-Brasil—what it had felt presumptuous to claim, when her claim on it seemed so weak compared to his own. She hadn't even been able to explain it to herself. But she knew now that she loved it for its wonder and its joy, its kindness and its beauty. She loved it because it brought the chance of mischief, the chance of miracles, the chance of something better. She loved it because it was good.

"Of course you do. But you hate it too. It never let you in, no matter what you did. What does it matter to you who controls the last few scraps left in the world?"

Hutchincroft growled at her side, but weakly. Biddy, risking a look at him, saw with alarm that he was truly fading, in a way that she hadn't realized his solid little body could fade. The tips of his ears were transparent, and his features indistinct, as though she was seeing him from a great distance away. Something really had happened to Rowan. Something terrible.

"I'll do my best to save him too, if you like," the Servant added. He must have seen the fear surface in her mind. "Familiars don't usually survive the deaths of their mages long, but there are always exceptions."

No. The answer was on her tongue. And yet she wavered, uncertain. Because if Hutchincroft could live after all—how could she say no, when it meant she would lose him? Would it be so dreadful when so much was already lost, to lose Hy-Brasil too?

Morgaine's voice came, unexpected. "You made me kill my familiar."

Biddy had almost forgotten Morgaine was there. She almost wasn't. She was curled on the floor, head resting on her arm, hair matted with blood. But her eyes blazed. Biddy remembered as if from a very long time ago sitting across from Morgaine in her townhouse, the first time they had properly met—how luminous she had seemed, and yet how carefully that light seemed curated to conceal something beneath it. This was what it had been concealing for seventy years. All the time, she had been furious.

"I didn't exactly *make* you," Vaughan said, in the tone of someone being very fair. "You chose to, in the end."

"Yes." Her breath caught painfully. "Yes, I chose. She was my soul, and you made me choose. You did exactly what you're doing to Bridget—pretended there was no choice at all. And I chose wrong."

"You chose sensibly." For the first time, he looked at her, not as the Servant of Magic, but as another mage. "I harvested my familiar too, Morgaine. I loved him, but we needed him. We needed every scrap of magic we could get. If you hadn't killed yours, we would have had to kill you and her together. Surely it's better to live than to die, all else being equal."

"All else *wasn't* equal," Morgaine said. "You're a monster. I should have resisted you with everything I had."

Some shadow flickered across Vaughan's face—anger, perhaps, or disquiet, or even hurt. It was smoothed away by the time he turned back to Biddy, as if it had never been.

"Well. Is that what *you* mean to do, then? You could. You could die right here, alongside Rowan O'Connell's familiar. But you're so young, and it would be pointless. Rowan wouldn't want it, you know. I was there with him, an hour ago. He was dying, and he wanted you to be safe more than anything in the world."

"I know." Tears burned her eyes, because she really did believe him this time. It was exactly how Rowan would die. "But it isn't just what he wants."

Real frustration cracked his voice. "Dear God, what do you think I mean to do with that island? I'm not a monster, you know, whatever Morgaine might say. I'm a mage, just as Rowan was—just as she is. I only want to study it—to learn its secrets."

"I know exactly what you want to do with it." She was on sure ground again now. "You'll do exactly what you've done with every scrap of magic all these years. Take what you can from it for your own ends, become more and more powerful, until at last you've drained it of everything it has to offer you and you'll look for something new. And you'll call it *using magic*." She shook her head. "No. No, I won't tell you."

"Why?"

"Because Morgaine wasn't wrong, and nor was Rowan. You *are* a monster. I knew it the first moment I saw you. Do you even remember when that was?" She didn't wait for him to answer. This was almost certainly going to kill her, and yet while it lasted every word was exhilarating. "It was downstairs, in the dining room. You walked past with Miss Finchley—you said in the Council chamber that you were looking the place over before you sent your wisps for me, but that was a lie, wasn't it? You had come for more magic, or perhaps to check the schism was secure. You never looked at us. Anna said you were a member of the board come to see that not too much money was being spent. And I hated you."

"I told you I took over this place to protect the schism. If the building had fallen into the wrong hands, it would have been lost."

"And when you did, you became responsible for the children here. You could have made life better for them. You could have given them better food, better teachers, a better life. You kept them miserable. I don't know whether you did it on purpose, in case their misery really was what was causing magic to break through, or whether you just didn't care. But I knew everything I needed to know about you then."

He considered her accusation seriously. "I don't see how I'm worse than any other person might have been in my position. I didn't make magic go out of the world, you know. I only did what I thought was best."

"You did what was best for *you*. You did it again when you found this schism. The first trickle of magic in seventy years, and you never shared it."

"I would, if it had been larger." Perhaps he honestly believed it. "But there's barely enough for one person here. What would have been the point in spreading it so thinly it could barely be felt? Isn't it better that it come to me, where I can make sensible use of it? It can't help everyone. All the magic in the world couldn't do that."

"So you decided to just let it help you."

"Yes." Whatever strange impulse had prompted him to ask for her understanding had passed. His face had hardened once again; his lips twitched in a smile. "Perhaps that does make me a monster. Most people are, you know."

Biddy said nothing. She hadn't been in the world long enough to argue that he was wrong—probably he was right. It made no difference. All that mattered was that she would die here, in this terrible room where her story had begun, and he would never find Hy-Brasil. She had nothing more to say.

Another voice spoke instead.

"What?"

It was the low, threatening rumble from her nightmares in the dungeon, but this time it was quiet with disbelief. He stood there in the doorway, amid the shadow feathers and skeleton beaks, like a great broken-winged bird of prey. Storm.

"Oh, you're here, are you?" Vaughan said dismissively. He was still looking at Biddy. Because of that, only she could see the wariness that had crept into his face. "Is Rowan dead?"

"He's dead."

Biddy's heart clenched; a sharp cry was wrenched from her, painful as a drawn tooth. It couldn't be true. It couldn't.

And yet Storm wasn't lying. She'd seen that in the dungeon, and she saw it now. Storm didn't have enough humanity left in him to lie. He had all the cruel honesty of a predator.

Storm barely seemed to hear his own words. He took a limping step forward into the light, his wings a twisted burden on his back.

"He told me to come here," he said. "He told me you knew where the schism was, and had known all along. He told me it was the only thing that made sense, that he'd been a fool not to see it and I'd been a worse one. He *laughed* at me. I snapped his neck. But he was telling the truth, wasn't he?"

All her life, Biddy had been gleaning Rowan's words for what he didn't mean to give away. Now, as her chest flooded with the worst pain of her life, her mind grasped one thing. Storm was here because Rowan had sent him. In his very last moments, somehow, he had guessed what the Servant knew and where he was going. He knew that Biddy would be there too. And he had sent Storm, because it was all he could do. Because Vaughan had been right. All he had wanted, at the end, was for her to be safe.

Somehow, he meant Storm to save her.

Vaughan showed no signs of having heard. "You know," he said thoughtfully. "Since you're here, Storm, I might just have you kill this one too, after all. More trouble than she's worth. I'll find what I'm looking for another way."

"Answer my question!" Storm's voice had risen. "You had the schism. For how long?"

Vaughan waved a hand. "A while."

"He's had it for six years," Biddy spoke up. In a surge of pain she barely felt, she got to her feet, careful to rest her weight only on her good ankle. A tiny hope was building in her chest. Vaughan would never see it—it was too small. Everything she wanted to do had crumbled; in its dust, she barely knew if she wanted hope at all. But perhaps, at least, she and Hutch could live.

The ravenstone was around her neck, under her clothes where Vaughan couldn't have seen it. She didn't know if the raven would be confined by the circle, as a human would be. But the Council had gone to a great deal of trouble to trap Rowan in a dream. Surely they wouldn't have done so unless a trap circle wouldn't work.

If she was right, if the raven's wings could carry her over the chalk, then she could take Hutchincroft and go. She needed just a moment of distraction. And Storm was here to provide it.

Rowan had wanted her to live.

"He was never going to give you the magic you needed," she said, and tried not to think of Rowan lying dead deep in the earth, tried not to choke on the words she was speaking to his murderer. "Just as he was never going to give you a place on the Council. He liked you better exactly where you are."

"Is this true?" Storm demanded.

"Oh, stop whining," Vaughan said, with a sigh. "I gave you what magic you needed."

"No," Storm said flatly. "You gave me what magic *you* needed. You gave me enough so I could do your bidding. But you told me that when there was magic to spare, you would fix me. You *promised* me. I did everything you asked, because I was waiting for there to be magic to spare."

"Shut up, Storm." Vaughan still wasn't looking at him. But Biddy was. She saw the fury blazing in his eyes, human in the blue and raven in the black.

"You had it. You had it all along. And you let me live like *this*."

The wings lying folded and heavy on his back snapped out with a crack like wet fabric. Biddy hadn't realized until that moment how enormous they were. They spanned the width of the room, black and monstrous, their quivering tips brushing each wall. Their feathers were thick in patches, but in some places the flesh was bare, in others torn open entirely so that the light of the schism shone through them. They took her breath away.

They could never fly, not really. But one great sweep was enough to bring Storm across the room, directly toward the Servant.

It wasn't clear what he meant to do. Perhaps he meant nothing at all—both eyes, human and raven, were on fire, and that flame might have crowded out all thoughts but a wild bird's desire to tear and kill. Either way, the Servant of Magic didn't hesitate. The bone wisps screamed toward Storm. At the same time, the Servant flung up a hand, and green light scorched the air. It was the light Rowan had flung at Storm in Morgaine's living room; the flash of green Biddy had seen at the bottom of the chimney. It hadn't held Storm for long then. But Rowan's had been fueled with thin scrapings of magic from trees and trinkets. The Servant had gorged at the crack between one world and another. His spell was blinding, like the burst of a second sun. Biddy threw her arm across her eyes on instinct; Storm stopped in mid-flight, suspended above the floorboards.

And yet he didn't draw back. As Biddy lowered her arm, squinting against the light, Storm somehow, impossibly, inched forward. The edges of his wings caught alight, curling up like paper held too close to the fire. The skeletons dived at him, sharp beaks pecking, bone claws scratching. Storm cried out just once, a bird's harsh cry, and then his face set.

The Servant's teeth bared in a snarl, his hand raised. Their attentions were utterly focused on each other.

This was it. She had the ravenstone around her neck; Hutch, weak and fragile, was on the ground beside her. She could catch him up in her arms, melt into the raven, be out through the door in seconds while they struggled. If she flew far and fast enough, she could make it to Hy-Brasil, with its rabbits and its trees and its waves and its castle. Perhaps Hutch *could* survive Rowan's death. Perhaps she could too. They could leave the world to its terrors, and hide away forever.

And yet she couldn't leave.

Behind her, the schism gaped, unguarded now as the wisps swarmed their master and Storm, incandescent and fragile and rapidly sealing once again. It was right there, in touching distance. They were so *close*. They had flooded it with everything Vaughan had stolen. Surely it would need very little to burst apart and bring magic pouring back into the world. But it wasn't any use. None of the artifacts she had taught herself to use were any help; their magic wasn't good enough, and nor was hers. She was nothing. She had nothing.

No. It came to her like the surge of the waves on the cliffs, swift and devastating.

She had something. She had the magic in her heart.

Living magic, Morgaine had said. Magic held within a living soul. She was no mage, nobody special, her parents could have been anyone at all. But a memory had been stored in her by a spell, long ago. The magic was still there—she could feel it underlying every beat of her heart. She had no way of releasing it on her own. But the schism was directly behind her. And though it was closing, it was wide enough for a raven to slip through.

That was how mages found their familiars. When they were the same age as Biddy was now, they stepped through the cracks in the world, and entered pure magic. It was where Rowan and

Hutchincroft had met, so long ago, when the world was very different. She knew it was possible for her to enter it too.

There was only one problem. She would never come out again. Hutchincroft had told her often: There was no time in magic, and no place. Young mages could barely find their way through it. Someone like Biddy had no chance at all. There was nothing to anchor them—nothing to anchor her. She would be lost, and then she would fade away.

That was what it took. The thought caught in her throat, bitter as unshed tears. If magic was to come back into the world, then it needed all of her.

She didn't want to. It sounded childish—it *was* childish, but she didn't want to. The Servant had been right, although she'd tried not to listen: She wanted to live. She was sixteen years old. She had only just met the world, and it was full of cruelties and wonders and complications that would take her more than a lifetime to understand. She wasn't ready to leave it. Rowan would never ask her to. He had said so himself: It wasn't her battle. She wasn't a mage. She had lived without magic all her life; no matter how much came back, it would never be for her. He had wanted her to be safe more than anything in the world.

And yet he would do it himself, in a heartbeat. Whatever else he had done, whatever mistakes he had made and secrets he had kept, when the world had lost its magic, he had given up everything rather than live as broken and compromised and self-hating as Morgaine and Storm had done—as Biddy herself would do, she knew deep in her soul, if she ran away now. And when the storm had come to take them all, he had given himself up for her and Hutch. He had known the agonies he was going back to, and he had been more scared than she had ever seen him, but he had done it, and he had done it with a smile, because he loved them and because it was the right thing to do. And now, despite everything she tried to tell herself, he was dead. She wondered if he had called for Hutchincroft in his heart before he died. She wondered if he had called for her.

All the magic in the world wouldn't help everybody. She knew that. And yet it would help some. Perhaps the mages didn't need magic back; perhaps some of them didn't even deserve it. But the girls asleep in this building did, the girls whose life she should have lived. The people in the slums outside the walls did, and those like :⎻.... ... ᴜver the world. Magic had never helped everyone, but there had been miracles once, when it had been in every stone and every star and every grain of sand. She had believed all her life that it was worth having in the world; she had believed it only moments ago, when she had told Vaughan he was a monster for hoarding it for himself. If she didn't believe it now, it was only because she was frightened, and she didn't want to die.

I will do everything in my power to open the schisms and restore magic to the world, she had promised the Púca. This was what everything meant. Not what was safe, what was easy, what she could afford to give. *Everything* meant her whole heart, with no promises in return. It meant too much, and it didn't care.

The room where she had met Rowan was afire with green light now. Storm could barely be seen in its blaze—he couldn't survive much longer. Morgaine lay on the floor, pale and still. Hutchincroft stood in front of them both, desperate and brave, almost transparent. Biddy looked at them all, and her throat and her chest tightened.

Rowan could do nothing now. Neither could Hutch, or Morgaine. There was only Biddy, and the opening behind her, and a single moment when the Servant's attention was entirely turned on Storm. No time, even, to say goodbye.

Her eyes were burning with tears; she blinked them away, so she could see. Her heart was pounding; she drew a deep breath, to calm it, so she could fly.

The ravenstone about her neck, as always, needed only the faintest push. Already she was transforming, feathers prickling, bones hollowing, arms stretching into wings. She tried not to think it was the last time she would ever feel her own body as it melted from her.

And she was right. She felt it before she even moved forward. The trap circle could no more hold her now than a line of ordinary chalk on the ground.

The schism glowed, softly, as though it were waiting for her.

She turned to face it, and with a flap of the raven's wings, she went to meet it.

Chapter Twenty

When Biddy entered the schism, the entire world convulsed. Most of London felt only a quiver beneath their feet, then a shudder as the ground split apart in a long, jagged line from Whitechapel to Westminster. Those in their beds woke with a start; those outside jumped aside with cries of fear as the earth parted. They didn't know that thousands of years ago a similar crack had split the earth on Hy-Brasil as magic had reached from a glittering schism to the yew tree where the last traces of its magic had been stored. They didn't know that this one led from a schism in Whitechapel to the stone in the vault of the Undercastle. They only felt shock and terror and a faint inexplicable wonder as the Thames surged and the cobbles fell.

Those with magic in their blood felt far more.

The schisms spidered across the earth, fault lines between one plane of existence and something beyond. They had been closed for seventy years, silent and waiting, so smooth they left almost no trace. Now, with a surge, they splintered apart, and magic teemed back into the world.

The way water leaks through a cracked bowl, Rowan had once said, but if so, the water was the ocean, endless and deep, and the surface of the bowl was the curve of the universe. The cracks opened in London, in Liverpool, in Wales and Scotland and Ireland; they opened in Europe, in the Pacific, in Asia and Africa and the Americas. On Hy-Brasil, the Púca waited by the ruins where the great fort had stood, and saw the sky gape wide.

Morgaine, drifting in and out of consciousness on a dirty floor of a Whitechapel orphanage, felt the shock of it; her eyes flew open with a gasp. The air was filled with magic. It poured from the schism on the wall, green and gold and glittering, catching the light from the windows like a hundred thousand specks of dust.

Vaughan Carlisle saw it too. The motes reflected in his glass eye as it widened, caught between disbelief and the first trace of awe he had felt in a hundred years. He froze—only for a moment, but it was enough. Storm, his mind consumed with the frantic fury of a wild bird, didn't hesitate. The blaze of light surrounding the Servant of Magic dropped, and Storm hurled himself forward.

Morgaine heard the cries as the two of them met, but she didn't turn her head. She watched as magic came back into the world.

———————————

Biddy saw none of this. From the moment she had passed through the schism, she had known nothing at all.

It wasn't like the dungeons of the Undercastle, after all. There was none of the terrible darkness she had feared. It was like melting into the trees on Primrose Hill as she had crossed the threshold into the secret library, only this time there was nowhere to cross to. She had simply dissolved. She had no body, no mind, there was nothing around her. It was like being underwater without the water, or soaring through sky without the sky. She wasn't sure how she was able to think at all, except that some stubborn kernel of herself was determined to hold on a little longer.

This is it, she thought, and marveled that she was not afraid. Perhaps she had already started to fade, and fear was one of the first things to go. Perhaps it was just that the magic so clearly meant her no harm. It was too big for her, that was all. She hovered in its midst, and waited for the end. She wondered if she had done what she had set out to do. She wondered if anyone was left to miss her.

And then, after what might have been a century or no time at all, details began to bleed into being around her. Flickers first, like sunlight glimpsed through leaves, the light the Japanese called *komorebi*. Yellow grass, then deep blue sky. They came slowly, but certainly, and she waited for them, wondering, without trying to catch them.

Finally, although there were no places in magic, Biddy found that she was standing somewhere, and although she had no body there, she was standing as herself and not the raven.

It was a field, vast and golden and sunlit. The only strange thing about this was that the sky above was deep black and studded with stars. The flat grass danced with flickering blue tongues of flame.

A boy, about the same age as Biddy, sat cross-legged in the grass. He wore a white shirt with ruffled sleeves and tan breeches under boots, the kind that Biddy saw in drawings in old books, and his chestnut hair was cut short. He rested his chin on his folded hands, patient, his eyes almost the same blue as the flames. Biddy's heart caught. She knew that face. It wasn't right yet, and it had never been so patient in all her years of memory, but it was the face she knew best in the world.

None of the blue flames paid him any attention, except one. That one, smaller and brighter than the others, hovered in front of him just out of arm's reach.

"You're supposed to chase me," the flame said at last, and it was Hutch's clear, precise lilt. It sounded younger than she had ever heard it, and even more worried. "You're a mage, and I'm a spirit. You're supposed to try to catch me."

The boy who wasn't quite Rowan, not yet, shrugged carelessly. "I'm supposed to," he agreed. "I thought I'd wait and see if you wanted to be caught."

"If you stay too long, you'll fade," the spirit said. It flickered, blue, uncertain. "It's very dangerous."

"Well, that's one way of looking at it."

"What's another way of looking at it?"

He stretched and sat forward. Rowan never could sit still for very long. "The way I see it, either you choose to come back with me and be my familiar, which I really hope you will, because you're the most wonderful thing I've ever seen. Or I'll stay and be lost forever in pure magic. That doesn't sound too bad. Either way, it's an adventure."

The spirit hovered, considering. "I think the way I said it first was right," it said at last. "Probably."

Rowan burst into delighted laughter. "Oh, I *really* hope you choose to come back with me." He sounded breathless, either from the laughter or because he was starting to flicker around the edges himself. But his smile was real, and full of mischief. Biddy found herself smiling as well. "We're going to have so much fun together."

Biddy.

The voice drifted toward her on the wind. It was Hutchincroft—her Hutchincroft. She knew his voice, older now; more importantly, she knew the note of mixed fear and relief and outrage from when she was a little girl and would wander off into the forest, the note that meant he had found her and loved her very much.

Biddy. There *you are. I thought I'd lost you* forever. *Stay still, I'm coming to you.*

"Where am I?" she whispered.

The only place I knew to look. I hoped you'd come here too.

"I thought you said there were no places in magic?"

There aren't. There's no time either. But there are moments. Every so often, something will happen.

"Is that Rowan?"

It was. And that's me. The note in his voice now was soft and proud. *We happened.*

Biddy thought of the moment she had flown through the schism. It seemed like a hundred years ago now, or perhaps no time at all. She had been thinking of Rowan and Hutchincroft, and loving them. Perhaps, without meaning to, she had called out for them in her heart, and her heart had found its way to them here.

She watched as the spirit that was Hutchincroft moved forward into Rowan's cupped hands. She watched him shiver, just once, and then in the blink of an eye he disappeared and the swirl of magic closed over him as if he had never been there at all.

"You went with him."

I had to. And suddenly Hutchincroft was in front of her, not a flickering flame but a golden rabbit with eyes the color of the sky. *The idiot was clearly going to just sit there until he faded unless I took him back. Besides, he was the most wonderful thing I had ever seen too. I had to.*

"Am *I* going to fade?" In that moment, she didn't mind. She felt strange and far away, but magic was all around her, and Rowan and Hutchincroft were part of that magic, and she could see how being lost could indeed be a great and wonderful adventure.

No. You won't. Because I am here to take you back too. Hold on to me.

Her limbs were clumsy and unfamiliar, but the feeling came back as she bent down and took Hutch's soft, warm fur in her fingers. "Is magic back in the world?"

It's back, he said. And she felt a joyful shiver ripple the air.

"What about Rowan? Did Storm kill him?"

Yes. But he needn't die. There was no doubt in his voice now, only resolution. *Not if we hurry. Hold tight, Biddy. We're going home.*

Chapter Twenty-One

The nursery was there, quiet and broken, glittering and over-bright, as she stepped back into the world. Its edges were sharp, glowing at first; she had to blink hard against them, the way she would in the first light of day. Her body solidified around her—the aches and weariness and the stabbing pain at her ankle returned, but muted, as though after a long soak in Morgaine's claw-footed tub.

As her eyes adjusted, the edges of the room softened. She saw the cradles back in their orderly rows as the infants within them slept. She saw that it wasn't light at all, except for a hovering globe in the center of the room. When Biddy turned back to the wall she had just passed through, there was no sign of the schism.

It's there, Hutchincroft said, without her needing to ask. He stood at her side, ears straight up. *I can see it. It's only visible to mages now it's open, that's all. And the air is filled with magic.* He sneezed sharply. *Too thick, if anything. Anything could happen around here.*

Biddy was about to reply when another thought struck her. "I can still hear you!"

Hutch flicked his ears with pleasure. *We've passed through magic together, you and I. We aren't mage and familiar, but we're bound now. We can hear each other.*

She couldn't keep back her smile. "That's what I always used to want, more than anything."

Me too, he said. *I'll only have to turn human for chocolate chip biscuits now. And bacon.*

"Bridget!"

Biddy turned at the sound of her name, just in time to see Morgaine scramble up from the ground, seconds before she was caught in a hug. She returned it, tightly at first and then more cautiously as the memory of Morgaine lying broken on the ground returned to her. And yet though Morgaine's hold was fragile and there was dark blood on her face, she was standing and smiling.

"I thought you were lost forever!"

"So did I." Biddy hugged her once more before she let her go. "You're better?"

"Only the broken bones," Morgaine said. "Storm..." She trailed off, a little uncomfortably.

Storm had an amulet to heal broken bones. He used it to torture and heal and then torture over and over again.

Storm.

He was lying on the ground by the door—where, Biddy realized belatedly, Morgaine had been kneeling. In the dim light he would have seemed only a great formless shadow, had she not been able to see the laborious rise and fall of his chest, and hear the faint, ragged gasps as he struggled to breathe.

"Vaughan's dead," Morgaine said, following Biddy's gaze. It was only then that Biddy saw a second mound underneath a blanket in the corner, and she resolved to look no further. She didn't need to see what those tearing claws had done to the man who had been the Servant of Magic. "I didn't even see the end. They were fighting when the world split open. When the light died and the dust cleared, Vaughan was dead and Storm was alive. But he's terribly hurt. I don't think he has a lot of time left."

"Good," she said bitterly.

Morgaine sighed. "He asked to see you, to apologize. Will you go to him?"

"There wouldn't be any point. I don't forgive him."

"I would never ask you to. I won't ask you to go to him at all, if you don't want to. It would just mean a good deal to him if you did."

"He killed Rowan. He tortured him to death. He doesn't deserve anything from me."

"He doesn't," Morgaine agreed. "I know. But if you gave it to him anyway, before he dies, it would mean a good deal to him. That's all."

Hutchincroft gave an indignant growl at her side, but Biddy, after a second's hesitation, nodded.

"Thank you," Morgaine said.

At first, when Biddy kneeled down next to the great winged body, she thought Storm was dead already. His face was broken and burned, sleek dark feathers and ghost-pale skin alike blackened and reddened by the Servant's flame. The space between breaths had slowed to the point it seemed no more would come. And yet when Morgaine spoke his name, his eyelashes flickered. She saw the gleam of blue and black beneath them, and then the pupils contract as they focused on her face. She remembered, unexpectedly, how beautiful he had been in the brief sliver of memory before everything had gone wrong.

One of the chosen ones, Morgaine had called him. It came to her unwillingly that she had once believed herself chosen for a great destiny too.

"They told me you had gone." His voice was hoarse and cracked, but both eyes were clear. "They said you went through the crack in the world."

"I did," she said. "I'm back."

He didn't question this. He was beyond questions now. It was too late for answers to matter to him.

"I'm sorry." His body twitched, his breath caught at a spasm of pain. "I'm sorry about Rowan, and about you. I was wrong. I've been wrong for a long time."

Biddy couldn't find it in herself to say it was all right. It wasn't, not if Rowan was dead, not when so many others had been killed over the years. But Storm's gaze held hers, filled with regret, and she felt herself nod stiffly. It seemed to be enough for him. He sighed, and looked once more at Morgaine. She knelt down beside him.

"I know," she said softly, though he hadn't spoken. He was beyond speech, passing beyond hearing. "I'm sorry too. Sleep now. It's over."

He smiled, just once, and then his eyes closed and he was still.

Biddy stood and looked at the twisted body, pity and relief warring in her heart. She thought of Storm as she had seen him in his own memories, young and angry and bitter. She saw him growing up, watching Rowan and Morgaine grow away from him and closer together, moving into a world he felt should have been his. She imagined the life he had led for the last seventy years, trapped below the earth as Vaughan mocked and manipulated him in turn, his body in pain and his brain on fire. And she did feel sorry for him, truly, almost against her will. But the memory of Hutchincroft's screams, the look in Rowan's eyes as the rain beat the windows in Morgaine's apartment, the fury of the magic that had tried to tear the memory from her heart—all of these things were difficult to forgive. Understanding a person wasn't always the same as forgiving them.

"Biddy," Hutchincroft's voice came, low and urgent. "We have to go right now. Do you still have the ravenstone?"

Biddy had almost forgotten it. She felt for the chain around her neck, and to her relief her fingers curled around the smooth black stone.

"Yes. Morgaine, I need to go to Rowan. Hutch thinks there might be a chance…"

"Go," Morgaine said at once. She sat up, firm and composed despite the blood and dust. "I'll handle things here. Every mage for a thousand miles will have felt that shock. I'll put a summoning rune on the door and call them."

Biddy scooped Hutch into her arms. "We'll come back when we can."

"Do." Morgaine hesitated. "Give Rowan my love, won't you? Even if—well, whatever happens."

"I will," Biddy promised. She knew that Morgaine didn't think that Rowan was alive, or wouldn't let herself think it. Perhaps she shouldn't either. But she had been through too much to be afraid of hope.

The ravenstone at her chest was more powerful than ever. She barely touched it with her mind before she felt her limbs elongating and feathers sprouting. With a single beat of her wings, and Hutchincroft nestled in her heart, she took off into the night.

The underground castle was smashed wide open. And not only the castle. From the air, Biddy could see the gaping scar across London, spidering from the orphanage in Whitechapel to the stone at the heart of Westminster. Thankfully the schism had opened at night, when the streets were relatively empty. Even so, crowds swarmed about it like ants. In one place a car balanced precariously on the edge where it had run aground, in another she could see police waving back the people pushing to approach. It ended right at the center of the Houses of Parliament, alongside Big Ben and the towering spires of Westminster Abbey.

Down there, Hutchincroft whispered in her heart. *Into the crevasse. Ignore the crowds. They won't care about a raven. And there's no magician in there who would dare to stop one.*

The raven didn't want to go beneath the earth. Its heart beat wildly, and its wings flinched back from the crack. But Biddy had passed through pure magic now; she knew who she was. She felt the pressure of its fear like a scrabbling of claws at her mind, but she was in no danger of losing herself to it. She soothed it quietly, and pushed on into the dark.

The dungeons were the deepest of all, and almost buried in rubble. After the raven's claws hit rock, Biddy twisted back into her own body. Hutchincroft jumped to the ground, soft and sure.

He's this way, he said, and nudged her gently with his nose. *We're nearly there.*

"Are you sure he's still alive? Storm said—"

I think I know better than Storm whether or not my own mage is still alive, Hutchincroft said, with an irritated flick of his ears. Biddy didn't question any further. She needed all her concentration for following Hutch through the ruined corridors.

※ ══════════ ※

The door to the dungeon had split open, and when Biddy squeezed through the crack, she saw a body on the floor. That was how she thought of it, *a body*, not a person, even though she knew at once who it was and she longed with all her heart to think otherwise.

Rowan lay crumpled on the ground. In some ways, he looked little different from when she had seen him through the scrying glass in enchanted sleep, what seemed a lifetime ago. There were few visible marks on him—a long cut extending from his temple to his jaw, a dark bruise swelling beneath one closed eye. His skin was pale, his hair and clothes stiff with dried sweat and blood, but that was nothing. What was different, what truly frightened her, was his face. It was blank and remote, and utterly still. Even in his deepest sleep, Rowan had never been so still.

She knew then that Storm had told the truth, and Rowan was dead.

And yet Hutchincroft didn't flinch, not even when Biddy dropped to the ground beside the body; not even when she put her hand to Rowan's neck and found him cold to the touch and not the slightest flutter of a pulse beneath her fingers.

"Is he gone?" she asked.

No, said Hutchincroft, who usually worried so much, and this time had no fear at all. *No, he is not. Because I am his familiar, and the magic of another world is flowing through me. And I am not letting him go anywhere.*

"Rowan says that magic doesn't work like that," Biddy said, though her heart lifted cautiously. "He said you can ask wild magic to heal, but it doesn't always do what you want, and it can't fix everything. It might not save him."

It will. Hutchincroft nestled on Rowan's chest, very gently, and laid his head flat against his heart.

Around them, the air began to stir. Biddy still couldn't see magic, but she had worked it now; she had spoken to it in the depths of the forest on Hy-Brasil; she had passed through a fracture in the wall and felt it teeming through her skin. She knew it well enough to picture the green-and-gold shimmer flowing through Hutchincroft from another world.

Magic could heal, but not on command, not for the asking. It couldn't ever bring back the dead. And yet, beneath Hutchincroft, Rowan's chest rose and fell—just once, slow and shallow, then again. His eyelids flickered; one hand twitched. Biddy might have been imagining it, but she thought she heard a soft sound, somewhere between a whimper and a moan, and her heart leapt.

"Please," she whispered, as Morgaine had whispered at the crack in the world. Without thinking, on instinct, she rested her hand on Hutchincroft's back. "Please, save him."

Something was happening. The long cut down Rowan's face knit together and smoothed; his limbs straightened. Color crept back into his cheeks, very slowly, like the changing of a season. She hardly dared to breathe.

And then Rowan flinched bolt upright with the strangled gasp of someone awakening from a nightmare or coming up from deep water. His eyes flew open, and they were as clear as they had ever been.

Biddy's own eyes filled with tears. She flung herself at him before she could stop herself, heedless of the damage that had only just healed, heedless of his clothes stained with dirt and sweat and blood, heedless of anything except the feel of him solid and real and whole. "Rowan!"

"All right, steady on!" he protested, but weakly. He hugged her just as tight, and she could feel him trembling. "I'm here. I'm back."

"I thought you were dead."

"So did I." She suspected his grip around her was for himself as much as her. He was still fighting for breath, and his voice didn't sound quite his own. "I thought you were dead too. Storm said they had you both, and they didn't need me anymore. It's about the last thing I remember him saying to me."

"He's gone." Biddy heard her own voice becoming sure and strong, and knew, strange as it seemed, that she was the one doing the holding and the comforting for now. "So is Vaughan. He had found the schism already."

"I know." He drew a breath, released it, drew another. "I knew when Storm said he could kill me that he must have done. It was the only reason he wouldn't need me alive. But I couldn't do anything about it. All I could do was try to send Storm to intercept him, but I had no idea what he'd do."

"They're both dead. It's all right now. There's magic in the world again, and you're safe, and everything's all right."

I knew it would be, Hutchincroft said. Biddy pulled away from Rowan, just enough for Hutch to wriggle between them. Rowan caught him up in one arm, and Hutch burrowed into his neck as though they would never be parted again.

"You did not!" Biddy protested.

Well, no, Hutchincroft admitted. *I only knew that I was still alive. It's very difficult to kill a mage when their familiar is still alive. Even in death, our souls are tethered to each other. It takes time for that tether to break, and I knew you would be holding on as tightly as you could. But we didn't have much time. Your body was dead. You were almost gone, and no magic could have found you then. Your hand's cold.*

"It is a bit," Rowan agreed. He buried it in Hutchincroft's warm fur, fondling his ears. "Give it a chance. It was dead a moment ago."

"Are you really, truly all right?" Biddy asked. "You don't have to be, you know."

He found a shaky laugh. "Well, that's good to hear. I'm probably a good night's rest and a strong drink away from really, *truly* all right. But I'm fine," he said, more seriously. "A moment ago I thought I was dead and you were going to follow me. I'm wonderful."

He looked it. His face was white and exhausted, it was true, but the light was starting to come back to his eyes, and it was the same twinkle she saw when she came down first thing in the morning and found him waiting for her in the kitchen with the day bright outside and the worries of the night burned away.

"And what about you?" he added. "What on earth have you been up to since I left? Don't think I haven't noticed that you and Hutch are talking now, by the way."

"We'll tell you later," she said, with a warning glance at Hutchincroft. "I'm fine, I promise. But later."

It wasn't that she didn't want Rowan to know what she had done, exactly. But so much had happened since he had been taken, she wasn't ready yet to face explanations and praise and recriminations. She didn't want to be the one who had brought magic back into the world just yet. Rowan seemed to understand, perhaps even more than she did. In any case, he nodded and drew her close to him, tucking her against his shoulder so that the sharp point of his chin rested on the top of her head. He was much thinner than she remembered.

"All right," he said softly. "Later."

She rested her head against him and let herself believe, for the first time, that everything really was over, or at least, something new and different was beginning.

Hutchincroft seemed to understand as well—at least, he said nothing about what she had done. Too soon, though, he pulled back and shook his ears.

I'm sorry, he said. *But we need to be back at the school. Morgaine needs us. There's magic everywhere, and the Servant isn't here. I imagine she'll try to take control of the Council, but she'll manage it far better with your support.*

"There's always something, isn't there?" Rowan mock sighed. He released Hutchincroft and ruffled Biddy's hair, the way he used to when she was much smaller. "Come on, then."

Before he got up, though, he paused. He bent to Hutch's eye level, and the two of them touched foreheads. "Thank you, my friend," Rowan said quietly.

Always, Hutch said, just as soft.

Chapter Twenty-Two

They didn't walk back to the Rookwood Asylum, or even catch the Underground. When Biddy suggested it to Rowan, since there was only one ravenstone, he smiled.

"I don't think we need to do that. Morgaine's summoning the other mages, didn't you say, Hutch?"

I did, Hutch confirmed. *It's the usual rune. You just have to find a door somewhere in this castle that hasn't broken. And a piece of chalk.*

They found the door easily enough, after picking their way back along the corridor: an oak door, leading to a small dusty broom cupboard. The chalk was more difficult. In the end, Biddy found a chunk of rock in the rubble that looked vaguely like limestone, and Rowan used the sharp end of it to scratch a rune in the wood.

"Doesn't matter," he said. "Nobody's going to be wanting this door for a while. Come on."

"Is that a rune lock?" Biddy asked, puzzled.

"The opposite. It's a rune door. You wouldn't have seen one before—they've been far too powerful to use for decades." Morgaine had mentioned them, she recalled, before they had gone on the Underground. "See that symbol? Morgaine's drawn exactly the same one on a door in the orphanage."

Biddy looked at it. "So?"

"So." Rowan was clearly enjoying himself. "Open it."

Biddy gave him a skeptical look, then pushed the door to the broom cupboard open.

Except it was no longer a door to the broom cupboard. It was the door that led to the infants' room in the Rookwood Asylum for Destitute Girls. Before them sprawled the cribs, the still-sleeping children, the narrow corridors, and the bleak wall that presumably gaped with a crack in the world she couldn't see. Biddy stared.

"We *are* mages, Bid," Rowan said. "Didn't you think we could do magic?"

Nobody else had arrived yet, as far as Biddy could see. The nursery had been cleared of debris, and the bodies of Storm and the Servant were gone—Morgaine's work, presumably. She was setting up the schoolroom chairs in the center of the room as though preparing for a lesson, the blood washed from her face, her movements brisk and efficient.

Both briskness and efficiency lasted exactly as long as it took for her to glance up and see the three of them. A smile lit her face, a smile that made Biddy realize she had never truly seen one there before, and in one movement she had crossed the room and flung her arms around Rowan.

He laughed as he caught her, possibly as much in surprise as anything else. "What's that for? Did somebody die?"

"Oh, stop it!" Morgaine pulled back just enough to see him. Her eyes were bright with tears. "Storm said he'd killed you. He meant it."

"I know." He kissed the top of her forehead, solemn now, and brushed her hair out of her eyes. "Don't cry. It's all right. Everything's all right."

"I'm sorry," she said. "I thought I'd never have the chance to tell you that. I should have gone with you all those years ago, on the day Vaughan took power. I knew I should have. But I was so ashamed. Tilda gave her life to keep me alive, and I knew what you thought of me for letting her do it."

"I'm sorry too," he said. "Because you're right, I thought everything you were imagining, and it was wrong. What Tilda did for you was none of my business. She loved you, and she was happy to do it. I'm glad she did. I just wish I'd been there earlier, so she didn't have to."

It was her turn to laugh. "God, you're so vain, aren't you? You honestly think you could have made all the difference?"

"Yes!"

"Oh, shut up," she said, and then they were kissing as though they would never stop.

Biddy looked away, embarrassed and amused and uncertain at the same time. She supposed that since Rowan wasn't really her father, Morgaine wouldn't be a stepmother, which was a vague relief. But it did seem that she would be *something*, after all these years. All at once, she didn't want the world and all its changes. She was exhausted and trembling, and she just wanted the three of them to be back on Hy-Brasil with the wind blowing against the castle and the waves crashing.

Hutchincroft must have guessed something of her feelings. He wrinkled his nose at her, and she smiled a little. It may or may not have been at Hutch's silent prompting that Rowan pulled back and turned to her, slightly breathless, hair rumpled from where Morgaine's hand had run through it.

"Biddy, you don't have to be here for this," he said, and grinned when she raised an eyebrow. "*This* being 'all the mages coming here in a few minutes to talk over the return of magic to the world,' obviously. You've got the ravenstone. Go back to the library at Primrose Hill. Nobody will bother you there."

"Rowan!" Morgaine protested, somewhere between amused and horrified. "You can't just keep giving a young woman a ravenstone like you're throwing her the keys to a motorcar!"

"Why not? She's clearly got the hang of it, haven't you, Biddy?"

"I think so," she said cautiously. She had yet to try it without Hutchincroft, and she wasn't sure, after all, if she was ready to leave. "But what about the children in the rest of the building? And the teachers?"

"They'll sleep right through," Morgaine promised. "No harm

will come to them. And whatever happens with the schism in this building, we'll make sure they're taken care of."

Biddy didn't have time to reply. The door opened, and a man stepped through; seconds later, it opened again and another followed. They both looked bewildered and half-asleep, their clothes in disarray as though they had dressed hastily and without looking in a mirror. Biddy recognized them both from the Council room, although all the faces not belonging to Morgaine or Vaughan were vague in her memory.

"Morgaine," one of them said, startled. His eyebrows, already raised, hitched farther at the sight of Rowan. "Good God."

"Thornton," Rowan said, as easily as if he were not wearing clothes stained by a week of blood and sweat and death. "It's been a while, hasn't it? Unless you were in the dungeon. Some of that's a bit of a blur."

"I—no." Thornton gave an involuntary shiver. "No, I...I never go down there. I don't quite understand—did Carlisle call this meeting?"

"Vaughan Carlisle passed away this evening," Morgaine said crisply. "I've taken on his duties for the time being, until we've resolved the current situation."

"What situation might that be?" the other gentleman asked. "And forgive me, but can I verify for certain that Vaughan is dead?"

Rowan laughed shortly. "Well, you can check his body if you like," he said. "It's probably around here somewhere—is that right, Morgaine? And the situation is that magic has returned to the world. You know that. You can both see it for yourself."

"Yes," Thornton said softly. His eyes were on the far wall. "I can. Who brought it back, may I ask?"

Morgaine opened her mouth to reply, but Biddy got there first.

"I did," she said.

The two men turned to her at once, startled. Uncertainty swept over her, but she held firm and let it break and disperse as she would a wave. There had to be an end to hiding. She wasn't a scared girl in a nightdress standing in front of the Council anymore. She was the adopted daughter of the magician of Hy-Brasil. She had carried the key to the last schism in her heart for sixteen years. She had ridden on the back of a Púca and seen the fair folk. She had passed through pure magic and come out again. She had brought magic back into the world. She didn't need to be afraid of two elderly gentlemen, one of whom had his waistcoat buttoned wrong.

"You're the girl with the spell," Thornton ventured. "Bridget, isn't it?"

"Bridget Hutchincroft-O'Connell," she said, and saw Rowan's smile soft and quiet out of the corner of her eye.

The door was opening again, but she had no desire to stay and see who would come through it next. There were nine more members of the Council—she had seen them all before. They had been carefully chosen, she now suspected, because they were no match for Vaughan. Which meant that none of them, not on their best days and especially not back-footed and bewildered in the middle of the night, could be a match for Rowan and Morgaine and Hutchincroft. She had done what she set out to do. Whatever happened among mages was no longer her fight.

"I'll see you later," she said to the three of them. She stooped to stroke Hutch's ears, and rose to give Rowan a final embrace. "Don't forget about the other people in this building, will you?"

"I won't," Rowan said seriously. "I promise."

She realized she believed his promises again—not because she thought he could make anything happen, as she once had, but because she knew now that he meant them, and that was what mattered. It made her smile as she turned to the far wall, ignoring the two Council mages and the one more who had just come through the door.

Her mind touched the ravenstone at her neck, and her body melted into the raven's as she flew out the open window and into the night sky.

⇌═══════════⇋

Biddy flew for an hour or so in lazy circles over London—not trying to escape, as Hutchincroft had warned her Rowan had once done, but just to enjoy the feeling of the wind through the raven's feathers and the touch of moonlight on her face. She was too sleepy to do so for long, though, and even with the streetlights, the night around was too black for the raven's eyes. As the sky turned to predawn grey she returned to the library amid the rowan trees, where a fire was flickering in the darkness, and the books and the warmth and the soft armchair felt wonderfully inviting.

She slept well and deeply, for the first time in days, and woke to slanting sunlight feeling almost as good as new. But she was still alone, and she had no way of knowing how long she'd be so. In the end, she took down a volume of fairy tales and tried to read it. It didn't help that it had to be breakfast, and she was getting hungry.

Biddy was curled up in the armchair, her thoughts far away from the book in front of her, when without warning Rowan and Hutchincroft stepped through the bookshelves.

"Right," Rowan said brightly. He was wearing fresh clothes now, and his hair at least looked as though there had been water splashed in its vicinity sometime in the distant past. "Ready to go back?"

She sat up, blinking, as startled and dazed as if she'd been asleep. "Back?"

"To the island. We've a long journey ahead of us, and not a lot of magic that could help us make it. There's a train leaving for Liverpool soon; we should be able to catch it—and, more importantly, we can miss the rest of the Council. They've stopped for breakfast."

We can have our breakfast on the train, Hutch said firmly. *I made sure of it. They have tea and muffins.*

Biddy was still catching up. "But I thought you'd be staying on the Council. Staying here in London. At least for a while."

Rowan laughed, and she caught the hard, glittering edge to it. "No. Not this time."

"Why? What went wrong?"

"Nothing went wrong." He must have seen that she wasn't going to be rushed past answers, because he leaned against the shelves, arms folded, and looked at her seriously. Some of his brisk energy faded. "We've done what needs to be done. The schism is secure, and there are far too many open now for any one person to take possession of. That great chasm across London can't be undone without attracting attention, but we've hidden every trace of the Undercastle again. Morgaine's taken the Council in hand, before you ask."

"So she's the Servant now?"

"She is. That, of course, is what took most of the time to sort out, never mind the truly important things, but yeah, she is. Though I doubt she'll use that title."

It looked very touch and go for a while, Hutch put in. *With some of them.*

"It was always going to be," Rowan said, "with Vaughan's death leaving the position open. Morgaine took charge, though, and I backed her up, and in the end we had the advantage of already holding the schism and of knowing what had happened when everyone else had just been shocked out of bed. We were lucky, too, that Vaughan was very good at eliminating rivals from the Council. Most of the mages back there aren't good for much."

Biddy thought of Algie and his monocle, colliding with them in the Undercastle and unable to tell she had been invisible, perfectly willing to believe he'd met somebody he hadn't because he hadn't looked closely at anyone he considered beneath him in decades. She thought of the vault with its magic locked away in stone, its dungeons and its secrets and its dust. It was beautiful, in its way, and yet she suddenly wished it had all been buried for good.

"Anyway," Rowan said, as though his thoughts had drifted as well. He briskly rubbed his eyes, which were starting to look heavy. "Most of them seem happy enough to go back to how things were handled before Vaughan rose to power—not that they have much choice, with so much magic loose in the world. They're relieved, and a little bit frightened, and on the whole I think they're well-intentioned. I just don't trust them."

"Not even Morgaine?"

"I trust Morgaine," he acknowledged. "But the rest of it... Councils and politics and laws...I played that game once. I'm not playing it again. I think they need someone to keep an eye on things from the outside more than they need another Council member."

"What does Morgaine say to that?"

"I haven't told her. I imagine she'll be furious with me, and she'll tell me I need to grow up. What she doesn't understand is that I *have* grown up, and I'm far too old to believe in working from the inside anymore."

"You should at least talk to her."

"I will, I promise. Actually, I doubt I'll have a choice. She has a real lock of my hair now to go with her dream ring. Next time I close my eyes, I'm in for it."

She won't have long to wait, by my reckoning, Hutch said dryly.

Rowan's eyebrows raised in not-very-convincing affront. "Are you trying to tell me I look tired?"

"No," Biddy said, and couldn't hold back a smile. "You looked tired a few hours ago. Now you look absolutely shattered."

"Oh, not you as well. Just because you brought magic back to the world and saved me from death, you think you can say whatever you like, is that it?" He yawned, which rather undermined his case. "It's just because I stopped to talk to you. It's catching up to me. I'm all right as long as I keep moving."

"That's your plan? You're trying to outrun a nap?"

"Actually, I feel more like I'm trying to outrun a coma. Just as well we have a train to catch." He straightened. "Come on! They'll notice I'm missing eventually. Don't you want to go back?"

Though he spoke lightly, there was a genuine question in his voice. She had, after all, been asking to come to the mainland all her life. It was safe for her now—the magic had gone from her heart, and if it hadn't, there was nobody who would care to find the secret buried in it.

Go back. Biddy thought about Hy-Brasil, with its castle and its rabbits and its forests and cliffs, and felt an odd ache in her heart. It seemed a piece of her childhood. She had been there only a few nights ago, but it seemed so much farther away.

And yet she did want it. She wanted it desperately.

"I'm not sure I can go back," she said carefully. "But I want to go home."

Rowan smiled, and there was a touch of sadness to it. "Well," he said, "let's get on the train for now. We can sort out the metaphysics later."

Chapter Twenty-Three

*I*n some ways, little changed at all. There had been magic in the world for a long time before the cracks had closed; now that it was back, the vast majority of people noticed nothing amiss. When they found their luck turning, they generally put it down to something clever they'd done that had finally paid off. When the very worst didn't quite happen, they were thankful, and asked no questions. When miracles happened instead, they never even knew.

And yet everything had changed. There were mages working spells once again. People who didn't exactly believe in magic but were desperate enough to hope found themselves calling on corner shops, on apartments with odd doors, on tiny cottages in mysterious woods. There was a pulse of magic beating and thrumming beneath the skin of the world, and it bled through in impossible ways.

It was very noticeable on the Isle of Hy-Brasil. Biddy had lived with Rowan and Hutchincroft since she was very small, but she had never lived with them as a true mage and familiar before. She hadn't known Hutch with the magic of another world flooding through him; she hadn't realized the burden of fear and worry he had carried without it. Now she would come downstairs every morning to books flying off shelves and dishes stacking themselves; the gardens flourished with vegetables in wild and unlikely colors; doors opened to the wrong places and butter had the tendency to turn into jam. (This last she had to talk to Rowan about, severely. "It's all very well on toast," she said, trying to ignore the twinkle in his eye, "but not on potatoes.")

The island itself seemed even more alive. The trees rustled in winds that weren't there, as though responding to autumns hundreds of years ago, and the black rabbits leapt and bounded in the fields as though fizzing with something just beyond the realm of human senses. It wasn't at all surprising: The schism that had once split the wall of the ancient citadel had opened once more. With the citadel wall gone, it hovered in midair a short distance from the twisted yew tree. Biddy couldn't see it, but she remembered where it was, and if she stood in front of it, sometimes she, too, felt a breeze on her face that was not from the sea, a breeze that smelled of moonlight.

She saw the Púca there once, a black rabbit with golden eyes watching amid the others in the fields at dusk. When she stopped and turned to face it, it inclined its head and scampered off into the distance. She didn't pursue it, but she didn't run from it either. She had ridden it now, and it had taken her where she needed to be. Someday, perhaps years away, perhaps at the very end of her life, she knew it would come for her again, and she would be ready. In the meantime, she was careful not to mention it to Hutchincroft. He was looking for revenge for his time as a spider, and nothing held a grudge quite like a rabbit.

Morgaine and Rowan must have had their fight and made up, because she called the island all the time—not through the dream ring, or at least not to Biddy's knowledge, but her face regularly appeared in the scrying mirror. She looked tired often, but happy in some way that went deeper than any of the transitory smiles Biddy had seen on her face before, a way that told Biddy whatever was tiring her was, at last, exactly what she wanted to be doing. She and Rowan would talk for hours, sometimes behind closed doors, sometimes with Biddy as well. Even though Rowan refused to be on the Council, he still flew out to join her in London at least once a week as new problems sparked unexpectedly into being. Not all

English mages were taking the change in regime as well as the old bewildered Council had at first, and there were new agreements to be negotiated with mages from overseas now they were all capable of spells once more. There were new mages to find and train as well—across the world, at least fifty had awakened in a rush the night the cracks split open. She didn't ask what else Morgaine and Rowan might be doing together, but she gave him another stern talking-to about it the first time he came back in the late hours of the morning.

"She has to be careful about marriage," she said. "And she doesn't want children. Things are difficult enough for her as a mage and a woman, and she has the Council to see to now. So be careful."

He had laughed at that far more than she thought the warning warranted, enough that it made her realize she hadn't heard him truly laugh in weeks. "I think we've got it under control," he said. "But thank you for the advice."

Biddy had been to stay with Morgaine once too—not by raven-stone this time, but by rune door from Galway. Rowan had taken her across in the currach, drawn the symbol on the door of an old boathouse, and pushed it open to the door Morgaine had set up in her own house. The world that all her life had been impossibly far away was now just a trip across the ocean and a step across a threshold.

"I'll drop by tonight and see how you both are," Rowan said from the other side of the door. "Enjoy."

She *had* enjoyed, and more than enjoyed. Morgaine had set aside as much of her work as she could and, as promised, had taken her shopping. The dizzying self-contained kingdom of Selfridges swallowed them up in the morning and discharged them that afternoon overloaded with dresses and hats and stockings, enough to make Biddy, by her reckoning, at least seven different people. They went to the British Library, and the Tower of London, and the great grey slab of the British Museum. One day, Morgaine had shown her the North London Collegiate School in Camden, where Biddy could go to school in the new term if she chose.

"You could stay with me and attend as a day pupil," Morgaine said. She was watching Biddy closely. "Half a year there, and you could go to university in September. If you want to, of course."

She *did* want to, or she thought she did. The idea sent a thrill through her like a rush of sea air. But she found herself hesitating, as she had on the threshold of Selfridges. It was a little *too* like being made someone new.

"What about Rowan?" she heard herself say.

"What about him?" She didn't wait for an answer. Morgaine, Biddy had found, often didn't. "Of course he knows I planned to suggest it, if that's what's troubling you. He thinks it's an excellent idea."

She nodded, and didn't say that in fact what troubled her was Rowan himself. However he tried to hide it, he hadn't been quite right since they had returned to the island. He was tiring more easily than he once had; like Morgaine, the lines around his eyes had deepened in the last few weeks, and he was coming back from Council meetings exhausted and frustrated. Unlike Morgaine, though, he couldn't seem to be *still*. He was constantly on edge, ready to flinch into motion at the slightest sound until she felt exhausted herself just watching him. Even though he rarely had cause to leave the island at night anymore, Biddy would wake at night and hear his footsteps pace the floor above her head; sometimes she would go downstairs and find him in the kitchen with a mug of tea, Hutch at his side, or in the library reading by the mage-lit fire. Nothing was wrong, he'd assure her, he just couldn't sleep. He had the quality of a taut bowstring, with no target in sight.

"Well," Morgaine said, and Biddy realized she'd been waiting for an answer, "think about it. You have time."

She did think about it, long and hard all that night and more when she woke up. Morgaine had to go to the Undercastle for the morning, and Biddy spent the hours without her wandering through the streets, not shopping or seeing any sights in particular, just letting the noise and the life wash over her like rain. She was walking down the great curve of Oxford Street when she heard her name, cutting sharp through the murmur of crowds and the rattle of cars and carriages. "Bridget!"

Something in her heart recognized the voice before she did, because when she turned she was completely unsurprised to be face to face with Anna Belenky.

Anna looked different to Biddy's memories. It took her a moment to realize that it was the clothes. She was no longer clad in the well-worn black dress from the orphanage; her suit was soft grey, neat and practical and well-made, and her hands were in crisp white gloves. Morgaine was right. It did make a difference.

"It is you, isn't it?" Anna said it with wonder, almost with fear, as though she were seeing a ghost or a miracle. Up close, her face had lost its unhealthy sheen, and her dark eyes were bright as they searched Biddy's face. "They told us you had been called away in the night. It was rubbish. You wouldn't have left without saying goodbye. Besides, I remembered the birds."

"What birds?" Biddy asked, though she knew, of course.

"The ones made of bone. The ones everyone dreamed of the night you vanished, the ones that never seemed like a dream at all. The ones that took you." She looked at Biddy with mingled humor and delight and just a touch of ruefulness. "I did think I might find you and rescue you one day. I suppose you couldn't wait."

Biddy had to smile at that. "I thought the same thing about you. But you seem to be doing very well."

Anna understood the question in her words. "It was weird. A few weeks after you left, one morning we all woke up and it was late, about nine o'clock. None of the alarms had gone off, nobody had stirred. And the place felt...different. Like a breeze had ruffled through it, churned everything up, and set them down again right where they'd been, only cleaner and brighter. After that, things started happening. There were cakes at breakfast, and nobody knew who had ordered them. The old ropes in the courtyard had vanished, and someone had left *snakes* in their place, God knows how. One of the girls—Lizzie Thatcher, do you remember her?— she got a letter from an aunt she never knew she had, inviting her to come to Wales and live with her. Good thing we taught her to read, wasn't it?" She didn't wait for an answer. "Nothing special happened to me, really, except I felt a bit better, and kept feeling it, and one day I thought that since I didn't seem so likely to die in the next few months I'd apply for a better job than the orphanage. I didn't expect anything to come of it. But a gentleman wants a governess, way out on the border between England and Scotland. He's an archaeologist, whatever that may be when it's at home. I'm going tomorrow."

Triumph buoyed inside her, and escaped in a laugh that she hoped didn't sound too wild. This was it, what she had been waiting for without even knowing it. This was why she had brought magic back, not for Councils or mages or even Hy-Brasil. *The chance of better*, Rowan had called a world with magic. It had worked. "That's wonderful."

"It's just a governess post," Anna said dismissively, but she couldn't hide the light in her own eyes. "I might have been better off staying at the orphanage, now it's changed hands—did you know about that? It's much better run now. Still. It's a change. You never know what might happen, do you?"

"Never." The kind of things, perhaps, that might have happened in books written by authors who still remembered magic.

They talked for as long as they could spare, and parted with an embrace. Anna's was as fierce and tender as her voice had been jaunty and careless, and Biddy found herself clinging to her as she might a fellow survivor of a shipwreck.

"Here," Anna said, as they parted. "Here's the address of my new place. Write to me. You'll be in London, yeah?"

"For a while," Biddy said, and she knew it was true. She'd be in London next year, among strangers, going to theaters and parties and shops and all the other things she had always read about. And then the following year she would be in university, studying science or medicine or law or whatever she decided to set her mind to. She loved magic, and she loved the little scraps of it she could master, but it couldn't solve everything. At university she could find ways to help keep people like Anna and her parents from dying in poverty and pain. She could try to change things, little by little, in her own ways. It all seemed possible—possible, and shining.

"You'll love it," Morgaine promised, when Biddy told her that evening. "I know you will. Rowan and Hutch will be fine, you'll see. It's not like you won't see them—they're here in London all the time lately. And Rowan knows you can't stay on the island forever."

The way she said it made her think Morgaine knew more about her concerns than she was letting on.

They did seem to understand when she told them, and to be expecting it. Hutch was delighted and dismayed in equal measures, clearly believing with all his heart that she would change the world but not quite sure why she couldn't do it here with them. Rowan seemed nothing but pleased for her, although there was an edge of distraction about it. He had been unusually quiet lately, and when his smiles came, they often felt pulled from a great distance.

"You'll love it," he told her, in such a direct echo of Morgaine, Biddy knew they had in fact been talking about her. "I might come enroll with you."

She raised her eyebrows. "At the girls' school?"

"Well, I *meant* at the university in September, but why not? I'm open to new experiences."

She told herself he would be fine, as he said he already was. Of course it wasn't possible to go where he had gone and come back unscathed, even though he had come back to a world full of magic. But he'd be fine.

Two weeks or so after she returned from London, Biddy woke to a lashing of rain and a wailing of wind outside the house, the kind of unexpected late-autumn squall that rattled the walls and split the skies with flashes of lightning out at sea. She snuggled deeper into the warmth of her bed at first, enjoying the feel of safety against the elements. Then, beneath the storm, she heard a soft moan from upstairs, and a smash of glass. Her eyes snapped open, and she was out of bed before she could even register what was wrong or why she'd been so stupid not to think of it at once. As she scrambled for the stairs, the wind seemed to rustle with the leaves of a thousand trees.

She understood why when she burst into Rowan's bedroom, not bothering to stop and knock at the half-open door. The room was alive with wisps—Rowan's wisps, born of tree and leaf. They swarmed, frenzied and useless and fierce, looking for an enemy that wasn't there. In the bed, Rowan lay in the grip of a nightmare.

Biddy had had the occasional nightmare herself since she'd come home. There were nights when the cold of the dungeons would creep over her sleep like a shadow, when the misery of the children's home would seep into the corners of her dreams. She saw the silhouette of Storm's wings in doorways, and felt the Servant's glass eye penetrate her skin. But unlike the terrors that had gripped her the week she'd been on Hy-Brasil alone, she'd always known even as she slept that these ones she had already conquered. The magic into which she'd disappeared had washed over her memories and colored them golden; the dark bits were leftover fragments, nothing more. She was home now, and she was safe.

Rowan wasn't safe. He was trapped once again. Despite the cold, his blankets were half on the floor, half entangled with him as he tossed in his sleep, trying to escape; his hair was damp with sweat. Wisps of leaves clawed their way from the wooden bedframe beneath him and joined the others in the air. Hutch sat in the center of the room, rigid and intent. Biddy was sure he was trying to wake him, but familiars didn't understand nightmares. They were too close to dreams themselves.

She dropped down on the bed at his side, ducking to avoid the swooping wings, and shook him gently.

"Rowan," she said, as calmly as she could. Rain slammed against the windows, and the leaf-birds around them swarmed with a furious rustling of wings. "Rowan, wake up."

He didn't respond, only twisted away, back arching.

"Please. You're safe. Storm isn't coming, he's dead, he can't hurt us. He can't hurt anyone ever—"

She broke off with an indrawn breath, more of surprise than pain: A wisp had stung past her cheek, clipping the edge with a paper-thin, razor-sharp wingtip, and when she clapped her hand to it, there was a smudge of blood on her fingers.

"Rowan!" Calm wasn't helping. She hit him on the arm, hard, as she had hit him all those weeks ago when she had gone into his dreams and found him trapped in a nightmare. "Wake *up*!"

This time it worked. He jolted bolt upright with a strangled gasp, trembling. His muscles were so taut and rigid that she nearly pulled back from him on reflex; he seemed ready to shatter at a touch, like the living glass in the first nightmare long ago. Instead, she rubbed his shoulder in gentle circles, the way he had calmed her when she was very small.

"You're back home," she said. "Storm's dead. It's all right. It's just ordinary rain."

"I know," he managed, through shudders. He rubbed his eyes with a shaking hand, blinking furiously, determined to wake up. "Thanks."

Hutchincroft jumped up on the bed between them. *Birds*, he said briefly.

Rowan frowned, then glanced up at the frenzied wisps, swore quietly, and snapped his fingers. They shattered at once, crumbling into leaves that fell in a shower over the bed and the floor. Biddy breathed an inward sigh of relief. They had been swooping too close to be entirely comfortable.

"Are you all right?" Rowan said, looking at her quickly. "They didn't attack you, did they?"

"No—really, they didn't," she added, as his hand went to the tiny cut on her cheek. "That's nothing. It was an accident. Are *you* all right?"

"Fine." He drew a deep breath, exhaled slowly, and almost, but not quite, managed to laugh. "So much for it being a calm night. Sorry to wake you. It's over now. Go back to bed."

Biddy blinked as he threw off his remaining bedcovers and got to his feet with a wince. "Where are *you* going?"

"Outside." Hutchincroft gave him a low growl of disapproval, and he rolled his eyes. The ravenstone was on the table; he scooped it up and put it around his neck. "It's just for a while, Hutch. I'm coming back."

"You can't go out!" Biddy looked over at Hutchincroft for support, and he gave a sharp, supportive thump. "It's raining!"

"Yeah, I noticed." He paused to stroke Hutchincroft's ears and to ruffle Biddy's hair, which was already ruffled enough. She'd forgotten to braid it that evening, and it hung loose past her shoulders. "I'm not going far. I mean it, go back to sleep. I'll see you in the morning."

She opened her mouth to argue, but he was already a raven, and then he launched himself from the window ledge and was gone into the storm.

⚬━━━━━━━━━━⚬

It was late in the morning before he returned. It wasn't like all the other times he'd vanished, across her childhood. Hutchincroft could tell her exactly where he was, so she didn't need to worry he was dead or hurt or never coming back. He hadn't even left Hy-Brasil. He was just flying, through the storm at night and then the calm, fair early morning, with no real purpose other than to get some space from himself. But she understood a good deal more about how people and particularly Rowan worked now, so she was worried anyway, for completely different reasons.

She was sitting on the lower branch of the great oak, watching the dappled patterns of light on the leaves, when Hutchincroft got to his feet and shook himself in a satisfied way. A moment later, Rowan emerged from the path between the trees.

"Morning," he called, with the twinkle of a smile that always made her want to smile back against her will. She didn't this time, but she was sure her reproachful look wavered.

"You are," he conceded. "But I don't know what you want me to say."

Neither did she. That was the trouble. It was impossible to guess at all the things being left unsaid. "It just—I thought bringing magic into the world would make everything better. I thought the island would be safe. I thought things would be—not perfect, but all right. But it doesn't always feel it. Sometimes I think things were better before, at least for you."

He laughed softly—a genuine laugh this time. She was learning, far too late, to tell the difference. "Does it really seem like that? It's not true. Of course there are troubles out there. Of course on my part there are going to be bad nights and days when I can't relax and I'm probably always going to hurt when the cold sets in because, Jesus, Storm was not messing about. But I promise, we are far safer now. Everything's as good as it's ever been in all the ups and downs of the world. If things don't seem all right, it's probably just that I've stopped pretending so hard that they are."

"That's the problem!" She swung her legs, frustrated. "I never realized how much you were pretending before. I never knew half the things that were wrong all my life. How am I supposed to know if they're wrong now?"

"That's fair," he conceded. There was no trace of laughter on his face now. "If it helps, I promise I'll let you know the instant something bothers me, and if you're worried, all you need to do is ask. But things are going well. It might be hard for you to tell, because you've had to take in a lot of ugly ghosts over the last few weeks, but they are. Biddy, I don't think you understand what you've done. Magic is back in the world now. It's everywhere, and everywhere it goes things are better and wilder and stranger. And you brought me back too. Whatever else came with it—whatever troubles or sleepless nights or bad dreams—they're nothing compared to that. I'll take every last one of them a thousand times over, and what's more, I'm grateful for them. All right?"

She couldn't speak suddenly around the lump in her throat, but she nodded quickly, and felt something like light or air fill her enemy as a potential friend. It meant learning how to dress, how to do her hair, how to make conversation. There was still so much she didn't know about the real world. And, rune doors or not, however often Rowan and Hutch flew through Morgaine's window, it would mean leaving Hy-Brasil. She would miss spring returning to the forest, the snow melting and green settling like a gentle blanket over the island, the baby rabbits emerging in the fields. She'd miss Rowan and Hutch.

"It was," she repeated, more quietly. "It is."

"Then go," Rowan said, and something in his voice told her he understood better than Morgaine ever could. "We'll be fine. We survived a long time before you were born, remember. We'll survive you going to school. It's boring here at the end of winter anyway. Hutch always sulks about the damp."

I do not! Hutchincroft protested, without looking up from the ground.

Rowan smiled. "And any time you want us, you just need to get us word. We'll both be there as quickly as a raven flies."

"I'm not sure it is a raven you turn into, you know," Biddy said. "Morgaine took me to the Tower of London, and the ravens there looked bigger. I think you might be a crow."

"Maybe," Rowan admitted. "I don't know very much about birds. I'm lucky it wasn't a sparrow."

She laughed. For a while, they sat in silence, with nothing but the whisper of the trees and the soft thud of Hutchincroft's feet as he investigated a thistle.

"Storm said it was your fault, what happened to him," Biddy said. The mention of the ravenstone had given her an opening, but she had been trying to find a way to broach the subject for a long time. "I don't think it was. You didn't force him to try to transform. It was his choice."

"It was mine too." Evidently, he recognized her remark for the question that it was. "I tried to tell myself afterward I didn't mean it to happen, but come on. I wasn't goading him to try it in the hope that he would succeed, was I? I wanted him to fail. And I knew the ravenstone better than anybody. I knew what failure looked like. We really didn't like each other by then, Storm and I. For a lot of reasons I stand by, and a lot more that were me being young and stupid. The trouble is, I can't be sure, looking back, exactly which one pushed me over the edge that day."

Biddy wasn't quite sure what to say. She wanted to tell him it was all right, because she loved him, and she was beginning to understand now, and certainly he had paid for it. But it wasn't her wrong to forgive. "I'm sure you were sorry."

"Are you? I'm not. I wished I hadn't done it afterward. I'm not sure that's the same as being sorry." He shrugged, uncomfortable. "Like I said. I wasn't always the kindest back then."

"It's so complicated," she sighed. She meant a lot more than just Rowan and Storm and Morgaine, and Rowan knew it.

"It is." He stretched and leaned back against the trunk of the tree. "It's all complicated and messy and wild and glorious. Which is why I'm glad you're leaving, for your sake. I want you to have all of it."

"I want all of it too," she said, and meant it. She wanted the whole world. Before she had stepped into the schism, she had thought she was going to miss it forever. "But I don't want to lose this. You and Hutch and the island and magic."

"You'll always have us," he said. "You'll just have other things, as well. Your world gets bigger. That's why they call it growing."

"Is that you being metaphysical?" she teased.

He raised his eyebrows, mock-hurt. "I was trying to be *sincere*, but all right, point taken. It came from Morgaine anyway. I don't actually know the first thing about growing, up or otherwise."

She didn't believe that, not anymore, but she smiled.

"Will you promise me something?" Biddy asked. "If I go away, promise me you won't use the ravenstone to hide if the nightmares get worse."

"I don't do that!" He frowned. "Have I been doing that?"

"You did last night. Hutch says you did last time, after Storm took you."

"That wasn't *hiding*, I just—" He caught himself, then nodded slowly. "All right. I promise. Will you promise *me* something, when you go away?"

"Is it to be sensible?"

He snorted. "I'd never ask that. Will you keep an eye out for trouble?"

A shiver went down her back, though she couldn't have explained the reason. "Why?"

"Magic comes into the world where it's needed. It's been needed for a long time, and it hasn't been able to break through. For it to find the strength to do so, at last—it's wonderful, but I think we should be prepared for what the next year or two might bring. That's all."

She nodded, very carefully. "So you want to send me out into danger again?"

He smiled. "You wouldn't have any fun otherwise."

"Well," she said, "I suppose you left home long before you were sixteen."

"I think you're seventeen now."

"We don't celebrate my birthday until the first day of winter," Biddy reminded him, but she knew what he meant. Seventeen was when mages came of age, when they passed through into pure magic, claimed their familiars, and entered the world. She felt seventeen.

"Still. I think you're ready."

The wind whispered through the leaves, bringing with it the bite of late autumn. Biddy laid her hand on the branch beneath her. It seemed to her she could feel the thrum of the world's magic easier here, where the breeze from the sea made the air a living thing. It was her imagination, probably, but never mind. That was a kind of magic too. So was what waited for her on the mainland, messy and wild and glorious, waiting for her to fall into it.

"I'll come back," she said. "For the summer, and at other times. Wherever I go, I'll always come back."

"We'll be waiting," Rowan said.

Acknowledgments

The first, fledgling version of this story was written during lockdown in 2020, and it was a bright light in a very dark year. It grew deeper and wilder over many drafts while the roots remained the same, and it has many people to thank for that.

As always, a special thank you to my agent, Hannah Bowman, for believing in what this book could be, and to my editor, Nivia Evans, for continually pushing me to get it there. I'm so very fortunate to work with you both.

To the amazing people at Orbit: Thank you to Lauren Panepinto, head of department, and Lisa Marie Pompilio, cover artist, for yet another incredible cover. You are absolute magicians. Thank you to Angelica Chong, assistant editor. Thank you to Bryn A. McDonald, Rachel Goldstein, and Kelley Frodel for their tact and care in copyedits. Because of them, I can promise that any repetitions left are completely intentional. In publicity and marketing, thank you so much to Alex Lencicki, Ellen Wright, Paola Crespo, Stephanie Hess, and Natassja Haught for helping this book find its people in the outside world.

As always, a lot of books go into writing a book, including all the ones Biddy remembers reading. This time, I owe special thanks to Peter Higginbotham's *Children's Homes: A History of Institutional Care for Britain's Young* (2017) for what became the Rookwood

Asylum for Destitute Girls, and Barbara Freitag's *Hy Brasil: The Metamorphosis of an Island: From Cartographic Error to Celtic Elysium* (2013) for introducing me to many of the stories of Hy-Brasil. Please don't blame either of these books for what I did with the information in their pages.

To my fellow authors on Twitter and Discord, it's an honor to navigate the wilds of publishing with you. To the Bunker in particular, thank you always for your humor, your intelligence, and your kindness. Special thanks to Rowenna Miller, time-traveling seamstress, for generously sharing her resources on women's fashion in the 1910s.

Thank you to the Menagerie: Miss Adler, our cat; Jonathan Strange, Mr Norrell, and Thistledown, our guinea pigs; and our merry band of outlaw mice. Special thanks this time to our beloved rabbits, Fleischman and O'Connell, without whom Hutchincroft would not have known how to periscope, ear-flick, binky, growl, thump, fight, nudge, implore, or give spectacularly skeptical side-eye. And in loving memory of Angel-cat and Much-mouse, gone but never forgotten.

Most importantly, thank you to Mum and Dad for your continual support and love, and to Sarah, for your patience and perception and ongoing belief that this story was worth telling.

Finally, if you've read this book: Thank you. It means everything to me. (If you're instead standing in a bookstore just reading the acknowledgments, I get it. I do that too.)

Meet the Author

H. G. PARRY lives in a book-infested flat on the Kāpiti Coast of New Zealand, which she shares with her sister, a cat, three guinea pigs, and two overactive rabbits. She holds a PhD in English Literature from Victoria University of Wellington and has taught English, film, and media studies.

if you enjoyed
THE MAGICIAN'S DAUGHTER

look out for

THE BOOK OF GOTHEL

by

Mary McMyne

Everyone knows the story of Rapunzel in her tower, but do you know the story of the witch who put her there?

Haelewise has always lived under the shadow of her mother, Hedda—a woman who will do anything to keep her daughter protected. For with her strange black eyes and even stranger fainting spells, Haelewise is shunned by her village, and her only solace lies in the stories her mother tells of child-stealing witches, of princes in wolf-skins, and of an ancient tower cloaked in mist, where women will find shelter if they are brave enough to seek it.

But then Hedda dies, and Haelewise is left unmoored. With nothing left for her in her village, she sets out to find the legendary tower her mother spoke of—a place called Gothel, where Haelewise meets a wise woman willing to take her under her wing.

But Haelewise is not the only woman to seek refuge at Gothel. It's also a haven for a girl named Rika, who carries with her a secret the church strives to keep hidden. A secret that reveals a dark world of ancient spells and murderous nobles, behind the world Haelewise has always known....

Chapter One

What a boon it is to have a mother who loves you. A mother who comes to life when you walk into the room, who tells stories at bedtime, who teaches you the names of plants that grow wild in the wood. But it is possible for a mother to love too much, for love to take over her heart like a weed does a garden, to spread its roots and proliferate until nothing else grows. My mother was watchful in the extreme. She suffered three stillbirths before I was born, and she didn't want to lose me. She tied a keeping string around my wrist when we went to market, and she never let me roam.

There were dangers for me in the market, no doubt. I was born with eyes the color of ravens—no color, no light in my irises—and by the time I was five, I suffered strange fainting spells that made others fear I was possessed. As if that wasn't enough, when I was old enough to attend births with my mother, rumors spread about my unnatural skill with midwifery. Long before I became her apprentice, I could pinpoint the exact moment when a baby was ready to be born.

To keep me close, my mother told me the *kindefresser* haunted the market: a she-demon who lured children from the city to drink their blood. Mother said she was a shapeshifter who took the forms of people children knew to trick them into going away with her.

This was before the bishop built the city wall, when travelers still passed freely, selling charms to ward off fevers, arguing about the ills of the Church. The market square was bustling then. You could find men and women in strange robes with skin of every color, selling ivory bangles and gowns made of silk. Mother allowed me to admire their wares, holding my hand tightly. "Stay close," she said, her eyes searching the stalls. "Don't let the *kindefresser* snatch you away!"

The bishop built the wall when I was ten to protect the city from the mist that blew off the forest. The priests called it an "unholy fog" that carried evil and disease. After the wall was built, only holy men and peddlers were allowed to pass through the city gate: monks on pilgrimage, traders of linen and silk, merchants with ox-carts full of dried fish. Mother and I had to stop gathering herbs and hunting in the forest. Father cut down the elms behind our house, so we had room to grow a kitchen garden. I helped Mother plant the seeds and weave a wicker coop for chickens. Father purchased stones, and the three of us built a wall around the plot to keep dogs out.

Even though the town was enclosed, Mother still wouldn't let me wander without her, especially around the new moon, when my spells most often plagued me. Whenever I saw children running errands or playing knucklebones behind the minster, an uneasy bitterness filled me. Everyone thought I was younger than I was, because of my small stature and the way my mother coddled me. I suspected the *kindefresser* was one of her many stories, invented to scare me into staying close. I loved my mother deeply, but I longed to wander. She treated me as if I was one of her poppets, a fragile thing of beads and linen to be sat on a shelf.

Not long after the wall was built, the tailor's son Matthäus knocked on our door, dark hair shining in the sun, his eyes flashing with merriment. "I brought arrows," he said. "Can you come out to the grove, teach me to shoot?"

Our mothers had become friends due to my mother's constant need for scraps of cloth. She made poppets to sell during the cold season, and the two women had spent many an afternoon sorting scraps and gossiping in the tailor's shop as we played. The week before, Matthäus and I had found an orange kitten. Father would've drowned him in a sack, but Matthäus wanted to give him milk. As we sneaked the kitten upstairs to his room, I had racked my brain for something to offer him so we could play again. Mother had taught me everything she knew about how to use a bow. Shooting was one of the few things I was good at.

"Please please please," I begged my mother.

She looked at me, tight-lipped, and shook her head.

"Mother," I said. "I need a friend."

She blinked, sympathetic. "What if you have a spell?"

"We'll take the back streets. The moon is almost full."

Mother took a deep breath, emotions warring on her face. "All right," she sighed finally. "Let me tie back your hair."

I yelped with joy, though I hated the way she pulled my curls, which in general refused to be tamed and which I had inherited from her. "Thank you!" I said when she was finished, grabbing my quiver and bow and my favorite poppet.

Ten was an odd age for me. I could shoot as well as a grown man but had yet to give up childish things. I still brought the poppet called Gütel that Mother made for me everywhere. A poppet with black hair just like mine, tied back with ribbons. She wore a dress of linen scraps dyed my favorite color, madder-red. Her eyes were two shining black beads.

I was a quizzical child, a show-me child—a wild thing who had to be dragged to Mass—but I saw a sort of magic in Mother's poppet-making. Nothing unnatural, mind you. The sort of thing everyone does, like set out food for the Fates or choose a wedding date for good luck. The time she took choosing the right scraps, the words she murmured as she sewed, made that doll alive to me.

On our way out, Mother reminded me to watch for the *kinde-fresser*. "Amber eyes, no matter what shape she takes, remember." She lowered her voice. "You'll want to warn that boy about your spells."

I nodded, cheeks flushing with shame, though Matthäus was too polite to ask what my mother had said under her breath. We hurried toward the north gate, past the docks and the other fishermen's huts. I pulled my hood over my head so the sun wouldn't bother my eyes. They were sensitive in addition to being black as night. Bright light made my head ache.

The leaves of the linden trees were turning yellow and beginning to fall to the ground. As we stepped into the grove, ravens scattered. The grove was full of beasts the carpenters had trapped when the wall was built. It was common to see a family of hares hopping beneath the lindens. If you were foolish enough to open your hand, a raven would swoop down and steal a *pfennic* from your palm.

Matthäus showed me the straw-stuffed bird atop a pole that everyone used for archery practice. I sat Gütel at the base of a tree trunk, reaching down to straighten her cloak. My heart soared as I reached for my bow. Here I was, finally outside the hut without Mother. I felt normal, almost. I felt free.

"Did you hear about the queen?" Matthäus asked, pulling his bow back to let the arrow fly. It went wild, missing the trunk to stray into the sunny clearing.

"No," I called, squinting and shading my eyes as I watched him go after it. Even with the shadow of my hand, looking directly at the sunlight hurt.

He reappeared with the arrow. "King Frederick banished her."

"How do you know?"

"A courtier told my father while he was getting fitted."

"Why would the king banish his wife?"

Matthäus shrugged as he handed me the arrow. "The man said she asked too many guests into her garden."

I squinted at him. "How is that grounds for banishment?" I didn't understand, then, what the courtier meant.

He shrugged. "You know how harsh they say King Frederick is."

I nodded. Since his coronation that spring, everyone called him "King Red-Beard" because his chin-hair was supposed to be stained with the blood of his enemies. Even as young as ten, I understood that men make up reasons to get rid of women they find disagreeable. "I bet it's because she hasn't given him a son."

He thought about this. "You're probably right."

I strung my bow, deep in thought. After the coronation, the now-banished queen had visited with the princess, and Mother had taken me to see the parade. I remembered the pale, black-haired girl who sat with her mother on a white horse, still a child, though her brave expression made her seem older. Her eyes were a pretty hazel with golden flecks. "Did the queen take Princess Frederika with her?"

Matthäus shook his head. "King Frederick wouldn't let her."

I imagined how awful it would be to have my mother banished from my home. Where my mother was protective, my father was cold and controlling. A house without Mother would be a house without love.

I forced myself to concentrate on my shot.

When the arrow pierced the trunk, Matthäus sucked in his breath. At first I thought he was reacting to my aim. Then I saw he was looking at the tree where Gütel sat. A giant raven with bright black hackles was bent over her.

I charged at the bird. "Shoo! Get away from her!"

The bird ignored me until I was right beside it, when it looked up at me with amber eyes. *Kraek*, it said, shaking its head, as it dropped Gütel on the ground. It kept something in its beak, something glittering and black, which flashed as it took off.

On the left side of Gütel's face, the thread was loose. The wool had come out. The raven had plucked out her eye.

A cry leapt from my throat. I fled from the grove, clutching Gütel to my chest. The market square blurred as I ran past. The tanner called out: "Haelewise, what's wrong?"

I wanted my mother and no one else.

The crooked door of our hut was open. Mother stood in the entryway, sewing, a needle between her lips. She had been waiting for me to come home.

"Look!" I shouted, rushing toward her, holding my poppet up.

Mother set down the poppet she was sewing. "What happened?"

As I raged about what the bird had done, Father walked up, smelling of the day's catch. He listened for a while without speaking, his face stern, then went inside. We followed him to the table. "Its eyes," I sobbed, sliding onto the bench. "They were amber, like the *kindefresser*—"

My parents' eyes met, and something passed between them I didn't understand.

Overcome by a telltale shiver, I braced myself, knowing what would happen next. Twice a month or so—if I was unlucky, more—I had one of my fainting spells. They always started the same way. Chills bloomed all over my skin, and the air went taut. I felt a pull from the next world—

The room swayed. My heart raced. I grasped the tabletop, afraid I would hit my head when I fell. And then I was gone. Not my body, but my soul, my ability to watch the world.

The next thing I knew, I was lying on the floor. Head aching, hands and feet numb. My mouth tasted of blood. Shame filled me, the awful not-knowing that always plagued me after a swoon.

My parents were arguing. "You haven't been to see her," Father was saying.

"No," Mother hissed. "I gave you my word!"

What were they talking about? "See who?" I asked.

"You're awake," Mother said with a tight smile, a panicked edge to her voice. At the time, I thought she was upset about my swoon. My spells always rattled her.

My father stared me down. "One of her clients is a heretic. I told your mother to stop seeing her."

My gut told me he was lying, but contradicting him never went well. "How long was I out?"

"A minute," Father said. "Maybe two."

"My hands are still numb," I said, unable to keep the fear out of my voice. The feeling usually came back to my extremities by this point.

Mother pulled me close, shushing me. I breathed in her smell, the soothing scent of anise and earth.

"Damn it, Hedda," Father said. "We've done this your way long enough."

Mother stiffened. As far back as I could remember, she had been in charge of finding a cure for my spells. Father had wanted to take me to the abbey for years, but Mother outright refused. Her goddess dwelt in things, in the hidden powers of root and leaf, she told me when Father was out. Mother had brought home a hundred remedies for my spells: bubbling elixirs, occult powders wrapped in bitter leaves, thick brews that burned my throat.

The story went that my grandmother, whom I hardly remembered, suffered the same swoons. Supposedly, hers were so bad that she bit off the tip of her tongue as a child, but she found a cure for them late in life. Unfortunately, Mother had no idea what that cure was, because my grandmother died before I suffered my first swoon. Mother had been searching for that cure ever since. As a midwife she knew all the local herbalists. Before the wall was built, we had seen wise women and wortcunners, sorceresses who spoke in ancient tongues, the alchemist who sought to turn lead into gold. The remedies tasted terrible, but they sometimes kept my spells away for a month. We had never tried holy healers before.

I hated the emptiness I felt in my father's church when he dragged me to Mass, while my mother's secret offerings actually made me *feel* something. But that day, as my parents argued, it occurred to me that the learned men in the abbey might be able to provide relief that Mother's healers couldn't.

My parents fought that night for hours, their white-hot words rising loud enough for me to hear. Father kept going on about the demon he thought possessed me, the threat it meant to our livelihood, the stoning I would face if I got blamed for the wrong thing. Mother said these spells ran in her family, and how could he say I was possessed? She said he'd promised, after everything she gave up, to leave her in charge of this *one* thing.

The next morning, Mother woke me, defeated. We were going to the abbey. My eagerness to try something new felt like a betrayal. I tried to hide it for her sake.

It was barely light out as we walked to the dock behind our hut. As we pushed our boat into the lake, the guard in the bay tower recognized my father and waved us through the pike wall. Our boat rocked on the water, and Father sang a sailing hymn:

> *"Lord God, ruler of all, keep safe*
> *this wreck of wood on the waves."*

He rowed us across the lake, giving a wide berth to the northern shoreline, where the mist the priests called "unholy" cloaked the trees. "God's teeth," Mother said. "How many times do I have to tell you? The mist won't hurt us. I grew up in those woods!"

She never agreed with the priests about anything.

Pulling our boat ashore an hour later, we approached the stone wall that surrounded the abbey. Elderly and thin with a long white beard and mustache, a kind-looking monk unlocked the gate. He stood between us and the monastery, scratching at the neckline of his tunic, as Father explained why we had come. I couldn't help but notice the fleas he kept squelching beneath his fingers as he listened to my father describe my spells. Why didn't he scatter horsemint over the floor, I wondered, or coat his flesh with rue?

Mother must have wondered the same. "Don't you have an herb garden?"

The monk shook his head, explaining that their gardener died last winter, nodding for Father to finish his description of my spells.

"Something unnatural settles over her," he told the monk, his voice rising. "Then she falls into a kind of trance."

The monk watched me closely, his gaze lingering on my eyes. "Do you suspect a demon?"

Father nodded.

"Our abbot could cast it out," the monk offered. "For a fee."

Something fluttered in my heart. How I wanted this to work.

Father offered the monk a handful of *holpfennige*. The monk counted them and let us in, shutting the heavy gate behind us.

Mother frowned as we followed the monk across the grounds. "Don't be afraid," she whispered to me. "There is no demon in you."

Through a huge wooden door, the monk led us into the main

chamber of the minster, a long room with an altar on the far end. Along the aisle, candles flickered below murals. Our footsteps echoed. When we reached the baptismal font, the monk told me to take off my clothes.

Father reached for my hand and squeezed it. He met my eyes, his expression kind. My heart almost burst. It'd been so long since he looked at me that way. For years, he'd seemed to blame me for the demon he thought possessed me, as if some weakness, some flaw in my character had invited it in. If this works, I thought, he'll look at me that way all the time. I'll be able to play knucklebones with the other children.

I stripped off my boots and dress. Soon enough I was barefoot in my shift, hopping from foot to foot on the freezing stones. Six feet wide, the basin was huge with graven images of St. Mary and the apostles. I bent over the edge and saw my reflection in the holy water: my pale skin, the vague dark holes of my eyes, the wild black curls that had come loose from my braids as we sailed. The basin was deep enough that the water would rise to my chest, the water perfectly clear.

When the abbot arrived, he laid his hands on me and said something in the language of clergymen. My heart soared with a desperate hope. The abbot wet his hand and smeared the sign of the cross on my forehead. His finger was ice cold. When nothing happened, the abbot repeated the words again, making the sign of the cross in the air. I held my breath, waiting for something to happen, but there was only the chilly air of the minster, the cold stones under my toes.

The holy water glittered, calling me. I couldn't wait any longer. I wriggled out from under the monk's hands and climbed into the basin.

"*Haelewise!*" my father bellowed.

The cold water stung my legs, my belly, my arms. As I plunged underwater, it occurred to me that if there was a demon inside me, it might hurt to cast it out. The silence of the church was replaced by the roar of water on my eardrums. The water was like liquid ice. Holy of holies, I thought, opening my mouth in a soundless scream. How could the spirit of God live in water so cold?

When I burst out, gasping, the abbot was speaking in the language of priests.

"What do you think you're doing?" my father yelled.

Finishing his prayer, the abbot tried to calm him. "The Holy Spirit compelled her—"

I clambered out of the basin, wondering if the abbot was right. Water rolled down my face in an icy sheet. Hair streamed down my back. I stood up, flinging water all over the floor. My teeth chattered. Mother fluttered around me, helping me wring out my hair and shift, trying to dry me with her skirt.

Father watched while I shivered and pulled on my dress. He looked at the abbot, then Mother, his brow furrowed. "How do you feel?"

I made myself still, considering. Wet and cold, I thought, but no different. Either there had been no demon, or I couldn't tell that it had left. The realization stung. I thought of all the remedies we'd tried so far, the foul-tasting potions, the sour meatcakes and bitter herbs. Who knew what they'd try next?

I met their eyes, making my own grow wide. Then I knelt in my puddle on the stones, making the sign of the cross. "Blessed Mother of God," I said. "I am cured."